SUDDEN DEATH

A DI FRANK MILLER NOVEL

JOHN CARSON

DI FRANK MILLER SERIES

Crash Point
Silent Marker
Rain Town
Watch Me Bleed
Broken Wheels
Sudden Death
Under the Knife
Trial and Error
Warning Sign
Cut Throat
Blood from a Stone
Time of Death

Frank Miller Crime Series – Books 1-3 – Box set

DCI HARRY MCNEIL SERIES
Return to Evil
Sticks and Stones
Back to Life
Dead Before You Die
Hour of Need
Blood and Tears

Where Stars Will Shine – a charity anthology compiled by Emma Mitchell, featuring a Harry McNeil short story – The Art of War and Peace

MAX DOYLE SERIES

Final Steps
Code Red
The October Project

SCOTT MARSHALL SERIES

Old Habits

SUDDEN DEATH

Copyright © 2017 John Carson
Edited by Melanie Underwood
Cover by Damonza

John Carson has asserted his right under the Copyright, Designs and Patents Act 1988, to be identified as the author of this work.

This is a work of fiction. Names, characters, places, brands, media, and incidents are either the products of the author's imagination or are used fictitiously. Any resemblance to actual events, locales, or persons, living or dead, is coincidental.

Without limiting the rights under copyright reserved above, no part of this publication may be reproduced, stored in or introduced into a retrieval system, or transmitted, in any form, or by any means (electronic, mechanical, photocopying, recording, or otherwise) without the prior written permission of the author of this book. Innocence is and

All rights reserved

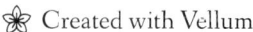 Created with Vellum

DEDICATION

This book is dedicated to Lt. James Nenni and Officer Laura Dunn of The Town of Newburgh Police Department

ONE

Friday morning. End of the week. Start of the weekend for Steven Hubbard would be at five o'clock.

He walked into his office building with a broad smile. Only eight hours to go and he'd have the most amazing time. Something to talk about that his friends wouldn't believe.

He didn't know he'd be dead in less than two hours.

Castle Court was a modern building, built on a gap site in Castle Terrace, just off Lothian Road.

Spectacular views of Edinburgh Castle! the brochure had touted, and for once, the estate agents had been right. The prime offices occupied by Hubbard's company sat cheek to jowl with the capital's most famous landmark. Although some might argue that the capital's most famous landmark was the statue of Greyfriars Bobby over on George IV Bridge. Tourists had rubbed the little dog's nose for luck so often the brass underneath all the dirt was shining through once more.

Whichever one it was, the castle was the only one visible from the office windows of accountancy firm, Alamo Management.

Accountancy was only one of the specialities in their portfolio, but the most important one.

Hubbard walked into the grand entrance hall, fully open to the ceiling five storeys up. It was as if the contractors had forgotten to add the centrepiece of the building, and stuck in two walkways up on levels four and five, connecting each half of the building.

Hubbard felt the briefcase bump against his leg as he walked. It was reassuring. Made him feel comfortable.

Especially today.

The day.

He nodded, smiled, and said good morning to workers from other firms. A staircase split off on either side. He took the left, mounting the wide, marble staircase. He liked to walk up. The corridor on the first floor looked down into the entrance lobby. He looked over at the other worker ants as they came into their colony.

'Morning,' a woman from the lawyer's office on level one said to him.

'Good morning.'

He smiled wider as he walked along the corridor. Up the next set of stairs until he reached level five.

Then he stopped.

He felt excitement, and a sudden rush of adrenaline shot through him as he thought about what he was going to do. The corridor wasn't open here, but there were windows looking down.

He crossed over the top walkway, hearing the noise of them talking way down below. Were they talking about him? They were. He just knew it. They were looking up at him, talking about him. Weren't they?

Fear, excitement, and rage all bandied for his attention as he ran all the way over the walkway and into the company's offices.

He was sweating, but the sweat was running thick and fast.

'Morning,' the receptionist said to him, smiling. Then she saw the look on his face and her smile dropped.

He turned right instead of left. *Senior Management.*

'Is everything alright?' Miss Smiley said, her mouth full of expensive teeth.

'Everything's just fine,' he said.

She stood up from behind the desk that was usually the barrier between clients and staff. 'You know you're not supposed to go along there? They won't be happy.'

He stopped and stood still for a moment, as if taking in her words. Then he slowly turned round. He was no longer smiling. 'What did you say to me?' He didn't say it harshly, just with an underlying tone.

The girl stood still, unsure of herself now.

God, he felt electrified. He could see the fear in the woman's face, and it thrilled him. He turned and walked fast, keeping a tight hold of the briefcase.

The door he wanted was straight ahead. He switched the briefcase to his left hand, and used his right to grab the door handle and turn it in one fluid movement.

'Sorry, sir,' the receptionist said from behind him. 'I don't think he's well.'

'Call security.'

Hubbard saw her disappear, and then he looked back at the man. 'We need to talk.'

It was easy. He opened the briefcase, and took the knife out. 'Open it.' He indicated the glass door that led out onto the balcony running the length of the building on this side.

'What the hell are you doing?'

'Open it,' he repeated, holding the knife higher.

'No. I won't.'

Hubbard stepped forward, and slashed his boss across the face. The man screamed.

'I said open it!'

The boss put a hand to his face, blood pouring through his fingers. He took out a key and opened the door.

The balcony offered an unparalleled view of the castle. They stepped out onto it. He turned to face Hubbard. 'What's wrong with you? You won't get away with this. I'll see you're arrested and fired.'

Hubbard didn't hear the man's words. He felt better than he'd ever felt in his life.

He sensed the receptionist watching him from behind as he rammed the knife into his boss's guts. Heard the woman's screams as the boss doubled over, blood spurting over the stone floor of the balcony.

Hubbard dropped the knife, and then grabbed hold of his boss, easily lifting the older, smaller man up to the balcony railing.

Then he felt a rush as he'd never felt before as he pushed.

He stepped back as the boss disappeared from sight. Screaming from behind him, screaming from in front, it was music to his ears.

Then he calmly picked up the knife, walked back into the office, put the knife back into the briefcase, and walked through into the corridor.

He casually stopped at the fire alarm box set on a wall. There was a little hammer on a chain to break the glass.

Steven Hubbard punched it.

TWO

Friday morning. End of the week. Start of the weekend for me would be at five o'clock.

'You got in late last night,' Kim said to me as I poured my second cup of coffee. I knew she wasn't meaning it in a nagging way. She wasn't my wife. Yet. We'd got engaged on Christmas Day, and to be honest, it seemed to have mellowed her a little. As if it had taken off the edge. We'd talked about getting married, but I had dragged my heels.

Catching a murderer sometimes makes you put your own life into perspective.

'Jesus, Bruce was putting them away. Percy couldn't keep up, so we poured him into a fast black. No doubt Suzy will be blowing smoke signals your way later today.'

'Tonight. We have a ladies' night out, remember?'

'Of course I remember.' I hadn't.

'Liar.'

'Mum, that's not a word we use indoors, remember?' Six-year-old Emma, Kim's daughter, my soon-to-be stepdaughter. I loved her with all my heart, and her father was okay with her living with me after I married his ex-wife.

'Sometimes, when I'm dealing with a hardened police officer, I have to get tough,' Kim answered.

'Frank's not tough. He's a big softie.' The little girl laughed and continued eating her cereal.

That was me put in my place.

'You're right, my wee doll. Frank's a big softie,' I agreed.

'Will you be looking after me tonight, Frank? We can watch a film. And you can make us popcorn.'

My father, Jack, walked into the kitchen. 'Are you making Grandpa Jack some popcorn too?'

'Of course we will.'

'And what film will we watch out of your collection of millions?' I raised my eyebrows at her.

'Really, Frank?' she answered. 'What have I said about you exaggerating? I have loads of DVDs, not millions. And I thought about *Sleeping Beauty* again, since you always call Grandpa Jack that when he's sleeping in the chair.' She got up from the table, rinsed her bowl out, and put it into the dishwasher.

'Wait, what?' Jack said, turning to look at the little person walking out of the kitchen to go and get ready for school.

Kim laughed. 'She's convinced Samantha has a cat in her flat and you tire yourself out playing with it. That's why you fall asleep in your chair.'

'Yeah, that's what it is,' he said, with a wry smile.

I buttered some toast and sat at the table with my coffee. 'You were in late last night,' I said.

Jack was a retired detective, and was dating Edinburgh-based crime writer, Samantha Willis, who just happened to live on the same level as us. That's how he'd met her.

'Listen, sonny, I'm a big boy now.'

'Oh, how the roles have reversed.'

'You're right though. I wish I'd come straight home from the pub. Don't get me wrong, I love seeing Sam, but she had a nice bottle of wine. If I hadn't seen it, I wouldn't have persuaded her to open it.'

'You're worse than a bairn.'

'Don't worry, I'll be out of your hair before you get married.'

'We're not rushing you, Dad.'

'I know that, but when you're starting married life, you don't want the old codger hanging around.' He made himself a coffee. Black.

'You've still got a few years to go before you hit sixty. Hardly an old codger. Old *sod*, maybe, but we're still a good bit away from *codger*.'

'Where did I go wrong, Kim?'

'I don't think it was anything you did, Jack,' she said, laughing.

'The gold band isn't on your finger yet, dear,' I said to her, giving her my best *smartarse* look.

'I think I'll move in with Jack and Samantha.'

'Sam doesn't have a cat.'

'We'll take Charlie.'

'I have no words for you.'

She laughed again as she left the kitchen to go and help Emma get ready for school.

'How's Bruce doing, now he's a dad again?'

'I thought he would enjoy going for a beer with me and Percy. Andy Watt was there too. It started off okay, but then he got all maudlin again. He wants to come back to active duty so badly, but the doctor hasn't given his approval yet. He needs to pass the psych evaluation, and he just can't right now.'

'Poor bastard. I can't imagine how he gets on with life every day after what he went through. An ear and three fingers cut off.'

'He's doing just fine. Physically. It's the mental side of things that gets to him.'

'He's seeing a psychologist though, isn't he?'

'He is. And she's doing well with him, but he's stuck in all day, even though the kids go to day care. Now Hazel's back with us, Bruce is at home with his thoughts and Jeremy Kyle. I'm going to have a word with Percy, see if he can swing Bruce coming back. Even if it's just sitting behind a desk to begin with.'

'Good idea.'

Later on, when I was thinking back on the conversation I had with my father, I wondered if my words had anything to do with the outcome of what happened.

And if anything I said would have changed things.

Or whether they would have stayed on that course and people would still have died.

THREE

Sometimes, the mornings start off slowly and I handle paperwork. Not the most glamorous part of the job, but that's the way it goes.

This Friday morning wasn't one of those mornings.

If I hadn't been feeling rough, I would have driven the car, but Detective Sergeant Andy Watt assured me he was fine. White-faced and drinking his third cup of coffee that I'd seen, but he was fine.

'Just don't get us killed,' I told him as he pulled into the kerb, too fast and too close to the patrol car that was blocking the road.

The fire trucks were sitting idly with their diesel engines growling in the cold March sun. I wished I'd put an overcoat on. The sun coming in through my window earlier had been lying to me. The wind ran up and started picking a fight.

What seemed like hundreds of people were milling around on the pavement outside Castle Court, a modern building overlooking its namesake, Edinburgh Castle. I looked up and wondered if anybody had witnessed the event.

People were right up against the *police line* tape, phones out recording everything that was going on. Forensics hadn't arrived yet. Neither had the pathologist. I wondered which one of them had picked the short straw this time.

A forensic screen had been put round the victim, and a blanket covered him. We lifted the tape and walked along this deserted stretch of pavement.

'This is getting worse by the minute,' Detective Chief Inspector Paddy Gibb said, coming up to meet me and Watt. He'd gotten here first, along with Detective Constable Steffi Walker. Hazel Carter was on the opposite periphery with a squad of uniforms, taking statements.

'Stabbed and thrown over the side,' I said to him, looking up at the balcony way up high. 'That's what I call pissing off somebody.'

'That's not all, he set off the fire alarm and walked out with everybody else. Now we don't know where he is.'

'Then we know who he is?' Watt said.

'Steven Hubbard. Aged thirty-two. Works in the finance department. We have a witness who said the assailant just walked in, and stabbed his boss in the guts after slashing his face. Then he threw him over.'

'He must have got blood on himself.'

'The lassie nearly fainted, Frank. She can hardly remember her own name. The paramedics are with her now. In the back of the ambulance.'

'Have the fire brigade cleared the building?' Watt said.

'This guy Hubbard set it off so there was no fire. I just spoke to the shift commander from Lauriston. They were first on the scene, and they said it was a deliberate set-off. No fire was detected.'

'It just helped him get out of the building,' I said.

Kate Murphy pulled up in her car and got to park near the ambulance.

'Morning, Kate,' I said.

'Hi, Frank. It's a bad one, I heard.'

'A witness says a stabbing before the victim was thrown over.' I turned and nodded upwards.

'I'll have a look. Did Doctor Wilson attend?'

'Not as far as I know. He's dealing with some drunks over at the station.'

'At this time of the morning?'

'It's Edinburgh.' Where drinking is a national sport, I wanted to say but kept quiet.

'When in Rome.'

She gave me a look that said things were different in the part of London she came from, but I doubted they differed that much.

'I'll have a look and then have a word with you,' she said, taking a forensic suit from the boot of her car and pulling it on. I walked over to the ambulance as Watt went inside the building with Gibb. Percy Purcell had left the station before me and I assumed he was also inside.

The woman was sitting inside with the doors closed, so her image wouldn't be shot and put on Facebook or any other media outlet.

I knocked and one of the paramedics opened one of the doors. I showed her my warrant card. 'DI Miller,' I said, stepping up into the vehicle.

The young woman sat on the side bed with a blanket wrapped round her, looking ghostly white as the male paramedic checked her over. I saw the woman was holding a cup of what I assumed was tea, and wondered who had fetched it for her. And whether the place did coffee.

'She's a receptionist for the finance company where the incident took place,' Steffi Walker said. She had been with the team for less than six months and was doing a great job. An ex-army medic, she was taking this sort of event in her stride.

'Miss...?' I asked the young woman.

'Tammy.'

'I believe you saw what happened?'

She looked at me and I saw the shellshock in her eyes. 'It was horrible. How could he do that? How could he just... stab him like that? Then throw him over the side?' Her voice was rising and I knew she was on the verge of a meltdown. She'd need to be taken to the hospital and given something to take the edge off.

'Are you able to tell me exactly what happened?'

She sipped some of the tea from the polystyrene cup before answering. 'He walked in as usual, but instead of going left to where the cubicle farm is, he turned right into the management section. I asked him what was going on and then he turned on me.'

I briefly looked at Steffi before carrying on. The young detective was taking notes.

'Can you describe to me what happened?'

She looked into my eyes and I could see a carnal fear there, like somebody who's stepped in front of a train and is pulled to safety at the last minute.

'I thought he was going to kill me. It was as if he were a different person.' Her hand was shaking as she looked into the tea. Then she started crying.

Steffi was up and took the cup from the woman. 'I've got it,' she said to me. I retreated out of the ambulance, confident my junior detective could handle the situation.

Inside the building, it was eerily quiet except for emergency personnel. Up on the top level, I found Paddy Gibb talking with Superintendent Percy Purcell out on the balcony, standing close to him as if he were contemplating throwing the boss over. He turned round when he heard me coming.

'Watch the blood there. Maggie Parks will have to go home and change her drawers if you fuck up her crime scene.'

Eloquently put, but Paddy was in a bad mood most of the time these days. He was due to retire so he could go and live with his girlfriend in Spain. The windy Edinburgh weather wasn't helping, accentuated by being up high.

'So he was stabbed here and thrown over,' I said, more out loud than to either man. Then I looked at Purcell. 'Do we have a motive?'

'Not yet,' he said, leading the way back in. I looked over at the castle again, knowing we'd send somebody up there to have a word. It was still an operating barracks, full of soldiers, one of whom could have been looking out of a window.

The crowd down below were still taking videos. The cars in the large, public, multi-storey car park opposite looked like scale models from up here.

'We have all patrols looking for him. We know what he looks like and we're getting somebody to find out where he lives.'

'Does he live alone?' I asked.

'We don't know much yet. The place was emptied when the fire alarm went off, and none of the workers are allowed back in yet. We'll get his info as soon as.'

'I think working in a place like this would make me go off my fucking head,' Paddy said. He had one hand in his pocket, no doubt cradling the packet of cigarettes that were a permanent feature there.

'I got a few of the staff to come back up here after we had one of the dogs go through the building with an armed team,' Purcell said. 'Early indications are he was working alone.'

'Workplace violence or terrorism?' I asked. It reminded me of the recent dealings I'd had with a suicide bomber.

'Workplace, unless we find out otherwise.' Purcell said.

My mobile phone rang. I looked at the number and answered it.

'Miller,' Robert Molloy said by way of introduction. He was an Edinburgh businessman, though some would use the term *gangster* but I used neither. *Pain in the arse* was my name for him.

'Molloy. How did you get this number?'

'Good morning to you too, detective. Now, I'm going to speak and you're going to listen. I heard on the radio a man was stabbed and thrown from the roof of an office building in Castle Terrace.'

'I'm not at liberty to say.'

Molloy's voice sounded rushed and angry, and not in the mood for conversation.

'I don't give a rat's arse what you're at liberty to say. I know you're looking for a bloke who works there. Steven Hubbard. Young man, wearing a suit, got blood on it. Wearing a silver watch.'

'What? Silver watch? What are you havering about, Molloy?' I'd walked away from Gibb and Purcell and lowered my voice. 'I'm at a crime scene so if you've got a point, get to it.'

'I know you're looking for this guy. And I know where he is.'

'You do? Where?' I looked over at Purcell and waved at him.

'He's on the roof of my fucking club. I'm in my office and the fucker just slashed one of my men. Come and get him before my son sends some of the boys up to throw the fucker off it.'

FOUR

I went with Purcell while Andy Watt took DS Julie Stott. George Street was just minutes away. Two patrol cars and an ARU were in front.

I was driving the car as if I'd stolen it. I avoided a tram rolling east on Princes Street, and a patrol car kept back any traffic waiting to cross Hanover Street.

'Mind the hubcaps,' Purcell said, as I took the turn too fast. He was white-knuckling the *Oh shit* handle.

'Hubcaps are long gone, Percy,' I said, trying to make it look as if I'd made the tyres squeal on purpose.

'You're going back to the track for fucking training.'

I ignored him as I shot to the top of the road, as much as the stalled traffic would let me, and we turned right into George Street, where Robert Molloy's *The Club* was located. All the vehicles were grouped near the entrance. The street was blocked off now. I got out of the car with Purcell closely behind.

We saw Steven Hubbard standing on one edge of the roof, the large knife clearly visible in his hand.

Inside, there were few people as the business hadn't opened yet. Staff were preparing for lunch duties. I was led upstairs by one of Molloy's men, and the man himself was waiting in his office.

The ARU boys were in front and also bringing up the rear.

'About fucking time. I almost called the control room in Bilston,' Michael Molloy said, turning back from the window. 'I would have got a quicker fucking response if I'd reported a cat stuck up a tree.'

'Frank's not here to listen to you whinging,' Robert Molloy said.

'That fucker came in here and went for one of my men,' Michael said, as if he hadn't heard his father. 'We couldn't stop him. He's like he's on something, but if you lot don't get up there now, the next thing that tosser will be on is the fucking pavement.'

'That's not the sort of thing I want to be hearing,' Purcell said.

'I don't give a fu—' he started to say, but Robert put up a hand.

'We haven't had the pleasure, Superintendent, but as you no doubt already know, my son was attacked not that long ago, and this is still raw for him.' He turned to look at his son and shook his head. *Fucking pavement* the look said.

'How did he get up there?' Purcell asked.

'There's a maintenance door that leads up to the roof. We have some repairs going on so there's easy access.'

'How did he know how to get up there?' I asked, watching as Watt and Julie Stott came in.

'Oh, goody, there's more of you,' Michael said.

'Shut up,' his father responded. 'It was me who called them, remember? Fuckwit.' Robert turned back to me. 'If he was looking for an easy place to run up, maybe he thought this was it. Somebody looking for access to a roof doesn't really have to look far.'

It made sense.

My phone rang. I took the message from control in Bilston. Arthur Stevens, one of our negotiators was on his way. I hung up and told Purcell.

'We should make contact with him,' I said. Purcell agreed.

Robert instructed one of his men. 'Show these officers up to the roof.'

'I'll post men down here in case he starts to come back down,' Purcell said.

'No need,' Michael replied. 'He won't get past us a second time.'

'It wasn't a suggestion.'

Michael shrugged.

We left the room, being led by a gorilla in a suit. Through a series of corridors and up some stairs.

'The fire brigade are in attendance,' Julie said.

I nodded as I approached the door. 'You with me, Andy?'

'Right behind you, boss.'

'Frank, I can go first,' Purcell said.

'No need. You three can follow, but I want one of you armed boys right behind us. Out of sight but close.'

The two armed officers nodded, looking as if they relished the idea of a bit of gunfire to liven up their morning.

I opened the door and was immediately assailed by the wind blowing across the rooftops.

Steven Hubbard was standing on the stone boundary wall that ran around the roof's edge. He had moved from the front of the building to the back.

'At last! You've come to play!' he shouted at me, waving the knife around.

'Knife,' I said, loud enough for Purcell to hear me. I heard him telling the armed boys to get up behind me.

'I'm here to talk to you, Steven. Why don't you step off that ledge and put the knife down?' It was a large knife, and if he ran at me I had to be sure to get my extendable baton out pretty quick. Or let the armed boys take him down.

We were at the south end of the building. The back of a hotel on Princes Street faced us. We were under a canopy of grey cloud, which looked menacing and full of ill will. Like the guy standing on the ledge.

I walked closer. I was on a terrace, which might have been more pleasant had this been a summer's day and I was sitting at a table with Kim, drinking a cold one. But I was freezing my nuts off.

Over on my left, sat a large, pyramid-shaped skylight. Hubbard was on my right, overlooking a small, private lane that ran up the side of Molloy's club. I knew it was there, but I didn't want to look over at it.

'What's your name?' Hubbard shouted.

I heard a scream from below as a pedestrian obviously looked up to see somebody standing on the ledge.

'I'm Detective Inspector Frank Miller.'

He laughed. 'Yes, sure you are. Where's the rest of them? The men you brought here.'

'They're waiting inside for us, Steven.'

'Stop calling me that! I left that name behind a long time ago. Why don't you step forward and we can talk about it?'

Christ. We trained for things like this, and trained again. One time we went to Redford Barracks in Colinton so we could practise riot training. The soldiers there were told to act as rioters and not hold back. Throw stuff at us as if it were the real thing.

It was hard, and they certainly did us proud, but training in such situations can only prepare us so much for the real world. Fear is our friend. Fear makes us sharp, keeps us alert, drives the adrenaline.

I felt the fear then. Not the sort of fear a member of the public might feel, but the fear that if I made a mistake, then my life might end. I wanted to think about Kim and Emma, but I had to drive them from my mind. Thinking about them would distract me, and that few seconds of distraction might very well give Hubbard the edge he was looking for.

I had confidence in the armed men who were in the stairway behind me, but again, we're talking seconds.

If Hubbard jumped off the ledge on my side, my baton would be out. And I knew how to use it. I would rather him die than me, so I would do all I could to defend myself. The old saying, better to be judged by twelve than to be carried by six was at the forefront of my mind.

'Come over here if you want!' he shouted at me, the knife pointing towards me, 'but I won't go back with you.'

'I just want to sit and have a chat, Steven. Nobody's going to harm you.'

'Damn fucking straight they're not, Zero. You think you know everything about me, but you don't know a fucking thing!'

Zero? What the hell was he talking about? His eyes were wild now, and I could see my chances of him coming off the edge were going down to... well, zero.

I wished the fucking negotiator would hurry up. I would be more than happy to hand things over to him so I could go and get myself a cup of coffee, but unless he was coming by helicopter, I was it.

'Who's Zero, Steven? I'm Frank remember.'

Christ I was getting colder by the minute. My face felt red and my nose was about to start running. As long as that was the only thing that was running.

'Yeah, right. He told me you were coming, but you and all the rest of them are going to get what's coming to you.'

He turned as if there was somebody coming up on his right, and he jumped down off the ledge onto the roof, slashing the knife through the air. Again and again.

I turned to the doorway to see Purcell looking out. *Are you fucking seeing this as well as I am?*

He nodded as if he could read my mind, or he was reassuring me the armed boys were about to be unleashed.

I only took my eyes off Hubbard for a split second, my hand going to the baton, which I took out. Now the time for tea and crumpets was gone. In its place was *Put the knife down and let me see your fucking hands!*

Hubbard slashed at the air, turning and jabbing as if there were a horde of men rushing him.

Then he stopped as suddenly as he had started. And turned to look at me. There was a wildness about him, and I could see the deep breaths he was taking. Sucking in air after his exertion. Preparing himself for the next fight.

With me.

'Put the knife down,' I told him, tightening the grip on my baton, and with a flick of my wrist, extending it.

He smiled.

'I'm a police officer. I'm telling you to drop the knife.'

Purcell stepped out now. He'd already deployed his baton. This was the visual, *Okay, we're here in number and we don't want to hurt you.* But we knew we would hurt him, not through choice, but through survival.

'Let's do it!' he screamed at us and started running.

Then something happened that was so unexpected I had to think about it over and over as I was writing my report.

Hubbard ran towards us then swerved and jumped back onto the ledge.

'I'll be back for you, Zero! You won't be so lucky next time!'

He spread his arms out, looked at us briefly once more, and took a dive off the roof.

FIVE

Screams came from below, in the lane at the side of Molloy's club. I shouted 'No!' at the top of my voice as I ran to the ledge, hearing a multitude of feet running behind me.

'Fuck's sake,' Purcell said as we looked over. The armed boys appeared, as well as more uniforms, and we all looked over at Steven Hubbard lying in the skip below, amongst the building material detritus, half of his head remaining on the metal edge.

Andy Watt and Julie Stott looked as well.

'Better get the paramedics to him. Cover our own arses,' Purcell said.

Arthur Stevens appeared as I stood back. He was an older man, weathered and experienced. He took out a packet of cigarettes and lit one, the wind snatching at the smoke he blew out.

'As situations go, I've been at worse,' he said, walking over to me, the cigarette bobbing up and down as he spoke. 'You, get your arse over to Harvey Levitt. Tell him, boss.' He looked at Purcell for support as he took the cigarette out and held it between two fingers. 'There are things going to be running through your head now, whether you want them to or not, and I will testify that nothing you did or said was wrong. I got here just before he started shouting. He was going to take his own life, no matter what.'

I was shaking. The cold or the adrenaline slowdown. Whichever one it was, I was already questioning if I could have done things differently. I was glad to be alive, but it didn't stop me from feeling we could have done more.

Now was the time to start picking this guy's life apart.

And find out who *Zero* was.

Hubbard's place was a flat in Leith Walk. Which itself was a long street, connecting the centre of Edinburgh to what was once a separate borough, the Port of Leith. The street was lined with shops, which had flats above them. I loved the place, feeling it was almost a village within the city. You could get drunk, get a sunbed tan and go shopping in a Chinese supermarket, all without having to jump on a bus.

Some places in Edinburgh were slowly losing their identity, and for the most part, Leith Walk was still the same. Change was inevitable and I wondered what the city would be like fifty years from now.

The old Shrubhill bus depot was gone, the place where the last of the old Edinburgh trams ran from. Now the new ones were housed in a brand new depot on the west side of Edinburgh near the airport. Shrubhill had been an icon on Leith Walk for years, before the bus company moved out and it was torn down for housing. Same with the social work building next door.

'Christ, Edinburgh should be called *Edinburgh 2.0*,' Purcell said, from the driver's seat. Clearly he hadn't been impressed by my stunt driving skills earlier and had insisted he drive, *Before you put us under a fucking bus.*

'I'm sure Aberdeen is changing as well, Percy. Before you know it, it will be one big housing estate and there will be no countryside left.'

'You're not kidding. But it's nothing compared to *Auld Reekie.*' He looked in his mirror to see if the others were still following in the cars behind. A patrol car was in front, two vans behind, along with Watt and Julie. And the armed guys. We were going to breach the flat, just in case.

'You should have seen the place when they were digging the road up for laying the tram tracks. It was a nightmare and then they decided to stop the trams short up at York Place.'

'I read about that. And now they want several million more to extend the run down to Ocean Terminal, where it was supposed to run to in the first place.' He looked at me. 'We're in the wrong game, Frank. Obviously diddling the taxpayer is the way to riches.'

'I don't know about diddling, Percy. Fuck me, say that loud enough and somebody will be pulling strings so you're policing a lighthouse on the Faroe Islands.'

Purcell laughed. 'Fuck 'em. They all think we don't know what's going on. We just can't prove it, that's all.'

The patrol car pulled into the side of the kerb and Purcell stopped, double parking. I looked out the back window at the other police vehicles behind, and the blue lights came on.

Steven Hubbard's flat was in a slim, detached tenement, the front door tucked in between an athletic shop and a bookies.

We all piled out in force, the uniforms running in with the ARU boys. Up three levels, and the breacher smashed the ram against the door which crashed back on its hinges. And then the armed boys did their stuff, which would have scared the shit out of me had I been sitting in front of the TV having a cup of tea.

The flat was clear.

We snapped on our sterile gloves.

The uniforms fanned out throughout the small flat. One of the team was taking photographs, but the forensics guy would do it in more detail later. Right now, we were looking for possible answers.

The TV was on. Paused. And it sent a chill through me as I looked. I nudged Purcell.

'Look at that.'

It took him a moment to see what I was seeing.

It was a video game. It had been paused at a point where some character or other was on the roof of a building. He was dressed in a suit, but the men who were coming after him were dressed in some kind of military uniform. He was holding a sword and was slashing at them.

The graphics on the game were good. Realistic. Certainly more realistic than when I was younger. Two men were obviously dead on the roof. Two more were advancing. It was night time, in an unknown city. The roof was slick with rain.

'Can you see a remote for this?' Purcell asked.

I saw a controller lying on top of an iPad. I opened the tablet and swiped to activate the screen. 'Look at this,' I said to Purcell. He peered at the screen. It was a video on YouTube, paused at the same point as the game was on the TV.

'I don't get it. You can play games on YouTube?' Purcell said.

'No, no. Emma does this sometimes when she gets stuck at a certain point in a game. Some YouTubers will play the game and video it and then upload it, so people can watch it. It's great when you're stuck, then somebody shows you how to advance in the game.'

I played the video on the iPad. The suit jumped off the wall onto the roof and started slashing at the military guys, killing them.

Gunfire cracked in the background. The figure turned round as I played with the buttons.

'Now I see how you spend your Friday nights,' Purcell said, his eyes glued to the flat screen.

'It's called living with a six-year-old stepdaughter.'

'I hear they're a lot better at this shit than a grown up.'

'Emma is.'

And then we both saw it. In the video game, the figure standing watching the suit.

The suit shouted something. 'Let's do it!' He started running towards the other figure then suddenly swerved and jumped back onto the ledge.

'I'll be back for you, Zero! You won't be so lucky next time!'

The character spread his arms out, looked back briefly and took a dive off the roof.

Just as Steven Hubbard had in real life.

SIX

We were getting a chief superintendent who would be the new divisional commander for Edinburgh, based beside us in the High Street. Jeni Bridge wasn't much older than Purcell but she had a wealth of experience. I had been expecting the woman to be the clichéd dragon, but she was far from it. Somebody had nicknamed her *Rottweiler*. She could be calm and friendly, but step out of line and you were on your way to getting a colonoscopy with a broom handle. But that was just a rumour, probably spread by jealous ex-colleagues whom she had leap-frogged on her way up the career ladder.

It just so happened she was coming in to sort out her office that Friday, so she could be right into her job come Monday morning.

Purcell took me in to see her.

'Inspector Miller. I've heard all about you,' she said, smiling and shaking my hand.

'I hope it was all good.'

'I'm going to leave you guessing on that one. Please, sit down.'

She looked at Purcell as I sat. 'Could you get us some coffee, Percy? I took the liberty of bringing in a Keurig.'

'Certainly.' He went over to the machine and switched it on, pottering about with mugs and the K-Cups.

Jeni made small talk while Purcell fiddled with the coffee, and he had three mugs ready in no time. Me? I used a kettle and wouldn't know how to switch a Keurig on, never mind find out where the little coffee pods went.

'This has been a terrible day,' Jeni said, as Purcell sat down.

'It certainly has,' I said, taking a sip of the coffee, which was pretty damn good.

'I'll read your report later, Frank, but give me a quick rundown on what happened this morning.'

So I did. We were already into the afternoon, but it seemed a lot longer.

'Video game?' she said. 'Do we know if he had any mental health issues?'

'We're going through all of that just now. It seems he suffered from depression after his father died. His mother is still alive and she said he kept to himself. Doctor Harvey Levitt is coming in shortly to go over this with us. Give us his professional opinion.'

'Who is this Levitt man?' she asked as there was a knock on the door. Jeni shouted to enter, and DC Steffi Walker came in.

'DCI Gibb sent me to let you know Doctor Levitt is here.'

'Thank you...?'

'DC Steffi Walker, ma'am.'

'Sit down with us, DC Walker. I want to meet everybody personally and since you're here, you might as well stay.'

Steffi closed the door and sat down. Purcell turned round and held up a mug. She mouthed *no thanks*.

'So,' Jeni carried on, 'this man, Levitt.'

'Yes, he's the force psychologist. He works for the University of Edinburgh, but he's on our payroll. He's been used many times.'

'Ah yes, Percy did say something about the team going to see the force psychologist after witnessing the young man jumping off the roof.'

'Nobody likes doing it. They see it as a snub on their manhood.' I looked at Steffi. 'And womanhood.' If that was even a word.

'It has to be done though. Rules are rules.'

I should have that tattooed on my person somewhere, I've heard it so many times.

'But you were saying about a video game. Tell me more,' Jeni said.

I looked between the two women. 'There was a video game Steven Hubbard had been playing in his flat. Well, we're assuming it was him who was playing it. We don't know for a fact, but the events taking place in the game were mirrored in real life when he was on the roof of Robert Molloy's club. He even called me *Zero*.'

She raised her eyebrows in question.

'It's the name of the main character's nemesis in the game. It's about an assassin in a city where there's no more law and order. It's called *Hitman Warrior: Zero's Return*.'

Her eyes lit up at that point. Recognition kicked in. 'I've heard of that. My teenage daughter plays videos all the time. I recently bought that for her.' She looked at Steffi. 'It used to be dolls until she discovered Xbox.'

'I can't say I play video games myself, ma'am, but I have two brothers who do.'

Jeni looked at me. 'So what's the connection between this game and our murder?'

'The game was paused where the hitman was on the roof, just like Hubbard was. It was almost as if he'd put himself into the role of the video game character.' I told her about the iPad and YouTube. 'He mirrored the game.'

Jeni blew out a breath. 'So somehow, he got it into his head he was playing for real. How the hell does this happen?'

'I'm hoping Harvey Levitt can tell us.' I drank some of the coffee and made a mental note to buy one of those machines.

'Get me a report as soon as,' Jeni said. 'I'm starting officially on Monday morning. Have it on my desk by then.'

'Will do.'

'It's probably too early for toxicology results to be back from the lab,' she said, hoping for a *No, I have them right here,* but having to settle for *You're right, it is too early.*

'If he *was* on something that would explain a lot.' I wasn't convinced though. I'd seen people who were high, and Hubbard didn't fit the bill.

We'll soon find out.

'We've been interviewing everybody at his work who knew him to talk to, and they all said he kept to himself. He didn't have any workmates he went out drinking with. We're talking to neighbours, but it's the same story there too. As I said, his mother says he kept himself to himself.'

'Any girlfriend? Or boyfriend?'

'We don't think he was gay, and he didn't go out with any girl we know of. Casually or otherwise. He might have sought the company of men of course, but if he did, then neither his mother nor his colleagues knew about it.'

Jeni leaned back in her chair. It was then I realised she was in casual clothes, which didn't make a difference, but was probably going to be the only time I would see her without a suit on.

'Does his mother give the impression she would be lying for him?'

'What mother wouldn't?' I said. 'But she's elderly, and I didn't get that impression.'

'No history of aggression in the workplace?'

'No. They said you would hardly know he was there. He was always polite to people.'

'Jesus. Then he snapped one day and killed his boss. I suppose we're lucky in this country we don't have easy access to automatic weapons.'

'Unless you're a scally,' I said to her.

She gave a brief smile that was one of resignation rather than humour.

'I'd like to come down and listen to what Levitt has to say. You can introduce me to him afterwards.'

'Of course.'

The four of us left the office and went down to the incident room. Since this wasn't a murder enquiry where we were hunting a perpetrator, all we had do to was look for answers as to why he did what he did. See if we could learn anything from it.

My fiancée, Kim Smith, is an investigator with the procurator fiscal's office. Yes, we work together. Yes, it's a pain at times, but we make it work. There are times when she's stuck in her little office in our investigation suite, just off the main incident room, but there are other times when we don't see each other professionally for weeks.

This wasn't one of those times.

Andy Watt was standing chatting with our new DS, Julie Stott. Moving from Glasgow CID, Julie had been with us for a month. In comparison, Steffi Walker was an old hand.

DCI Paddy Gibb stood at the front of the room, talking with Harvey Levitt. Probably asking the doctor how best to give up smoking, although Levitt's area of expertise was the head. Maybe Gibb thought his head needed examining.

'Right, everybody here?' Gibb said. He made eye contact with everybody, as if he were doing a head count. Jeni Bridge stood at the back, not wanting to take away the focus from the investigation.

'Good. Most of you know Doctor Harvey Levitt, the force psychologist. He's going to give us his take on things.'

The slim, bearded man was very affable, and had helped me get through some rough times, but he was as sharp as a stick.

'Thank you all for being here, and listening to what Paddy here sometimes calls my *drivel.*'

He smiled as we laughed. Gibb looked over at Jeni as if to say, *He just made that up.*

'Without seeing the tox results, it's difficult to give you an exact opinion, but let me give you both sides of the story. If the killer was on something, and by his neurosis, it would be some kind of amphetamine, then his behaviour could certainly have been one of detachment. His mind had placed him somewhere else and he was acting out a role that wasn't real life.'

Jeni looked at him. 'So what would make him do that if the tox results come back negative?'

'Psychosis. Bipolar disorder, perhaps, which used to be known as manic depression. I've been told the procurator fiscal is asking to see his medical records, but we don't know at this moment if the subject was indeed afflicted by this. However, his mother did say he had suffered from mild depression after the subject's father died, but then he seemed fine after '

'And that sort of thing would make him do what he did?' I asked.

Levitt turned his attention to me. 'It affects different people in different ways, but for this man, yes, it could have made him so introverted the only way he could have come out was through the video game character. It's not typical, but it can happen.'

'He was a timebomb waiting to go off,' Julie said. She was a confident young woman and I had noticed her and Steffi Walker getting along well. And Hazel Carter had taken them both under her wing, being the most experienced detective out of the three of them.

'It could be. It happens to people all the time. They've studied people in America, workers who suddenly become active shooters, bringing a gun to work and killing their co-workers.'

And that was that. We would just have to wait and interview anybody else we could think of to see if Hubbard was a closet psychopath.

As it turned out, the tox screen came back negative. By the end of the working day on Friday, we knew whatever had gotten into Steven Hubbard, it wasn't drugs. Nor was he psychotic. He'd been suffering from depression after the death of his father, but his mother said he had picked himself up after a while. Something that millions of people suffered from every day.

So what had made him kill somebody before killing himself?

SEVEN

'Don't wait up,' Chip Haines said to his wife.

'Why? Aren't you coming straight home?'

'Now, if I was, I wouldn't have just told you to not wait up.' He smiled a sarcastic smile as he pulled on his jacket.

Wendy knew he stood in front of the full length mirror and adjusted the belt with his gun on it. After twenty-five years, he still got a kick out of looking at himself in the mirror with his full kit on.

'Where are you going?'

He was smiling at himself, but wasn't smiling when he turned to her. 'One of the boys is having a poker game at his house.'

'Which one?'

'Which boy or which house?'

'Don't be a wise ass.'

'Christ, Wendy, what is this? The Spanish Inquisition?'

'I was just asking, that's all. You've been going out a lot recently.'

He stared at her for a few seconds. 'After what we've been through, I just need to have a distraction.'

'Some distraction, drinking, gambling and—'

'And what?'

'And staying out late.' She'd been going to say *whoring* but stopped herself.

'It's *my* life.'

With that, he left the house to start his 3–11 shift. She had liked it better when he worked the early shift, 7–3, but three months ago, he'd chosen the back shift instead. Another nail in the coffin they called their marriage.

She wondered why he was going in two hours early. He didn't even want to spend time with her when she was home for lunch.

Wendy was a teacher in a private nursery and Chip's shift had worked fine until he changed it. She'd read about couples going stale, but she never thought she'd have it happen to her. She wished she'd never come to New York now, and had stayed back home in Connecticut when she was younger.

Things had been even more strained since Ryan had come home from college last summer. He was struggling to find a job, although Chip accused him of being a slacker. Ryan had been for interviews, but nobody had picked him up. He wasn't remotely interested in flipping burgers or working in *Bed, Bath and Beyond*. Retail work wasn't for him, he said.

Wendy hated it when her husband and son got into a fight, but it was always her fault for not taking Chip's side and for babying Ryan. She was a mother, it was what mother's did.

It wasn't all the fights they'd had in the last nine months, but her husband's new after-work activity that played on her mind all the time.

Ryan was down in the basement, watching TV on the big screen all night.

She was already in bed, ready to put the light out when she decided she had to go out. Ryan was still downstairs. She told him she had to go out for a bit but she wouldn't be long. He told her he was tired and would be going to bed shortly.

Dressing in old sweatpants and sweatshirt—*Yeah, that'll look attractive if he sees you, girl!*—she drove out to the police station in Newburgh. She couldn't park in the front public lot, so she parked next door in the lot of what used to be the police station-cum-courthouse-cum-town hall. Now it was just the building permit office and fire inspector's office. It was well-lit and some of the official cars were parked there.

Wendy parked next to an old-model Jeep Grand Cherokee with *Fire Marshall* written on the door. Her car was inconspicuous, and if any of her husband's colleagues stopped to ask what she was doing, she would tell him or her she was waiting for Chip. They wouldn't question her, as most of them knew her.

So she sat and waited, with the lights out, listening to *90s on 9* on her Sirius XM. She liked the 80s as well, but they were playing some romantic songs and it made her want to cry.

Just after eleven, she saw cars start to come out. Chip's was the fourth. *Maybe he had called his girlfriend before he left.* Then she told herself to stop thinking this way. She wanted to give him the benefit of the doubt, but she'd read if your spouse starts to suddenly change their habits, then there's a good chance they're seeing somebody else.

So she drove behind Chip's Ford Explorer in her Toyota. Luckily for her, there were plenty of these cars about, and the streets weren't lit around here.

Chip drove up to Route 300 and turned right. She followed, thinking about what buddy's house he could be going to. She knew most of the officers, and Chip was close to the guys on his shift. It wasn't a huge department, with only forty-three staff on, which meant they got close.

And she had socialised with many of the wives and girlfriends of the other officers. So she knew where most of them lived.

And when Chip turned down a street in a nice part of Fostertown, she couldn't think who lived there. Chip pulled into a driveway. She had no choice but to drive past. Then she saw a house with no cars in the drive and no lights on. She pulled in and turned the engine off, cutting the headlights. She thought Chip would be too preoccupied to notice nobody got out of the car.

She watched as security lights came on. Then lights behind the glass in a front door. And then a woman answered. She was obviously pleased to see him as she hugged him. Maybe she was the one going to be dealing the cards.

Wendy sat in her car and cried. She'd been a good wife and mother and this was how he treated her. She put the car into reverse and backed out of the stranger's driveway. Put her headlights on and drove home. Although it wasn't home anymore was it? It was merely the house she and her husband shared.

She sat in her own driveway, feeling more lonely than she'd felt in her entire life. She walked up the stairs to her front door. She'd left the TV on to make it sound as if somebody was home, even though Ryan had been downstairs.

She expected to see the basement lights off, but they were still on. She thought her son had probably fallen asleep, so she walked down to the next level. The TV was on, but the sound was low. They had a spare room down here and another bathroom.

'Ryan, you in there?' she said outside the bathroom door. No answer.

She opened the bedroom door and switched the light on.

Then she screamed and screamed.

EIGHT

It had been nearly three weeks since Steven Hubbard had hurled himself off the roof and the press had moved on to a politician who had been sexting an underage girl.

Bruce Hagan was a DS in my team and Hazel's other half. He was missing three fingers and an ear after being attacked by a killer, and was on a slow road to recovery. It wasn't the physical injuries that bothered him, but the mental ones. He'd been on long-term sick for nearly nine months.

That Saturday afternoon, we went for a pint.

'Christ, Frank, I wish to God they would let me back on the team. I'm going off my fucking head at home. The baby goes to day care, Jane's at school, and all I have to look forward to is watching daytime TV. I sometimes wish the bastard had killed me.'

We were sitting in Tanner's bar in Juniper Green. It was a great little local bar for Bruce, being only minutes' walk from Barberton Mains where he and Hazel lived.

'I want you back on the team, Bruce,' I said.

'But?'

'But nothing.'

'Come on, boss, spit it out for fuck's sake.'

I swallowed some more lager. 'Well, it's all this talk about wishing how he'd killed you that's stopping you, Bruce. You want the truth, that's it right there in a nutshell. You're blowing your own chances.'

'What? Pish. I just get fed up that's all.'

'I can't imagine what you went through—'

'Damn straight you can't,' he said, interrupting me.

'As I was saying, I can't imagine it, but it couldn't have been that bad.'

We were in a corner near the front of the pub. It was quiet with only a few blokes sitting near the bar.

'What do you fucking mean, *It couldn't have been that bad?*'

'I'm just saying, Bruce. You have it made now; you have Hazel, you have the kids. What more do you want?'

'I want to stop fucking dreaming about what he did to me! That's what I fucking want.'

'You're seeing a psychologist. Surely she's helping you. Or don't you want help? I think you just want to throw yourself a pity party. Have everybody say, *Oh, look at poor Bruce.* Well, I'm not saying that, because I don't pity you.'

'A fucking pity party? If you weren't my fucking boss, I'd knock—' He didn't finish his sentence. He just sat there and slumped his shoulders. 'Now I see what you're doing. I react just like that with the psychologist too. Jesus, I'm sorry. I just get angry. I want to throttle the bastard who did this.'

'He's dead, Bruce. You're alive. You won. Take that as first prize and go and piss on his grave. Don't let the bastard win, not when he's not even around to see it.'

'You're right, of course. Sometimes I think I need a good kick up the arse. And I think you just gave it to me.'

'I want you back on my team, Bruce, but the brass are not going to let you come back until you can prove you won't beat the shit out of anybody who pisses you off.'

He drank some lager. Then looked at me. 'I've been a silly sod. All this time in therapy and all it takes is one good drink with you to make me understand.'

'It's going to take a little bit more than that, but now I think you're on the right road. Work at it, and I promise you, you'll be back with us.'

'I've been working hard at it. Jill, my therapist, has told me she's pleased with my progress. I only see her once a week now. The doc has taken me off my meds. When I get stressed, I can work through it on my own now without popping some pills.'

'I'm glad to hear it.'

'I'm going to make this work. I thought I was finished as a copper. The more I thought like that, the more I felt down. I couldn't pick myself up.'

'And now we know you can.'

'You're not just my boss, you're a good friend.'

When I got back home, Kim told me Jack was over at Samantha's flat and he wanted me to go over.

I knocked on the door and Jack shouted to me that the door was open.

When I went in, Sam was sitting on the couch, crying her eyes out, with Jack's arm around her shoulders. She was getting hysterical.

'What's wrong, Dad?' I said, feeling myself tense up.

'Sam just got bad news from her sister. Her nephew Ryan died last night.'

Saying the words out loud made Sam cry even harder.

'Sorry, love,' Jack said.

'Good God, I'm so sorry to hear that, Sam. Is there anything I can do?'

'Make sure the apartment is okay, son. Sam has to go home to be with her sister. I'm going with her. I got us a flight on British Airways leaving tomorrow morning, via Heathrow. We'll have to pack some stuff.'

'Will do.' I wanted to ask how he'd died, but was sure my father would tell me later on. 'What time does your flight leave?'

'Ten to seven, then the Heathrow flight leaves at nine forty. We get there just before one, local time, so it'll be six here. A couple of hours or so to get through customs and up to Newburgh. Should be about eight, your time.'

'Call me and let me know what's happening.'

'I will. I'll leave all the details later.'

'I'll drive you to the airport in the morning.'

'Thanks.'

'I'll leave you both to it.'

Sam stood up then and put her arms around me and held me tight. 'Thank you so much for caring.'

'You're family, Sam. Although you and Jack aren't married, you're still family to us.'

She let me go and smiled a weak, watery smile.

I went back home and told Kim what had happened. 'Jesus, that's rough. Poor thing. I hope she knows we're here for her.'

'I told her, but they're leaving for New York in the morning.'

She was thoughtful for a moment before going into the kitchen. 'Since you're cooking, I ordered Chinese.'

'Did you hear that, Emma?' I shouted through to the living room where Kim's daughter was playing with Charlie, our cat. 'Your mum doesn't like my cooking.'

'I heard her, Frank. And it's been noted. It wouldn't surprise me if she's already on Santa's naughty list.'

'Well, just keep up with your homework to make sure you're not on it.'

'Let's not be silly. Santa knows I'm a good girl.'

I laughed, then my thoughts went back to Sam and my laughter drifted away.

'Life goes on, honey,' Kim said to me. 'We can laugh and love and still remember people who aren't with us anymore.'

I wasn't sure if she was referring to my deceased wife or Sam's nephew. Either way, she was right. For those of us left behind, life goes on.

NINE

Jack felt tired as they picked up their cases from the carousel at JFK. He had wound his watch back five hours. 'Now we get to live the last five hours all over again,' he said. 'Who says there's no such thing as time travel?'

Samantha smiled but wasn't in the mood. He pulled the cases as they headed through customs. As Samantha showed both passports to the customs officer – her American one on top – he looked them over quickly.

'Just the two of you?' he asked, as a drug-sniffing beagle was making the rounds.

'Yes,' she answered.

'Welcome home,' he said, handing the passports back. Then he saw a lone traveller with a passport from God knows where, and she heard the officer asking to look through the man's case.

'I should have brought some haggis through,' Jack said.

'It's not always that easy. And as much as I love you, I don't want to see you behind bars for smuggling in haggis, even if it is your national dish.' This time she smiled a tired smile. 'It is still banned in this country.'

Jack had booked a Chevy Tahoe SUV and they weren't long getting the paperwork done at Enterprise, then it was on the road. It was sunny although still cold in New York State, so the drive was uneventful.

Almost two hours after landing, they were at the Marriott off Route 17K. Overlooking the runways for Stewart International Airport.

As Jack started to unpack, Samantha called her sister from the room's phone, and started crying all over again. Half an hour later, they were driving to Wendy's house.

It was in a quiet neighbourhood in the town of Newburgh, not far from Orange Lake and only minutes from the hotel. Jack saw the sign for Gold's Gym and wondered if Wendy and her family used it.

Rock Cut Road was an area of working class homes; a lot of people commuting every day, taking the ferry across the Hudson to connect with the train at Beacon. Manhattan was less than two hours away. As Wendy and Chip worked locally, neither of them had to worry about the commute.

They lived in a detached, bi-level on a fairly large lot. Woods were behind them and on the other side of the road, and there were some sparse trees between them and their neighbours.

'Wendy said Chip liked the privacy of this house when they bought it,' Samantha said, as they pulled into the driveway. The double garage was integral at the side of the house. 'It was private without being too isolated.'

'It's a nice place,' Jack said, parking the Tahoe. When they had been over to NYC back at Christmas time, Wendy and Chip had come down to the city to spend time with them. They had promised the next time they were in New York they would come up to Newburgh to visit. Little had he known the next time he visited, their lives would be altered.

Samantha reached over and squeezed his hand. 'This year is going to get better for us. After I was such an idiot last year, thinking you could have done that to me.' She shook her head. 'I am so sorry, Jack.'

'You have nothing to be sorry about. We can't change the past, but we can look forward to the future.'

They both saw Chip open the front door and walk down the wooden steps from their porch onto the stone pathway that led to the garage. He was in his late-forties but the last day or so had aged him.

Samantha went over to greet him, and hugged him as Jack got out and walked over to the man who may or may not become his brother-in-law one day.

'Chip. I wish we were meeting under better circumstances, my friend.' He shook Chip's hand.

Chip only nodded, trying to keep his emotions in check. 'Come in. I have the coffee pot going. Wendy's inside. She's a basket case.'

Inside, the house was warm. Wendy was sitting on the couch and jumped up as if something had bitten her as Jack and Samantha walked in. She rushed over to her sister and they held each other.

Chip went away to make coffee and came back with a couple of mugs a few minutes later.

Wendy was drying her eyes. She took her mug and sipped at the hot liquid.

'I'm so sorry, Wendy,' Jack said. 'This was awful news for us.'

Chip handed the second mug he was holding over to Samantha.

'How was it awful news for you, Jack?' he said, his face darkening. 'You didn't know Ryan. Never met him. How the fuck would it be awful for you?'

Jack felt his face reddening slightly, but he had been in this situation many times before, when he'd had to deliver the news to a family that a loved one was gone. 'I'm here for Samantha.'

'Oh, another nice little vacation for you, is that it? It must be nice jet-setting on somebody else's dime.'

Jack saw Samantha's eyes widen just before she stood up. 'You listen to me, Chip Haines; we came over here at Christmas after Jack paid for us both. Yesterday, I asked him to come with me as I didn't feel like making this journey alone. Jack paid for the airline tickets. Jack paid for the hotel. Jack paid for that fucking Chevy out there for us to ride around in for as long as we need to be here. So cut the crap. We don't need to hear this.'

'Well, aren't you the big man? Big, Scottish detective. Well, you aren't the only one who's a fucking cop round here!'

'Chip!' Wendy shouted.

'You know what? I don't need you sniffing round here. My wife and I will be fine without you. Samantha the fucking big shot and this big fuck—'

Jack stepped in front of him. 'You've said enough.'

'You talking to me like that in my own home?'

'Listen, son, I've been toe-to-toe with a lot harder fuckers than you. You don't want this, I can assure you. You're upset, I can see that, but keep yourself in order.'

'Who do you think you are?'

'I'm the man who would go to prison for her.'

Chip was about to say something else, but sneered instead and stormed out, grabbing a jacket on the way. A few minutes later, he screeched out of the driveway and took off towards Route 52.

'I'm sorry about that, Wendy,' Jack said, stepping back from the window.

'It's not your fault,' Wendy said. 'We're going our separate ways soon.'

'God, no,' Samantha said. 'Things are strained right now, but you have to be strong for each other.'

Wendy looked at her. 'It's not Ryan being dead that caused this. Chip's off to see his girlfriend. He was with her last night as well.'

'Girlfriend?'

Wendy sniffed and used her paper hanky again. 'I don't know how long it's been going on, but it's a while now.'

'Jesus, I'm so sorry,' Jack said.

'Twenty-five years we've been together. He has one more year as a cop then he can retire. We had plans for our future, but they've all gone now.'

'I know this is gonna hurt talking about Ryan like this, but where did they take him?' Samantha said.

'The Orange County Medical Examiner is based in Goshen.' Wendy looked at Jack. 'About twenty miles from here.'

'Have they done the autopsy yet?'

Wendy nodded. 'Yesterday. It was an overdose, but they won't get the tox samples back for a few days. They can tell, apparently.'

Samantha clasped her sister's hand. 'Did you know he was taking anything?'

'No! That's what's so strange about all of this. I know he was a bit down after leaving college. He was a qualified engineer. He just couldn't get a job right now. He kept saying he was waiting for the right one to come along. He graduated last summer, but he seemed upbeat. He had his friends, and they played around with their cars. He had everything to live for.'

Jack looked out the living room window. Thought back to when his own son was growing up and all he had to worry about was Frank drinking underage. He turned back to the women.

'Would you mind if I had a look round downstairs? Samantha said Ryan was down there when you found him.'

'No, go ahead. Second door on the right. There's a light switch just inside.'

He was glad she hadn't questioned him. He couldn't quite put his finger on it, and thought it was the detective in him, but he wanted to see the place for himself. Not out of morbid curiosity, but to run a professional eye over it.

The basement level was what they called a finished basement. Made into a usable space, unlike some other houses that weren't finished and owners used the space for storage.

It was big, taking up one half of the lower level, the other half taken up by the integral garage. There was a main TV room with a large screen sitting against one wall with a sectional couch facing it. A pool table sat over in one corner, with a little bar near it. Sliding glass doors were on the back wall. Over on the right were three doors; a closet for keeping cleaning materials in, a full bathroom, and a spare bedroom where Ryan had died.

By habit, Jack always carried a nitrile glove with him. It was a habit he'd tried to kick, but it was almost like breathing for him. He pulled it out and used it to turn the door handle and open the door.

The smell of death hit him first. The room was a mess. The sheets had been thrown back. Paramedics had left their own nitrile gloves on the floor. He moved around the room, opening drawers in a chest of drawers, but finding only winter sweaters.

A wardrobe held only winter jackets. A little night stand had a clock radio and a lamp on it. A paperback was in the only drawer. There were no burn marks on the carpet or any sign of white powder. He looked in a small rubbish bin. It had a couple of dead AA batteries, but nothing else. No cotton buds, cut cigarette filters, lighters, pen parts or straws. No burnt foil. There were no black smudge marks on the light switch or door handle.

He went into the bathroom and checked there as well, finding nothing. No signs Ryan had been in here shooting up.

After walking around searching the place for another ten minutes, he went back upstairs and asked Wendy if he could look in Ryan's room.

This room was more cluttered. He saw a glasses case and opened it, but it contained nothing more than a pair of sunglasses. After spending another fifteen minutes going through the whole room, he went back to the women.

'Wendy,' he said, sitting down on the couch and looking at her, 'can I ask you a few questions about Ryan?'

'Sure.' Her voice was thick with emotion, and when Jack looked over at his girlfriend, he was glad to see she wasn't looking quizzically at him. She understood.

'Did he seem to be losing weight?'

'No.'

'Frequent colds or being ill?'

'No.'

'Did he seem anxious, or did you notice a change in his personality?'

'No.'

'Poor hygiene or sudden hair loss?'

'No.'

'Change in routine or was he sleeping badly?'

'No.'

'Was he suddenly isolating himself, in urgent need of money or maybe nodding off?'

'No.'

'Did he wear long sleeves in warm weather?'

All his questions were answered with no hesitation. Although some family members couldn't give a toss about their kids, he could tell Wendy had, and she would have noticed something.

'Sorry, it's just the detective in me.'

She smiled at him and started chatting with Samantha again, her hanky never far away from her nose.

It was only then that Jack decided Ryan had been murdered.

TEN

'You got that soup ready?' Chef Cogliarri said to her.

'Yes. It's almost done.'

'Almost isn't good enough. We open at twelve! You are a disgrace to my kitchen! Get a move on!'

It was pumpkin soup with coconut and lime. It wasn't mixing rocket fuel, Mel Carpenter thought as she put the finishing touches to the large pot.

Cogliarri always added a little hint of Italian to his accent. She'd overheard him telling the restaurant manager one day that he was originally from some small, Italian village where his grandmother taught him how to cook. Which flew in the face of reality. She'd heard from one of the other chefs Cogliarri was in fact from Maryhill.

'When's the queen coming?' she asked the head chef, who had turned his back on her.

'What did you say?' Which came out as, *What deed you say?*

'I asked when the queen was expected. You know the prince doesn't like to be kept waiting.'

The chef looked at her while some of the others stopped working. 'Back to work!' he shouted at them, before turning his attention back to the insolent young girl standing before him.

'Are you trying to be funny?' he said, leaning in closer. His breath was stale, and she looked at the beginnings of stubble spreading across his jowls.

'Of course not. But if the royal party turns up and things aren't ready, his lordship will be handing you your notice. Don't say you weren't warned, matey.'

She walked away, heading along the corridor that led to the pantries.

Cogliarri was dumfounded. 'Get back to work!' he shouted again, but everybody was already making busy.

Mel was in one of the pantries but she didn't know what she was looking for. Then she heard the door open and the head chef came in.

'What the fuck was all that about, you stupid cow?' he said, but she was nowhere to be seen. He could have sworn she had come in here. She was small, so maybe she was behind one of the higher racks. He walked back farther, looking between the racks, along each narrow aisle.

'Mel! Get your arse out here!' There was no Italian now, just pure Glaswegian.

'I know you're working for the other side!' she said.

Cogliarri spun round and saw her standing before him.

'What the fuck is wrong with you, you stupid bitch?' he said.

She pulled the front of the rubber apron down and pulled her chef's shirt open, exposing her naked breasts. Cogliarri stared at them for a few seconds, and his focus was on them, not the tin Mel had in her hand. She raised it and squirted it at him. Too late, he lifted a hand but the lighter fluid tore into his eyes, burning them. He screamed as she stepped forward with the lighter.

'Nothing personal, but I have to protect the queen. I'm one of Her Majesty's agents.' Cogliarri didn't hear her words as his hands scrabbled at his own face. Then Mel flicked the lighter and she held it to the chef's jacket, its flame still burning as it hungrily sought out the fluid that covered the man.

Mel had turned and buttoned herself up. She kicked over one of the containers that now held more gasoline, the liquid having been brought in days ago and stored in these containers for this very purpose.

She ran out, closed the door behind her, and locked it. There was a window in the door and she looked through it, watching as the man screamed, his face and body on fire. He came up to the door, his skin melting, his screams seeping through.

She'd put containers of cooking oil in the corridor next to the boxes of fruit and veg that had been delivered that morning. Nobody questioned it as they were going to be using them at lunchtime. She also stored a lot of the paper bags the food had been delivered in. Now, she emptied the cooking oil onto the papers and lit them.

She unscrewed the tops of more containers, kicking them over, again being careful not to let the flammable liquid touch her.

Another lighter, another fire.

She hurried through to the kitchen. 'Fire! Fire!' she screamed, and the others started running and panicking when they saw the corridor go up in flames.

She ran over to a counter top where a large knife was sitting.

'What's going on, Mel?' one of the chefs said.

'The whole place is going up,' she said, and as the man looked over her shoulder, she picked up the knife and rammed it in. His eyes widened in terror. She pulled out the knife and rammed it in again. He fell to his knees and she kicked him over, throwing the knife to one side.

The fire alarms were going off now. She needed to hurry.

The restaurant manager came down just before they opened, as he always did. He saw the young chef on the floor, lying on his front and moaning.

'What's happening?' he screamed, then he saw the flames for himself. 'Help me get him to his feet!' he shouted, pointing to the chef.

Mel grabbed his hair and spun him round, shoving his face into the huge pan of boiling soup, holding onto him as he fought back. Then she just as quickly pulled him back. Soup dripped off his face, as did his skin. She picked up another knife and rammed it into his guts. He screamed like a dying animal, and Mel threw him aside. He collapsed on top of the chef.

Mel ran for the stairs. She had to get to the train station.

The crowds were thick. Patrons of the restaurant, hotel guests and staff were all being ushered out of the hotel onto the North Bridge.

All they saw was a woman wearing chef's whites. Casually walking along in the middle of the road as traffic was being disrupted by the crowd of people rushing to get out of the burning building.

ELEVEN

'Happy birthday, Mummy!' Emma shouted, as she rushed into the kitchen with Kim's gift. A plush, toy cat. Something I suspected Emma would get more fun out of than Kim would.

'Thank you, honey.'

I held out the large package I had for her and placed it on the kitchen table. 'Happy birthday.' I gave her a peck on the cheek, watching as Emma screwed up her face.

'Thank you.' She opened the cat first and then the leather jacket I'd bought her. She tried it on and gave the little toy a squeeze.

'Wow, twenty-nine. Another year and you can say you're in your thirties, like me.'

'At least I'll be a married woman by then.'

Getting married again at twenty-nine was fine, she said, but the big three-oh, not so much. The state of my life and Hell would very much have similarities should I not get into the spirit of exchanging vows, she'd told me one night.

I know it was wrong to compare Kim to Carol, and I didn't do it often now, but sometimes something would come into my head and I would find myself thinking of her. She would have been a few months older than Kim, had she lived long enough. My smile slipped for a moment and it must have showed.

'You okay, Frank?'

I smiled harder. 'Of course.'

I could see in her eyes she didn't believe me, but she let it go. Emma had already left to go and see if Charlie wanted to play before she had to go to school.

'Are we still going out for a meal tonight?' she said.

'Yes, we are. And if McDonald's is busy, there's a good chippie I know down on Broughton Street.'

'Wow. You certainly know how to impress a lady, Frank. And here was me going to impress you. I might have to revise that plan.'

'You always impress me, Kim.'

'Too late, tightwad. Now you'll have to earn it.'

'Oh boy. I suppose I'll have to take you somewhere they sit down to eat now.'

'Smartarse,' she said, laughing. Then she put her arms around my neck and kissed me.

I gently pulled away from her. 'Okay, future Mrs Miller, I have to get ready for work.'

'Me too. My dad said he'll pick up Emma on his way home from the office. Then we can go to Pizza Hut downstairs then come back upstairs for a good bit of how's your father.'

'Really?'

'No. Pizza Hut means fun time will be suspended until further notice.'

'You drive a hard bargain, *Miss* Smith.'

'It's *Mrs* Smith actually. I kept his name even after I divorced him.'

'Being right all the time must be tiresome for you. I'll see you later.'

Turned out I saw her much sooner than I expected.

Later that morning, I had put on my overcoat to step out for lunch with Andy Watt and Julie Stott. We were about to leave the office when the call came through. A hotel fire on the North Bridge. It was the Hilton Edinburgh Carlton.

Of course, patrol cars would be on the scene, and traffic would be diverted and crowd control would be implemented. Nothing for MIT, or so I thought.

But we were going to get involved. Hazel Carter grabbed her jacket from the back of her chair. 'There's a jumper on the North Bridge,' she said.

'And they're requesting us?'

'She appears to be a chef, she has soot marks on her uniform and the place is going up like a—'

'House on fire?' I said. Hazel didn't laugh but shook her head. If I was her husband, she would have inserted the word *Twat* at the end of her sentence, I'm sure. But I'm not. I'm her boss, though I knew I was skating on thin ice.

'Watt, you can come with me,' DCI Gibb said.

'As long as I can drive, Grandpa,' he said under his breath.

'What?'

'I said, the traffic will be backed up.'

'Is that what he said?' Gibb asked me.

'I think so,' I said, shooting Watt a look. 'Okay, let's get round there. I'll take Steffi and Julie. Two cars. Let's not scare the girl. She might be in shock, so let's give her the benefit of the doubt. Let's go. Julie, with me.'

And so we went round to the North Bridge, literally thirty seconds from the station on a normal day, but it was a few minutes as we skirted round the first fire engines to attend. What traffic was on the bridge heading for the High Street was now stuck. Uniforms couldn't turn the traffic round for the woman standing on the ledge.

We didn't have our sirens on, and we didn't drive as if we were racing. We just pulled into the side of the road and got out of the cars.

She was on the Balmoral side, with views over Waverley station to the west. The Bank of Scotland HQ was up on the Mound over to our left. The castle ahead. The Scott Monument poked up from Princes Street like an accusing finger. If this woman had climbed up to take a photograph of Edinburgh city centre, she couldn't have chosen a more perfect spot. But she wasn't there for a photo shoot. She had other things on her mind.

Over on the other side, an east wind blew in from the North Sea unabated, ruffling her hair and fluttering her white uniform. She had climbed onto the side by the stone wall that held the North Bridge plaque, and was staring into space.

I scuffed my shoe on the pavement before I got too near to her, not wanting to get up close without her knowing I was there. She turned round and looked at me.

And smiled.

'You're late,' she said. Then stared back towards the castle. I looked over at Julie, who didn't take her eyes off the woman.

'Can you come down here and we can talk?' I said. Arthur Stevens had been called and I was glad to see his car pull up. He got out of the car and patted down his pockets as if he couldn't find his cigarettes.

Fuck me, Arthur, I thought. If this girl had indeed been close to the fire in the hotel, then the last thing she needed to see was somebody pulling out a lighter.

Thankfully, he pulled out his phone.

Watt, Gibb, and Hazel were farther down from us. 'Come down and we'll get you a nice cup of tea,' Gibb said. 'Get you warmed up.'

She ignored him and turned towards us again. I saw stitching on her breast pocket. *Mel*. The other side had the hotel's name on it. But it was the blood that covered the front that drew most of my attention. A crowd of onlookers had started to gather down at the Princes Street side, being held back by a diligent uniform and police tape.

'Can I call you Mel?' I asked her. 'My name's Frank.'

'I thought you would have been here sooner. You promised, and now that place is on fire. I think I might have done it,' she said.

Christ, I didn't want her to start confessing now, not until we were recording it, or Norma Banks, the PF, wouldn't be able to have it admissible. I hoped Arthur Stevens had his phone on record mode.

'Mel?' Stevens said, walking up close to me. 'Do you think we could talk?'

She smiled at him. 'Of course we can. You're the lord's new footman, aren't you? I've seen you around town before.'

Oh shit. Flashbacks to Steven Hubbard standing on Robert Molloy's roof hit me then.

'That's right, I am. I have a message for you.'

She brightened at this. 'What is it? Has the queen arrived?'

'She's nearly here,' Stevens said, taking a step closer. 'She wants you to be waiting for her. If you let me help you down, we can both go and meet her.'

'Why are you here? Shouldn't you already be at the palace?'

'I was sent for you. We can all go together.'

'I burned the palace. It was a trap. They wanted her there, but I made sure there was nothing left for the queen to go to. Now she can safely come back with me.'

Mel's smile dropped and she looked towards the castle again. 'I must hurry. Whatever would the queen say if I were late again? And my father. He would be so disappointed.'

'Let me help you down, Mel,' I said, but didn't move towards her.

'No, follow me. I know a quick way,' she said, and stepped off the edge.

Julie screamed. Or maybe it was Arthur, I couldn't be sure. Steffi Walker rushed forward and tried to leap up onto the parapet, but Hazel held her back. One slip, and she would have been over as well. Julie was more cautious when she approached.

'Arthur, grab my belt,' I said to him as I got my belly up onto the edge. Stevens held on as I looked down onto the glass roof of Waverley station. Mel had smashed a few panels of glass as she hit them, and the steel frames had smashed her before she fell through the gap onto the platform below, where her skull was caved in.

Screams from below. Screams from above. 'Right, Arthur,' I said, and felt the negotiator's grip on me loosen.

'Two in the space of a month,' Stevens said, pulling out his cigarettes. I wondered if he was in competition with Paddy Gibb, to see who could get a hacking cough first. Stevens coughed, to let me know he was in the lead.

'Let's get down there,' I said. Whoever that poor girl was, she deserved our best attention. That was my initial thought.

Until we discovered what Mel Carpenter had done.

TWELVE

Down in the train station below, nobody else was hurt by Mel jumping off the bridge, except for a few cuts from flying glass.

'There's nothing we can do at times,' Arthur Stevens said, which smacked of covering his own arse.

The young girl had landed on the road next to a platform. It had taken a while for forensics and the pathologist to get there. The city centre had ground to a halt as firefighters took care of the hotel above us.

Jeni Bridge came down. She had settled into her position well, which wasn't surprising as she'd had the same role in Glasgow.

'Christ I could do with a fag,' she said to Stevens, hinting that she would settle for one out of his packet if he was dishing, but he wasn't biting. She looked at me. 'I don't want to hear how bad it is for my health, or how expensive they are nowadays. I'm addicted to the damn things, Frank. Deal with it.'

'I wasn't going to say a word, ma'am.' Which was a lie. I was going to tell her the head of forensics – DI Maggie Parks – would chew her a new arsehole if she caught her smoking near a crime scene and flicked the butt away. And that was exactly how it would be treated until all the evidence was gathered. Norma Banks wouldn't want any *T*s left uncrossed on this one.

'What the hell makes them do it?' she said. A sheet, surrounded by a forensic screen, covered what was left of the girl called Mel. Blood spattered across the tarmac, seeping out from under the sheet.

'She was acting out of the ordinary, just like Steven Hubbard,' I said, by way of explanation.

'Something set her off. Paddy Gibb and Purcell have been talking with the station commander. He says the fire was set deliberately. They were lucky the whole building didn't go up. She used an accelerant to start it. Witnesses say she sprayed somebody with a liquid, probably lighter fluid.'

'So, it was premeditated. She must have somehow taken petrol in to use it as an accelerant. And she would know the cooking oil would go up as well.'

'We finally got hold of a manager who gave us a name. Mel Carpenter. She was a sous chef in the hotel. Quiet. Somebody who kept herself to herself.'

'That hotel is part of a large chain, so I'm assuming the human resources files were kept on a server offsite and not up there.'

'You assume correct, Inspector. We have Watt onto it now. We need somebody to go and talk to next of kin.' She looked back over at the sheet-covered body. 'We're going to have to identify her by dental records. You can get that information from the next of kin too. Watt has the details. I'll leave you with that and check in with you later.'

'Yes, ma'am.'

'I'm going back to the station, although the way the traffic is I'd be quicker walking. In fact, maybe that's a good idea.' She took her packet of cigarettes out in anticipation of being out in Market

Street, at the side of Waverley, where she could finally light up. It was all uphill to the station from here, whether she took Fleshmarket Close opposite the exit, or walked up Cockburn Street. Maybe the thought of a drag would spur her on.

My phone rang and I took the call, ending it just before Kim came up to me.

'Chatting up other women?' she said, looking at Jeni's retreating back.

'She's forty-five, according to her profile. I mean, I like older women, but I don't feel sleeping with her would get me up the ladder quicker.'

'I said chatting up. You're getting way ahead of yourself there, cowboy.'

'I heard she set fire to the hotel,' Kim said, sombre now.

'We just got her details from the hotel HQ. She has parents who live in Fife and she has her own apartment down in Powderhall.'

'Who's going to see her parents?'

'Percy just sent me a text. He's going with Steffi Walker. Give him a call and arrange for him to take you.'

'No, I have other things to do. Norma wants me to find out what went on at the hotel. Are you going to the girl's flat?'

I nodded. 'I'll take Julie. Andy and Hazel are with Paddy over at the hotel.' With a ton of other police. 'Oh, and I have some bad news for you,' I said.

'Okay. I'm listening.'

'Guess where I had dinner reservations for tonight.' I looked up in the direction of the Carlton.

'Oh shit.'

Half an hour later, Kate Murphy had released the body for transport to the mortuary.

As it turned out, Mel's mother and father lived in North Queensferry, on the other side of the Firth of Forth, in the Kingdom of Fife. Purcell had been quite happy for Steffi to drive. Apparently, she was a better driver than I was, or, as he put it, *You can't be any worse than Stirling fucking Moss.*

The sun was shining, but a wind blew in from the Forth. Steffi looked out the back window. There was a patio with a stone balustrade running around it. Dalgety Bay was in the distance, across the Firth of Forth. It was a modern house in a modern development, priced for its view.

'What's Mel done now?' Carpenter said. He was a tall man, probably ex-military.

'We're still investigating,' Purcell said, 'but we believe she took her own life this afternoon.'

Her mother sat down heavily on the couch, followed by Carpenter. The man looked at Purcell. 'What do you mean, *you believe?*' Gone was any form of arrogance now.

'Sir, this is not easy, but your daughter jumped to her death from the North Bridge this afternoon.'

'No!' her mother screamed. 'She wouldn't do that!'

There were tears running down the old man's face and he appeared to have aged in the space of a few moments. 'Calm down, Nettie. Let the police officers tell us what happened.' He looked at Purcell. 'How can you be so sure?'

'Some of our officers were there when she jumped,' Steffi said. 'We had a police negotiator there talking to her, but she didn't listen.'

'Well, he wasn't very good then, was he?' Nettie shouted, trying to stand, but held back by her husband.

'It's not their fault, Nettie. Don't blame them.' Carpenter held his wife firmly before looking at Steffi. 'She was supposed to be at work in the hotel. We heard about the fire and couldn't get through to her. We were worried.'

Nettie was sobbing hard but stopped to look up, sniffling. 'So, you're saying there was a fire in the hotel where she worked, but she didn't die in the fire?'

'Yes,' Purcell said.

'She got out but then committed suicide. This doesn't even make sense!' Her voice rose again and she thumped her fists up and down. 'I won't believe she did this.'

Carpenter pulled her in closer again. Looked at the two detectives. 'She's had problems for a long time, but we thought she'd got over them.'

'I'm sorry to have to ask this, but we're going to need dental records to help identify her,' Steffi said.

'Oh God,' her mother said, and started crying hysterically again.

'Her dentist is in the town. I'll give you his number,' Carpenter said. 'And I'm assuming we won't be able to see her?'

'I'm sorry. Sometimes the old cliché is true; best to remember her how she was.'

'Well that's just fucking great!' Nettie shouted. 'Now we can't even say goodbye to her because she's all fucked up!'

'Nettie, I'm going to call the doctor. You need to take something.'

'Don't bother. I've still got enough of that shit lying around here. I'll pop some later. God knows he gave me enough of them the last time!'

'We had some problems with Mel a while back. She disowned us. We haven't seen her for a while,' Carpenter said.

'She was a beautiful girl, but she just had problems. All the medicine in the world couldn't help her.'

'She was doing better though,' Carpenter said. 'She's had problems for years. We even saw a bit of an improvement after she went to that place.'

'What place?' Purcell said.

'It's called *Paradise Shores*. It's a wellness retreat. It's for de-stressing your life.'

'Which is a fancy name for rehab clinic,' Nettie said.

'It's not full of junkies, as my wife might suggest, but for people with depression problems. It's not an asylum, I can assure you. Mel had issues with her self-esteem, that's all. She just needed her confidence boosted.'

'The health spa and the wellbeing clinic are in the same place?' Steffi asked.

'Yes. It's in a former castle up in the Highlands. Some small town I can't even remember the name of now. But some people go there to de-stress, and there are therapists there too, if you want to book a session.'

'We can find it.' Steffi scribbled some notes.

Carpenter got up and walked over to an old-fashioned sideboard, picked up a personal telephone book, and flipped through the names until he got the number for Mel's dentist. 'He'll have Mel's X-rays. I believe he sent them to her new one when she moved to Edinburgh.' He wrote it down on a small piece of paper and handed it to Purcell.

'Was there anybody special in her life?' Purcell asked. 'A boyfriend. Girlfriend. Any special friends?'

'She wasn't gay and she never talked about a boyfriend. She did have dinner with somebody a few weeks ago. A man. She didn't say where she met him, but she seemed excited about seeing him.'

'Did you ask his name?' Steffi asked.

Nettie looked at her. 'She laughed and told us to mind our

own business. It was nothing to do with dating, she said, but this man made her happy, whoever he was.'

'Somebody from work?' Purcell suggested.

'Could be. She saw him twice. Then she never spoke of him again. She seemed so much happier though, as if she'd turned a corner.'

Purcell looked out the tall windows for a moment. It was indeed a beautiful view. Maybe one day he and Suzy could afford a place like this. If he won the lottery.

'Thank you for your help. And again, I'm sorry for your loss. We'll be in touch about Mel's personal effects.'

Nettie stood. 'I want to go to her flat. I want her stuff.'

Steffi stepped forward and put a hand on Nettie's arm. 'We have officers going through her flat just now.'

'I want to go. She's my daughter! They're her things!'

'I know. I understand. But it's something we have to do.'

'Come on, love,' Carpenter said. 'I'll make you some tea.'

'We'll see ourselves out.' Purcell placed a business card on the coffee table.

Outside in the driveway, Purcell looked around for a moment before they got in the car. 'It just goes to show, no matter how much money you have, you're not always happy, eh?'

'I wouldn't know, sir. I'm only a DC.'

'I wouldn't like to see the state that woman will be in if we find out for sure Mel torched the hotel.'

Purcell's phone rang as Steffi drove away. After listening to the caller, he hung up.

'That was DCI Gibb. The fire brigade just found two bodies burnt in the kitchen. A liquid was poured all around the place and set alight.'

'Maybe she went over the edge, mentally. I know there's a lot of people who want to tell their boss to shove it, but don't.'

'Are you trying to tell me something, Officer Walker?'

'No, but maybe Mel wanted to and went one step further.'

'Her parents think she was happier than she'd ever been.'

'I used to tell my parents that when I was in the army. Sometimes I was more scared than I've felt in my life, but I didn't tell them that.'

We never do, Purcell thought.

THIRTEEN

As a precaution, we took an ARU with us when we went to Mel Carpenter's home. Two people had seen her spray lighter fluid at the rapidly spreading pool of gasoline, just before the whole kitchen was engulfed.

It wouldn't be beyond the realms of possibility for her to have rigged her apartment.

We were down in Powderhall, an area of Edinburgh that had been famous for its dog racing many years ago.

'My dad would remember this place when it was the greyhound racing stadium,' Julie said, as she followed the ARU Mitsubishi into the housing estate.

'More flats,' I said. 'They're springing up everywhere.'

'Where we are now, there used to be an old scoreboard. Gigantic it was. There were men inside putting up the results, back when numbers were painted on placards and slotted into position so the punters could see. Then it went electronic. My dad has loads of photos from here he used to show us.'

'The Edinburgh Monarchs motorbike racing was here too, wasn't it?' I said, as we stepped out of the car.

'It was. There was a dirt racing track inside the dog racing circuit. Most Friday nights they would race here.'

It seemed as if Edinburgh was evolving into something else entirely, reinventing itself as it slid into the twenty-first century. I wondered what the next fifty years would bring, but by then I'd either be pushing up the daisies or daytime TV would be the highlight of my day.

More uniforms were behind us as we went up one flight of stairs. The uniform smacked the door back with the battering ram and we stood back. Nothing happened.

The armed boys cleared the flat.

It was nice inside, a modern, two-bedroom affair, with one of them having an en suite. There was nothing remarkable about the place. Nice, new furniture, obviously bought by Mummy and Daddy if a sous chef's wages were anything to go by.

We looked for any evidence that would let us into Mel's head, but there wasn't anything obvious.

Except the TV.

A show had been playing and it was paused.

'It's the DVD player,' Julie said, picking up the remote.

I had a sinking feeling in my gut as she hit play. The setting could have been Edinburgh a few hundred years ago, but I recognised the show. It was a fantasy programme. *Kings and Queens*. A young woman darted furtively through some woods, while a palace burned in the background. She stopped when she saw some men approach her. They talked about the queen's arrival.

'Let me take you there,' the young woman said. 'I know a quick way.' She was standing on the top of a wall, with branches of trees around her. She stepped off the wall.

One of the men ran forward and jumped onto the wall, obviously expecting to see the woman lying at the bottom of some cliffs, or a mountain or something. I didn't watch the show, despite the rave reviews for it.

The camera followed the man as he jumped up, and then the viewer could see the girl didn't jump into oblivion at all, but down onto a set of stairs that led down through the clouds. They were barely discernible from the hillside.

The first man called to the other and they both jumped, landing on the steps and disappearing through the cloud.

'Jesus,' Julie said. 'Did you just watch what I watched?'

'I was with you every step of the way,' I replied, and she looked at me to see if the pun was intended, but it wasn't.

'First Steven Hubbard, and now this girl. One playing a video game and one watching a TV show. What the hell's going on, sir?'

'I wish I knew, Julie.' She had paused the show again.

'Take the DVD out. I want to take it as evidence.'

We found the box for it, and I put it in and slipped it into an evidence bag.

I left instructions for the uniform patrol to stay until the joiner turned up to fix Mel's door. She wouldn't be around to file a complaint, but her father would, I was sure of it.

We went back to the station. Before I entered the evidence, I wanted to show Purcell and Gibb what we had found.

I played it in the conference room.

'It's the DVD of a TV show called *Kings and Queens*. It's a fantasy show.'

'I've heard of it, but I haven't watched it,' Purcell said, a little too convincingly, as if we were accusing him of sitting watching porn in his underpants.

'I watch it all the time,' Gibb said. Jeni Bridge looked at him. 'What?' he said, shrugging. 'It just pulls you along. There's a lot of fighting in it.'

'I took you as more of a cops and robbers sort of a man,' Jeni said.

'I see enough of that in here.'

'I saw him as more of a *Coronation Street* sort of man,' Purcell said.

I played the DVD before they roped me into the conversation. 'Mel was talking like this as she stood on the bridge earlier. Then she said she was going to show us a better way to go. Then she stepped off. The character on the show looks as if she's stepping into thin air but in fact, she steps onto a set of stairs you can only see from a certain angle.'

I showed them what I meant.

'So, was she like Hubbard?' Jeni asked. 'Depression?'

Purcell answered. 'Yes. Stemming from low self-esteem. She went to a private wellness centre, called *Paradise Shores*. I had one of the DCs look it up. It's in a converted castle, in Golspie, run by an American and his wife. They're both psychologists. It looks pretty upscale.'

'It sounds like a brothel my ex-husband visited while he was in Thailand,' Jeni said. We looked at her. 'No, he didn't, but I wish he had so I could have screwed him in the divorce.'

'So we assume she was unstable, just like Hubbard was?' Gibb said.

'It would appear so,' Jeni said. 'I've seen it before, when people just leave reality behind for a moment. Although we'll reserve judgement until the toxicology results come back.'

I doubted very much they would find anything other than prescription meds when we got the results.

My mobile phone rang. I talked to the person on the other end and then ended the call.

I left the conference room with Julie.

'Where are we going?' she asked me.

'To see an old woman.'

Steven Hubbard's mother lived in Broomhouse. It was a better area than it used to be, close to the government buildings on Broomhouse Road

'The DVLA used to be in one of those buildings,' I told Julie, as we turned left at the lights. 'Before they moved it to Edinburgh Park. Then a few years later, they closed all the offices in the UK.'

'Why would they do that?'

'Some clown politician figured they could save a few million a year. Considering they bring in billions every year, the money they saved was a drop in the ocean. It looked good for him though.' I didn't like politicians. Most of them were slimy bastards, out to line their own pockets. Maybe Purcell was right. Diddling the taxpayer certainly lined your own pockets. I'd yet to meet a politician who actually worked for the people who put them in power.

'So where do people go who need help?'

'The post office, mainly.'

'Jesus. In my local one, it's two old women who run it. I can only imagine what a fiasco that was when they first had to take over.'

We stopped outside Mrs Hubbard's house, a little terraced affair opposite some new houses that had sprung up.

'Old Mother Hubbard,' Julie said, getting out of the passenger side. The old woman had one of her curtains parted and let it fall back when she saw us arrive.

Inside, she led us through to her small living room where she had been keeping watch.

'How are things with you now, Mrs Hubbard?' I asked her.

'The press have been awful. One young man from some

manky magazine wanted an exclusive on Steven. Wanted me to dish the dirt on my own son. They've treated me like a scumbag. And my neighbours treat me like a leper. Nobody talks to me, and I've had eggs thrown at the house. Like it's my fault.' Her lips trembled as she spoke to me.

'I can have more patrol cars from Corstorphine swing by,' I said, making a mental note to do so whether she wanted it or not.

'It's okay.' She looked at Julie. 'I have the kettle on. Tea or coffee, hen?'

'Coffee, please, Mrs Hubbard.'

'You, Detective Miller?'

'The same, thanks. Do you want a hand?'

'No, I'll do it.'

While she busied herself, we sat down. The living room was simply furnished. The small, flat screen TV clashed with the old sideboard that was obviously an heirloom. I felt sorry for the old woman. This was often the way. The family would suffer the wrath directed at a dead relative who had done something nefarious.

'This is a nice house,' Julie said, looking at a china cabinet filled with knick-knacks.

'Where do you live, Julie?' I asked, realising I didn't know. It was something I should have made an effort to find out but hadn't.

'East London Street.'

'The New Town? Nice.'

'What about you, sir? Or is that a question I shouldn't be asking?'

'I live in the Old Town. In Royal Mile Mansions on the North Bridge. My wife and I bought it before she died.'

Her eyes went wide. 'Oh God, I'm sorry. I didn't know.'

'It was a few years ago. She died on duty. She was a detective, like me.'

'Jesus. I'm so sorry.'

'Don't be. Working as a team, you get to know the people you work closely with. Now Kim lives with me, her and her little girl. Emma's going to become my stepdaughter this summer.'

'That's nice.'

Mrs Hubbard came back in with three mugs. Then she pottered about, looking through an ottoman that was sitting to one side of the chair. She took out a leather-bound book then sat down.

'Some stuff was taken away from Steven's flat for evidence. Then I got a call telling me I could go in and take whatever I wanted. He wasn't a fiction reader, but he liked to look at books about history and all sorts of non-fiction stuff. This was in his bookcase.'

She held up the book for us to see.

'It's a diary. He wrote down thoughts in it, things he did and was planning to do. I looked through it, not to be nosey, but to find a connection with him. Does that make sense?'

It did, and I told her so.

'Then I came to a bit where he said he was going to a place called *Paradise Shores*. I thought it was a resort in Ibiza or something, but no, it's a place in the Highlands. Some wellness centre, they call it. I thought it was strange. It didn't seem to be the kind of place he would want to go to. Then I found out why. He was seeing a girl. I didn't even know about her.'

'Does it mention her name?' I asked.

'Yes. Her name is Mel. There's not a last name, but he mentions that she's a chef in the Carlton Hotel on the North Bridge. And when I saw it had been set on fire today, and they thought it started in the kitchens, I remembered this book.'

I saw Julie looking at me. We hadn't given out Mel's name to the press. 'Did you ever meet this woman?' I asked.

'Yes. A week ago at Steven's funeral. She came up to me afterwards, dressed in black like a widow. She smiled at me, shook my hand and told me she was a friend of Steven's. It was only when I was looking through the book yesterday I realised this was the same woman.' She looked at me. 'I'm assuming she's the one who jumped off the bridge today.'

'I'm so sorry, Mrs Hubbard, but I can't talk about it. This is an ongoing investigation—'

She held up a hand. 'I suspect it is. Steven mentions in here he was going to this *Paradise Shores* place with her.' She looked lovingly at the book before passing it over to me. 'What Steven did wasn't normal. Find out why he did it, Inspector.'

FOURTEEN

'See what you're getting yourself into?' Samantha said to Jack.

'What do you mean?' He was sitting on the small couch in their hotel room, flipping through the TV channels. The remains of a bagel and cream cheese sat on a plate on the coffee table in front of him. He was jet-lagged after yesterday's flight, knowing his body would take a few days to get used to the time difference.

He and Samantha had slept in late, and when he looked at his watch, he saw it was already mid-afternoon in the UK.

'You couldn't ask to get involved with a more dysfunctional family.'

He muted the TV. 'Just because your sister's getting a divorce doesn't make you dysfunctional.'

'It would have been nice to come back here and it just be a normal visit.'

'It's life, Sam. Nobody's perfect.'

She walked over to him and leaned over, kissing him on the cheek. 'You know I love you, Jack Miller, don't you?'

'Of course I do. I love you too.'

'I'm going to shower.'

He watched her walk into the bathroom, and knew he felt something for her he hadn't felt for any woman since his wife. He'd loved Beth with all his heart, had been broken-hearted when she died, and he'd sworn to himself he'd never get heavily involved with another woman again. Then Samantha Willis walked into his life.

He kept the volume off but continued flipping. A tabloid talk show called *Maury* came on. It was a talk show a bit like Britain's *Jeremy Kyle Show* except these young people were on here to find out who the father of their children was. He put the sound back on for a second. The audience were booing some young guy who looked as if he couldn't hold down a job. He denied being the little boy's father. The host, Maury Povich, was passed a brown envelope from a producer. The young man on the stage was told he wasn't the father of the boy.

The young man danced about the stage, and the young woman rushed off. It turned out this man was the fifth one who had been DNA tested, and she was sure he was the one.

Jack switched the TV off. Picked up the phone and dialled a number in Edinburgh.

'Neil? It's Jack.'

'Hey, Jack. How's things going over there?' Neil McGovern said, from his office in the Scottish Parliament Building in Edinburgh.

'Sam's sister's in a bad way, which is to be expected. Her husband's an arsehole though.'

'Do tell.'

'He's been having an affair. He went to see this woman on the night his son died. That's why Wendy was out; she was suspicious so she followed him after his shift. She saw Chip go into a woman's house. Then when she got back home, Ryan was dead.'

'Have they confirmed it was an overdose?'

'Yes.'

'But?'

'How do you know there's a "but"?'

'I know you, Jack.'

Jack took a deep breath and was momentarily distracted by Maury. 'Two "buts", Neil. One, I think Ryan was murdered.'

'Wait a minute; murdered?'

'That's what I said, murdered.'

'You sure this isn't the old murder squad detective in you giving it yahoo? Seeing crimes where there aren't any?'

'Nice psychology there, but hundreds have tried long before you, my friend, and not one of them succeeded. Making me doubt myself.'

'You're not doubting yourself though, are you?'

'Of course not.'

'Talk to me then, Jack. I'm all ears.'

'I had a look round the room where the boy died. There was no sign of any past drug use, or attempts to hide it. Same with his bedroom. Yet, he had a needle mark on his arm and a little bag of pills was found near him. Fentanyl.' He went on to describe what he had been looking for and what he had found. 'And his mother said he was acting normally. And he'd been drinking that night, which meant he could have been overpowered more easily.'

'I've known some drug addicts, Jack, and he doesn't sound like one to me. On the face of it, I would agree with you.'

'I also need a favour.'

'And now we get to the point.' McGovern laughed.

'I'm that predictable.'

'You are that, old son.'

'Maybe you could make enquiries with your pals over here.

There's a car keeping us under observation. A dark blue Chevy Impala.'

'You obviously have a plate number, or my friends would be searching for the next ten years.'

'I do.' He read it out to him.

'I can't promise anything, but I'm owed a few favours. How many in the car?'

'Two of them. I was thinking it was maybe detectives from Chip's department, the Town of Newburgh Police, but they're stretched to bursting from what I've heard, so I don't think they have the manpower.'

'I'll get onto it later today and call you the same time tomorrow. Let me know if anything gets freaky there. I have friends in Albany too.'

'Will do, Neil. Thanks, buddy.' He cut the call and was sitting watching another couple arguing on the tabloid talk show when Samantha came out of the bathroom, rubbing her hair dry. She was wearing a bathrobe and normally he might have tried to undo it, but nothing could be further from his mind.

'Did I miss anything?' she asked.

'You did actually. It seems some guy called Cameron really is the father of Chanelle's daughter.'

Its official name was International House of Pancakes, but everybody called it by its acronym IHOP. A restaurant chain, the local one was at the Target Plaza on Route 17K, which was a horseshoe-shaped strip mall, with Target as its anchor store.

Pancakes ordered, the server brought them a carafe of orange juice. And two cups of coffee. 'It's been a long time since I was here,' Samantha said, cradling the cup and looking out the window. It was windy outside, grey clouds scudding by, heading north.

'It's my first time,' Jack said, pouring the OJ.

'You've never been to one at all?'

'Don't make it sound like I haven't been with a woman before.' He smiled at her as he passed her a glass.

Samantha laughed, then stopped as if she had brought an image of her nephew to the forefront of her thoughts. 'I still find it hard to believe Ryan's gone,' she said.

'A death in the family is never easy.'

'I can't believe he was a drug user. I'm not saying he was an angel, but he never showed any sign he wanted to take heroin.'

'He could have gotten involved with somebody at college.' Jack hadn't told Samantha his thoughts on the subject, not wanting to rock the boat in their relationship. He was tormented, torn between telling her what he thought and keeping his mouth shut, when Samantha made the decision for him.

'I know I'm only a crime writer and you were a real detective, Jack, but I wanted to tell you something. Please keep it to yourself.'

'Okay. Anything you tell me, stays between us.'

She was about to reach over and grab his hand when the server came with the food. Jack topped up their coffee cups from the flask.

'You were about to tell me something,' he said, digging into his pancakes.

Samantha looked at him as if she wasn't sure how to carry on. 'Look, you might think I'm way off bat here, but... I think Ryan was murdered.'

Jack washed down his pancakes with coffee. 'I have to say I'm relieved.'

Samantha raised her eyebrows for a second. 'That isn't the

reaction I was looking for, to be honest. I thought you would tell me I'm a paranoid aunt who was being dramatic.'

'I say relieved, because everything is pointing to Ryan being murdered. We don't know for sure, of course, but he didn't display any of the signs associated with drug use.'

'I know some people die from an overdose, but they're usually using the substance. It doesn't make sense that Ryan would want to try it and then take too much at one time.'

'It does happen, especially with fentanyl. It's fifty times more potent than heroin, and some people mix it. But they're usually the ones who are looking for a stronger fix.'

'I feel sick, to be honest. I can't express this feeling to Wendy, but on the other hand, I would feel guilty if I didn't.' She picked at her own food.

'We can't mention it just now. Let's see what the medical examiner has to say about the toxicology results. One step at a time. We don't want to jump in with both feet.' Jack looked up for a second, just in time to see the Chevy Impala that had been following them, drift by the side of the restaurant, heading for the back parking lot.

He patted his jacket. 'I've left my wallet in the car,' he said, standing up.

'Oh, I see how it goes; you leave and they'll have me washing the dishes when you don't come back.' She smiled a weak smile at him.

'I'll have the car running outside. Come running when you hear me honk the horn.' He laughed as he made his way out.

He'd parked the Tahoe round the side of the restaurant in one of the slots facing the main road. When he got out, he could see the Impala had pulled in next to him. He stood where he was for a moment, seeing a pair of feet on the other side of the big SUV. Then the feet disappeared and the Impala reversed out. Jack ducked back. This side lot was one-way, so he knew the car would have to drive right round to come back out. When the blue sedan moved out of sight, he jogged up to the car.

He took out the key fob and had the doors unlocked before he got to the car and jumped in behind the driver's seat, where the darkened sun glass would hide him.

He watched the Impala with the two men in it approach the traffic lights at the exit and turn right.

He stepped out and felt around in the front wheel arch and found what he was looking for.

A magnetic GPS unit.

'Sneaky bastards,' he said to himself. He opened the driver's door and left it on the seat and went back inside.

'Look,' Samantha said as Jack sat back down, 'I hope I didn't sound paranoid. I don't want you to think I imagine every death to be murder.'

'Of course not. That's why I wanted to look at Ryan's room, and asked Wendy those questions. It was what I would have done in Edinburgh, back in the day.' He drank more coffee.

'I like travelling with you, Jack. I just wish this was under better circumstances.'

'I'd like to try Florida.'

'Maybe we'll go in the fall when it's not so humid.'

'How about a weekend in Amsterdam when we get back?'

'Sounds good.'

'Listen, Sam,' he said, after the server brought over their bill, 'I went out to the car because I saw somebody drive past.'

'Who?'

'I'm not sure. I saw them before, outside Wendy's house and again in our hotel car park. I saw them drive by the window just now. When I went outside, they were at the side of the Tahoe.'

Samantha looked at him. 'Did they come in here?'

'No. They left a magnetic GPS unit under the front wheel arch.'

She looked shocked for a moment. 'That sounds like something the feds would do.'

'I know. Now they won't have to follow us because they'll know wherever we are. But I've got a surprise for them.'

He paid at the front desk and they left the restaurant. When they got in the car, Jack drove round into the main parking lot, on the Target side. He drove past an articulated truck parked in a corner. Curtains were drawn round the inside of the cab, suggesting the driver was asleep.

Jack turned the SUV around and pulled in close to the forward facing truck, and stopped for a second. He took the GPS unit and stuck it under the trailer, hearing it clink onto the metal. Then he drove away.

'I don't know where that truck's going, but whoever is tracking us is going to be scratching his head.'

'They'll figure it out soon enough that we found it.'

'It might buy us some time.'

Samantha's throwaway mobile phone rang. She could hear shouting and screaming on the other end before a voice spoke.

'Sam, it's Chip. You'd better come now. Wendy's about to be arrested.'

FIFTEEN

They headed north on Route 300, then took east on I84. Then the exit for 9W and they were in the Fostertown area within fifteen minutes. By which time, Wendy was sitting in the back of a Town of Newburgh Police Ford Explorer.

Chip was there in civilian clothes, but three of his colleagues had turned up in three patrol cars. He was standing on the doorstep of a large, detached one-level house. He walked down the path when he saw the Tahoe approaching.

A sergeant – that morning's patrol supervisor – was sitting in an older version of the SUV Jack was driving. He got out as Chip reached the road.

'Chip, what's going on?' Samantha said, as she got out of the big car. She looked at Wendy sitting on the hard plastic seats that were standard fare in the back of the police SUVs.

'I was here with my friend when Wendy turned up and started going mental. Shouting and kicking the front door. I had to call the patrol supervisor to come and take care of things.'

'You couldn't take care of it yourself?'

'No, he couldn't,' the female said as she approached. 'Your sister is lucky I'm not going to press charges.'

'Maybe if you left her husband alone, then Wendy wouldn't have to come here.'

The woman pulled out a police badge and practically shoved it into Samantha's face. 'I'm a police officer, honey. Chip and I work together.'

All the anger Samantha had felt building up on the drive over left her like air rushing out of a balloon. 'So what now?'

The sergeant stood next to Samantha. 'We're going to release Wendy into your care. If she starts this nonsense again, she'll be in Orange County Jail. Do I make myself clear?'

'Yes.'

Jack walked up to Samantha after he had snapped off a photo of Chip's girlfriend. He made it look as if he was checking a text.

'Who are you?' the sergeant asked.

'I'm retired Detective Chief Inspector Jack Miller. Samantha's friend.' Jack stood at six-foot-five and towered over the sergeant.

'You can take her away, but I don't want to get a call to come up here again. Is that understood?' he said to Samantha.

'Yes.'

He opened the back door of the patrol SUV and helped Wendy out. Then he took the handcuffs off.

'Really, George? Handcuffs?' Wendy said.

'It was for your own protection, Mrs Haines.' The supervisor closed the back door of the car as Samantha led her sister away.

'Jesus Christ, Wendy, what the hell were you thinking?' Samantha said to her sister as they got into Wendy's old Chrysler minivan.

Wendy just started crying as Jack followed them. Samantha drove, knowing her sister was in no fit state. It didn't take long to get to Wendy's house and she parked Wendy's car outside the left hand door while Jack parked near the pathway to the house.

With coffee made, they sat in the living room, Wendy looking rough, her eyes red and her face puffy.

'Do you want to tell us what's going on?' Samantha said.

'You can see what's going on, Sam. My life is falling apart.' She drank some of the black coffee. Looked at her sister. 'Chip didn't come home last night. I knew where he'd be. So I went over to confront him, to tell him to get his stuff the fuck out of my house. But that bitch started in on me. I swear to God, if she wasn't a cop, I would have kicked the shit out of her.'

'You're not going to gain anything by going over there.'

'Apart from satisfaction, you mean?'

Samantha stood. 'Have you been to a funeral home to arrange things yet?' Just saying the words out loud seemed so unreal.

Wendy shook her head. 'No. I was supposed to go with Chip, but he told me I could take care of it on my own. He's too busy fucking that whore of his.'

'We'll help you, Wendy,' Jack said.

'The medical examiner will have to release him first. After the autopsy is done. Until then, we'll have to wait,' Samantha said.

'We'll be here for as long as it takes,' Jack said. Then his thoughts turned to the blue Impala again. And the two men who were driving it.

Then a thought struck him. 'Did Ryan have a lot of friends?'

Wendy looked at him. 'He had a few. Why?'

'I was just wondering. Have any of them been to see you?'

'No. They weren't those sort of friends. It was a bunch of guys who hung around together, working on cars mostly. Ryan liked to tinker with his own car.'

'Where is his car?'

'It's in the garage.'

'Do you mind if I go and have a look at it?'

'No, of course not. There's a door leading into the garage from the basement room.'

Jack walked downstairs and found the door. There was a short corridor. He flipped the light switch and saw a door on the right and one in front of him. The right was the laundry room. Straight ahead was the garage. Another fumble on the left and he found the light switch for the garage.

The fluorescents lit up the double space. There were no windows offering any light, but it was well illuminated. He looked at the old Honda Civic and suddenly the hairs on the back of his neck went up.

Somebody had obviously already had a look at the car. The seats had been cut open, the boot had been left open and the tools were scattered on the concrete floor behind the car, along with the carpet. The backs of the seats had been cut open. Carpeting in the front of the old car had also been ripped up.

Whoever had come in here had been looking for something, but two questions sprang to mind; what had they been looking for?

And, more importantly, how had they gotten in?

The garage doors were locked.

He walked back into the basement and had a look around. The back door and all the windows were secure.

Whoever had done this had a key.

He went back upstairs and asked Wendy where Ryan's keys were.

'I have them. Why?'

He explained what he had found.

'Who the hell would do that?' she asked, shock written all over her face.

'Somebody was looking for something. They obviously thought Ryan had it.'

'How did they get in?'

'Who else has a key?'

'Me, Chip, and Ryan were the only ones who had a key. Oh, and my neighbour next door, but she's in her sixties. A widow. You don't think...?'

'No, I don't think your neighbour would do that to Ryan's car.' He looked at Wendy. 'Where is this place where he hung out with his friends?'

'It's over in New Windsor. They all chipped in to rent it. They're a nice bunch of boys. A couple are a bit older, one of them is married. I've never heard Ryan say a bad word about them.'

'I'd like to talk to them. I'm assuming they know about what happened to Ryan?'

Wendy nodded. 'Chip said he would talk to them. They won't be there until this evening though. They work during the day.'

'I'll go tonight.'

He wondered if somebody had it in for Ryan, but he suspected it went deeper than that. Maybe one of the friends would be able to help him.

He'd soon find out.

SIXTEEN

Inspector Suzy Campbell came into the flat and dropped down into a chair. Bear, their German Shepherd came bounding over.

'How were things today?' Percy Purcell said, coming through from the kitchen with a ladle in his hand.

'I'm bloody knackered. I thought going back to uniform would be a good thing, but I sometimes think it's harder than being a detective.'

Purcell walked over to her, shooing the dog out of the way and gave her a kiss. 'You need some special Percy loving.'

'I need a gin.' She got up. 'I got fooled by that *special loving* talk before.'

'Hey, if I was to market that, women would be lining up for a sample.'

Suzy laughed. 'It better make us millions, Percy, or you'll be going down in my estimation.'

He raised his eyebrows and smiled. 'Just take a look at the goods, and tell me this isn't worth a million pounds.'

'You're enthusiastic if nothing else, I'll give you that.' She walked over to their cabinet in the corner where they kept the booze and poured herself a G&T then followed Percy back into the kitchen to get ice.

'How's Angie Rivers?' Another detective who worked with Suzy in uniform.

'I think she misses Aberdeen, but the fact that I'm here helps her.'

'I'm surprised she wanted to come down here in the first place.' He stirred the stew he was making, taking another sip of the gravy. 'Not only an amazing lover, but a master chef in the kitchen as well. What a guy.'

'God, your modesty amazes me.'

'I hope that's not all that amazes you.' He put the spoon in the stew and turned to her, bringing her in close for a hug, kissing her passionately.

'Jesus, as much as I'd like you to take me through to the bedroom, I need a shower. And there's a dog watching us.'

Purcell looked at Bear. 'You need to know when to look away, son.' The dog chuffed at him and ran to get his rubber ball.

'So, maybe later tonight,' Purcell said to Suzy.

'I think your ambitions are getting ahead of your abilities. You're going for a pint with Frank later, aren't you?'

Purcell looked past Suzy and rubbed his chin. 'Decisions, decisions. Stay in with girlfriend and make wild, passionate love to her? Or go for a drink with a colleague?'

'Go for a pint. It'll last longer and won't put so much strain on your heart.'

Purcell looked at her. Blew out some air in resignation. 'You're probably right.'

Suzy laughed as she threw the ball for Bear. 'Your dad said he's going to Facetime before dinner.'

'I'll call him now then. I don't want the old sod calling me when I have you in an embrace.'

'Take a cold shower first.'

Purcell laughed as he switched his iPad on and called his father.

'Oh, there's Mister Bear!' Lou Purcell said from Aberdeen. The dog wagged his tail when he heard Lou's voice.

'Good afternoon to you too, old man,' Purcell said.

'Okay, don't get all jealous on me now. I miss you too. That's why I can't wait to come and visit you.'

'I said you needed to get a pet when I left.'

'I don't have time to look after a dog.'

'You looked after Bear when I was staying with you.'

'That was different. I knew he would be moving out one day. Besides, my social life is getting busier by the minute.'

'Uh oh. I don't like the sound of this.'

'Listen, son, I'm in my early sixties. Not quite ready to be pushing up the daises.'

'Christ, I wish you wouldn't talk like that.'

'It's a fact of life. You're only on this planet once, so you might as well enjoy yourself while you're here. I mean, having only one girlfriend at your age is fine, but—'

'Aw Jesus, here we go with the love-life tales. Be careful not to hold on to your little blue friend for too long or your fingers will get stiff.'

'Eh? What kind of talk is that in front of Suzy?' Lou waved. 'Hi, Suzy love. Is he looking after you okay?'

'He's doing a great job, Lou. He's even cooking dinner tonight.'

'Good for you. I hope it's not that stew like he cooked for me once. I was shitting through the eye of a needle for days afterwards.'

'Aw, for God's sake. You never had food poisoning off me, old man. You should try washing your hands before eating.'

'You never cooked for me more than one time.'

'She's better looking than you,' Purcell said, stirring the stew again.

'So anyway,' Lou said, carrying on, 'as I was saying, life's too short.'

'Why do I get the feeling you're going to tell me you've dumped Elizabeth?'

'Why are you so negative? Always looking on the dark side.'

'What's her name, Lou? This new Judy you're going out with.'

'Judy? I've not heard that expression in a long time.'

'Grandpa used to say it. When he was telling me about the birds and bees and introducing me to lager.'

'What? That old sod. I knew you were drinking as a teenager.'

'Just get on with it, Dad. Tell me who she is. And how did Elizabeth take the break-up?'

'Now, I never said I had broken up with Elizabeth. *You* said that. And this other lady is just a friend. For now.'

Purcell turned to look at Suzy. 'Can you believe this?'

'I'm going for a shower. See you later, Lou.'

'Bye, Suzy.'

'So, tell me what's going on,' Purcell said.

'Well, it's somebody I used to work with. We connected on that tweeter thing.'

'It's called Twitter, ignoramus.'

'Whatever. Tweets, twits, twats, it's all the same to me.'

'Give me the edited version, Lou, my stew's getting burnt.'

'Is that a euphemism for—'

'No it's not.'

'Anyway, Margery and I reconnected and we're going to meet up.'

'When?'

'See, that's the thing; she doesn't live up here.'

'Wait a minute. Hold your horses right there. That's why you wanted to come down here for a visit. I knew you were up to something! Missing me, my arse.'

'Well, I miss Bear.'

'I'm not having you come down here and using this flat as a knocking shop.'

'Hardly a knocking shop! I just asked Suzy if I could stay in your spare room. Like you stayed in mine, for the longest time while you were getting your divorce settled.'

'You're my father. It's what parents are supposed to do.'

'I agree. We look after each other. That's why I'd like to come and spend some time with you.'

'So you can come down here and entertain some filly? I won't be a part of your sordid affairs.'

'I told you, Margery and I used to work with each other. We're meeting for lunch and we'll catch up.'

'If Elizabeth finds out, she'll cut it off.'

'Don't be so bloody manky. A man can have some female friends without wanting something from them.'

'That's true. However, I know what you're like.'

'Keep your mind above your waistline and you'll be fine. So, when can I come down?'

'Look, Dad, we're busy with work right now, Suzy is still unpacking her stuff—'

'Liar. She showed me my room for when I come down. She even has the bed made. She showed me on this camera.'

Purcell gritted his teeth and stirred the stew. 'It's not like I don't want you to visit—'

'Me asking was just an FYI. I've already bought my bus ticket. I'll be there tomorrow.'

'I don't want this place used as a sex den.'

'What have you been smoking? I told you, at my age, we enjoy having a conversation and a good cup of coffee. Just wait, you'll be old one day.'

'I'm looking forward to it.'

'You say that now, but just wait 'til you have your family feeding you and wiping your arse.'

'*I* won't be wiping your arse.'

'So you'd rather see me in a home where they give you a good belting for shitting the bed?'

'Christ, I'm making stew here! God, now I'm going to call for pizza. You and your bloody talk about getting old.'

Lou laughed. 'Bye, Bear. Grandpa will see you soon!' He waved at the camera.

'He's not even in the kitchen. He said he couldn't care fucking less if you came down and he's sick of your shit.'

'Language, you wee bas—' But Purcell had already cut his father off. That was all he needed, Lou snoring away in the next room while he, Percy, was trying to get his end away.

He'd need to sit down with his father and have a talk about boundaries. No walking about in his Y-fronts when he felt like it. No stinking out the bathroom before he and Suzy had used it in the morning. No prank phone calls. The stew was starting to smell burnt.

'Balls!' he shouted out in frustration.

Then Bear came firing back into the kitchen with his ball.

SEVENTEEN

'Have you heard from Jack?' Kim asked as I loaded the dishwasher.

'I was talking to him earlier. Remind me to give you the number on their burner phones. They just bought them in Walmart.'

'Burner phones. You make them sound like they're gangsters.'

'That's what he called the disposable ones they bought. They don't want to be without a phone over there.'

'Makes sense. So what was he saying about Sam's nephew?'

I stopped for a moment. 'He thinks Ryan was murdered.' I explained to her why my father thought this.

'It could very well be, but what would the motive be and who would want to kill him?'

'That he doesn't know. There's something not right though, and my dad being an ex-detective, he finds it hard to switch off.'

'I hope he doesn't get into trouble, if there are shenanigans going on.'

'He can handle himself.' I finished loading the machine and turned it on.

'Are you still going out tonight?'

'I am. We thought it would be a bit more informal if Bruce met us for a drink.'

'Us?'

'Me, Percy, and Jeni.'

'Oh, it's Jeni now?' She smiled and slipped her arms round my waist.

'Chief Bridge when we're in the office.'

'Maybe I'll get to meet her one day. She skipped off before I could introduce myself at Waverley.'

'You never know. But tonight, it's all business.'

'I bet you say that to all the girls.' She kissed me on the lips.

'Yuck!' Emma said, coming into the kitchen.

I parted from Kim and smiled at the little girl. 'What are you up to, tiger?'

'Well, I'm just making up my birthday list. I'm not sure if I want a new car or a diamond ring like Mummy's.'

'You're too young to drive and your future husband will have to buy you a ring.'

'Yuck again! Boys are horrible. Except you, Frank. And my daddy. You're both okay, but those boys in my class are horrible. Kevin sits there and picks his nose and when I look over, he pulls his finger out and pretends he's not doing it. He's disgusting.' She looked at me as I was smiling. 'I'm not even kidding you, Frank. Laugh if you must, but you don't have to sit across from him.'

'I'll try to remember that. Now, you go and make up a new list. Maybe Charlie will buy you a present too, if you ask him nicely.'

'You think he would?' Her eyes widened at the thought of our cat buying her a gift, and she ran back through to the living room, calling out his name.

'Now Charlie *is* going to buy her a gift,' Kim said, laughing.

'He was going to anyway. He told me.'

'It's just as well I came into your life, Miller, or you'd be known as the daft old cat man.'

'Hey, when it was just me and Jack living here, the cat never answered me back. And he never got jealous when I petted another cat.'

'Get out of here,' she said, slapping my backside.

I wrote down the temporary phone numbers for the American mobile phones Jack had bought.

I put on a jacket as the wind was making it feel a lot colder than it was outside. 'I'll see you later,' I said to her, and she smiled back at me.

I'd gone to see the force psychologist, who was always at our disposal, and talked to him about Kim making comments about other women. He'd told me she might never get over the fact her ex-husband had cheated on her. There would always be a little insecurity on her part, and I would just have to accept that if I wanted to be with her. It was my job to constantly reassure her, and over time, it might get better, but some people who have experienced infidelity, never get over it.

Logie Baird's bar was quiet. A few of the regulars nodded to me. It was my local, or one of them I should say. It was where I went for a quiet pint, sometimes on my own, sometimes with Kim.

Tonight, I was meeting some of my colleagues.

Percy Purcell was propping up the bar, talking with the young barmaid who was serving. Alison was an attractive twenty-something, with blonde hair. A few years younger than Kim. I wondered what my fiancée would think if she came in here and found me innocently chatting to her.

Purcell saw me coming and waved me over. 'What are you having?' he asked.

'Since you're paying, I'll have a glass of the most expensive whisky you have, Alison,' I said.

'Give him a bottle of Budweiser, Ali,' Purcell said, peeling off a tenner. Then we both saw Jeni Bridge walking in. She was dressed in jeans and a sweater with a leather jacket. You would never know she was a cop.

'Whatever the lady's having, Ali,' Purcell said.

'That's very good of you, Percy,' Jeni said, smiling. 'Just a half of lager.

We got our drinks and sat at a corner table.

'Here's to us,' Jeni said, raising her glass.

'To us, ma'am,' Percy said.

'It's Jeni out of hours, Percy. That goes for all of us. You too, Frank.'

'I'll drink to that,' I said.

The door opened again and we all looked at it, as if the main feature was about to start, but it wasn't Bruce.

'I hope Hagan isn't giving a taxi driver a doing or anything,' Purcell said.

'He isn't likely to go off track with this, is he?' Jeni said.

'No, I'm just saying. Bruce is fine now. I wouldn't have suggested this if I thought he couldn't handle it. I also talked with Harvey Levitt, and he said Bruce should be okay.'

Famous last words, I thought.

I looked at my watch. It was early. Only 7:25 pm. I wondered how Jack had got on with his own endeavours.

The door opened again and in walked Hagan. He couldn't have looked more annoyed if his hair was on fire. He strode over to the table then broke into a smile.

'Bloody taxi driver tried taking me the long way, but I told him who I was and threatened to have his badge taken from him. He gave me a discount.'

Purcell closed his eyes for a second, wishing he hadn't made an earlier comment about Bruce smacking a taxi driver.

'Bruce, this is Chief Super Jeni Bridge. She's our new divisional commander.'

'Pleased to meet you, ma'am,' Hagan said, grinning and holding his hand out. Jeni shook it, aware some of the detective's fingers were missing, but she didn't blink. She was also aware his right ear had been cut off but the prosthetic – or *pathetic ear* as he called it – was covered by his hair, which he kept long.

'Pleased to meet you, Bruce. And call me Jeni. This is an informal meeting.'

'Sit yourself down and I'll get you a pint,' Purcell said.

'I'll take a bottle like Frank's got, if you don't mind,' he said, sitting down, placing himself between me and Jeni.

'How's your daughter settling into living in Edinburgh?' I asked Jeni as she toyed with the half pint she had sitting in front of her.

'It's hard, but she's adapting very well. She goes back through to Glasgow to spend some weekends with her father, but she likes it here a lot.'

She didn't elaborate on what the former husband did for a living, but none of us were interested.

Purcell came back with a bottle and handed it to Hagan, holding on to it for a second longer than was necessary and he raised his eyebrows slightly, as if they'd spoken on the phone and Purcell had promised the detective sergeant certain parts of his body would be hurting if he drank too much and showed us up.

'I believe you're a new father,' Jeni said, smiling.

Hagan took a swig from the bottle and thumped it down onto the table a little too hard. 'I am. This is our second one. I have a wee girl, and now a wee boy.'

I could see Purcell was gritting his teeth. If *we* could see Hagan had already been drinking, then Jeni could too. This was a fucking disaster. I'd trusted Hagan and I could see he was going to get drunk and say something he'd regret. Maybe I had rushed him into this.

He took another swig of the beer and laid the bottle back on the table a bit more gently. 'Sorry, sometimes I try too hard not to let something fall and the opposite nearly happens. And no, I haven't been drinking tonight before I came out. I just feel as if I've been given a new lease of life.'

I'm sure I sat with a look of surprise on my face.

'So, what's this job you want me to do?' he asked.

'You're going on holiday,' Jeni said.

'What's the catch?'

'You're going with me,' I said.

EIGHTEEN

Jack found the street address for the rented garage where the group of young men tinkered with their cars. That was the good news.

The bad news was, the place was a burnt-out shell.

He couldn't get parked close by for the fire trucks and police cars but managed to get parked in a side street a few blocks away. He walked back towards the garage and the group of onlookers, filming other people's misery with their mobile phones.

'What happened here?' he asked a young woman who was holding her phone up.

'The place caught fire. Nobody's saying anything. There's a detective there. He's from the Newburgh Fire Investigation Unit.' Jack looked at her, the question of how she knew obviously written all over his face. 'My mother went to one of the Citizen Police Academy courses.'

Jack nodded and thanked her. There was a group of young men standing about.

'Man, that's fucked up,' he heard one of them say. 'I put almost ten grand into that fucking Civic, and now it's up in smoke.'

'Did you guys know Ryan Haines?' he asked the young man.

'Yeah. You a cop?'

With this Scottish accent? I don't think so, son. 'No, I'm a friend of his mother's.'

One of the older guys in the group, a man with a bald head, a thick beard, and glasses, stepped forward. 'We're friends of Ryan's. Still can't believe he's gone.'

'It was sudden alright. His mother's devastated. She didn't know he was on drugs.'

'Ryan on drugs? None of us touch that shit, man. A couple of guys we used to hang around with OD'd on smack. We like having a drink but when we're down here, we work on our cars. We had a TV and a games console. We had a laugh in here, but none of us touched that shit. And if we find out who gave him that stuff—'

'I know how you feel. You'd like to avenge his death. But it doesn't alter the fact he was found with a bag of drugs next to him.'

'I'm telling you, Ryan wasn't into that.' The man took a step forward as if he were going to square up to Jack. Big mistake, Jack thought.

'I believe you, friend. What's your name, anyway? I'm Jack. I'm Ryan's Aunt Samantha's friend.'

The man nodded as if sizing Jack up. 'Cool. I'm Aaron. That's Matt. Moody. Tango.' He pointed to the others who nodded to him in lieu of a handshake. 'So, you were a cop at one time.' It was said matter-of-factly.

'That obvious, huh?'

'Oh yes,' Aaron said.

'You're right. I'm a retired murder squad detective. His mother isn't convinced he was a user either. So tell me then, was there anybody Ryan was hanging about with who could have given him the stuff?'

'We would have known,' one of the others said. A shorter man with dark hair and Latino looks. 'We're here most nights, either on the cars or gaming. We don't need to take any of that shit. It's just for losers. Sure, Ryan was having a hard time finding a job, and his time was taken up by the new woman in his life, but he was an ace guy.'

'I don't think his mother knew about a girlfriend,' Jack said.

'Hardly a girlfriend. A MILF, according to him. Although he was still working on getting to know her better.'

'You got a name for her?'

'Nah. Some blonde chick. I only saw her once when she was dropping Ryan off here. She peeled out of here when I opened the door. We teased him about her, but he said she was just a friend, not a girlfriend, but we knew he would be in there if he got half the chance.'

'What kind of car was it?'

'A Honda CR-V. Looked like '15 or '16. The new style. A chick's car.'

'Yeah, a *She*R-V,' the guy called Moody said.

Jack took out his burner phone and opened up the photos. Showed the young men the picture he'd taken of Chip Haines' girlfriend standing at her house. 'Is that her?'

'Yeah, that's her.'

'Was there anything belonging to Ryan in there that I can tell his mother she won't be getting back?' Jack said.

'His Civic. Man, he put a lot of money into that. He said he was going to sell it when he got it finished. It was almost there. Just a few tweaks and a new paint job and he would have got about eight grand for it.'

'That's a tidy sum,' Jack said.

'Until you realise he put in about ten grand. He started with a shell and put the engine in it and everything else.'

'Why wasn't he keeping it?'

'He was going to take the eight grand and put it down on a new Civic. They have a fast one coming out and he wanted that.'

'The Type-R,' Tango said.

'So what happened here do you think, guys?'

Smoke was still pouring out of the building, but the fire department had it under control. The main company was Vail's Gate, but they had a mutual aid system where other departments would be called out to help.

The girl who had been filming came over to join them. 'This is Gears. She's Aaron's girlfriend,' Moody said. 'She's one of the boys. Doesn't mind getting her hands dirty under the hood.'

'You say the nicest things,' Gears said. Jack wanted to know her real name but didn't push it.

'Do you guys own this building?' he said instead.

'Nah. We just rented it from some dude. He gave us a good rate as long as we paid on time.'

'I'm assuming there were other cars in there?'

'Fuck, yes,' Gears said. 'I was working on an old Scooby.'

'That's a Sub—' Moody started to say.

'Subaru,' Jack said. 'I might be old, but I'm not an old fart.'

'Yeah, dipshit,' Aaron said, slapping Moody's arm. 'We had a few cars in there. Projects we were working on. Our own cars were outside, thank fuck.'

'You guys had any trouble from anybody recently?'

'Nah. We're no angels, but we don't go looking for fights. That's for the little a-holes that go drag racing. We go to car meets, where hundreds of people turn up to look at all the cars,' Gears said.

'There was the trouble with Gremlin's family,' Tango said.

'Who's Gremlin?' Jack asked.

Aaron's face twisted for a second. 'He was some guy we met over at Bear Mountain Park when there was a car meet. He seemed okay. Had a nice Acura Prelude, but then he turned out to be a douchebag. He was taking heroin. Tried to get us into it so we told him to fuck off. Next thing we know, his wife finds him face down in their kitchen. Not even Narcan brought him round, he was so far gone.'

'You said you had trouble with his family?'

'Yeah. His father and one of his brothers came round here one night, looking to pick a fight. They blamed us. Us, for fuck's sake! They accused us of selling him the smack. Bunch of fucking rednecks.'

'Got an address for them?'

'Nah. We only know where Gremlin lived. He rented a house with his wife in New Windsor.' Aaron told him the address. 'I think his wife still lives there.'

'Do you think Gremlin's family could have been responsible for this?' Jack nodded towards the garage.

'Who knows. I wouldn't put it past them. That detective bloke has their name anyway. Next time they come looking for us, we won't be so polite.'

Jack looked over and saw the detective looking at him. 'You guys coming to the funeral?'

'Of course, man. Ryan was a good guy.'

'Does his mum have your number, Aaron?'

'No. But she follows us on Facebook. Get her to PM me. I'll let the others know.'

The detective walked over to us. 'You know these people?'

'I do now.'

'What's your name?'

Jack knew he didn't legally have to give the man his name, but didn't see the harm. 'Detective Chief Inspector Jack Miller, Lothian and Borders Police, murder squad. And you are?'

The detective looked at him for a moment. 'Stick around. I might want to talk to you shortly.' He turned and walked away.

'Yeah, watch me,' Jack said. 'Good meeting you, Aaron. I'll see you at Ryan's funeral.'

'Later, bro,' Aaron said, fist-bumping Jack.

It was getting dark as Jack walked back over to the Tahoe.

He looked right at the detective as he drove away.

NINETEEN

'Aw, man, none of that 80s pish,' Bruce Hagan said, reaching over to fiddle with the car's radio.

'Leave it, you bloody heathen,' I chastised him.

We were crossing over the Kessock Bridge, bypassing Inverness city, going over to the Black Isle.

'Do you know there are dolphins in there?' Hagan said.

'And Nessie, too. Let's not forget about her.'

'I want to go over the story again.'

'What's to tell? It's the truth. I'm a police officer who's having a hard time adjusting after being attacked by a serial killer and I need help.'

'You might want to put on your not-quite-so-happy face.'

Hagan flipped the sun visor down and began practising faces.

'Jesus, Bruce. You don't want them to put you in a strait jacket, do you?'

Hagan laughed and flipped the visor up again.

We were making good time and would have made better time if Hagan hadn't insisted on stopping at Pitlochry to use a toilet.

Which then turned into a stop at the bakery on the high street for pies and a doughnut.

So that's why it took almost four hours to get to our destination, an hour north of Inverness.

Paradise Shores. 'Shithole Shores, more like,' Bruce said, as we left Golspie and travelled another mile to the health spa housed in what was once a private castle. I think he was having doughnut withdrawal. This wasn't the French Riviera, and the rain lashing off the roof of our car did nothing to convince us it was.

It was a huge building and I could only imagine the money it would have needed to be kept in the family hands, which is why it was sold off in the first place. I'd done a bit of research on the place the night before, and it had some impressive history, but like thousands of other private castles and estates all over the UK, it was too costly to keep. Some were abandoned, while others, like this place, were sold off.

There was a clock tower in the middle of the building, and I could see a modern extension on the right-hand side, but it had been designed to blend in with the original property.

I stopped the car at the front door, and it looked like a fancy hotel. It even had a doorman. We got out of our car and I popped the boot.

'Good afternoon, gentlemen,' the man in the fancy suit said.

'Good afternoon,' I replied.

The man turned round and indicated for a bellboy to come out and deal with our bags. A suitcase and a holdall each.

'Very nice,' Hagan said, walking in ahead.

'I'll have somebody park your car,' the doorman said. 'Your keys will be left behind reception.'

'Thank you.'

I followed Hagan in. He was standing around waiting for me. 'I think Hazel would like this place.'

'I think she'd prefer somewhere warm for your honeymoon.'

'I never said anything about a honeymoon.'

The reception area was busy but not crowded. 'Frank Miller and Bruce Hagan,' I said. 'We have reservations.'

'Welcome to *Paradise Shores,*' the girl said, smiling.

'Thank you.'

She clicked her keyboard and gave us two cards. 'Those are your rooms. Your bags will be taken up. I'll print out a copy of your schedule for the week. Your first appointment is tomorrow, but feel free to check out the establishment this evening. Doctor Sharp and his wife will be around tonight. You'll get to meet them later. They like to introduce themselves personally to each of our guests here.'

'What about meals?' Hagan asked.

'All the hours for the restaurants are in your welcome pack. There are set meal times for our three restaurants, and there is twenty-four-hour room service for an extra charge. All the other meals are included.'

The bellboy had our bags on a fancy hotel cart. 'This way, gentlemen,' he said, his accent definitely not Scottish. More South London than anything else. 'My name's Tom, if you need anything, give me a shout.'

'Like what?' Hagan said, his brow furrowing.

'Excuse me?'

'I said, like what?' Hagan had gritted his teeth.

Tom's smile faltered for just a second. 'Like a magazine, or newspaper, something to eat. Just give me a call.'

'Relax, Bruce. He meant room service,' I said.

Then Bruce suddenly smiled as if he'd been winding the bellboy up. 'I know.'

Christ, this young guy's going to think we're a couple of psycho hitmen.

We went through the main doors towards the rear of the building, following Tom through to the back where there was a long corridor that stretched both left and right. The back wall was made up of windows. We turned left and made our way along to a sign that said *Lifts*.

There was a set of bay windows in the middle with a few chairs set around a table. It was ideal for gazing out to the Dornoch Firth in the distance – on a good day. This afternoon, there was heavy cloud with a driving rain. Nobody was sitting at the table.

'You're on the fifth floor,' Tom said, as one of the lift doors opened.

'This is a big place,' Hagan said, stepping in behind the bellboy.

'Five floors up, three floors down. The bottom two floors are for storage and maintenance. They're off limits.'

We were in 502 and 503, with an adjoining door, on a corner. I tried the door between the two rooms to check it was locked, having already promised Hagan a kick in the nuts should he find himself sleepwalking.

You should be so lucky, he had told me.

I looked out of my window. The castle sat atop a bluff, with ornamental gardens below. It was as if somebody had taken a giant ladle and scooped out part of the clifftop and left behind the gardens. A road ran along the edge of the beach, before turning into the woods that surrounded the property, then ran out of sight on the right, where the cliffs weren't so steep.

The gardens would look spectacular in better weather, but right now, they were being drenched, and the sea looked cold and angry.

I unpacked and plugged in the little kettle. It was late afternoon and I was famished. I took out my welcome pack and checked to see what time dinner would be. Three restaurants the receptionist had said. The little brochure showed a swimming pool and gym in the south wing. That was the extension I had seen when we drove up.

There was a little cinema that showed classic movies every afternoon and evening. I wasn't interested in the James Cagney movie showing the following afternoon but I wanted to have a look around. In fact, after dinner, Hagan and I would both be having a look around.

I went downstairs to the bay window and used the payphone, inserting my credit card into the machine.

'Hi, honey,' Kim said. 'I sent you a text, but you didn't answer.'

'That's because no phones are allowed here. They took them from us when we checked in.'

'What? They can't do that.'

'They can and they did. It's in the very fine print. It's for privacy. They did say if we didn't want to come in, we would get a full refund, but that offer was only good while we were standing in reception. We had no choice.'

'How are you calling me now?'

'They have payphones.'

'Talk about old school.'

'It is what it is.'

'What about your iPad?'

'They took that too.'

'Jesus, how are you going to amuse yourself?'

'There's a TV in the room with cable. And there's a library with a bunch of old paperbacks.'

'How are you ever going to survive without the internet?'

'I'll try.'

'Apart from that, how is the place?'

'It's a big castle. There are three restaurants. We're scheduled for dinner in the *Dornoch* in about half an hour.' I looked at my watch. Already five thirty and the day was slowly slipping away. I wondered how cold it would be compared to Edinburgh.

'How's Bruce faring?'

'He seems in good spirits. Now he's officially back on the team.'

'Great. I'm taking Emma to Hazel's place tonight for a couple of hours. Just a women's get together, so we can all talk about you.'

'Nothing new there, then,' I said. 'Have you heard from Jack?'

'Yes. I told him you were away and he understands, but he's going to check in with me. He went to a garage where Ryan hung out with his friends and they all tinkered about with cars. It was set on fire.'

'Jesus. Were they having problems with somebody?'

'They don't think so. It's horrendous to think somebody in Samantha's family ended up this way.'

'Maybe Jack will find something out. I'd like to know what the local PD think about it.'

'I'll ask Jack when he calls tomorrow.'

'Okay. I'm going to go and get Bruce then we'll go down to dinner. Give Emma my love.'

'She's playing with Charlie just now. They've both had their dinner.'

'Okay. Take care.'

'I love you, Frank, you know that, don't you?'

'I know. I love you too. Both of you.'

'I'll talk to you tomorrow.'

'I'll call you in the morning. Make sure the milkman's gone before I call.'

'Where you think I could find the time or energy to entertain the milkman, is beyond me. Emma will want to talk to you. She's missing you already.'

'I miss her as well.'

After I hung up, I put on a blazer. Dinner was smart dress they'd said in the confirmation email they'd sent before we left Edinburgh. I knocked on the adjoining door with Bruce's room, but there was no answer.

I tried again, but nothing. Had he fallen asleep? I knocked again, harder this time. Still no answer. My heart started beating faster. Kick the door in? What if he was in the bathroom? Okay, he knows we are going down around five thirty, heading to the bar.

You would think a place that helps people with addictions wouldn't have a bar, but before you could order a drink, you had to hand over your room card, and if they saw you were on a special programme, you didn't get served.

I looked at my watch again, went over to the window and looked out. The rain had stopped, but the sky was dark with full clouds, making it darker than it would normally have been, although I doubted the evening darkness was far behind. A couple of hours and it would be fully dark.

I left my room, went out into the hallway and up to Bruce's door. I knocked hard but got no answer.

Fearing the worst, I made my way downstairs to get security to open the door.

I hoped I hadn't misjudged Bruce and he had killed himself.

It turned out, that was the least of my worries.

TWENTY

I found Hagan at the bar, surprisingly well turned out. He'd changed into a shirt and tie, with a dark blazer.

'Here he is,' he said as I approached. I locked eyes with the young woman he was sitting with.

'Bruce, you didn't tell me you were coming down,' I said.

'What? You my dad now?' He laughed, but I saw a hardness in his eyes that wasn't there before. Or was my imagination getting the better of me?

'I was going to buy you a drink, but I can see you already have one. How about you, Miss...?'

'Felicity. Felicity Kendal.' She smiled and held out a hand for me to shake.

'Thank you, but a soft one. I'm waiting to go to dinner with my friend.'

'There's two of them,' Hagan said, grinning and putting his bottle of Becks down and taking a sip from the glass of amber liquid that was obviously accompanying the beer.

'Coke?' I suggested.

'That would be fine.'

I looked at the barman who had been hovering. 'Pepsi okay?' he asked.

She nodded. 'And one for my friend? She'll be along in a minute.'

'Of course. And I'll have a lager.'

'Another Becks,' Hagan said, the short glass back on the bar again. The dark green bottle was in his hand now and he was waving it about. The barman looked at me and I shook my head.

'Let's just take it easy there, big man. We want to have a nice dinner without falling over the table.'

'Yes, Dad.' He looked at Felicity. 'See how he talks to me? Like he's my fucking dad.'

I could tell Hagan had come down to the bar long before I had. I looked over at the door leading into the bar and saw a security man dressed like a bouncer. Two more were at the entrance to the castle. No doubt there would be more.

'Bruce. A word in private, if I may.' I looked at Felicity. 'If you'll excuse us for a minute.'

'Uh, oh, now I'm in trouble.' He took a swig from the beer bottle and thumped it down on the bar. I took him round the corner into a hallway that led along to another lounge bar where games could be played.

I found a quiet spot over by one of the windows. This view was similar to the one my room gave. I turned to Hagan who was grinning like an idiot.

'What the fuck are you playing at?' I said to him.

He made a funny face and held up his hands, one of them with a glove on. 'I'm just trying to fit in. Make it look like I have a drink problem.'

'You're doing a good job. Just don't overdo it. Later on, we can regroup.' I stood up straighter. 'For fuck's sake, you do remember why we're here, don't you?'

'Of course. But you have to understand, I've been cooped up in the house since this happened. This is like going away to Spain with my mates. Without the sunburn.'

'We're here to get you help. You better make this work!'

'Relax, Frank. You need to take a chill pill. Or at least have a Glayva on ice like I'm having. Man, that's like a hoor wearing silk panties; they slide down so easily.'

'Get a grip. I don't need you getting pished. No more drink for you for the rest of the stay.'

'What? Come on. I'll just have one or two.'

'You'll have no more. When we go back through to the bar, you'll order an orange juice. And that's what you'll stick to for the rest of our time here.'

'*You* ordered a pint.'

'Never mind what I do. Get back through there and behave yourself.'

'Aye aye, Captain,' Bruce said, and brushed past me as he walked away and went into a toilet.

Back in the bar, Felicity was sitting beside another young woman. This one was blonde, with her hair pulled up in a ponytail.

'Sorry about my friend. We're here to get him help,' I said to Felicity. The barman was earwigging as he dried a glass. The bar was quiet, and I had no doubt it would get a bit busier later on.

'There's no need to apologise,' Felicity said. 'Allow me to introduce you to my friend; this is Penny Blair.'

'Pleased to meet you,' I said, shaking her hand.

'Frank's here with his friend, Bruce.' She looked around her. 'He was here a minute ago. Where did your friend go?'

'To use the bathrooms. He'll be here in a minute.' Just don't draw too much attention to yourself, Bruce, I thought.

Too late for that though.

TWENTY-ONE

'You might want to see this,' a young man said. He was sitting in front of a bank of monitors and had zoomed in on two men in one of the lounges.

'Who are they?' Vincent Woo said. Despite his Asian surname, his accent was very much Oxford educated.

'Police officers.'

'What?' Woo said, his voice full of alarm.

'Don't worry, their images were run through facial recognition. They're guests here.'

There were several operators in the confined room. All of them sitting in front of monitors, watching the common areas of the castle, inside and out.

'Bring up their profiles,' Woo said.

The operator brought up both Miller's and Hagan's profiles. Woo read the details.

'Okay. There's nothing to worry about. They're genuine, but keep an eye on them. And alert Doctor Sharp. He'll want to be kept in the loop. And disable that payphone in the back corridor.'

'Will do. You might want to look at this as well.' The operator brought up another video of a man and a woman arguing.

'Good Lord, I don't need to be kept informed about every little thing. You're paid to keep an eye on security round here, not to bore me with drivel. That man has mental health problems and he's been a patient of Doctor Sharp for a week now. *Melissa Sharp*.'

Woo put a hand on the man's shoulder. 'I don't need to tell you to tread lightly there, my friend.'

The operator made the video disappear. He'd rather go swimming naked in a pool filled with piranha fish than get on the wrong side of Melissa Sharp.

TWENTY-TWO

'You'll have to excuse my good friend here,' Hagan said, when he came back. 'He's a real stuffed shirt.'

The young women smiled at him.

'He seems just fine to me,' Penny said.

'You don't know him like I do, darlin'.'

Felicity and Penny had agreed to share a table for dinner.

'Bruce is just kidding, of course,' I said, managing to smile and grit my teeth at the same time.

'Let's make a toast; to new friends.' He raised his bottle and clinked the glasses of the two women. He'd completely ignored my order for him to drink orange juice. 'So, you're both here for the health spa?' he said.

'Yes. We thought it would be a nice wee change. Escape from Edinburgh,' Felicity said.

'We're from there! Small world, eh? So what do you two do for a living? It has to be modelling, right?' He grinned and chugged back on the beer.

Penny smiled. She was the younger of the two. Blonde, blue-eyed, good looking. She could have been a model.

'I'm a manager for a travel company,' she said.

'I'm a department head for a major bank,' Felicity said.

'Yeah, well, come up to my room later and I can give you an interview. If you know what I mean?'

I clamped my hand down on Hagan's left thigh and looked at him.

'Wow, look at Frank, getting jealous here. Easy, cowboy, there's plenty to go round. Although I didn't know you swung that way.' He guffawed and drank more beer.

I knew it would be a good night if I didn't knock him out before going to bed. He was playing his part too well.

The two women were gracious enough to look at their menus while I leaned over and whispered in Bruce's ear.

'Didn't we just have a talk? Take it fucking easy.'

Hagan's brow furrowed and he stood up, swaying on his feet, knocking his chair over. 'Fuck you. I'm going to the bar. I'm not hungry anyway.'

One of the security men came over with a waiter, one of them ready to take our order and the other ready to start swinging. I stood up. 'It's okay, pal, he's just had a little too much to drink,' I said to the security man.

'We don't allow intoxication in the restaurant,' he said, looking as if he was itching to smack Hagan.

Form a line, I thought, picking up Hagan's chair.

'I'll have a word with him. He's seeing Doctor Sharp tomorrow. I'll see he behaves until then.'

The man nodded, a silent agreement between us; *I'll back off but I'll be here anyway.*

'I'll see you up to your room, Bruce,' I said, putting a hand on his arm.

'Get your fucking hands off me,' he said, jerking his arm away. 'I need to have a pish.' He stormed off.

Christ, I couldn't have felt more stunned if I'd tried. I could feel my face creeping into the red zone.

'Please don't worry about it, Detective Miller,' a voice behind me said.

I turned round and was looking at the face of Charles Sharp himself. He was holding out a hand for me to shake.

'Doctor Sharp. I wasn't expecting to meet you until tomorrow. Although they did say at reception you liked to introduce yourself to everybody.' I shook his hand.

'I've already met the ladies there. In the bar, earlier. I thought I would introduce myself over a fresh orange later on, but I was informed about a commotion in the *Dornoch* restaurant.'

It sounded strange, hearing a Scottish name pronounced by an American.

'I do apologise—'

Sharp held up a hand. 'There's no need. Some of us are here for guidance after all.' He turned to the waiter, still smiling and gave an almost imperceptible nod of his head. 'Please join me later in the bar.'

'Thank you. I will.'

'Enjoy your dinner.'

I sat down after he walked away. 'Again, my apologies,' I said to the women.

'There's no need,' Penny said.

'Forget about it,' Felicity added.

We ordered our food and made small talk. Bruce hadn't come back by the time our food was brought out, and I didn't want to order anything for him, having a feeling he was only after liquid satisfaction.

'We're going to have a walk around and get the lay of the land,' the young women said after dinner. 'I'm sure we'll see you around... detective,' Penny said, smiling.

'Enjoy your drink with Doctor Sharp,' Felicity said

In the bar, Sharp was talking to an older couple. He excused himself and waved me over when he saw me approach.

'Detective Miller. Would you like a drink? I only drink non-alcoholic drinks, but don't let me stop you.'

'I'll just have a Pepsi, thanks,' I said, wanting to keep a clear head. 'Again, I apologise for my friend. He's been having problems lately.'

'And that's why you're here. Please don't worry. We don't work miracles here, Detective Miller, but we like to think we can put people on the straight and narrow. Help them focus more in their lives. And I believe that's what you put on your application form? Needing your friend put in the right direction?'

'Yes, Bruce had a bad time of it.' I looked around to make sure nobody was sitting close by. I explained about Bruce being attacked by a serial killer and how he narrowly escaped with his life, and how he had been having problems since it happened more than six months ago.

'I'm sure we can work with him. I have him in for an hour at ten tomorrow.'

'I'm glad. He was in therapy but nothing seemed to work.'

'We'll do our best with your friend. There are different methods we can try, but I have to tell you now, his treatment will be confidential. I hope you understand?'

'Of course. I just want what's best for my colleague.'

He stood. I followed suit. 'It's nice to meet you, Detective Miller.'

'Likewise.'

First impressions. I didn't like the man. This was going to be fun.

TWENTY-THREE

'Can we go and play with our dolls, Mummy?' Jane asked Hazel.

'Of course you can. But play quietly. Daniel's just gone down to sleep.' Hazel looked at Kim. 'I wish I could sleep like a baby.'

'I bet.' Kim poured the water from Hazel's kettle into the two coffee mugs as Jane and Emma went upstairs to play with the toys. 'How are you doing, mixing work with being a new mother?'

'It's tough,' Hazel said, getting the milk from the fridge and pouring it into the two coffee mugs. 'I never thought it would be this hard though. It was easier when I had Jane.'

'Well, you didn't have any other kids to worry about when she was born. Daniel came into the world with another sibling.'

'It's something I have to get used to.'

They took their coffees back into the living room. The TV had been muted. A soap opera played out in front of them.

'How are you and Bruce doing?' Kim said, putting her mug down on a side table next to her chair.

'I know *I'm* doing fine. I don't know about him.'

'Am I missing something here, Haze?'

She took in a deep breath and let it out slowly. 'I suppose you'll find out soon enough; Bruce and I have split up.'

Kim sat up straight in her chair. 'What? When?'

'It was after New Year. We brought in the bells together, he started drinking too much, and we had a huge fight. That was the start. Things went downhill after that.'

'And he left?'

'He did. He told me he didn't have to put up with a nagging cow like me. So he packed a holdall and left. He came back for the rest of his stuff one day when I was at work.'

'I don't understand. Frank had a beer with him on Saturday and he met him in Tanners. Just up the road. Is he staying close to Tanners?'

'He's staying *in* Tanners. You might not know this, but he knew the owner from way back, and the flat above the pub wasn't being used. Except for storage. So the stuff was taken out and now he's renting the place.'

'Hell's teeth, Haze, you should have told me.'

'I thought it would blow over. That he would realise just what he has to lose. But then when I met him in town one day, he walked away and then a woman stepped out of the shadows and they were holding hands when they walked up the High Street.'

'Bastard. After all you've been through together.'

'He's never been the same since… well, after what happened to him.'

'I know, but it doesn't seem to stop him going out with other women. Do you know who she is?'

Hazel's face turned red and she looked down at the floor for a moment. 'I saw them get into a car together. I took a note of her car registration.'

'And you ran it through the system.'

'I did. I'd get fired if I was caught, but at this moment in time, I couldn't care less.'

'I won't say anything. I know Frank wouldn't either, as long as it wasn't done for nefarious purposes.'

'I just wanted to know who would be interested in him.'

'Who is it?'

'Amanda Cameron. She's one of the barmaids in Tanners. He doesn't have to go far for a shag and a pint. She's younger and better looking. What the hell she sees in him I don't know.' There was bitterness in her voice, which Kim could understand.

'So what's next for you both?'

'I don't know if we have anything left to salvage. He gives me money for the kids. He hasn't made any demands. Nothing at all. I think he feels like a failure, so he wants to stay away.' She drank some of her coffee.

'Maybe being back on active duty will make him come to his senses.'

'God knows when that will be.'

'Didn't he tell you?' Kim said.

'Tell me what?'

'Hazel, he started back today. He's on an operation with Frank and a couple of the others.'

'No, he didn't tell me. Bloody typical. I'd find out when I walked into the incident room.' She looked puzzled. 'I'm surprised Jill White, his therapist, signed off on that.'

'What makes you say that?'

'His fucking temper. I was living with him and I didn't see a blind bit of difference. Mood swings, getting drunk.'

'What? Did he hit you?'

'No, I'm just surprised Jill sanctioned this. If she didn't, he wouldn't be back. Are you sure he's back on active duty?'

'Yes. He's away with Frank to Golspie. Some of the team are there.'

Then Hazel smiled. 'I get it. It was just me. He's got it made now. Back at work. New girlfriend. No responsibilities. Just hands over the cash and lets me have the sleepless nights. Selfish bastard. No wonder Jill thought he was ready to go back to work. I was the one dragging him down.'

'Maybe when he's back working with you, he'll feel differently.'

'I'm putting in for a transfer. Back to uniform. There's no way I'm going to be working with him.'

'You can't do that. Frank won't let you. He's worked with you for years. You're a valuable part of the team.'

'I can't work with Bruce. Not the way he is.'

Kim nodded. And she knew which one would be leaving Miller's team.

She called *Paradise Shores* and was told Miller was out of his room but a message could be left for him. She left a message for him to call her. Then she called Percy Purcell.

She was already getting a bad feeling about this.

TWENTY-FOUR

'I'm looking for my friend,' I said to the concierge at his little station near the front entrance.

'Of course, sir. I saw him leave a little while ago.'

I took out a note and palmed it to him. 'Any idea where he went?'

'I called for a taxi for him. He wanted to go to a pub.'

'Which one?

'The County Hotel, just up the road. They have a public bar.'

'Thank you.'

I walked over to the two women. 'My friend Bruce has gone to the pub. I have to go and get him.'

'I'd like to go too, if I could,' Felicity said.

'Sure. The more the merrier.'

'I'm going up to the room,' Penny said.

We took my car and the grounds of the health spa looked completely different after dark. The main drive was surrounded by thick trees on either side, and might have looked foreboding to somebody with a fear of the dark. A track on either side led into the trees.

'Service roads,' Felicity said.

I smiled at her. 'I'm glad you've been doing your homework, Sergeant.'

Julie Stott had slipped into the role of guest Felicity Kendal very well. As had DC Steffi Walker, or, as the castle management knew her, Penny Blair.

'How are you both settling in?' I asked Julie.

'Fine, sir. I like Steffi a lot, and I know I'm the transplant from another division, but she's helping me blend in with the team.'

'You come highly recommended, Julie. And it's Frank, while we're here.'

'What do you think of the place?' she asked, as I turned right onto the A9, the main road north.

'It seems nice on the surface, but I'm getting a feeling about the place.'

'Me too. I don't like it. I'm glad I'm not picking up the tab.'

'I'm not sure if it's because we know of two killers who were here, or if it just isn't my sort of place. Maybe if it was in Florida or something.'

'Try and get us a gig in Florida next time, Frank. That I could deal with.'

'What's wrong with the north of Scotland?' I asked her with a grin, flicking on the windscreen wipers as rain started to hit the car.

The County Hotel was quite a large establishment, situated right on the main road, set back a bit, with a car park in front. A sign said there were vacancies. I wondered if it got busy in the summer. I parked up and we could hear the commotion before we even got through the front door.

'Fuck you!' Bruce Hagan shouted, throwing a stool at another patron. His shirt was hanging out and blood was running out of one nostril.

The stool hit a table and scattered the glasses on it.

'Bruce!' I shouted, and grabbed the next stool he'd picked up.

He spun round and drew his fist back then stopped when he saw it was me.

A man who had been lying on the floor, stood up and landed another punch on Hagan's face. Then he turned to me.

'Police!' I said, bringing out my warrant card.

He thought about it and backed off. The man's friends stepped forward, but I stepped between them and Hagan.

'Back off! If anybody else takes a fucking swing at us, you'll all be spending the night in the cells.'

They thought about it. 'He fucking started it!' one of them shouted. 'We were minding our own business when he started in on us.'

The barman was standing holding a baseball bat. 'Put that away. Is it true what they said?'

'Christ, he's like a fucking madman,' the barman said, putting the bat away behind the bar. I had the feeling he only had to bring it out when visitors were in town. 'We never had this trouble until that fucking place opened up down the road.'

I heard the sirens a couple of minutes before the door burst open. A sergeant and four constables strode in.

'We'll take it from here,' he said to me, as the barman pointed to Hagan.

'Things just got out of hand,' I said, showing him my warrant card.

'I said, we'll deal with it, *Inspector*.' The man was well over six feet, broad-shouldered, and clearly wasn't used to dealing with upper ranks. He had a shock of red beard on his face.

I knew the sergeant was within his rights to do what he had to do with Hagan.

'He's a police officer,' I said, taking him aside. 'He's been through the mill, so we're getting him help down at the wellness centre.'

'That's as may well be, but I'm lifting him right now.'

'Come on, sergeant, cut him some slack. I'll have a word with him.'

'There will be a fucking riot if I don't lift him.'

'Jesus.'

The sergeant asked the barman to come over to the door as the other uniforms tried to calm things down. 'Who gave the first punch?'

'Him,' he said, pointing to the man Hagan had decked.

'Not the copper?'

'No.'

The sergeant nodded. 'I'll still take him in. Drunk and disorderly. I have to live here, after you yahoos go home.' He turned to a constable. 'Right. Get him in the van. You'll sober up overnight in the cells. Drunk and disorderly.'

'What? Away t'fuck.'

'You want to add assaulting one of your colleagues to the charge?'

Hagan relaxed. 'Okay, have it your way.'

The sergeant led the men outside and stepped to one side with me. 'You better watch it with that one. You can pick him up nine o'clock tomorrow morning.'

'I know this is your patch, sergeant, but let's not get confused by who has the higher rank. Understand?'

The sergeant walked away as Hagan was hustled into the back of the van, and the posse took off.

Julie came out. 'Now that's not going to look good,' she said.

'I have to make a call. I'll use the phone in here. Watch my back.'

We went back inside and some of the locals glared at us as they picked up the furniture. I found the payphone and dialled a number I'd memorised.

Thunder boomed overhead and I could hear rain starting to crash down.

'Percy? It's Frank. We've got a problem. Hagan's been arrested. Drunk and disorderly.'

'What? Aw for fuck's sake. How the fuck did that happen?'

'He was pished earlier and caused a rumpus in the castle restaurant at dinner.'

'Jesus Christ, was there a big commotion?'

'The doctor who owns the place came over.'

'Well, that's just brilliant. Has the whole plan gone tits up?'

'No. This Charles Sharp sees Hagan has a problem. Hagan told me he was just play acting, but between you and me, I don't think he is.'

'Leave it with me. Call me tom—'

The phone line was dead.

'Does this happen every time it rains?' I asked Julie. 'The phone going dead?'

'The wires are not underground up here. Maybe a tree brought a line down. There's a big storm coming in.'

'What about mobile phone coverage?'

'Up here? This is not the big city. We're lucky to get one bar on a good day.'

We went back outside and into the car. 'There's nothing we can do until morning.'

'Do you think Bruce will be able to handle the rest of the stay, boss?'

I looked at her before I drove off. 'I hope so. Or we're all screwed.'

TWENTY-FIVE

Rain lashed off the windows as Charles Sharp stood looking out into the darkness. There wasn't much to see, but there were plenty of pictures running about inside his head. He was holding a glass of malt in his hand, in one of the crystal tumblers he kept only for that brand of whisky. God that was one thing the Scots got right; nobody could imitate Scotch.

'Penny for them,' Melissa Sharp said, coming up and standing beside him.

'Remember that vacation we had in Cape Cod?' he said, not turning round.

'How could I forget?'

'This weather reminds me of that place. The heavens opened that Saturday and we stayed in the hotel all day.'

She gave a small laugh. 'We had fun though.'

He turned to face her. 'We did. It was special.' He held up his glass, knowing she was fond of a glass of wine.

'Not tonight. Mama's unsettled. I have a feeling we're in for a sleepless night.'

'Christ, I hope not. I have new clients in the morning.' He walked across the huge living room to the roaring fire. It was a feature he loved about the mansion, his oasis away from the castle. Logs spat and crackled, the flames dancing as if they were alive.

'Do you think we should call the doctor?' It always sounded funny to Sharp, asking her if she thought they should call the doctor, since they were both doctors themselves.

'I already did.' She pulled the floor-to-ceiling drapes closed, banishing the night. Rain still battered the glass as if demanding entry. It was accompanied by a high, whistling wind.

'Do you miss America?' Sharp asked her.

'I do. But I love being here, too.' She smiled a tired smile. 'Why? Do you miss America?'

'Of course I do. But I miss New York more than I miss my hometown.'

Charles Sharp was brought up in Texas. His father owned an oil company and had wanted his son to follow him into the business.

Charles Sharp wanted to be a doctor and had followed that path. That's why he had other people run the business for him, now his father was gone and he owned the business.

'I fear time is running out.'

'The last ones were close.'

'We went down the wrong road.'

'Do we have anybody here this week?'

Sharp looked across at her. The room was dimly lit by table lamps, just the way he liked it, but it was the light from the fire that warmed him, not just physically, but mentally too.

'There's one who's come to my attention. I'm seeing him tomorrow. I'll get a better feel for him. And there's a woman, too. I'm not sure about her, but we're going to try her as well.'

There was a knock on the front door.

JOHN CARSON

Sharp got up and walked through to the entrance hall, a grand affair with a large, sweeping staircase on one side.

Thunder boomed, and lightning slashed across the night sky. He opened the door and a dishevelled figure stood looking at him. He was dressed in a long raincoat, a soaking wet hat sitting on his head. Sharp thought the man could very well have been a time traveller from the nineteen thirties.

'Come in. You'll catch your death standing out there.'

The doctor walked in, and Sharp had a look out into the dark, but doubted he could have seen anything even if it wasn't raining, far less when there was a downpour.

The doctor lived in a house farther down the track. Sharp had had it refurbished especially for the doctor so he could stay close by without having to live under their roof.

'How long has she been like this?' he asked, shaking off his wet coat after laying his medical bag down.

'About an hour,' Sharp said.

The doctor picked up his bag. 'An hour? You should have called me sooner.' He started marching along the hallway that led through to the back of the house, Sharp behind him.

'I couldn't. It was too early. The first lot of meds wouldn't be out of her system.'

'I told you before, it's okay if they overlap.'

'I'm not comfortable with that. I don't want to see her suffer.'

'I hope she's not in too much pain. I'll give her something for it.'

They reached the doorway, and Sharp took out a key and unlocked it. They went down a narrow flight of stairs. *Keeping her out of sight in the basement, I see* Solomon had said the first time he'd come here.

'It's her own space,' Sharp had said. He'd thought the doctor would refuse to work for him, but after he'd handed over the envelope with the cash in it, the doctor suddenly decided he would enjoy working here.

He had been offered the cottage as well, after Sharp had discovered the doctor's previous experience. The cottage offered him shelter and protection, both of which could be swiftly taken away should the doctor deem it fit to resign his post.

Although both men knew there would never be any resignation accepted, not after what the doctor had seen and done here.

The hallways were narrower down here. The rooms smaller. But at least the room he was going to was big enough to run around in, should he find himself being chased.

The shouting and screaming was getting louder and more frequent.

'You'll have to help me. I'll give her something to calm her, then the next dose can be administered. You ready?'

Sharp nodded and put the key in the lock. The shouting stopped. He felt the hairs go up on the back of his neck. He turned the key, then the handle, and pushed the door open.

The woman stood looking at him. Hair a mess. Spittle running down her chin. Eyes wide and jittery.

'The doctor's here,' he said.

She smiled, her mouth a grotesque slash in her face. Looked at Solomon with puffy, bloodshot eyes.

And screamed again.

TWENTY-SIX

There was a Starbucks on Route 300 right around the corner from the hotel. It was after nine o'clock and the line for the drive thru was constant but not backed up as it would have been in rush hour.

Jack had put on a light windbreaker. The sun was out, but it was weak with a chill wind blowing through the area.

He bought two coffees and turned round by the Chili's restaurant. This was a small strip mall, with some stores and a couple of restaurants. He stopped and took a sip from his coffee, looking around him. A grey, military plane was flying low on its approach to the air base.

There was no sign anybody was following him.

He drove off, heading back to the Howard Johnson. They'd checked out of their hotel the night before, and booked into this other one; it was just down the road, but Jack had felt better about doing that. Not that it would make much difference. If whoever was following them had the resources to stick a GPS unit on their car, they would certainly be able to find out what hotel they had moved to.

In the room, Samantha had showered and dressed in the time he had been away.

'Listen, Jack, I'm sorry I haven't been attentive to you, but I just haven't been in the mood to fool around.' She put her arms around his neck and kissed him. 'I still love you though.'

He laughed. 'Honey, I love you too. And I'm not some animal. I understand why we're here.'

There was a knock at the hotel room door. Jack silently stood back and walked over to his holdall and took out his hammer. Before checking in the night before, he'd driven round to Home Depot and bought the tool. He couldn't get his hands on a gun, so this was better than nothing.

He looked through the peephole and then stood back, opening it and smiling.

Neil McGovern stepped in. Looked at the hammer and smiled. 'I'd rather have a coffee, old son.'

'Neil! What are you doing here?' Samantha said, pleased to see him, and giving him a hug.

'I heard they served good Starbucks in this part of the world.'

'Have mine,' Samantha said. 'I haven't touched it.'

'I'm just kidding. I had plenty on the plane. The British Government use only the best on their private service.'

'You flew over here on a private jet?' Jack said, closing the door.

'I was going to come over on business next week, but I just moved things around a little.'

'Have a seat.'

McGovern sat on the little two-seater couch.

'Did you fly into JFK?' Samantha asked.

'No, I flew into Stewart Air Force base. Homeland Security have offices there. They just don't advertise it. I deal with them a lot, so it wasn't a problem for me to land there on my way down to the city. They even gave me a driver to chauffeur me around.'

Samantha was looking worried. 'What's the urgency, Neil?'

'Nothing for you to worry about. I have everything in hand. In fact, two of the men who are helping me are outside having a chat with the two men who've been following you.'

'What? I thought I'd put them off by putting the GPS unit on a trailer.'

Jack sat down on the edge of the bed next to Samantha.

'They're DEA, Jack. They're not put off easily. They're in a plumber's van this time.'

'Why the hell are the DEA following us?'

'Because you're connected to Ryan Haines.'

Samantha put a hand to her mouth before speaking. 'What the hell did he get himself into?'

'Dunno, yet. I'm going to find out. I made a call to a friend of mine in HS, and he's going to get back to me. However, I do know your nephew was hanging out with a young man who also died of an overdose six months ago.'

'Why would the DEA be involved in that?'

'They're usually after the supplier. It seems they've had your nephew or his supplier on their radar for a while now. I'll try to get more information, but in the meantime, I'm having a message sent from my friends that you're family and have nothing to do with whatever operation they're working on and to back off.'

'Do you think it will work?'

'I have no doubt.' McGovern stood. 'I wish I could stay, but I do have important work down in Manhattan. However, here's a number where you can reach me.' He handed Jack a business card.

'Thanks, Neil. I'll give you the numbers of the phones we bought.' He recited the numbers, and McGovern put them into his phone.

He then gave Samantha another hug. 'Give my best to your sister. Please convey how sorry I am for her loss.'

'I will. Thank you for everything, Neil.'

McGovern walked out of the room with Jack, along the corridor to the doors that led out to the back car park, past an ice machine and a vending machine. The back entrance was made of a glass wall with doors in it. Jack looked out and saw two men standing next to a plumber's van. The driver of the van looked over before driving off. McGovern walked out with Jack and they spoke to the two men from Homeland Security.

'They got a phone call while we were talking to them. They won't be back,' the lead one said.

'Thanks, guys. I appreciate your help,' McGovern said.

'No problem. We'll be at the base. If you need us, give us a call.' The man handed Jack a business card.

'Thanks, buddy. It's good to know somebody's got my back in a foreign country.'

'The colonel says you owe him a steak dinner,' the man said to McGovern.

'Tell him from me, I already have the table booked.' He smiled and shook the men's hands and watched as they walked back to their nondescript black sedan and drove off.

'The colonel is in charge of the Manhattan office. I can't say any more than that, but he'll enjoy his dinner tonight.'

'I can't thank you enough, Neil. When I called and asked you to run that plate, I didn't expect this.'

'The DEA can be a little sensitive. Whatever it is they have planned, I'm sure you're not going to be in their way.' McGovern walked down the steps and another car started up and drove over to him. 'Keep in touch, Jack.'

And with that, he was gone.

TWENTY-SEVEN

Kim dropped her daughter off at the primary school just down the High Street, five minutes from their flat. It was just like being a single parent again. She had gotten used to that for a while, but now she was living with Frank and was about to be his wife, she much preferred to have him around.

After dropping Emma, she drove up to the station.

In the incident room, Paddy Gibb was standing talking to Andy Watt.

'Ah, the wanderer returns,' Watt said, smiling.

'Miss me, Andy?'

'Of course. I'd rather see your smiling face than that sour puss of your fiancé's.'

'I'm sure he'll be touched you're missing him too.'

'We were just talking about the post-mortem reports from Kate Murphy. Andy was down there when the PMs were being done,' Gibb said.

'I'm going to start eating salad for lunch. Jean said I should try and lose some weight for when we go to Florida in the autumn.'

'I told you she thought you were a slob,' Gibb said.

'She said I needed to tone my muscles. Nobody says she thinks I'm a slob.' Watt shook his head and held up his hands in exasperation. 'Did you hear those words come out of my mouth, Kim?'

'Don't get me involved in any of this.'

'Bloody slob. What does your girlfriend think of you?'

'I'll have you know, she thinks I'm perfect the way I am,' Gibb said.

'There's no accounting for taste.'

'Shut up. She's got class.'

Watt rolled his eyes. 'As the boss was saying, those two blokes, the head chef and the maître d', were both stabbed to death. They had no soot in their lungs, so they were dead before the fire got a hold of the kitchen.'

'Christ, they must have really ticked her off,' Kim said. 'But I wonder what made her kill. Are the tox screens back yet?'

Watt picked up a sheaf of papers from his desk. 'Nothing in her system except prescription meds. Fluoxetine.' He turned to Gibb. 'Prozac.'

'I know what it is, smartarse.'

'Apart from that, nothing.'

'Maybe she just went off her head.'

'Don't forget she was friends with Hubbard. Who just happened to go off his head,' Gibb said.

'And they were both at the *Paradise Shores* wellness centre,' Watt said.

'And that's why Frank is away there with Bruce and the others.'

'Talking of which, has he checked in with you today?' Percy Purcell asked as he came out of his office.

'Not yet. He called using the payphone in the castle last night.'

'Didn't he take his phone?' Gibb asked.

'He did, but no phones or computers or anything else that can connect them with the outside world are allowed.'

'What?' Watt said. 'That's shite. What if there was an emergency? What do they expect them to do, blow smoke signals? Sounds like a right dump.'

'It's all part of the healing process, they say,' Kim said, but still she had a worried look on her face.

'He called me from the pub last night,' Purcell said. 'He had gone out with Julie, looking for Hagan. They found him in a hotel bar, knocking seven shades out of a few young locals. He had the better of them too. Then he was arrested by the plods up there. I'm going to rip somebody a new arsehole when this is over. I tried calling them, but now even the local police station isn't answering their phone.'

'It's away in the wilds, so what can you expect?' Gibb said.

'It's not the North Pole. They're civilised up there. Besides, I got onto BT and asked them what had happened up there and they said there were several outages but they were having a problem locating them.'

'I hope they get it sorted soon.'

Kim was looking worried. 'I hope Frank's going to be okay. He's up there with Julie and Steffi, but Bruce was supposed to be backup too.'

'I'm going to have a word with Jeni Bridge,' Purcell said, walking away. Kim caught up with him.

'Is everything okay, Percy?'

'No. Old Happy Harry is coming down from Aberdeen on the bus today. I mean, it's not as if I haven't seen him for a long time.'

'You mean your dad?'

'Yes.'

'Lou's obviously missing you.'

'Yeah, he probably wouldn't even notice I'd gone unless he was talking to me on Facetime.'

'That's not true.' She put a hand on his arm. 'Trust me, he's missing you.'

'He told me he's been in touch with an old friend of his. A woman. So he's coming down here to hook up with her.'

'He wouldn't have done that if you weren't here.'

'We'll see.'

'I have to go and see Jill White about Bruce.'

'I thought she signed him off for coming back?'

'She did. I just want her opinion on something. Can you spare me somebody to come along?'

'Take Andy with you.' He looked over at the other two detectives. 'Watt, saddle up. You're going with Kim.'

'Thanks. I'll catch up with you later, Percy. Oh, and before I forget, tell Suzy we're still on for Friday night.'

'You girls and your drinking sesh. I don't know how you do it. But I don't want you to feel guilty about taking my fiancée out and leaving me home with my old man.'

'I won't.' She smiled at him and headed out with Andy Watt, leaving Purcell shaking his head.

'So, where are we off to? Nice cup of coffee somewhere, a couple of hours diddling about then back to the office? I like your style, Kim. Getting me out of there for a skive—'

'The Astley Ainslie. I want to go and see Jill White.'

'You need to fine-tune your skiving skills, missy. I mean, if it was afternoon, we could have gone for a pint.'

'Is that what you normally do, Andy?' she asked with a wry smile.

'No.' He had a disgusted look on his face. 'I was talking about a friend of mine. In fact, if you really want to know, it's your boyfriend who does that. There, you made me say it. I hope you're satisfied.'

Kim turned her car off Morningside Road and headed for the Astley Ainslie hospital, where Jill White, Bruce Hagan's therapist, worked. She suddenly felt sad about Hazel's relationship going south.

'Did Hazel sign in this morning?' she asked.

'Not yet.'

'Did she call?'

'Not as far as I know. Why?'

'I'm worried about her, Andy.'

'Then call her.'

She pressed the Bluetooth phone button on her steering wheel and told the voice recognition feature to call Hazel.

Kim's heart was beating fast now, thinking Hazel had maybe done herself in. Took a bottle of pills maybe, or just slit her wrists. What if she was so depressed that—

'Hello?'

Hazel's voice sounded through the speakers in the car.

'Hazel, it's Kim. I was checking that you're okay.'

'I'm fine. Bloody flat tyre as I was about to leave with Daniel to go to the babysitter. I would change it myself, but I can't leave the baby alone. I'm waiting for the AA to come. I called Paddy and he said not to worry.'

'Oh, okay. You still up for a night out with Suzy and Kate Murphy on Friday?'

'Kim, I am counting the minutes. I'll be in as soon as.'

'See—' The call was disconnected.

'I'll bet Hagan's relieved to be up north, eh?' Watt said. 'Not having to look after the kids. I never had to do that myself. My ex was always around for that. I'm waiting for my eldest to give me a wee ankle biter. *Grandpa*. At my time of life, that word sounds just perfect. Jean's lucky, she's got one already.'

'How is living with her turning out?'

'You know, I thought moving into her place in Colinton would be awkward, but she lets me treat the place like it's my own.'

'She lets you throw your dirty skids on the bedroom floor, you mean?'

'Sounds like somebody's been snooping about in my bedroom.' He laughed. 'Too late to get jealous now, girlfriend. I've got Jean and you've got Frank. Let the cards fall and all that.'

'DS Watt, you never fail to amaze me.'

'That's what Jean says too, but we're on first name terms. However, for your information, I do manage to get my dirty clothes into the laundry basket.'

'You'll make a good husband.'

They drove down Canaan Lane and left through the main entrance to the Astley Ainslie hospital.

'I wonder who thought it was a good idea to have two psychiatric hospitals in Morningside?' Watt said. 'It's a wonder the residents allowed that.'

'Maybe the hospitals were here first.' Kim drove through the grounds until she came to the one-storey building at the back, where she knew Jill White worked.

'The lunatics running the asylum. I thought that was only American politics!'

'The world has gone mad,' she replied, as they got out and went into the hospital.

'I'd like to speak with Jill White,' Kim said, showing her ID to the receptionist.

Five minutes later, they were walking through the building to the office at the back. The place had an antiseptic smell, even though they didn't deal with medical problems.

'Kim! Good to see you again,' Jill said, as they walked in. 'And you've brought Sergeant Watt. Good to see you again, Andy.' She came round the desk and gave them a hug. 'Please, sit down. Coffee?'

'Thanks. Black for me,' Watt said. He hated taking milk from somebody else, in case it was off and had bits floating in it. Bits were for orange juice not out-of-date milk.

'Thanks, Jill. Same for me.'

Jill flicked the kettle on and made chit-chat while the coffees were being made.

'You've lost weight,' Kim said.

'I have. I've been working out since... well, you know.'

Miller and his team had tracked down the men who had abducted her son, years after the event took place.

She handed them their hot drinks and sat down again. She was in her thirties but slimming down had taken some years off as well as pounds.

'So, what can I do for you?'

Kim reached into her jacket pocket and brought out some sheets of paper. 'I know you're bound by patient confidentiality, but since you wrote the report, all I want to do is go over it with you.'

'What report's this?' she asked, taking the sheets from Kim.

'Giving the all clear for Bruce Hagan to return to work.'

Jill read it with a puzzled look on her face. 'I don't understand. Where did you get this?'

'Bruce had to give it to our new divisional commander, Jeni Bridge. She had to sign him off for his return to work.'

Jill sat back in her chair and looked at both of them. 'I didn't write this.' She gave the sheets back.

'What do you mean?' Kim looked at the top sheet again, and flipped through to the second page. 'It's got your signature on it. This is an official report, on paper with the hospital's name on it.'

'I mean, I didn't write that report, Kim. Look, I can't talk about specifics, but let me tell you, Bruce is far from ready to return to work. I wouldn't let him anywhere near a police station, far less let him back on active duty.'

Watt looked puzzled. 'Are you saying Hagan forged this document?'

'That's exactly what I'm saying, Andy.'

'How the hell can he do that?'

'Simple.' She got up and walked over to her printer, opened up a box, and took a sheet of paper from it. She handed it over to Watt who glanced at it before passing it to Kim. It had the hospital name and address on the top.

'I have to write reports and letters all the time. When I'm ready to print, if it's only the front page with the name of the hospital on it, then I put one of those in the machine. If it's more than one, like the one you have, then I'll put in however many pages I need, with only the name of the hospital and our telephone number printed across the bottom and only the top one will have our header. Anybody could have taken some of those sheets and written a letter at home and printed it off from a home printer.'

'What about your signature?' Kim said.

'That isn't my signature.'

'How could Hagan have gotten the pages?' Watt said. 'Was he alone in here?'

Jill thought for a moment. 'Yes. I got called outside for a few minutes one day while Bruce was in here. He could have taken the pages then. Even if he folded them, he could have straightened them out for the printer and folded them again, this time with the words printed.'

'Christ, Jill, I need you to be honest with me now, because Bruce is away on an undercover job with Frank. Is Bruce dangerous?'

'Only to himself.'

'When was the last time you saw him?'

'It was weeks ago. He's finished here. He said he felt a hundred per cent better and he wasn't coming back.'

'And you believed him?' Watt said.

'No, of course not. I called his doctor and told him, but he said Bruce was a changed man. That he was weaning him off his meds and he wasn't concerned about Bruce coming back here. So what can I do? Without the GP's willingness to send him here, my hands are tied. This is a voluntary psychiatric hospital. Nobody can make Bruce come here, not even your new commander.'

'If he wanted back on duty, he'd have to still come here,' Watt said.

'Clearly he had other ideas,' she said, nodding to the paper in Kim's hand. 'You should give Frank a heads-up as soon as you can.'

'That's just the thing,' Kim said, 'we can't get a hold of him.' She told her about the restrictions at the castle. And how Bruce had been arrested already.

'I said Bruce is only a danger to himself, but now I see how clever he can be, I'm not so sure. And now he's fighting? You better get hold of Frank as soon as.'

TWENTY-EIGHT

I was up early, tempted to go for a swim in the pool in the gym, but in the end, I watched some TV before going for a shower. After a quick bite to eat, I drove down to the police station on Main Street in Golspie. Obviously neither of the two women could come with me as nobody knew they were undercover police officers.

Not surprisingly, it wasn't a big place. It looked like a double-fronted shop with a door in the middle. If it hadn't been for the *Police* sign hanging above the door, you might have thought it was a closed newsagent. Vertical blinds hung in the window, blocking the view from outside.

I parked the car outside and went in. The desk was being manned by a young constable.

'Help you?' he said.

I showed him my warrant card. 'DI Miller, Edinburgh MIT. You have one of my men in your cell.'

The burly sergeant came through from the back. 'I'll deal with this. Follow me, Miller.'

I went round the back of the desk and through the door the uniform had appeared through, feeling my temper rising.

'What's your name, I said, when we were in a short corridor.

'Angus McTavish. Why?'

'Well, McTavish, I don't know how the fuck you run things up here in the sticks, but back in civilisation, we call our superior officers *sir*.'

'Do you now? Well, I've been a copper for thirty-five years, so when I come across one who's superior to me, I'll call him *sir*.'

He opened a door and walked in and sat behind his desk. 'Now, what do you want?'

'I need my sergeant out of your cell.'

'Do you now?'

I was trying to stay calm but this man was pulling my chain. I picked up the phone on his desk and was glad to hear a tone. I called a number. McTavish yawned and took out a piece of paper from a filing tray.

'Ma'am? It's DI Frank Miller. I'm at Golspie police station, here to collect Sergeant Hagan, but I'm getting no co-operation from Sergeant McTavish, who runs this place.'

'Is that right?' Jeni Bridge said. 'Put him on.'

I handed the phone over to McTavish. 'My boss wants a word.'

'Does she now?'

'Take the fucking phone,' I said, gritting my teeth.

He took it. 'What?'

'This is Chief Superintendent Jeni Bridge, from Edinburgh.'

'Good for you.'

'What? You listen to me, fucking McTadger. My officer is there to collect one of my other officers, so release him right fucking now. If you don't, I will be right onto Stirling and speak to my old boss who happens to be the chief constable. I found out one of my officers was arrested last night and I did some background on you. Three disciplines, one misconduct. I could shag your career with one phone call. So get my officer released and don't let me ever find out you disrespected a senior officer again. Do I make myself clear, you ginger-headed ballbag?'

McTavish's face had turned almost as red as his hair. 'Yes, ma'am. I'll see to it that he's released right away. No charges were brought. We just had him cool off a bit overnight.'

'Get it done right now.'

'Yes, ma'am.' He handed the phone to me and got up from behind his desk as if his arse was on fire.

'That seems to have done the trick,' I said to Jeni.

'After Percy called me last night, I did some background checks on the reprobate. Listen, Frank, and this is not meant to be rumour spreading, but were you aware Hagan has left Hazel?'

I was stunned for a moment. 'Left her, as in split up?'

'That very definition.'

'I wasn't aware. He hasn't said anything to me.'

'Just keep an eye on things. It may affect his decision making. We're going to have a talk about his future career when you get back. I can't do anything about it right now, as we've spent a lot of money putting this together, but you have my authority to make a decision to pull the operation if things get out of hand.'

'I will. The phones are a bit iffy up here and we're not allowed our mobile phones. If I need to contact you, I'll go to the pub up the road. There's a payphone in the castle, but I don't trust—'

The door opened and McTavish ushered Hagan in.

'I have to go. That's Bruce with me now.'

'Be careful,' she said, hanging up. I replaced the receiver.

'Jesus, my fucking head,' Hagan said.

'I just need you to sign his release form,' McTavish said, no doubt wanting to see the last of us, but still going by the book.

Outside in the car, Hagan yawned. 'What the fuck were you thinking?' I said to him.

'Don't get all *Grandpa* on me now,' he said, reclining the seat back.

'Fucking *Grandpa*? If this operation wasn't so important, I'd have your arse booted out of here.'

'Jesus, you're worse than my dad was. Lighten up, Frank. We're here to have a good time.'

'We're working, for Christ's sake!'

He brought the seat back up. 'Call this work? Lying in a fucking coffin was work! Having my fucking fingers and ear cut off was work! This sitting in the bar lark is far from work! I don't even want to hear about it, not from you, not from any of you fuckers in Edinburgh.'

I knew then I had made a big mistake. In wanting to do something right, I had done something terribly wrong.

'Fasten your seatbelt. We need to get you back and freshened up. You have an appointment with Charles Sharp at ten.'

'Ah yes, my meeting with Chuck. Tell him I'm still a nut job and here to find my inner peace. What a load of pish. He'll be as daft as the rest of those other fuckers. Especially that daft cow, Jill White.'

I was about to drive off when I jumped on the brake again. 'What did you say?'

'What? Did I say something out of sorts about your precious Jill? I know you were working on the abduction of her boy. Did you get close to her? And by close, I mean, were you shag—'

I reached over with my left hand and grabbed him by the front of his shirt. 'You ever say that again and I'll—'

'What?' he screamed. 'Cut my other fucking fingers off? Cut my other ear off?'

I let his shirt go and knew then this whole operation was

fucked. Hagan had tricked me into letting me think he was okay for active duty when he clearly wasn't.

I drove back up to the castle wondering why Jill White had signed him off, fit for duty.

But deep inside, I had an idea how it happened.

And it was too late to do anything about it.

TWENTY-NINE

'Andy, I need to go somewhere,' Kim said, as they got back in the car.

'I'm in no hurry to get back. Stop by Greggs if you like. I could murder a Scotch pie.'

'I think you've murdered enough Scotch pies.'

'Well that's nice. I offer to buy you brunch and you throw it in my face. You know, when Miller kicks you to the kerb, don't come running to me. It'll be too late—' Watt saw the tears running down her face. 'Jesus, Kim, I was only kidding. Of course you can come running to me.'

She laughed and sniffed back the tears. 'Hazel and Bruce have split up, Andy.'

Watt became serious. 'What? How did that happen?'

'He left her. What with all that's been going on, him coming to therapy and everything, it was too much. He left her.'

'What's her name?'

'What?'

'You heard. There's always a woman involved. Look at

Hagan's position; he's messed up physically and mentally, and he's probably throwing his weight around—'

'She never said that.'

Watt held up a hand. 'Let me finish. Throwing his weight around and being a general pain in the arse. So he goes out to the boozer and meets a woman. Of course, he's charming and polite to her. He's in a different zone. He's in the danger zone now. The danger of getting caught. It's exciting, because now he's cheating on his wife. Or almost wife, in Hagan's case. There's always a woman.'

'She's the barmaid at Tanners bar in Juniper Green.'

'There you go then. It happens more often than you think. A man's unhappy at home and the next thing, he's sleeping with the local barmaid. It happened to my mate. He was sleeping with the local barmaid. She was new. Laughed at all his jokes, and the next thing, he's left his wife for her. She turned out to be a real hoor. And he got engaged to her too. He kicked her into touch pretty sharpish, but by then it was too late. He'd lost everything.'

'I want to go and see her in the bar.' She looked at the clock on the dashboard. 'The pub will be open.'

'You don't have to ask me twice to go to a pub.'

They drove off, up Comiston Road where she took a right along to Greenbank Drive.

'What are you going to do at the pub?' Watt asked.

'Don't worry, Andy, I just want to see what she looks like. I'm not going to slap her around.'

Watt was quiet the rest of the way as they skirted over Glenlockhart and Kim turned left onto Lanark Road, and ten minutes later they were in Juniper Green. Once a village, it had been sucked up into Edinburgh a long time ago.

Tanners bar was set back from the main road. It had parking for a few cars and there was a vennel leading to the rear car park.

The frontage was painted a light shade of brown. As was the door that led up to the flat above the pub.

'That's where Bruce lives now,' Kim said, pointing to the door.

'Above the pub?'

'Yep. Not only screwing the barmaid, but living above the pub.'

'We don't know for how much longer.'

'How do you mean?'

'Come on, Kim. How long do you think he's got when he comes back to Edinburgh? Forging a document from a therapist to get back on duty? They'll kick his arse out the door.'

'On the contrary. I think he's being very smart. Imagine the publicity; detective who was attacked by a serial killer he helped bring to justice, kicked off the force. The force rep will say he didn't know what he was doing, and he got mixed up because he was so keen to get back to work.' She looked through the windscreen at the brewery sign above the door. 'There's no way on God's earth they'll boot him out the door. Especially if he actually discovers there's some shenanigans going on at that health retreat.'

'Christ, I think you're right,' Watt said, as they got out of the car. 'They wouldn't let him back, but if he somehow conned his way back to work, then he could show them he was fit. Very clever.'

Inside, the place was quiet, waiting for the lunchtime build up. There were a few customers in, a couple of them sitting at the bar. A young woman was serving.

'I wonder if that's her,' Kim said, in a low voice.

'Remember, she hasn't done anything wrong.'

They went up to the bar and the young woman smiled. 'Can I help you?'

'Are you Amanda?'

'Jesus,' Watt said in a whisper.

'Yes, I am. Do I know you?'

'No, but you probably know a colleague of ours, Bruce. Bruce Hagan.'

'Is there something wrong?' She looked worried. Then she turned round to a man behind the bar. 'Can you hold the fort for a couple?' she asked.

'Sure. It's not like we're rushed off our feet.'

Amanda walked round the bar and indicated for them to follow her. She took out a key and unlocked a door in the short hallway that led through to the bathrooms and the restaurant. There was a stairway that led up to another door. She unlocked that and stepped inside. It was the entrance to the apartment above.

They stood in the living room, looking down onto Lanark Road.

'This is where Bruce lives,' Kim said.

'It's where we both live.'

'Oh. I didn't know you were living together.'

'So what's wrong with Bruce? I thought it would be too soon for him to go back to work. But he insisted he was okay to go back, even though he was going up to the Highlands. He is okay, isn't he?'

'Yes, as far as we know, he's fine.'

'So what's this about?'

Kim could feel her face going red. 'We just wanted to make sure he was okay after the break-up. He's been vulnerable lately and feeling down, so we wanted to speak with you, to make sure he's handling everything okay.'

'Handling what? Going back to work?'

'Everything. Life in general. Look, we're his friends as well as his colleagues, and we're just checking up on him.'

'Oh, I see, you're friends of that bitch too, I suppose. The one he lived with. Did she send you round here?'

'No, not at all. As I said, we're friends of Bruce too. Nobody sent us here.'

'He's a good guy, and we want him to know we've still got his back if he needs anybody to talk to,' Watt said.

'You do know he has two children, don't you?' Kim said, her face feeling more flushed, but now it was her temper making it that way.

'Of course I do. She didn't appreciate him. When he would come in here, we would talk and he told me how rotten a cow she was.'

'And you felt sorry for him and started sleeping with him.'

'I fell in love with him. He didn't sleep with me until he was away from her. Not that it's any of your business. I make him happy, that's all that matters.'

'Meantime, his wife is stuck at home with two young children, one of them a baby, while he's out fucking about.'

'Wife? Hazel isn't his wife, honey, *I* am.' She held up her left hand to show the band of gold. 'We got married three weeks ago.'

THIRTY

I sat with the two women in one of the lounges. I'd given Hagan instructions to meet me in there as soon as he'd freshened up and had something to eat.

Felicity Kendal and Penny Blair. Or as I knew them, DS Julie Stott and DC Steffi Walker.

'You do know Felicity Kendal is an English actress from the 70s?' I said to her.

'Of course. My grandpa used to talk about her all the time. He had a crush on her.'

'Well, Charles Sharp is American so maybe he hasn't watched much UK Gold.'

Julie smiled. Then a thought jumped into her mind. 'How was Bruce?'

I noticed a couple poking their heads in to have a quick look, and seeing there was nothing much happening, left again.

'I swear, if I didn't know better, I'd think he had a twin and the wrong one came up. He was like a different person, let me tell you.'

'What do we do now?' Steffi asked. 'I don't think we should cancel the operation because of him.'

'We'll use it to our advantage. His behaviour fits in with why he's here, so maybe he's doing us a favour.'

'That's true.'

'Are you allowed to go in with him when he sees Sharp?' Julie asked.

'No. It's a doctor patient thing. I was thinking of having a walk around the property. We could split up and cover more ground. They have walkways down in the gardens and there's tracks that lead into the woods.'

'Sounds good. Why don't we go and freshen up and we'll see you in the TV lounge? We can leave from there. That way, we'll know where we all are,' Julie said.

'Agreed. Bruce's appointment is at ten so shortly after that. He'll be in for an hour the doc says.'

'Great. Come on, Penny, let's go.'

The two women got up and left the lounge. I sat at the table and looked out at the sea in the distance, having a sinking feeling in my stomach. Not at being here on the operation, but what I knew would happen to Bruce when we got back to Edinburgh. His career was finished, but we had spent too much money on getting in here, so I had to keep my fingers crossed he didn't blow it. That's why he hadn't been told about two of my team being here. He hadn't met Julie or Steffi before now and didn't know them as coppers, and it had to stay that way.

I got up and left, heading for the *Dornoch* restaurant where they were still serving breakfast. There was a coffee bar as well as waiter service, so I grabbed a quick cup. Bruce should have been finishing up, but there was no sign of him. I grabbed a passing waiter.

'Have you seen my friend, Bruce Hagan?' I told him Bruce's

room number. It was how they checked. He took out a little pocket computer and looked at it.

'I'm sorry, sir, but there's nobody from that room number been in here.'

Fuck. Now I was starting to think he'd gone up to his room and fallen asleep. I made another coffee and rode the lift up to our floor. Knocked on Bruce's door after laying one of the coffees on the carpet.

Bruce answered the door. 'Frank! I was just coming along to see you. Is that for me?' he said, grabbing the coffee from my hand. I picked mine up off the floor and went inside.

'I thought you were going to go and have some breakfast?' I said, kicking the door shut.

'Breakfast is for wimps. I have all I need right here.' He had made a coffee from the kettle that was on the little coffee station on the dresser. And had added a little whisky to it, from what I could see.

'Christ, did you not learn anything from last night?'

'Relax. Hair of the dog, that's all.' He opened the bottle and poured a measure in and took a drink.

'Bruce, give me the bottle.'

'What? Away with yourself. I just need it to steady my nerves, that's all. I'm seeing this quack, and I don't want to be sitting in there like a window licker. I want him to see this is just a passing phase. That I'm getting better.'

'I don't think you are, Bruce. Getting better.'

'What? Don't talk pish, Frank.'

'I'm being serious. I don't blame you, but I think you might have rushed things a little.'

'Rushed things? Didn't you sit down in Tanners and give me a right good rollicking? That's what I needed. Now I just need this wee dram to take the edge off. I'll be fine, you'll see. In fact, you can walk me down to his office and watch me go in. You'll see, Frank. Everything will be fine.'

Was I being a bit unfair to Hagan? Bringing him up here and expecting him to be like he used to be? I felt guilty. I don't know how I would be if I'd gone through what he had, so I decided to back off. Maybe cut him a bit more slack.

'Okay, I'll go down with you, but just to make sure you're okay, not because I want to babysit you.'

'Thanks, Frank. You're the best friend a man could ever hope for.' He stood looking at me with his hand out. We shook and I went back to my own room, telling him to give me a shout when he was ready to go downstairs.

THIRTY-ONE

Jack was with Samantha in Wendy's house. She'd had the call and wanted them to go round.

'The medical examiner released Ryan.'

Samantha hugged her sister and they both cried for a minute. Jack looked out the window to see if there was any sign of the DEA, but if there was, they must have been hiding up in the trees opposite the house.

'What next?' Samantha said.

'I already called the funeral home. They've gone to Goshen to pick him up and I have to go to their place to go through things with the funeral director. Will you both come with me?'

'Of course we will,' Jack said. 'I'll drive you wherever you want. Is Chip coming too?'

Wendy shook her head. 'No. He says I can deal with things. He's probably busy with that whore of his.'

'Did Ryan ever meet her?' Jack asked.

'No. Why?'

'I just wondered.' That wasn't what his friend knew. They had all said they recognised her when he had shown them the photo he'd taken of her with his phone.

'Did the ME say what Ryan's cause of death was?' Samantha asked.

'Yes. It was an overdose of fentanyl. I remember Chip and I talking one night, about the drug epidemic in this country. Fentanyl is so potent if you had two little piles of it sitting side by side, exactly the same looking, one could be more than the other by a fraction and it would be enough to kill you. Ryan injected heroin laced with fentanyl.'

Samantha briefly looked at Jack as she hugged her sister again. 'Where's the funeral home?' she asked as they parted.

'Out in Wallkill,' she said. 'It's the place that dealt with Mum and Dad.'

Samantha nodded. Wallkill was a little town farther west, not far from Newburgh. Their mother and father had lived there after selling their large Connecticut family home.

Wendy looked at her watch. 'It won't take us long to get there but we should leave now.'

Outside, there were cars passing in a constant stream, but there was no sign of anybody spying on them. Hopefully McGovern had sorted the DEA out for good. They got in the Tahoe and pulled out onto Wendy's road and headed for the west section of Route 300, which would take them right into Wallkill.

The day was dull, but the roads were dry and it would have been a good day for sightseeing had that been the reason for their trip.

They approached Route 52 and went straight across on the green light and that's when Jack saw it; the large pickup truck approaching fast from behind. It was a heavy duty model, larger than the normal sized ones, with orange markers on the roof just above the windscreen. It had a chrome, crosshair-shaped front grill. It was dark in colour and the windscreen had been tinted slightly.

It didn't worry him at first, because a lot of guys drove pickups fast, but then he saw it was getting closer and closer after they went through the lights. Jack's opinion was he wouldn't be pushed along any road just because somebody was in a hurry.

This part of Rock Cut Road dipped into a valley. It was a typical country road, trees lining each side, with the occasional house.

It was here the pickup driver made his move. He floored it and hit the back of the Tahoe. The women screamed while Jack fought for control, gritting his teeth and mentally promising the driver a good kicking if he got out.

'Hang on!' he shouted, and floored the car, but the truck kept up and smashed into the back of them again. Jack had seen this in movies, and now he was on the receiving end, he knew what it felt like.

Then he saw what the driver was trying to do as the pickup went onto the other side of the road. The Pit Manoeuvre. Or the Precision Immobilisation Technique, a manoeuvre created by the Fairfax County Police Department in Virginia. A police car would hit the back end of a car, causing the driver to spin out and lose control, usually flipping the car over.

Jack knew the guy was going to do this because he hadn't moved forward, but was keeping the front of his truck level with the back of the Tahoe. This being a full-size SUV with a high centre of gravity, Jack knew they would roll over if the truck hit them.

'Hold on!' he shouted, and rammed the brake pedal down. A split-second later, the truck driver made his move, but instead of hitting the back of the Tahoe, he hit the front.

The SUV still spun round, but they didn't roll over and as they spun round a few times, Jack caught glimpses of the big pickup swerving all over the road; he thought for a moment the driver would lose control, but he managed to keep it on the road.

The brake lights came on. The Tahoe stopped spinning, and Jack assumed the other driver would come back; he was alright with that. Unless the guy was armed, he was going to get his head kicked in. But another car appeared on the horizon and the pickup roared away, throwing a plume of black smoke into the air. A diesel engine.

The Tahoe was sitting in their own lane, half on the road and half on the shoulder. 'Are you alright?' he said, turning to look at the women. Samantha had a bleeding nose, but Wendy was unconscious.

The curtain and side airbags had gone off and the next thing Jack knew, an operator was talking to them through the OnStar telematics.

'Do you need help sent, Mr Miller?'

When he had rented the car, he had temporarily registered for the service.

'Yes, we need help. We've been hit by another vehicle and there are multiple injuries on board.'

'I'm sending help now.'

Jack had to climb over the centre console to get out of the passenger door to get to the back to help Samantha with her sister.

'Did you see that crazy bastard?' she said, cradling Wendy. 'He nearly killed us!'

That's what he was trying to do, Jack thought, but didn't voice it. He'd have to call Neil McGovern and give him an update.

Things just got a lot more serious.

THIRTY-TWO

'What do you think of the castle?' Charles Sharp said to Bruce Hagan.

'Meh. You've seen one, you've seen them all. I couldn't care fucking less about historical crap.'

Sharp was looking out the window, his back to the detective. Another sunless day. He missed the time they lived in Southern California. They'd been there for a while, trying to find a cure for Mama, but it had been a bust. Now he was in this place. Looking out onto a dark sea. At least it wasn't raining.

He turned to face the policeman. 'I want you to start *being* interested in castles and historical stuff, Bruce. And you will be. I've read your file and what you went through was horrific, but it can be less debilitating with my help. All I need is your co-operation and willingness to take on board what I have to say.'

Hagan guffawed. 'A miracle worker, eh? Just like the medicine men of old. Roll up, roll up, get your cure-all here.' He was slumped in the chair and looked at the doctor with more than a little scepticism.

The room was covered with dark oak; wall panels, ceiling and doors. All except the thick, plush carpet. Which was dark brown, staying with the theme.

Two small, wall lamps helped light the room, along with the natural light from the window, but if you closed your eyes and opened them suddenly, you could be living in the fourteenth century for all you knew. 'I know you want help, Bruce, or you wouldn't be here. But I understand your frustration.'

'Do you?'

Sharp walked over and sat on a chair opposite, keeping a smile on his face. 'It's my business to understand. I've helped many people and I can help you.' He made direct eye contact with Hagan. 'I can read you and I see behind the gruff exterior you display, there's a man wanting to be able to go back to who he was. Am I right?'

Hagan was silent for a moment then he sat up in the chair. 'You're right, of course you are, but I don't see how you can help me any more than the people I've already been to.'

Sharp smiled and held his hands out sideways. 'So you think all car mechanics are the same? They do the same job, they were all trained, but wouldn't you agree some are better than others?'

'I suppose.'

'Of course you do. Think of me as the master technician as opposed to somebody who's no better than an oil changer.'

'Okay. I'm listening.'

'Over the next week or so, I will delve into your past, not only the past where recent events happened to bring you here, but right back. Sometimes people have childhood fears that are dredged up. Sometimes not.'

'And if I don't have?'

'Then all the better! That means we have a smaller parameter to work with. Either way, your therapy will be intense here, Bruce, but you will go away feeling like a new man.'

'Sounds like a miracle.'

'Not really. We have it inside all of us. Like the woman who suddenly gets the strength to lift a car off her little boy. If we dig deep enough, we can find what we're looking for. We just need to know where to dig.'

'Okay. That's what I want to hear.'

'Would you like some water before we begin? You look a little... how shall we put it...?'

'Hungover.'

'Yes. Hungover. I'll get you some.' Sharp stood, went over to a dresser at the back of the room, poured Hagan some water and handed him the glass. 'I am always amazed at how good the water tastes in Scotland. Where I come from, I wouldn't let a dog drink it. That's why we always had filtered water. But I digress. Tell me a little about when you were a boy. Just so I can get to know you better.'

Hagan started telling him all about growing up in Edinburgh before he and his family moved to Fife. Sharp was taking down notes, and Hagan started yawning.

A short while later, Hagan had dozed off. Sharp stood quietly, walked over to a panel in the wall, and gently pushed it. Inside was a small room. Doctor Solomon sat, waiting patiently, reading a car magazine.

'He's asleep now. Do what you have to do.'

Solomon nodded and walked into the large room, holding a little, black zipper case. 'Is the door locked?'

'Of course not. I expect a pipe band to come in any minute now. Of course it is. Now, hurry up.'

Sharp looked at his watch; there was a little time before the session ended, but he always made sure none of the appointments clashed. The next one wasn't due for another hour. That way, if he did find a subject, he would be able to do this.

Solomon took Hagan's left trainer and sock off and opened the little zipper case. Took out a syringe, squirting some of the clear liquid into the air before spreading two of Hagan's toes and inserting the syringe there.

When he was done, he put the syringe away and stood with the small case in one hand.

'Could you...' Sharp nodded towards the shoe and sock. 'I deal with the mind, not the body. I have you for that.'

Solomon tutted and put the sock and shoe back on.

'How long will this take to get into his system?'

'By the time he wakes up, it will have taken effect.'

'Outward signs?'

'Nothing more than he was already showing. This is a different formula however, so we will have to wait.'

'What about the rest of it?'

'As long as he drinks that spiked water you gave him, he should have the full dose by the end of the week.' Solomon looked at Sharp. 'Did you give him anything last night?'

'No. Why?'

'He was fighting in the bar in the hotel. McTavish told me this morning.'

'Christ. Maybe this will stop all that.'

'If not, I can add a little something to the cocktail, but I don't think you want him too incoherent.'

'I most certainly do not.'

'What about the other woman?'

'She's getting the same. We'll be monitoring her closely.'

'This is a far more potent strain. You wanted me to accelerate the program so that's what we did. They're working hard, but with such time constraints I don't think—'

'That's right, don't think, doctor. You're not paid to think.'

'Call me if you need me. I'd better go. The clock's ticking and he'll be awake soon.' Solomon departed the room the same way he'd come in.

Ten minutes later, Hagan was wide awake, stretching and yawning. 'Sorry, did I doze off?'

'Just for a little bit.'

'Jeez, I think that's the best sleep I've had for a long time.'

'It's the fresh Highland air that does it for most people, although I suspect the alcohol helped you along.' Sharp smiled.

'I suppose you want me to cut out the drinking?'

'This is not a prison, Bruce. I can only suggest you modify your drinking habits so we can let you concentrate on getting better.'

'I will.' He stood up and winced. 'I really do have a hangover. My head feels like it's going to explode.'

'Stress and not enough sleep. Just take it easy for this upcoming week and we'll see a new you.' He watched Hagan lose his balance for a moment and panic gripped him, thinking Solomon had overdone it, but then Hagan straightened up and smiled.

'When's my next sesh with you, doc?'

'My assistant will help you with that, but I'd like you to come to a group session tonight. It's an informal get-together with people who are in the same situation as yourself.'

'Group therapy?'

'I prefer to call it a welcome party. Shall we say seven o'clock?'

'I'll be there.' Hagan left the room.

THIRTY-THREE

'It's beautiful here, isn't it?'

I turned round at the sound of the woman's voice behind me. She was maybe in her late forties or so. I could have been wrong. A woman in the bar one night, who I'd never met before and who was very drunk, had asked me how old I thought she was. She looked sixty, but I thought I'd be kind and tell her she looked as if she were fifty.

I'm only forty, cheeky bastard, she had told me before storming out.

So this woman could have been anywhere between mid-forties and mid-fifties.

'It is. I can't believe how peaceful it is.' I'd walked through the gardens down at the base of the castle while Hagan was in with the doctor. Through an arched hedge and some more gardens until I came to the service road that ran round the perimeter of the property. The beach was ahead of me, and the sound of the sea rolling up the sand was music to my ears.

'I'm Melissa Sharp, Charles' wife.' She smiled and held out a hand.

I shook it, feeling her grip strong, her hand warm. She smiled before letting go.

'Do you always greet newcomers down on the beach?' I asked, smiling back at her.

She gave a quick laugh. 'I usually have a stroll down here at this time, when the weather permits. So, no, I don't always bump into people down here.'

'I was just curious. I wasn't meaning to be rude.'

'I know.'

Her accent was American. I had read up about them, how they had met at Harvard Medical School and decided to get married and start their own psychiatric business together. How her husband was very rich. She was very nice with a beautiful smile that I suspected could charm the birds out of the trees.

'Do you mind if I walk with you for a bit?' she asked.

'Not at all.'

'How long have you had this place?' I asked her.

'A couple of years.'

A wind was blowing in off the Dornoch Firth. I dug my hands deeper into my jacket. 'Why Scotland?'

'Believe it or not, America is full of Americans who have ancestors who come from Scotland. Although I have an American accent, I was born here. In Inverness. We moved to America when I was seven.'

'How does your husband feel about living here?'

She kicked at a stone on the beach. The tide rolled in gently, far enough away so we didn't have to worry about our shoes getting wet.

'He loves Scotland.'

'But?'

She smiled wryly at me. 'But I don't think he wants to end his days here. This is a business venture for us. We're making money at it, but sometimes all that doesn't matter when your heart is somewhere else.' She bent and picked up a stone that had been rounded by the rolling sea over many years. Her left hand arced out and let the stone go, but I was watching her more than the stone. She was graceful and elegant, like the butterfly tattooed on the inside of her left wrist.

The stone sank rather than skipped, depositing it back from where it came. Maybe it would be a thousand years before it made its way up onto the shore again.

'It seems a popular place,' I said, picking up a stone and throwing it in beside its brother.

'It is, in the summer. We wanted a place where people could come, and leave refreshed, mentally as well as physically, and now business is booming. More so in the summer months, but we may just have it purely as a hotel one day.'

'You have an advantage with this view.' I looked into the distance as a huge mansion house came into view, sitting on the top of the cliff ahead of us.

'You like our house?' she asked.

'It looks fantastic.'

'It was built a long time ago, but not by whoever built the castle. It was added a couple of hundred years ago.'

As we walked farther along, a dark green Land Rover appeared as if by magic out of the trees. I couldn't see the service road from here, but obviously it led up to the house.

'That's one thing about owning the place,' Melissa said, 'we have staff to deliver our groceries.'

'I'll have to see if my wife will get on board with having staff,' I said.

'How long have you been married?'

'I'm not. Yet. This summer sometime. We live together.'

Melissa suddenly stopped. 'You'd do anything for her though, wouldn't you?'

'Of course I would.' I saw her eyes were bright, as if she were about to start crying.

'I have to go, Frank. I hope your colleague improves while he's here.'

'Me too.'

'Charles works wonders.'

'That's good to know.'

'I'll see you around.'

I watched her walk away across the sand and go in through the entrance to the gardens. I strolled off the beach, onto the service road, and started wandering through the forest. Most of the property was covered by trees, which would be a great relief from the sun, for those who visited during the summer.

I had just started round a corner and the road split two ways, left and right. I took the right and was suddenly on a steep part of the road. No wonder they had to use Land Rovers to deliver groceries. There was a parking area at the side of the house, but the track itself came out into a small car park in front of the mansion house.

A man dressed in black, carrying a doctor's bag, came out of the front door. I was about to ask him how to get back to the castle when a young woman appeared and they started arguing. The man in black shouted at her. She started crying and rushed back inside, slamming the front door. He was about to step into his little car when he suddenly stopped and looked in my direction. I ducked and stepped behind a tree.

I heard the car door slam, the engine start, and the wheels spin on the gravel drive.

I came out from behind the tree and walked up the slope into the car park. The car had already turned a corner and disappeared. I skirted the driveway, following where the car had gone. Once again, the road forked, left and right.

I took the right, and farther along I saw the little blue car. It was parked in front of a small house. Maybe it belonged to another member of staff. I remembered looking at a satellite view of this place and saw there were buildings scattered around the property. Obviously they had staff living in the grounds. The castle didn't run itself.

Then suddenly I heard a faint howl. Like a muted scream. Coming from the mansion house.

I strode back towards the old, stone building, not bothering with stealth now.

The front façade of the house was quite impressive. It was a three-storey affair, the third level probably servants' rooms, once upon a time.

I walked up to the front door, the wind blowing through the trees as the weather was starting to turn once again. My feet crunched the gravel like the car had done as I kicked and scuffed my way over.

When I got near the door, it suddenly opened.

A woman was standing there. It wasn't the woman who had been arguing with the man just a few minutes ago.

'I'm DI Frank Miller. I thought I heard screaming coming from the house.'

'You heard wrong. Why are you here?'

'I'm staying at the castle.'

'Then go back there. This is off limits to visitors.' She slammed the door shut. I looked at the windows and upstairs, the face of the younger woman looked back at me, then she quickly closed the curtains.

I walked away again, and once more, just as I reached the fork in the road, I heard the scream again. This time, I kept on walking.

THIRTY-FOUR

Mobile Life ambulance service had attended the scene of the crash and taken Wendy and Samantha to St Luke's hospital ER in the city of Newburgh. One of the paramedics told Jack Samantha's nose didn't look broken, but he was more concerned about Wendy.

'So this truck,' the police officer said to Jack, 'did it have any plates on it?'

'I didn't see any.'

'You mean you couldn't make it out?'

'No, I mean, it wasn't displaying any. He had taken them off.'

'So you saw it was a man?'

'Just generalising. He or she, took them off.'

'And the windows were blacked out?'

'Yes.'

'And you're sure it was a Dodge?'

'An old one, but yes, a Dodge.'

A few cars had turned up along with the ambulance, including State Police cruisers. Orange County 911 dispatch had a computer system that sent the message to the nearest police cruisers, whether it was a State Trooper or a Town patrol.

'Those guys will be assisting us with the accident recreation.'

'It wasn't an accident.'

'We're treating it as one until we can look into this further.'

'To see if I made this up, you mean?'

'Not at all.' He turned round when another unmarked cruiser pulled in. 'Here's a detective now.'

As luck would have it, the detective was the one who Jack had met the other night at the garage fire.

'My name's Sergeant Chris Nolan, Town of Newburgh PD. Didn't I see you at the garage fire the other night?'

'Yes you did.'

'The retired detective, right?'

'Correct again.'

'So what's going on here?'

'Somebody tried to kill us.' He was expecting scepticism, and it might have happened, but Jack sensed this detective knew he wasn't dealing with just any Joe off the street.

'So run it by me.'

Jack looked at the man who had his badge clipped to his belt, in front of the gun that sat in its holster. He wore sunglasses, even though it wasn't that sunny outside, and was chewing gum.

Jack ran through what had happened. He didn't mention he thought he knew who had tried to run him off the road.

'You cut somebody off at the lights or something?'

'No. We just left Wendy Haines' house. Chip's wife. You know him, don't you?'

'Of course.' He looked around him then back at Jack. 'So, if it wasn't road rage, what's your gut telling you?'

'I have no idea. We just came from Scotland to help Wendy. She's my girlfriend's sister.'

'Well, obviously somebody's mad at you if it's not random.'

No kidding.

'I can assure you I haven't deliberately pissed off anybody since I've been here.' Which wasn't quite true; he hadn't made a new friend in Chip.

'A tow truck is coming to take it away to our pound. I'll have somebody take some of the grey paint chips off it.'

Jack looked at the creased side of the bright red Tahoe and was glad the car wasn't his. 'I've called Enterprise and they're bringing another one out to me.'

'Okay. We'll be a while here so if the guy comes back, then we'll deal with him, but he's probably long gone now.'

I wish he would come back, Jack thought.

'We'll need you to come to the station and make a formal statement,' Nolan said.

'Okay. I'll be round later. First, I have to get to the hospital to check up on the women.'

He didn't have to wait long for Enterprise as their local office was just down the road.

One of the patrol officers waved the agent through. 'Everything okay, Mr Miller?' he asked.

'Apart from somebody trying to murder us, I'm fine.'

The agent looked to see if Jack was joking or not, and when he saw that he wasn't, he got away from the scene as quickly as possible.

THIRTY-FIVE

Kim was sitting in Percy Purcell's office. 'What the hell do we do now?' she said.

'Technically, it's his private life, Kim. There's not a lot we can do. It's none of our business who he gets married to, and unless it affects his work, then there's nothing we can do.'

'You see that's what I really came in here to talk to you about. Jill White didn't write the release to return to work.'

Purcell sat up straighter in his chair. 'Are you sure?'

'Of course I'm sure. I spoke to her. She was the one who told me.'

'Christ. Hold that thought.' He picked up the phone on his desk and made a call. 'Ma'am? It's Purcell. I have Kim in here with me, and you need to hear this.' He listened to the reply before hanging up.

'Jeni Bridge wants us in her office right away.'

They strode along the corridor to where Jeni's office was. She called them in after Purcell knocked.

'Sit down,' she said, indicating the chairs in front of her desk. 'So what's so important, Percy?'

Purcell looked at Kim. 'You tell her.'

'I was at the Astley Ainslie hospital. I just wanted to talk to Jill White, because I wasn't convinced Bruce was really fit to return to work. He's away from Hazel.'

'Really? How do you know that would affect his work?'

'I didn't, not really. I just had a feeling. After Percy said Bruce was arrested last night for drunk and disorderly, I wondered why Jill thought he was okay. So we went to talk to her and she said she didn't write the report allowing him to return to work.' She had a copy in her hands and passed it over to Jeni. 'He forged her signature.'

'What? Oh Christ, Percy, we really do have a problem.'

'To say the least. He got himself arrested last night. He was fighting in a bar.'

'I know. Frank called me this morning from the station. I had to chew out the sergeant up there.' She sat back in her office chair and threw her head back. 'Talk about a baptism of fire.' She looked at the others. 'We can't do anything about Bruce from here.' She looked at Kim. 'Does Hazel know?'

'I don't think so.'

'Good. That information stays in this office for now. However, two more of my officers are up there, and Frank doesn't know what he's dealing with. I don't like that at all, Percy.'

'I don't like it either, ma'am.'

'I would send you up there, but Hagan knows you and he might cotton on that something's wrong if we're sending backup.'

'DC Walker and DS Stott are there already, and we deliberately didn't reveal them to Hagan,' Purcell said.

'And they're more than capable officers, but let's not lose focus of why they're there in the first place. They're a team of four. If they find nothing's going on, then that's fine. Job done. Come home. But if there's something shady about the place and the good doctors who run it, then they're a man down. If we'd known Hagan had been blowing smoke through his arse, then we would have had somebody else there.'

'I'm fucking mad at this,' Kim said. 'Frank could be in danger for all we know. Just because Hagan is trying to be bloody clever.'

'What do you mean?' Jeni asked.

'I was talking to Andy Watt about this. What if there *is* something going on up there, and we make the arrests. Even if we found out Hagan had forged a report, we would be like *Oh, super, Bruce. You were a naughty boy, but you did a good job, so we know you really are fit for work. Welcome back!* So he gets to come back to duty through the back door, meantime risking the whole operation. And he gets arrested the first fucking night they're there.'

Purcell put a hand on Kim's arm. 'Take it easy, Kim. We need to focus now. It might be nothing was going on and *Paradise Shores* really is just a wellness centre.'

'And the Loch Ness Monster comes into the Dornoch Firth for kids to ride on.' She looked at him. 'You don't really believe nothing happened there, do you?'

'No. Something happened to Steven Hubbard and Mel Carpenter when they were there. What, I don't know, but hopefully we'll find out.' Purcell looked at Jeni. 'What I do know is we can't have officers putting the team in danger. Frank is more than capable of dealing with Hagan, but it's the unknown that worries me.'

'Agreed. I'm sending backup there.'

'I'm not sure there's anybody Hagan doesn't know. And we can't trust him not to blurt something out, especially if he has a drink,' Kim said.

'And it's too short notice to get in an outside team and bring them up to speed.'

Jeni tapped her steepled fingers against each other. Looked at Purcell. 'Our computer department put together a couple of legends for Walker and Stott, didn't they?'

'Yes. The women went over them in detail before they left. They memorised everything, so if any detail is checked, then it will hold up.'

'There wouldn't be any time for somebody new to be brought up to speed. Or to have them slip into a new persona.'

'It was supposed to be a four-man team up there. Now it's down to three. Plus one who we now know isn't supposed to be there, and who could jeopardise the safety of the other three,' Kim said.

'I'm going to let it play out just now,' Jeni said. 'We can't go blundering in there and throw this operation out the window.'

'I'm worried sick now.'

'I know how you must feel.'

'No you don't. I know Frank is more than capable of looking after himself, but they didn't invade the fucking beaches at Normandy with one soldier.'

Jeni leaned forward and rested her hands on her desk. 'Is there anybody we can send up there who Hagan doesn't know?'

'I know one person, but I'm a bit reluctant to let her go in there alone.'

'She won't be alone, she would be liaising with Frank and the others.'

'I could ask her, but she's under no obligation.'

'Who is it, Percy?'

'My fiancée, Inspector Suzy Campbell. She's based down in HQ at Fettes just now, but she was a detective up in Aberdeen.'

'Do you think she would be willing?'

'I'm sure she would.'

'We could get her briefed today, get her up to speed.'

'I don't know if our computer guys could get her a legend made up in time.'

'I know somebody who could,' Kim said. 'A guy who now works with my dad, Ian Powers. He's one of the best and he's helped Frank in the past. I'll call my dad and see if he can arrange it.'

'Good. Let's get this done. Percy, call Suzy and ask her. If she says no, we'll try for a Plan B.'

'Right.' He took his phone out, called Suzy, and got right through to her. After he explained what he needed she agreed.

'She's on board,' he said, hanging up.

'Great. Have Ian Powers create a new job description for her. Make up some stuff and have her go over it. Then we'll think of somebody we can send with her.'

'I'll get onto it right away.'

'If the place has no rooms available, have him delete somebody else's name and get her in there.'

'Will do.'

'And when Bruce Hagan gets back here, I'll sit down with him and give him the bad news regarding his career.'

THIRTY-SIX

I was waiting for Hagan in Julie's room. Steffi came through the connecting door. Their rooms were similar to the ones Bruce and I had.

'How is this going to affect Bruce when we get back to Edinburgh?' Julie asked.

I was looking out the window. It was more or less the same view I had from my room. We were all on the same level. I turned to face the two young women.

'I don't know.'

'Come on, sir,' Steffi said. 'We know it's not going to be good news. He got arrested for being drunk. I'm not saying I condone it, but—'

'How would you deal with it if you were in Jeni Bridge's shoes?'

'It would depend on how the rest of this operation went.'

'There you go. There's your answer. You would have to look at the big picture. Bruce sacrificed a lot for the force. It will very much depend on what happens here. She might just take him aside and have a word with him.'

'It's a very difficult position,' Julie said. '*Conduct unbecoming a police officer* is how they would get him out the door.'

'That's correct. But all the factors would be taken into consideration.'

'Let's hope they're lenient with him,' Steffi said.

'What did you do while Hagan was in with Sharp?' Julie asked me.

'I had a walk down on the beach, trying to get the lay of the land. I was joined by the lovely Melissa Sharp.'

'How does she seem?'

'Very pleasant, actually.'

'I wonder why she joined you on the beach?'

'Maybe she didn't have any appointments or something. I thought they were both doctors. Maybe it's a quiet time of year.'

'Maybe she was just sounding you out,' Steffi said.

'I had thought of that. I didn't make her any the wiser though.' I leaned back against the window frame. 'Let me tell you though, I walked up to the big house where they live and heard screaming coming from in there.'

'Screaming?' Julie said.

'It was muted, but it was definitely screaming. I went to the door, but a woman answered and told me I was mistaken.'

'We should give it a closer look,' Steffi said.

'Good idea,' Julie agreed. 'After dark. We can go for a walk tonight.'

I looked at my watch. 'Bruce should be finished by now. I told him to come straight to his room for a debrief.'

'You don't think they have the rooms bugged, do you?'

I shrugged. 'There's no way of telling unless you know what

you're looking for, but bugs can be so small nowadays, they can practically hide them in your toothpaste.'

My room and Bruce's were only a few doors away, and I heard the lift doors dinging as they opened. Then we all heard the yell.

I ran over to the door and yanked it open. In the hallway, Hagan was on his knees, his hands wrapped around his head, forehead touching the floor, yelling.

'Bruce! Are you okay?' I said, rushing over to him, followed by the two women.

Steffi stepped in. Being an ex-army medic, she kicked right into action, kneeling down beside him.

'Bruce, tell me where it's hurting,' she said.

'My head! My fucking head is going to explode!' His feet beat a tattoo on the floor and Steffi couldn't get him to let go of his head.

Suddenly, he keeled over and for a moment, I couldn't see his chest rise and fall; I thought he'd gone into cardiac arrest, but then he opened his eyes and sat up just as Steffi was feeling for a pulse and had started giving him mouth-to-mouth.

'There's a time and a place, darlin',' he said to her. Then he took some deep breaths, puffing in and out.

I reached out a hand to help him up but he got up lightning fast.

'Are you okay?' I asked him.

'I'm fine, squire. How about you?' He was sweating profusely but he had a grin on his face.

'Is your head okay?'

'It's fine. How's yours?'

He kept his hair long, and now it was slick with sweat and a mess.

'Christ, Bruce, you were screaming in agony. You sure you feel okay? I can get them to call a doctor,' Steffi said.

I noticed a subtle change in his demeanour then. 'Mind your own fucking business, bitch.'

'Enough, Hagan!' I said.

'Come on, Frank. People poking their noses in where they're not wanted. Makes me fucking sick.'

'I'm sorry,' I started to say to Steffi, but Hagan spun round.

'Don't you dare fucking apologise for me! You cu—'

'Hagan!' I shouted at him, stepping in between him and Steffi, thinking he was going to lift his hand to her.

That stopped him in his tracks but his eyes looked glazed. He stood looking at us, and I was glad he didn't know who Julie and Steffi really were.

Then I saw the blood trickling down from his nose. 'You're bleeding,' I said to him.

'Yeah, well, you might be bleeding in a minute.' He turned round and stormed away, going into his room and slamming his door.

'I'd better go and see if he's okay. I'll see you ladies around later on.'

'Nice seeing you again, Frank. Maybe we'll see you in the bar later?'

'Count on it.'

I walked along to Hagan's room and banged on the door. 'Bruce! Open the door.' There was no answer. I was worried something had happened to him. 'Bruce, open the door, or I'll have somebody open it.'

I tried the handle in frustration. The door opened. I went in. His room was as if it had been turned over. Clothes everywhere. Garbage lying about. Bed unmade. It hadn't been like this before. It was as if he'd taken a mad turn and thrown the stuff around.

Then I heard the shower running.

I opened the connecting door and went into my own room. Sat

on the bed for fifteen, twenty minutes and went back through after knocking on the door and getting no response. The shower was still running. 'Bruce? You okay?' I shouted, knocking loudly on the bathroom door, loud enough to wake an elephant.

No answer.

I opened the door. The extractor was running but still there was steam everywhere. Either Hagan liked his showers boiling hot, or else...

'Bruce!' I shouted. No matter how loud the noise of the running water was, he would have heard me.

I stepped forward and grabbed hold of the shower curtain and pulled it.

THIRTY-SEVEN

Lou Purcell was sitting on a bench in the waiting area of the bus station in St Andrew Square when Percy went to pick him up.

'You *must* be hungry, sitting there eating a manky old sandwich,' Percy said as he approached his father.

'I made this myself,' Lou said.

'That's what I meant.'

'Sit down while I wash this down with my tea. I don't want people to think I'm a paraffin lamp.' Which was slang for *tramp*.

'For God's sake,' Percy said, sitting down on the bench. 'And the term is *homeless person*.'

'I don't go in for all that PC crap. When did *fifteen amp* rhyme with *homeless person*? Is that what the snoots call them nowadays?'

'It's just not right calling unfortunate people by those names.'

'One of those pish-stained fuckers just tried to cadge a couple of quid off me. He was wearing better shoes than I was!'

'What did you say to him?'

'If you must know, I told him to fuck off. I don't think he's too happy, because now there's two of them. They're standing behind you, over there. Waiting to mug us when we leave.'

'You and your bloody big mouth.'

Lou balled up the cling film and fired it into a bin, drank the dregs of his tea and put the cup back on his flask, putting it back into his holdall. 'Right, I'm done. Let's go. You got a car waiting?'

'I have actually, because I'm busy, not because you think you're royalty.'

They both stood up and the two men started coming towards them. Percy took his warrant card out. 'Police. If you get close enough to read this, you're leaving in an ambulance.'

They looked at each other before turning around and traipsing in the opposite direction.

'I knew you would take care of them, that's why I told them to sling their hook.'

'Just get a move on before I arrest you.'

'Bloody charming. My piles are killing me from sitting on that hard bus seat and all I get is lip. What about a hug for your old man?'

'Bugger off.'

'Bear will give me a hug, I'll bet.'

'I've taught him to hump you when you visit.'

'That poor bloody dog. He knows Grandpa didn't corrupt him.'

'Well, he's living in civilisation now.'

'Oh I see, Aberdeen was okay when you dragged me up there. *Come up with us, Dad*, they said. *You'll love it*, they said. Then they have a big barney and Paula fucks off with the milkman.'

'It was an accountant, if you remember, you senile old sod.'

'Enough of the name calling, you wee brat.' He shivered in the chill wind that was blowing through St Andrew Square. 'Where's the car?'

'In the taxi rank. It has an orange light with the word *Taxi* written on it.'

'Tell me you're kidding.'

'I'm kidding. Get a move on.'

They turned right and walked down the hill to where the police car was sitting. 'This isn't a taxi service mind. My new boss said it was okay, but I won't be taking advantage of her.'

'Sure you won't.' He opened the back door and slung his bag in. 'This is me you're talking to, Percy.'

'Get in. And tell me all about this old floozy you're trying to take advantage of.'

'Clearly this is the result of *spare the rod and spoil the child* in action.'

Percy started the car and drove away from the rank.

'I'm insulted that you think that's all I'm after from a woman.'

'Just tell me about her. Like, does she prefer an axe or a carving knife to get rid of her husbands?'

'You're very funny.' He looked out at the alley of shops that was Multrees Walk, in what was once the exit for the bus station, many moons ago. 'Maybe I'll buy her one of those fancy handbags out of that shop.'

'Louis Vuitton? You've got to be kidding me. They're thousands of pounds. She'll milk you for everything you've got if you get her one of those.'

Lou looked at his son. 'Really? Nice attitude. I'd buy Suzy one, because to me, she's worth a million dollars.'

'You know what I mean.'

'No, I don't. Maybe we could expand this conversation over dinner tonight.'

'Or maybe you could have that conversation all to yourself in the scabby old hostel in the Grassmarket.'

'My lips are sealed.'

'Listen though, Suzy's going to be going away for a few days on an operation.'

'So it's just us boys at home? Just like the old days.'

'Don't remind me.' He took George Street and cut down Dundas Street.

'Jesus, this place hasn't half changed. What happened to that eyesore on the corner of St Andrew Square near Jenners?'

'They tore it down.'

'And put up that modern monstrosity.'

'You need to get with the times, Dad. Things change. I think it looks good.'

'Well, we'll see if it's still standing in a few hundred years' time when all the Georgian buildings are still going strong. They knew how to design houses back then. They had class.'

'Well, the flat we bought is a modern one, right round the corner from St Stephen's Church.' Purcell didn't want to tell his father people had been murdered in a flat in the same building, a case they had worked on just a few months earlier. He suspected it was the reason the people had sold up and moved out and why they let it go at a good price.

'What about when you have kids?' Lou asked. 'Wouldn't you rather see them running about a back garden?'

'Dad, we're not even married yet.'

'You're in your forties. You don't want your kid to be embarrassed when he goes to school. Other kids will think you're his grandpa.'

'Thanks for the input, Dr Spock.'

'I'm just saying. You'll be retired by the time he gets to college. Then he'll be giving you lip and you won't be able to skelp his arse or he'll slap you about.'

'Was that your worry when I was growing up?'

'I don't think I did too bad. Look how you turned out.'

'I can't argue with that.'

Purcell pulled into the lane and approached the underground car park. The automatic gate lifted.

'Very swanky. I'll bet Professional Standards wonder how you can afford a place like this.'

'It's called a mortgage, Dad.'

They parked and rode the lift up to the fourth floor.

'I have to admit, this is better than staying in a hot—'

Bear came bounding out of the living room and jumped all over Lou. 'My boy! This is more like it! Why can't you greet me like this?'

'He's just putting on a show. He talks about you behind your back.'

'Just show me where the dog treats are kept and where the kettle is.'

'We have Hobnobs if you're hungry.'

'Don't worry, I'll find your stash of chocolate digestives.' He looked at his son. 'Kettle.'

Percy showed his father where the kitchen was. 'I have to go back to work. We'll have Chinese for dinner. Try not to burn the place down.'

THIRTY-EIGHT

There was only one ER serving Newburgh and its surrounding environs, now Cornwall campus had closed. So, it was busy after Jack parked the car in the multi-storey car park and took the pedestrian bridge over.

'How are you doing?' he asked Samantha, when he finally got through to the emergency bays. Security was tight; sometimes they had to go into lockdown when a gang member had been brought in and there were members of another gang waiting outside to finish him off.

'I'm fine. Because it was a head injury, they X-rayed me pretty quickly and same with Wendy. One of the male nurses said she was okay. The doctor told me she must have fainted. It's the stress that did it, not the crash. She didn't hit her head hard enough to knock her out.'

'I'm glad you're both okay. You had me worried.'

'Did they get the guy who was driving the truck?'

'Not yet. They're looking for him, but there must be a million of them. And to be honest, I don't think they're going to be looking very hard.'

'Why not? Wendy's a cop's wife.'

'Estranged wife. I spoke to a detective who I saw the other night at the fire at the garage where the young people hang out. He seems to be a bit... defensive, is how I would describe him.'

'You don't think he's interested?'

'I just get a feeling about him.'

'I'd like to have a word with that bastard who ran us off the road, let me tell you.'

'You and me both, Sam.'

'I want to get the hell out of here. I'm just waiting for the doctor to write my release.'

'Any medications?'

'No. Just Tylenol for pain.'

Shortly after that, the doctor came in and Jack popped into the next bay to see Wendy.

'Christ, Jack, I feel like I've been hit by a Mack truck.'

'We *were* hit by a truck, just a smaller one.'

'Did you get hold of Chip?' she asked.

'He's not answering his phone, Wendy.'

She shook her head, her lip trembling as she started to speak. 'We were happy together, Chip and me.' She looked at him. 'What the hell happened?' The question was rhetorical.

The doctor came into the bay and told her she was free to go. A nurse would be in with paperwork shortly.

With everything in order, they left the ER.

'I'll have to go to the funeral home sometime today,' Wendy said. The car was the same as the one that had been wrecked, only this one was black. 'I'll have to give them a call.' She took out her phone and found the number online before dialling.

'I was worried about you,' Jack said to Samantha, who was sitting in the front passenger seat.

She reached over and grasped his right hand. 'I'm so glad you're here. I don't know what I would have done if I was here alone with Wendy.'

'I know you, and you would have managed just fine.'

'I'm glad you have confidence in me.'

'Of course I do.' He winked at her.

They drove straight up Route 17K, eventually coming to Wendy's road. It was blocked off by a police car. They were a long way from where they'd had their accident, so it couldn't be anything to do with that.

'What's going on?' Jack said, after rolling the window down. A State Police officer walked up.

'You can't go up there. The road's been closed.'

'My sister-in-law lives there.' He told the officer her number.

'Stay there.' He walked away, and spoke on his radio. After a couple of minutes, he came back. 'You can go along. There's a detective waiting for you. You can only go as far as the Town PD car.'

He stood back and let Jack drive through. The road was quiet with no traffic, but as they rounded the corner, they saw why nobody was getting in. There was a house fire.

Jack drove up to the police car blocking the road. The detective waiting for them was none other than Chris Nolan, the same one who had been to the scene of their accident earlier.

He approached as Jack stopped beside the patrol car. Several fire trucks from different volunteer companies were in attendance. Wendy's house was well alight.

'Oh my God, no!' Wendy said as she stepped out of the car. She was about to walk round the patrol car when Nolan stopped her.

'You can't go anywhere near the house.'

'What the hell happened?' Samantha asked.

'We don't know yet, but we'll get to the bottom of it.'

'You get around,' Jack said, not liking the man at all.

'I'm one of Orange County's fire investigators. I multi-task.'

'Do you come out to every fire?'

'When I get a call to come out from a patrol officer or the Fire Marshall. It's too early to say, but considering somebody tried to run you off the road this morning, and then your house goes up, then I think it's time for me to be involved.'

Jack's first impression had been that Nolan was a colleague of Chip's and they would close ranks, but now he got a feeling Nolan was on the up and up.

'Nothing on the truck, I suppose?'

'Nothing,' Nolan said. 'Could be the guy's hiding it in his garage. Who knows? If he takes it in for repair to any reputable garage, we'll get a call as we've already circulated the details.'

Jack looked at the flames licking through the roof of the house and the firefighters battling it.

'This wasn't started that long ago, obviously.'

Nolan looked at his watch. 'The first 911 call came in about fifteen minutes ago.'

'We were in the ER, before you ask,' Jack said. 'They have paperwork and we're on their security cameras.'

'I'll check it out, obviously, but I don't have you at the top of my list if it's arson.'

'What am I going to do now?' Wendy said.

'We'll get you a room in the hotel. If they don't have any vacancies, you can share our room.'

'Don't forget to buy some new clothes. The way that fire has a hold, there's going to be nothing left,' Nolan said.

THIRTY-NINE

Hagan was gone.

I wondered how he could have just disappeared until I found the connecting door between our rooms unlocked. And my own room door unlocked. The rooms were on a corner of the building, so our doors were in different hallways. He had slipped out round the corner from where we had been standing.

He was standing at the end of the hallway, leaning against the wall, one hand cradling his head.

'Bruce!' I shouted.

He looked over at me, and then his eyes widened in shock, as if he didn't even know who I was. Then he was suddenly running. Away from me towards the end of the hallway, and then he was through a door I hadn't noticed.

I ran after him, my feet muffled by the thick carpet. The door was a fire exit leading to stairs. I went through it into the light grey stairway, and could hear shoes thumping on the grey rubber on the steps, going down. I looked over the railing and could see Bruce running down, a couple of floors below me. He was moving fast.

'Bruce!' I shouted again, taking off after him. It was well lit with signs pointing down.

The rooms were in the new wing on the right of the castle. On the ground floor was another door with *Authorised Personnel Only* on it.

I shot through the door into reception and saw one of the reception staff filling in a brochure stand. 'Did you see my friend come through here? Bruce Hagan?'

She looked at me. 'No, nobody has come out that way.'

I turned back and went to the *Authorised* door and turned the handle. It opened.

This stairwell was lit, but wasn't painted in a light colour and there weren't so many lamps on the walls. I stopped and listened for a moment, but I couldn't hear anything moving below. I ventured down another two levels and realised I was in the bowels of the castle. There were what seemed like hundreds of pipes running along the ceiling and shooting off in different directions. It was cooler down here. The floor was wet and the light was dimmer.

'Bruce!' I shouted. Nothing. There were no signs of any maintenance people. No sign of life.

Where the hell had he gone?

I walked through a warren of passageways, stopping every now and again to listen. There was no sign of Bruce. I don't know if it was my imagination or not, but it seemed to be getting darker.

Then I saw another door. A black, steel affair. Open. I walked forward, wishing I had my phone so I could use the flashlight built into it. I looked in. Ambient light from the passageway showed me there were more stairs.

I heard a foot shuffling on a metal step farther down.

'Bruce? Is that you, Bruce?'

More shuffling of feet on the steps.

I shivered, not from the low temperature, but from what felt like an ice cube sliding down my back.

Yet my face was sweating. I had no light, no weapon, no means to call backup. And my friend was down there, suffering from God knows what. In that instant, I felt sorry for Hagan. He'd had a rough time of it, and it all started because he wanted to prove himself to the team when he came back to Edinburgh six months ago.

I felt I had let him down. Despite me going to Purcell and fighting Hagan's corner, I should have known better, should have taken Hazel aside and asked her opinion. Now, more than likely, Hagan would be booted out of the force for good. They would dress it up as something else, sweeping it under the carpet so it wouldn't look as if they were getting rid of a mentally disabled officer who was hurt in the line of duty and who was a hero – but get rid of him they would.

This was not how this operation was meant to go. That thought was going through my mind as I took the first step down into the darkness. I fumbled about, barely seeing the handrail. The staircase was circular. And not very wide. Enough room for two people to pass, but a crowd would get stuck.

How many crowds do you think come down here? Keeping a tight grip on the handrail, I made my way down into the darkness, step by step, staying as quiet as I could. If Hagan was down here, I didn't want to spook him.

'Bruce, are you there, buddy?' I said, my voice barely above a whisper. One step. Two steps. *We all fall down.*

I was going round and round, one step at a time. There was a faint light at the bottom, but not enough for me to make anything out.

Then I heard a noise above me, from where I had just come. My heart was tripping in my chest. I could barely see in front of me. I was torn between going down to see if Bruce was there, and going back up in case that was him I'd heard.

I decided to go down farther, as that was where I'd heard the noise coming from originally. Farther down, round and round. It was getting slightly lighter. The light was coming from what I thought might be a doorway at the bottom of the stairs. I looked down, hoping to catch a glimpse of Hagan, but couldn't see any sign of him.

I gripped the dirty handrail as if my life depended on it, careful where I was stepping. Then I was at the bottom. The light was faint through the doorway. It was another steel door. Beyond it, I could barely see more old-looking pipes on the ceiling.

Then I felt a gloved hand touch my face and I jumped, but it was a cobweb. I swiped it away and edged forward into a narrow hallway.

'Bruce. It's Frank. Let me help you get out of here. Come on, we can talk about this.'

Nothing. He had to be in here. There was only one doorway and I had heard somebody moving about.

Some of the old lights were out down here. Only one at the doorway was lit, and one at the far end. I had to duck as I moved forward, in case I bumped into one of the pipes.

Then, all of a sudden, I came into a wide room. Except it wasn't a room, it was a tunnel.

Or to put it correctly, a sewer.

The stone was greasy looking. A little trail of water ran past in the wide trough. The smell was rank. I looked to my left, farther into the tunnel, but it was pitch black, as if the tunnel was sucking all the light from the little lamp at the end of the passageway.

Looking right provided the same view.

There was a passageway straight across, but it was dark in there too, as the light bled away into the distance. Had Bruce gone along there? Why would he do that? But then again, if he was experiencing some problem with his head, there might be something going on he couldn't control.

Then the lights went out.

I have never experienced such a lack of light before. I waited to see if my night vision would kick in, but if it was going to, it was taking its sweet time.

Then I heard it. Just off to my right. Or was it from straight ahead, coming from the other passageway? I was disoriented. No, it was coming from straight ahead.

Movement. Feet shuffling on the cold, stone floor. I wanted to move, to get away from the noise, and fuck Bruce, he could make his own way out. My hand felt a wall to my right, but I couldn't move. I didn't know which way to go.

Then somebody was walking through the water that ran through the tunnel. How close was I to it? Pretty close, if I was where I thought I was. Getting closer. Until there was the sound of wet feet on stone.

It was fight or flight time, and since I had nowhere to run to, I was damn well going to fight.

I'd always told my old man, there wasn't one person who walked this earth that I feared. They were human beings like I was, nothing more, made up of flesh and blood, skin and bone. They might know how to fight, but I also knew how to fight, where to hit them for maximum effect if my life was in danger. I knew my adrenaline would be in the driving seat, as it was now.

Feet shuffled close to me, and the noise echoed slightly round the chamber. There was no light, so he didn't know exactly where I was, just as I didn't know where he was. If it was Hagan, he would surely answer. If it was somebody else, I would give my position away by calling out his name.

I'd shouted after him already, so if he was fully aware, he

would know I was down here. If he wasn't, then I would have to overpower him to get him back upstairs, although God alone knew how I would achieve that.

First things first, find out what I was up against.

Then two things happened.

First, a lamp came on. An old-fashioned lamp. But it had modern LED lights in it.

Second, I saw who was holding it. I assumed it was a woman, from the way she was dressed. She was facing away from me. It had been dark, and I only had a split-second to see her after the light came on, and she was dressed like a woman, so that was what my brain processed. Black tights, a black skirt, and black shoes that were soaking wet after she walked through the water.

She was wearing a cloak over her with the hood pulled up. She had walked through the dark, but why hadn't she put the lamp on sooner? I didn't have the answer, and I wanted to call out to her, but I didn't want to scare her.

I shuffled my foot on the ground. I'd been standing here with the lights on just a few seconds ago, and if she had been watching from the other passageway, then she would have seen me, so it was a reasonable assumption she knew I was there. So me scraping the stone floor with my shoe shouldn't come as a surprise to her.

'Hello?' I said. There was no other noise down here and my voice reverberated round the chamber.

She didn't turn round.

I made the same noise with my shoe again and inched closer.

Still nothing.

Closer still. 'Hello, miss? I'm a police officer. I'm looking for a friend of mine.' I got even closer to her and reached out a hand.

I touched her shoulder through her cloak. She spun round as if she really didn't know I was there.

I thought then that I had died and gone to the very gates of Hell itself.

The woman's hair was long and straggly, but it was her features that were horrific. Her eyes bulged as if they were going to explode. Her skin was falling off as if she'd been scalded. Her lips were pencil thin, but her teeth were big and yellow and a foetid odour came out of her mouth.

She screeched, her eyes going even wider, if that was possible.

She dropped the lamp and flew through the water. I couldn't speak for a moment. 'Miss!' I called out and was about to follow her when a hand reached round from behind me, covering my nose and mouth with a cloth, and just as I reached a hand up to grab the arm, everything went dark for real this time.

FORTY

'You're checking out early?' the girl at reception asked the woman.

'Well, did you figure that out all by yourself, little lady?' Mabel Hollingsworth gritted her teeth, wishing the painkillers would kick in soon.

'I'm sorry, Mrs Hollingsworth. I hope you enjoyed your stay with us.'

'It's *Miss,* you little fucking bitch.' She knew the girl was silently laughing at her. Looking at her in that way they all do; *ugly old cow.* That's what the kids shouted at her when she walked to the bus stop. That's what one of her patients said to her one day. Her hands had almost gone round the old woman's throat, but she had stopped herself.

The receptionist kept her smile in place, but Mabel knew, just fucking *knew* the little whore was laughing at her. *How about I reach over there and wipe that smile from your fucking face?*

'Oh, I'm sorry, *Miss* Hollingsworth.'

She was saying it in a tone that suggested she wasn't sorry at all, not one little bit. And see the way she dragged out the S on the end of the word?

'*Oh, I'm sorry, Miss Hollingsworth,*' Mabel repeated, in a voice one would use to mock somebody. 'Just get me my fucking bill.'

'Is there a problem?' the front-of-house manager said, coming across when he heard the foul language.

Mabel turned to him. She'd dealt with fuckers like him before. All balls and no brains.

'If I want to talk to you, then you'll know about it, you little wank, because I'll be looking right at you and my mouth will be open and words will be coming out. Just like right now.' She poked him in the chest. 'Until then, get out of my face.' She gritted her teeth at him.

'I'm sorry, madam, we can't have you using language like that in front of the other guests.'

'Is that fucking right? So what are you going to do about it?'

'I'm going to have to ask you to step away from reception while we prepare your bill.' He put a hand on Mabel's elbow, as if he were about to physically escort her away from the front desk.

Mabel was quick. She moved with a speed that belied her looks, and shrugged off the hand but with her own hand, she grabbed the man's wrist, twisted his arm and leaned in close to him.

'You ever put your hand on me again, fuck face, and not only will I twist your arm right out of the socket, I'll twist your prick off and make you eat it. Do I make myself fucking clear?'

'Yes, yes,' the manager said, his knees bending.

'This man is assaulting me!' Mabel screamed, letting the manager go and stepping back. 'Call the police!'

A security guard came over, quickly followed by Charles Sharp.

'Miss Hollingsworth, whatever's the matter?' Sharp said.

'That man!' She pointed to the manager who was now indeed on his knees, rubbing his arm. 'He accosted me! He *touched* me! The dirty, filthy bastard!'

'Look, why don't we step through to my office. We can talk about this, and why don't we talk about your bill through there?'

'I'm going to have him arrested.' Her face was on fire. As if her whole skin were melting. 'I need a cold drink,' she said.

'And we'll get you one. Right through here.' He turned to the guard. 'Show Miss Hollingsworth through to my wife's office. She doesn't have a patient scheduled.'

'Ma'am, this way,' the guard said, picking up Mabel's bag.

Sharp turned to the manager. 'Are you alright?'

'Yes, yes, I'm fine,' he said, getting to his feet. He knew there were people in here who were going through some difficult times.

'Make sure everybody is okay in here and I'll make it up to you.'

The manager nodded. Sharp walked away, through the back towards his office.

Mabel was pacing the room. 'Try to relax,' he said to her. 'You won't be receiving a bill. I am disgusted how that man put his hand on you, and he's being arrested as we speak. My security team have taken him away. I can only apologise.'

'It's not good enough. Fucking touched me! You know, those old bastards in the home where I work will sometimes get their willies out? One man was playing with himself, right in front of me! I don't want to see that! Next time, I'll fucking cut it off.'

Sharp indicated for the guard to leave and he did so, just as Solomon came in with his medical bag.

'You remember Doctor Solomon?'

'How could I forget? Fucking letch.'

Worry lines were etched over Solomon's face as he stepped

towards her. 'Mabel, I need you to listen to me. You have a headache right now, correct?'

Mabel stood, her nostrils flaring as if she were a bull about to charge. 'You fucking dirty bastards are all the same. You want me to take my clothes off so you can fuck me right now. Well, I'm not having it. I've lived without a man's joey until now, and I don't need you putting your joey inside me.'

Solomon put his hands up. 'I'm not here for that. I have something that can take your headache away instantly. You won't feel any different, I promise you, but the headache will be gone.'

'I don't fucking think so, you cocksu—'

Sharp grabbed hold of her, pinning her arms behind her back while Solomon took out a syringe and quickly shoved the needle into Mabel's arm, pressing the plunger as fast as he could.

'How long does it take?' Sharp asked as Mabel started to kick and thrash. She was a fifty-nine-year-old woman but strong enough at the moment to knock out a world champion boxer.

'Not long,' Solomon said.

'Well, fucking help me then, instead of standing there like a lemon.' Sharp was sweating.

Solomon stood and smiled. 'You could do with the exercise, Charles.'

'I swear to God, I'll—'

Mabel relaxed, and Sharp guided her over to a chair. She sat down with a thump, her breathing heavy, but she was visibly relaxing.

Sharp took Solomon aside. 'What the hell *is* that?'

'It's something that counteracts the first dose we gave her. It just helps them overcome the headaches. Like Hagan, sometimes their body has an overreaction to the meds. It's mixed with a sedative.'

'What about Hubbard and the Carpenter woman?'

'They had the follow-up as we discussed, but we have a new follow-up. What I just gave her is like putting an additive into your petrol tank to make your engine run smoother.'

'When can she be given the next lot?'

'She can be given it any time. After twelve hours.'

'Has it been twelve hours since she was given the first dose?'

Solomon looked at the clock on Sharp's wall. 'Not quite. Nine hours maybe. That's why I was going to give it to her tomorrow.'

'Give it to her now.'

'What? No, I can't do that.'

'Didn't you say it was safe for Mama's meds to overlap?'

'That was a different one. She hasn't even had the first dose of the new one.'

'Give Mabel the second dose before she leaves. And make sure she's driven down to Inverness to catch a train. Have one of the security guys do it. Pay for her ticket and make sure she gets on the fucking train. That way, we'll be shot of her until it's time for you to go and see her.'

'As you wish. But get me glass of water. I have some tablets she'll need to take to overcome the initial nausea.'

Sharp walked away to fetch a glass while Solomon, rifled about in his bag and took out another syringe. He walked over to Mabel, who was obviously feeling the effects of the first injection. He took her other arm and injected the liquid into her. Then he stood up.

Sharp came over with the glass of water, and Solomon helped Mabel take the tablets. 'That's it, done. I'll go and see her a few days from now, see how she's holding up.'

'Right, tell them to get her down to the infirmary while she's still dopey. I don't want my wife finding us administering this shit in here. Say she felt faint or something, if anybody asks. Then get her onto the train later and make sure she gets her connection to Glasgow from Inverness. Get somebody to go with her.'

'Okay, I'll tell them.'

A few minutes later, Mabel was led from the office.

Sharp left his office feeling drained. He wanted to go and see Mama now, just to give her a hug. But he knew he couldn't.

She might kill him.

FORTY-ONE

'Frank!' I heard a woman's scream. Felt hands grasping at me. A bright light assaulted my eyes when I opened them. Just for the briefest second, I thought it was the woman from the tunnels. I tensed but strong hands had a grip of my arm.

'Take it easy, sir,' I heard a man say.

My eyes were fuzzy. Like they are when you wake up from a deep sleep at three o'clock in the morning with the dog barking, thinking there's an intruder in the house.

Christ, my head hurt as if it had been hit with a club. I opened my eyes fully, then squinted against the harsh light. I was lying in a stairwell, the first one I'd chased Hagan down.

Julie was there, and so were two men in black. Security men, I assumed.

'Help's on the way,' Julie said. Then a door opened and Steffi came in with a first aid bag and knelt down beside me. I could have kissed her right then. She started taking things out of the bag. Then she was shining a light in my eyes.

'The doctor's on his way over,' she told me. 'Try not to move. You have a head injury.'

'What?' My head was killing me, and I put a hand up to the front, just above my eye and felt the blood there.

'There's blood on the wall where you fell,' Julie said. 'You must have tripped and hit your head on the wall.'

I looked at her and she gave me a look back that told me everything I needed to know; she was voicing that opinion for the benefit of the security men.

'I remember coming down here, looking for my friend, then... nothing.'

Steffi was dabbing at my head. 'You know first aid, then, Miss..?' one of the security men said.

'Yes, I do,' she replied, ignoring his inference that she should supply him with her name.

The door opened again, and a thin man came in, followed by Melissa Sharp.

'Detective Miller, what happened?' Melissa said.

'I seem to have fallen down the stairs.'

'Don't move until I have you checked over,' the man said, crouching down. 'I am Doctor Solomon.'

I looked at Steffi as she backed away. She didn't want to give the game away, so she couldn't reveal she knew more than just first aid, but I'd felt her hands on my arms and legs, assessing me, and she stood watching the doctor intently.

His cold, thin hands did the same as Steffi had. He asked me if I hurt when he squeezed and I said no, but my head was on fire.

'You hit your head a bit there, so maybe we should take you down to Main Street where the hospital is.'

'I'm fine, doc. I have a headache, that's all.'

He did the *flashlight in the eyes* thing like Steffi had done and seemed satisfied. He stood up. 'Help him to his feet,' he ordered the security men.

The two men were obviously body builders and grabbed an arm each and hauled.

'Easy, easy,' Solomon said. 'You're not in *Weightlifters R Us* now.'

Both men slowed down and kept hold of me as I stood up. I actually felt fine, apart from the sore head.

'We have a small infirmary here for minor injuries. I'd like it if you went along to get cleaned up,' Melissa Sharp said.

'I'll come with you,' Steffi said.

'Are you a friend of Mr Miller's?' Melissa asked.

'I am now.'

Melissa looked disapproving for a second but then nodded.

They began to lead me out of the stairwell. 'I was looking for my friend, Bruce,' I said. 'Have you seen him?'

'My husband wants to talk to you about your friend, detective. He's waiting for you in the infirmary.'

We left the stairwell and crossed the reception area and through another door. Turned right and along to a lift. Melissa entered a code number into a keypad and the doors opened. We went down three levels and the door opened into what could only be described as a small hospital ward. A receptionist sat behind a desk facing us. She smiled at Melissa but was given nothing in return.

'It's along here,' she said. My entourage followed me. There was a hospital bed in a side bay.

'In here,' Solomon said. I sat on the bed, and Steffi came in with me. There were curtains across the doorway, but they were left open. Solomon went away, assuring me he would be back.

The security men stood outside to one side. I felt like a prisoner being taken from Saughton prison back home.

Charles Sharp appeared. 'Well, well, well,' he said, smiling. 'I was coming to see you when I got the call telling me you had fallen.'

I just nodded and didn't say anything about going downstairs. Not yet. Not until I could square it away in my own head that I hadn't just dreamt the whole thing.

'It seems I took a tumble and knocked myself out.'

'Why didn't you just take the lift down?' he said, the smile still in place.

'I was looking for my friend, Bruce. He went down the stairs. Have you seen him?'

'Yes. He's quite safe, but we have to have a talk in private about him.'

I looked at Steffi and she got the message and left.

'Is she a friend of yours?' Sharp asked.

'We met her and her friend when we came here. She's a nice girl. Very attractive.'

He gave a brief laugh. 'Well, this isn't prison, Detective Miller. 'Guests can – how shall I put it? – *meet up*, if they like. And young Penny is very attractive.'

I was about to ask who Penny was when I remembered that was the name Steffi was using. Christ, my head did get a good battering.

Solomon came back with a nurse. Looked me over again. 'How's your head now?' he asked.

'Actually, it feels a lot better.' It was true. Whatever headache I'd had was gone.

'It looks like you just bumped the wall when you fell. Nothing to worry about. Just a little superficial scratch. The nurse here will sort you right out. Call me if you need me. Through the reception, of course.'

He walked away and a look passed between him and Sharp.

The nurse cleaned me up and put a plaster on the cut, just below my hairline. 'That can come off in a little while. You'll be fine.'

She left the bay, and Sharp stepped closer to me. 'We have Bruce resting in a bed in one of the rooms down here. It seems this whole process is overwhelming him a bit, so I had Doctor Solomon give him something to help him sleep. He'll be awake before dinner, then I want to have a chat with him.'

'Is this normal?' I asked him.

'Yes, perfectly. When patients start to open up about their experience, it's like a floodgate opening. The next thing they know, they've opened the gates wide and it all comes rushing out at once. We want the flow to be a little restricted, more controlled. Some patients are fine, others like Bruce need a little help in controlling their emotions. Which is why I'm going to give him the psychological tools to deal with his mental and physical trauma. He'll rest here this afternoon, and he'll be cared for. If he can make it to the group session this evening, then fine, if not, I will be talking with him every day, but sometimes when the emotions start to flow, people get overwhelmed.'

'Can I see him?'

'Best not, for now. I'll get him to eat his dinner in here and I'll have my wife get him some fresh clothes.'

He guided me out of the bay and into the corridor. 'You have to understand, Frank – you don't mind if I call you Frank? – Bruce is in a delicate place right now. Imagine him sitting in a set of scales. One side can give him the peace to move on with his life and deal with the trauma he faced. The other side can have him lowered to a place of despair and misery. My experience will give him everything to deal with his life, I can assure you.'

'So, you're saying that you have the magic cure, doc?'

Sharp smiled wider. 'No, I'm not saying that at all, and I'm not suggesting for one minute everybody who comes here goes away fully *cured* for want of a better word.'

'Like Steven Hubbard and Mel Carpenter?'

His smile dropped a little. 'I can't discuss any patients, I'm sure you understand.' We started walking towards the reception, the security guards and Steffi behind us.

'Let me put it to you this way, Frank; when you were at school, did you like some teachers more than others?'

'Of course.'

'Some teachers were better than others, yes?'

'Yes.'

'I may not have a magic wand, but I am a very experienced psychiatrist. Think of me as a better teacher.'

He was still smiling as we reached the lift and he entered numbers into a keypad. The doors unlocked and slid open. 'My men will see you upstairs, Frank. Take care of your head.'

Steffi and I were ushered into the lift. Sharp was still looking at us as the doors slid shut.

FORTY-TWO

Charles Sharp sat behind the desk in his office. Melissa sat in the chair he usually used when he was talking to a patient. It was along the corridor from his own office. He hadn't told her about Mabel Hollingsworth going nuts in reception, although he had no doubt she would find out soon enough.

'So what happened, Charles?' Melissa said, taking a sip from the glass of whisky he had given her.

'I was never happy to know two policemen were staying here. I told you they were going to be trouble. And did you hear him mention Hubbard and that Carpenter girl? Christ, I thought Solomon was going to look after them? Some job that was.'

'He did his best. He did exactly what we asked him to.'

'Christ, what are those people in the lab actually doing? They said they were close to a breakthrough!'

'They are, but you have to give it time. Maybe Hagan is the one.'

'Well, we'll see, won't we?'

'You can't rush these things, Charles. I would wait until we see how this first lot goes through his system before giving him the additive. I don't want anybody else getting it.'

'Too late for that.'

She sat up and looked at her husband, the muscles tightening in her jaw. 'What do you mean?'

Sharp played around with his own whisky glass, slowly turning it in his hands on the desktop. 'I already told Solomon to issue it.'

'Without me knowing about it?'

'You would have given me attitude. Told me to stop what I was doing, that it was too risky.'

She put her glass down on the little side table. 'Well, of course it's too risky. Didn't you see what Hubbard did? Or Mel? She set fire to the hotel. After killing the head chef. Good God, Charles, Mel could have burnt the hotel down with all the guests in it.'

'Well, I don't want to wait. Mama is getting worse by the day.'

'I know she is, but we have to be sensible. Now we have two policemen in the castle, one of whom is obviously deranged. And the other one was caught sneaking around down in the basement.'

'Jesus, it was just as well the CCTV guys were on the ball, or we might never have known Miller was down there.'

He looked at Melissa. 'We're going to have to do something about Mama wandering about.'

'Miller saw her.'

'He *thinks* he saw her. He saw something, but one of the boys took care of him.'

'You're lucky Miller didn't have his brains bashed in by those thugs.'

'*Those thugs* as you so eloquently put it, are ex-army and very highly trained. They know what they're doing.'

'Do they?'

'Of course they do. They knew enough to take Miller back to

the stairwell, and smack Miller's head and smear the blood on the wall to make it look like he hit the wall. They're not stupid.'

'Gorillas in suits.'

Sharp suddenly shot his chair back. 'I'm sick and fucking tired of you being negative all the time. Why can't you just be on my side?'

'Why do you think I'm sitting here? I'm on your side! And don't use that language in front of me, please. It belittles you.'

'Too strong for your little Scottish palate?'

'You're a complete bastard, Charles. You know I would do anything for you, but right now, Mama is why we're doing this. Don't ever lose sight of that!'

Melissa got up from her chair and stormed out of Sharp's office. The secret door behind his desk opened.

'I think she might have a point,' Solomon said, stepping into the room.

'I don't pay you to think.' Sharp was looking out the window. 'Where is it all going to end?'

'You tell me. As you said, you don't pay me to think, but you do pay me to inject the subjects. I'll go and see her in a couple of days in Glasgow. Give her the supplements.'

'Make sure you do. We don't want anybody else setting fire to a hotel.' Sharp turned back to look at the doctor. 'You enjoy this, don't you?'

Solomon smiled. 'What do you think?'

'I think maybe you enjoy this a little bit too much.'

Solomon started laughing. 'I loved my work at Porton Down. Retirement didn't suit me.'

Sharp rubbed his hand over his face. 'God, I'm tired. When this is over, I want to go to the Caribbean for a holiday.'

'I can give you something.'

Sharp laughed. 'I've seen what your *something* does. Which reminds me, has Hagan had the part two yet?'

'No, I have all the following samples ready to go.'

'Delay it. I want him a bit more compos until we decide what we're going to do with Miller. Maybe an accident would be best.'

'We should have taken care of him down in the basement.'

'And have half of Police Scotland up here looking for him? No. For the same reason, we're going to let Hagan come back to normal. How long before it wears off?'

'I have no idea. This is a new version. I tweaked it.'

'Tweaked it? How?'

'It's a different formula.'

'Christ. He's a police officer.'

'A police officer who has gone so far over the edge, he's never coming back. Not even your best therapy can deal with him. Am I right?'

Sharp looked at him before answering. 'I've never seen somebody like him before. People like him have usually killed themselves by now. The genuine ones.'

'That's something to think about.'

'It would be a first.'

'It would take the pressure off. Then Miller would go home in one piece and nobody would be up here looking for him.'

Sharp contemplated it. 'I don't know. It's risky.'

'Time's running out, just remember that. For everybody, especially Mama. We have to get this right and we're knocking on the door. Think how Melissa would feel if Mama came back to her.'

'How we would both feel.'

'Yes, of course.'

'I'll give it some thought.'

'I'd best go.' The doctor walked over to the door to let himself out.

'Solomon?'

The doctor stopped and looked at Sharp. 'Yes?'

'Tell me, how many did you kill?'

'How many? Or how many do they know about?' He laughed and let himself out.

FORTY-THREE

I was sitting on the edge of Julie's bed, recounting my story. She had the good grace not to share a look with Steffi, a look that might suggest I had indeed banged my head.

'Christ that sounds horrendous.'

'Right, spit it out,' I said to Julie. 'I want your opinion. Don't fabricate it, just tell me how it is. What you're really thinking.'

'Well, boss, seeing an old woman down there in the tunnels? What if you did bang your head and you imagined the whole thing?'

'How about you, Steffi?'

'Okay, let's just say you really did go down there, who is the woman and where the hell did she come from? And who grabbed you from behind?'

'Good points. Now, if I had dreamt that, then it was a very vivid dream. I don't know what happens when you knock yourself out, what goes through your mind and all that, but there is one question in all of this, what the hell is going on with Bruce? Did I really hear him down there, or was that somebody else?'

Julie made a face. 'I didn't know Bruce before he was attacked last year, but if you want my opinion, whoever said he was ready to return to work, needs firing.'

'I agree. We need to make contact with Edinburgh, but just when you need to make a call, the bloody phone lines are down.' The castle had had no phone lines operating when I was at reception earlier. The payphone was also dead.

I stood and went to the window, looking out into the dark. 'Bruce was supposed to be going to some group therapy session about now, I think.' There were a few lights in the distance, the only sign of civilisation, the only indication there was life somewhere other than in this castle. I turned back to them.

'We need to go back down there. Now, I've described that place in detail, so when we go down, you'll see if I was imagining it or not. That way, we'll know for sure.'

'Let's suppose you did go there,' Julie said, not quite convinced, 'then if they saw you earlier, it's safe to assume they'll see you again.'

'Not if we have a distraction.'

'Like what?' Steffi said.

'You could go to one of the fire exit doors and push on the bar. They're alarmed. Just pretend you accidentally bumped into it. Or say you tripped or something. While you're dealing with the security, Julie and I will get down into the basement.'

'What about getting back out?'

'We'll deal with that later.'

'When are you thinking of going?' Julie asked.

I looked out the window. 'No time like the present.'

Sharp made a phone call. Then looked at the doctor.

'The Hollingsworth woman was taken to the train. They said she looked a bit dopey. Is that normal?' Sharp said to Solomon.

'You tell me what normal is. It was a mild sedative she had. By the time the train's scooting south, she won't remember her own name.'

'What?'

'Relax. I mean, she won't remember all of this, in your office, or being down in the infirmary. It's just playing with her short-term memory. Very short. She'll remember being here, but she'll recall having a good time at the spa, not you fighting with her in your office.'

Sharp shook his head. 'We need to start accelerating this program. Hagan was supposed to be in group therapy tonight—'

'And he should be. We don't want Miller poking about again. And I'll make sure Hagan has enough meds so he can get back to his own room tonight.'

'Where's Miller?'

'Not in any of the public places, the bar or the lounge. He was in the restaurant earlier, having dinner with those women he met here.'

'Oh, yes, the nosey ones. Maybe he's trying to get them into bed. Playing for the away team now.'

'Like you did.'

'That was different. Melissa and I—'

Solomon sniggered. 'Dress it up any way you like.'

'Don't you try to fucking psychoanalyse me. Stick to the pills and the needles, doctor.'

'I'm just saying. It's what happens when people go away on a trip.'

'Not everybody has your sordid viewpoint. Anyway, make sure Hagan is up and about. Group therapy starts in half an hour, but

I've changed my mind. I don't want him going to it, I want him in here with me. My wife can take the group.'

'He's already up and raring to go.'

'Good. Let's tell him there's been a change of plan.'

FORTY-FOUR

'I've called in sick,' Chip Haines said to his girlfriend, Lois.

'Poor thing. You've been through a lot.'

He was sitting on her leather couch, the one he had thought was fun to have sex on, but which was now only cold and had an annoying squeak. Chip had felt the old buzz when he had come home with Lois one morning after their shift had ended. He had everything most men would kill for; a good-looking wife, a decent son, a good job and a house that was almost paid off.

But he wasn't getting the buzz.

Lois gave him the buzz.

She was younger than Wendy, extremely hot, and loved it when he did things to her Wendy would have baulked at. And yet... here he was, with his new love and he felt empty inside.

'They could have killed her,' he said, taking a swig from the beer bottle.

'But they didn't. Whoever "they" are.'

'What the hell had Ryan got himself into?'

She sat beside him and put a finger over his lips. 'Don't, Chip. We can't think like that.'

'It's true though.' His lips trembled and tears rolled down his cheeks. 'Wendy hates me, my son is dead, and now my house has been burned down.'

'He didn't get himself into anything. It was an accidental overdose. You and I are both cops, we know this is an epidemic. Young kids are dying every day. How often have you been called out to an overdose this month alone?'

'I can't remember. A few.'

'I've been out to more this month than in the whole of last year. It seems every week young men and women are getting hold of this stuff and ruining their lives with it.'

'My son wouldn't have taken that stuff.'

Lois put a hand over one of his. 'We don't know they're doing it. A lot of families are like that. They don't know their loved ones are taking drugs behind their backs. You know that as well as I do.'

'You don't understand, Lois. After Ryan came home from college, we grew close. Not that we weren't close before he went away, but with him being in the house all day, we bonded more. I would have known if he was using drugs.'

'They don't advertise it, honey. Have you never spoken to a family who say they didn't know their kid was using?'

'You don't get it. I *know* he wasn't using. I think he was murdered, Lois.'

His girlfriend sucked in a breath. 'Don't say that. It will eat you alive.'

'There's no other explanation for it.'

'You're in denial, that's all. You're reacting to your grief.'

'Don't patronise me!' he said, jumping up.

Lois stood and put her arms around him. 'That's the last thing I would do and you know that. I loved Ryan too. He was going to be a part of my family, when you and I got married. We talked about it, him and I.'

'When?'

'What?'

'When would you sit and have a chat with him?'

'A couple of times I bumped into him at Joe's Pizza round from the station.'

'I thought the young crowd hung around in Denny's?'

'Not at lunchtime.'

Chip nodded. 'He was a good kid.'

'Look, I've been meaning to ask you this for a while, but how do you feel about leaving here?'

'Newburgh?'

'Yes, Newburgh. We could move down south where it's cheaper. We could be happy down there, with nobody to tell us what to do.'

'We both have a few years before we retire.'

'You have two. I have three. Three years then we could go and live somewhere we won't have to shovel snow out of the drive.'

'I don't know.'

'Come on, just think about it. We won't have to be bothered about anybody. It'll just be you and me.'

Chip stepped back from her. 'That sounds good. Maybe it will do us the world of good getting away from all of this. First of all though, I'm going to talk to the chief in the morning. Tell him my thoughts about my son being murdered.'

'Just be careful, sweetheart. If he was murdered, then we don't know who to trust. I'm getting scared.'

'Don't worry. I can look after myself.'

Lois hugged him and watched him walk out the front door. It would be the last time she ever saw him leave the house.

FORTY-FIVE

The alarm beeped incessantly, and I knew we had to move now. 'Come on, let's get down here,' I said to Julie. We were standing behind the *Authorised Personnel Only* door, the one I had gone through earlier in the day.

'Jesus, this is a part they don't put in the brochure,' Julie said.

'Come on, we don't have time.'

We started down the dingy stairway for two levels then stopped at the corridor with the pipes. 'Down here on the left, will be a steel door that leads into a circular staircase, which leads down to another doorway.'

'Okay, let's go.'

We jogged along, keeping our heads low, and there it was; the doorway. With the staircase.

'Sorry I doubted you, boss.'

This time we each had a little flashlight. Julie said she always packed a couple in her bag whenever she went on holiday, in case of a power cut. I wished I had thought of that.

I looked over the banister and the lights were back on below.

Somebody had wanted to prevent me from going into that other tunnel across the sewer, and had gone to great lengths to convince us all I had fallen.

I couldn't wait to get hold of the guy who had put something over my mouth and knocked me out. A big guy, if he had carried me back up there by himself. Or maybe he had help. I'd be sure to ask Charles Sharp.

We went down the old, rusty staircase as quietly as we could, shining the lights ahead of us. Then we reached the bottom and the doorway.

I turned to Julie. 'Straight ahead is the sewer. That's where the woman crossed.'

'Okay.'

'You alright with going ahead?'

'Of course I am. Jesus, I'll lead the way if you want. Big girl.'

I laughed. 'I like you already, Julie. You'll go far.'

'I'd like to go as far as Jeni Bridge, that's for sure.'

'And you will, one day. Right now, we have to cross that sewer.'

We walked along the corridor, our flashlights casting shadows. The lamps on the walls were old and dimly lit.

'I wonder who has to come down here,' Julie said. 'I won't be applying for a maintenance position here any time soon.'

'You and me both, sister.'

We came to the sewer and I shone my light across to the other tunnel. It was pitch black after the length of the light. 'The pits of hell,' I said.

'As far as bolstering morale goes, you might want to take a refresher course.'

I laughed and heard Julie rustling about in her jacket pocket. She brought out four carrier bags.

'Where'd you get those?' I asked her.

'When I bring shoes, I bring carrier bags to put them in for going home. I don't want dirty soles touching my clothes. And I am not stepping in that shitty water in my good boots. Put the bags on and we'll dump them on the other side.'

I couldn't argue with that. We did as she said and put our boots into the bags, tied them loosely at the top and waded through the water, which was only a couple of inches high. At the other side, we took them off carefully and laid them to one side.

Then Julie brought out a travel bottle of hand sanitiser.

'Remind me to go on holiday with you next time.'

'I'm sure Kim would be pleased to hear you talking like that, big guy.'

'You know what I mean.'

'No, I don't. Explain it to me.'

'I was just—'

'I'm kidding, boss.'

'Remind me to give you an early annual appraisal when we get back. And I have to be honest, it's not looking good for you.'

'Promises, promises.' Then she suddenly put a hand on my shoulder. 'Put your light out,' she whispered.

Instinct made me trust her and as we both turned our lights off, I saw a flashlight in the distance, coming down the stairwell we had just come down.

'Let's go,' I said, switching my light back on. A quick sweep showed us this tunnel had more pipes in it. Julie grabbed hold of the carriers and shoved them behind a pipe then we started running. The tunnel bent sharply round to the right. That's why it looked pitch black when I had shone the light across the sewer.

The tunnel was straight for a ways, before turning right. We ran a few hundred yards, then as the tunnel veered right again, we saw the old, iron door ahead of us. I stopped, my breath coming fast, but I wasn't feeling the effects. Julie looked as if she was just getting warmed up.

'Keep running or see what's through here?' she said, seeing the door wasn't completely closed.

'I've always been a sucker for seeing what's behind the closed door,' I said. I grabbed hold of it, expecting to put my weight behind it, but it opened easily and didn't squeak. I shone my light through the doorway. The tunnel carried on for a few feet, and at the end of it was a set of stone steps.

'Come on, Julie,' I said, hearing footsteps running behind us in the darkness. We ran forward, up the stone steps, which ended at a landing. An iron ladder was attached to the wall.

'Watch our backs. I'll go up.' The flashlight was a small, pocket affair, and I could easily hold it in my teeth as I climbed. The ladder was maybe fifteen feet high. At the top was a round, iron cover. I held on with one hand and shone the light about. There were two holes, obviously for putting lifting tools in to lift it off from the other side. I pushed, again expecting to feel a ton weight, but it wasn't that heavy.

I put the flashlight into my pocket and pushed. It lifted off easily, albeit with a scraping noise, and slid to one side. 'Come on up,' I said to Julie.

She climbed faster than I had. I clambered out into the cold, wet night. The rain had eased off, but the long grass round this manhole was wet. As I looked down, I saw the light from the flashlight of whoever was following us.

'Quick,' I said quietly to Julie, 'help me put it back. Quiet as you can.' I put my finger into one of the holes and Julie did the same and we put the lid back on, laying it gently down.

Then we heard shoes clanging on the ladder. Somebody was coming up. I sat on the iron cover and indicated for Julie to do the same. It wasn't a big cover and I had to put my arm around her so we could sit close. I reckoned between us, we weighed around 350 pounds. Maybe whoever was below us could bench press that weight, but not from the angle he was at.

The cover didn't even budge. We sat there for a few minutes, figuring the guy wouldn't want to stand there all night if he couldn't open it. I told Julie to stay seated. I moved so I was kneeling, put my eye to the hole, and then saw the light below, just moving out of sight.

'He's gone. Here, take this,' I said, as I pulled out two balaclavas.

'As fashion accessories go, I've always dreamt of one of these, as well as a pair of Jimmy Choo heels.'

'Well, I'm glad I could get you at least one of those.' We slipped our balaclavas on and took our bearings. We were in the woods somewhere.

'She couldn't have come out here, surely,' Julie said.

'Maybe we should have carried on deeper into the tunnel. Maybe that's where she went.'

'We should go back down. Whoever followed us will surely have gone back the way he came.'

'Let's try it,' I said, then I heard it, just the barest movement behind us, above the noise of the wind.

'Stay right where you are,' a voice said, 'or I'll shoot.'

FORTY-SIX

Steffi Walker had opened the door in the gym and walked back to the reception area.

'I'm sorry, I tripped and knocked against the door and it opened,' she said to the man behind the desk.

'Somebody from security will be along shortly. It's happened before. It's not a problem.'

'I do apologise.'

'Can I take a note of your name for the report?' he stood with a pen poised over a notepad.

'Penny Blair. I'm a guest here.'

'The security room will just want to know what happened. It's not a big deal, honestly.'

'Thank you so much.' She walked out and along the corridor to where the lifts were. When the doors opened, two burly security men stepped out and hurried to the gym. Steffi stepped in and pressed the button to go to one of the lounges to wait for Miller and Julie.

On that level, she stepped out and walked up to reception. 'I'd like to make a phone call.'

'I'm afraid the phone lines haven't come back on at this time, madam.'

'Let me ask you; what would happen if there was an emergency here?'

The girl looked at Steffi as if she were daft. 'We have our mobile phones.'

'So you're allowed them but we're not?'

'We're staff, madam.'

Steffi realised she was appearing belligerent. 'I'm sorry. I'm just a bit on edge.'

'Of course, I do realise how hard it must be. I'm always on Facebook when I'm not at work. This day and age, we're always on our phones, aren't we?'

'It's like a third appendage.'

Steffi turned away and headed through to the bar. She hoped Miller was safe. She bought a drink and sat and stared at the television in the corner.

Being a police officer meant everything to her now. Her time in the army was meant to get her experience in life, to *toughen* her up, as her father put it. He'd done a few years in the army himself. He'd encouraged her, even though she'd felt guilty for leaving him behind when he was on his own. Her mother had been gone for three years when she left for training, but he'd said his wife would have loved to have seen her daughter in uniform. She hadn't lived long enough to see it.

Her experience did count when she went to join up. She had sailed through the training at Tulliallan, the training college near Stirling. She had worked hard and when Percy Purcell saw what she could do first hand, she had been drafted straight into MIT, much to the annoyance of some of her colleagues.

So, now she was sitting here in a bar having opened an alarmed door. Big deal. Two of her colleagues were creeping about in the bowels of the castle while she sat here twiddling her thumbs.

Well, she could be doing something a lot more useful. Like creeping about herself.

She left the bar and walked out the front door. As if she was just going for a jog. She was wearing running gear so it wouldn't look out of place.

She started running, cutting through the car park, and turned right, connecting with the service road and running down it, towards the gardens. There were buildings way over on the right-hand side, but as she got farther down, she could see a light in the distance. Then as she went even farther down, it disappeared from view.

She saw a rough track cutting away from the service road down at the bottom and she jogged along it. The woods were thick here, and she was beginning to think her imagination had gotten the better of her when she saw the light again.

It was an old house, tucked away at the end of the track as it snaked into the woods. She moved closer, careful where she was stepping, until she got closer to it. There were lights on in two of the upstairs windows. It was three storeys high. The ground floor looked as if it was made out of reinforced concrete.

As she moved closer, she saw an old, wooden basement door, sitting at a forty-five degree angle, surrounded by overgrown grass and bushes.

She had researched this place on a history website before they came up. It said some of the buildings were used during World War Two. Sunderland flying boats were kept down in Alness, but the castle was used as a coastal defence post, making sure an enemy attack was thwarted before it got close to Alness. Each of the little towns up and down the coast had coastal defence measures in place back then.

This looked as if it had been a war building. Maybe it had housed armed personnel.

She ducked and ran across an open area towards the basement door. Then it came to her; this was a coal chute. The fuel used back then to heat the house was coal, and this is where it would be delivered.

She fought through the grass and bushes, hoping to get a closer look inside one of the windows that was set into the wall by the chute.

But then she saw the chute didn't have a lock on it. Should she go in? Maybe it wasn't legal, but she might find something she could later direct the others to, if they had to get a search warrant.

She gently lifted one side of the double doors and went down a set of steps, closing the door behind her after she took out her small flashlight. The stairs led down into a damp, dark cellar with no sign of any coal. They had obviously updated their heating system years ago.

She took out a little pocket flashlight. Like Julie, she had come prepared.

There was a door, which appeared to be locked, but next to it was a doorway. A tunnel. She started walking along it, then she started jogging when she saw how long it was. Then it turned to the left and kept going. And going. She was starting to sweat. Then she started to get a panicked feeling, as if she had gone into someplace and would never get back out again.

Then it forked. Left or right? Left. So she ran some more, and the tunnel weaved again and then she came out into a short corridor. She thought it ended at a stone wall but then she saw the opening on her right. A doorway. She looked round and saw the old windows set into the wall on her left.

They were rounded at the top, with bars on the outside. Hadn't she seen these windows from outside? Yes. They were set below the other levels of the castle windows, but they were high up from the ground. She looked out of one of the windows, but it was covered in grime. She couldn't see anything in the dark but a lighthouse in the distance, winking its light at her.

She didn't want to go any farther along, so she turned back and jogged the way she had come, connecting with the main tunnel again.

She knew she should just go back. After all, she hadn't found anything. Yet, the other tunnel was beckoning her. She would wonder what was down there if she went back now. It was right there! *Go!* she told herself, and before she knew it, she was running along this one too.

It sloped down, turned, and sloped down some more. She tried to visualise the outside of the castle, and could see the hillside it was built on. This tunnel must be inside the hill. Curious as to where it came out, she carried on until she came to a dead end. There was a small, metal grate built into the wall.

As she got closer, she saw it was a vent, built into a door. She stepped up to it and it led into an old-fashioned kitchen. *Wartime chic*. Yet, it had modern appliances on the countertop.

She found the handle by pointing her light down. Surprisingly, the door wasn't locked. The hinges didn't squeak as she'd expected they would. Then she was standing in the old kitchen. This must have been another house for wartime staff.

It was dimly lit. The smell of cooking hit her. Dirty dishes were in the old, farmhouse sink. A coffee pot was sitting brewing, its little red light like a beacon in the semi-dark.

A corridor was just outside the kitchen. Also dimly lit. She had already switched off her flashlight and moved along quietly. On her right was a staircase.

It was a bit brighter round the corner. She peeked round and saw large windows on the right-hand side. Moving quickly, she rounded the corner and slid up to the first window, keeping herself against the wall and looked round.

It was like a cell. A rubber-covered mattress was on the floor. A door was on the other side of the window, which was at waist height. She ducked down and moved quickly to the next one. Slowly, she moved her head up, peering over the edge of the glass.

It too was empty.

Then a face shot up from the floor, baring its teeth at her.

'Jesus,' she gasped, jumping back.

It wasn't a monster she was seeing, but a man. Unruly hair, wild-eyed look, spittle and drool coming from his mouth.

He was looking right at her. It was a face she knew.

Bruce Hagan.

She stepped sideways away from him, standing in front of the next window. Which wasn't a cell. It was a laboratory.

With people in it. Wearing white lab coats. One of them looked, pointed, and shouted something.

She turned and ran, Hagan angrily smacking at the glass as she ran past him.

She had to get out of here, whatever the fuck *here* was.

Steffi ran down the corridor she had just come along and didn't stop when she got into the kitchen. Her eyes only had a second or two to register the man standing in front of the door she had come out of. And the other man standing near the coffee pot. She didn't see the man who had come down the stairs and was now coming in behind her.

She started fighting them, but they were big, with big muscles. They outnumbered her. They restrained her, one getting her arms behind her back while another sat on her legs after they got her down on the floor.

She saw a man in a white lab coat come in, a needle in his hand.

'I'm not going to lie,' he said, 'this is going to sting.'

Then there was only darkness.

FORTY-SEVEN

'Take it easy, mate,' I said.

The man was about my height, dressed in camouflage clothes. Holding a shotgun.

'I'm not your fucking mate,' he spat, stepping closer to me. 'You bastards have made a big mistake coming here to turn this place over. I'm going to make you regret it.'

He thought we were housebreakers.

The barrels of the shotgun were now only six inches from my face. I was holding my hands up, but not straight up in the air. Bent at the elbows. Timing was going to be everything and I could feel myself shaking as the adrenaline was rushing through me.

How much do you want to see Kim and Emma again? I was about to make my move when Julie made a retching noise and bent over.

The next move was his downfall. His face creased in disgust as he thought Julie was being sick. It was designed to knock him off kilter, just for a second.

It worked.

He swung the gun towards Julie, but as he shifted his weight to do it, I reached out as fast as I possibly could, grabbing the gun and moving it skywards away from Julie's direction.

It went off as he squeezed the trigger. His back was to the slope of the hill and as he turned sideways, he was already falling, but I couldn't let him point the gun at us again. I held on fast to the barrels and as he fell backwards into the rough, I went with him.

I rolled over holding on tight, but as we rolled, I came to a stop with him on top of me. He yanked at the gun, but I still held on. He couldn't see my face for the balaclava, and I thought for a second he was going to try to take it off, but he had more deadly intentions than that.

'I'll kill you and make you disappear, you bast—' he started to say just before the open palm of Julie's hand smacked him in the side of the face.

He fell sideways, and as I let the gun go, it went off again, the buckshot flying harmlessly high into the air.

'You're welcome,' she said, reaching out a hand to me and pulling me to my feet.

'I had it under control.'

'Sure you did, boss.'

Our attacker had rolled farther down the hill in the dark, and I didn't know when he would be coming back. Or loading his gun.

'Up this way,' I said, seeing a light through the trees.

We struggled through the undergrowth and the trees, then we both saw the lights on in the mansion house. The hill at the back of the house sloped away, which is what we were on. There was no back garden to talk of, but I remembered seeing a side garden. Maybe whoever built this wanted it as close to the cliff as possible.

'Is that Sharp's house?' Julie said, as we struggled up the hill.

'Yes. He and his wife live in there.' It looked even bigger when we were looking up at it from our angle. Then I saw the lights I'd seen from farther down. They were basement lights.

There was a small track through the woods, leading down to the side of the house. Next to it was a parking space big enough for a large vehicle. There was a door leading into the side of the house, on the basement level, an old van parked there, with ladders on the roof.

'Maybe a place where the plumber can get down into the bottom of the house,' Julie said.

'Thanks for that, Captain Obvious.'

'I wish soldier boy had kicked you in the nuts now.'

'You don't mean that,' I said, taking off across the small parking area. I could hear Julie running behind me.

'I do. Just for being a smartarse,' she said, catching up. We looked round the van and could see some basement windows lit up. We crept forward, ducking low, until we got to one of the windows.

We both heard the scream at the same time.

A face shot up to the window from the side.

I reeled back for a second and thought Julie might have screamed, but she was more professional than I was. She didn't flinch.

It was the woman I'd seen earlier. The long hair was unkempt. She'd bared her teeth at us, and it was clear she hadn't seen dental work in a long time.

She screamed again, and then we heard soldier boy coming closer. I tapped Julie on the shoulder and pointed to the driveway I'd gone down earlier that day, the track that led down to the shoreline.

We ran as quietly as we could, sticking to the side of it. We stopped for a moment, ducking into the tall grass and listening.

Lights came on above the front door. A man wearing black

opened the door and looked out as the soldier came into the small car park we'd just left. Then he was up onto the main drive.

'Have any of your cronies been outside wearing balaclavas?' he said, his voice shouting above the wind.

'Shut up. And put that fucking gun away, you clown.'

'Don't you speak to me like that—'

'Or what?' The man in black grabbed hold of the soldier.

'Get your hands off me!'

'Was that you shooting your gun again?'

'Of course it was. I was fighting two bloody Ninjas back there!'

'Piss off, you little freak. If I hear that gun going off again and disturbing everybody, I'll shove it up your fucking arsehole.' He shoved the man away and stepped back inside, closing the door.

'I'd like to see you try!' soldier boy said.

The door opened again. 'What did you say?'

'Nothing.'

'Bugger off.'

The soldier disappeared back down the hill.

'Who the hell do you think he is?' Julie whispered.

'God knows. But let's get back before he makes a phone call to somebody.'

'The phones don't work, remember?'

'Not for us, anyway.'

She was about to walk away when I saw the headlights of a car coming toward us along the service road that went past the smaller house in the distance. 'Car!' I said, as I grabbed Julie's arm and hauled her into the long grass.

We stayed down as a dark green Land Rover came towards us and drove on by, going down the track that led to the shore.

'I wonder who that is?' Julie whispered.

'Let's not wait around to find out.'

We cut through the woods until we came to the edge of the castle's car park. We took our balaclavas off and slipped them into our pockets. 'Follow me,' I said to Julie, and crouched as I ran across to where my car was parked. We took our jackets off and threw them in the boot. I took my keys out and opened the door. Julie got in the other side. I started it up and drove back along the road that led to the mansion house, but cut off to the left, along the other road that led to the smaller house.

I kept the lights off, until I was sure there was nobody home in the small house, and I drove past slowly. I'd seen there was another road leading away from the smaller house, which meant the occupant wouldn't have to drive all the way down here to get to his house, when there was a shorter way.

I drove along in the dark, my eyes adjusting to the gloom, and after a few minutes, we came to the end. It led out onto the main road leading to the castle. I turned left towards the castle itself and then put the lights on.

Two minutes later, we were pulling in front of the castle entrance.

'Finger-comb your hair,' I told Julie, waiting for the concierge to come out, which he did.

'Can you park the car?' I said to him, slipping him a tenner.

'I'll have one of the lads do it right away, sir,' he said.

We walked inside, just two people coming back from a drive. The cameras watched us enter, so they wouldn't think we had just been creeping about in the woods, fighting with a man with a shotgun.

A bulky man stood at reception, a young woman by his side. He turned round as we entered.

I couldn't believe who I was looking at.

FORTY-EIGHT

Charles Sharp came into the office and the security guard stood to one side.

'You can wait outside,' he said, dismissing the man.

Bruce Hagan sat in one of the chairs, his breathing heavy, his eyes bloodshot. He'd just been brought up. Plans had changed after they caught the girl sneaking about.

'Good evening, Bruce. How are we tonight?'

'I don't know about you, but I feel like I'm on fucking fire inside.' He moved his fingers rapidly, as if this would help.

'Here, take these,' Sharp said, taking out an amber pill bottle and opening it. He shook two tablets into the palm of his hand. He handed them to Hagan and fetched a glass of water from his sideboard.

Hagan washed them down. 'What are these?'

'They'll countcract your feelings of anxiety, Bruce. You feel like you're on fire because you're dealing with your feelings head on.'

'I want to go to my bed.'

'And you can go back upstairs after this session of course, but I feel it would be beneficial for you to talk about things. Today, your stress overtook you and we had to take you down to the infirmary. You don't want that again, do you?'

'No.'

Sharp sat behind his desk and picked up a pencil, tapping it against his teeth.

'Fingers down a blackboard,' Hagan said.

'What?' He stopped mid tap.

'Tapping your fucking teeth like that is like fingers down a blackboard. It's making the hair on the back of my neck crawl.'

Sharp tossed the pencil onto the desk. He looked over at Hagan and could see his eyes were brighter now, more sharply focused.

'What would you say if I told you I knew exactly what was wrong with you?'

'That's what I'm here for, doc. Get my brain running on the right track again and I'll shake your hand and tell you, you are a marvel of modern medicine. That's not going to happen though; you're not going to be the fire exit door when the rest of the building's on fire.' He tapped the side of his head. 'You're not going to be the last life jacket just as the ship's starting to tilt.'

'Interesting metaphors, Bruce. Is that how you see your life now?'

'Of course I do. So nothing you can say to me will be the golden key to get out of here. When I leave here, I'm still going to be mentally attached to you through your words ringing in my ears, but something will come along and upset the balance and you won't be around to talk me off the ledge.'

Thunder cracked in the distance, rolling east.

'I'm going to give you mental tools, Bruce, so if something does happen to upset you, you'll be able to reach in and know what tool will help you. It will be automatic in future. I won't need to be there in person.'

'If you say so.'

'I do.' He looked at the pencil, but didn't pick it up. 'We're practising psychiatry as it was a hundred years ago, with advances so few, they're hardly worth mentioning. Freud was ahead of his time. Nietzsche thought outside the box.'

'Two of the most famous psychiatrists that ever lived and now you're going to be number three?' Hagan scoffed at him.

'My thinking is so far advanced it will be a long time before anybody understands. That's why I want to tell you exactly what's wrong with you without you thinking I should be a client in here.'

'Go on, doc. I'm listening but I'm not hearing very much so far.'

'It's not everybody who could take on board what I'm about to say.'

'Doc, if you procrastinate any longer, I'll be the one taking out a pencil, but it won't be to tap my teeth with, it will be to shove through your eyeball.'

Sharp felt a cold feeling running down his spine.

'I want you to listen to my words very carefully, and digest them. Try not to dismiss them out of hand. Okay?'

'I'd prefer it if you would stop flapping your gums and get on with it.'

'Okay, here we go.' Sharp smiled and looked Hagan in the eyes. 'You're experiencing what I like to call a glitch in your personal association with time and relative dimension.'

'What did you say?' Hagan scowled like a fighter who's just been insulted in the pub after downing ten pints.

'Come on, Bruce, you're not a stupid man. Listen to what I'm saying. I, Charles Sharp, don't exist.'

Hagan continued to look at Sharp. Then he burst out laughing. 'What? You're having a laugh, right?'

'No, I'm not.'

'Is this some kind of new primal scream therapy, where you play with the patient's mind and the only screaming they hear is in their own head?'

Sharp kept his face straight. 'I know you were in that coffin, Bruce, and that man did terrible things to you, but deep down in your subconscious, you think you were at fault. *If I hadn't done this, if I'd only done that.* It's what people tell themselves.'

'You weren't there. You didn't see what he did to me. Have a look!' He swept his hair back to show where his missing ear used to be. 'That happened because I got careless!'

'You think you went into that room that night, but you didn't.'

'What? How can you sit there and feed me this garbage?' Hagan's face was beginning to feel flushed.

'I agree, you were there, but not in the way you think.'

'What do you mean?'

'I'm talking about the parallax view, Bruce. The sideways glance that is your life.'

'This is getting weird for me, I have to tell you.' Then he gripped his head and let out a yell.

'It'll pass, Bruce. Just ride it out.' Sharp sat back and saw Hagan fall onto the floor and curl up into a foetal position, wrapping his arms around his head.

The secret door opened and Doctor Solomon stepped out. 'Christ, he's having a bad reaction. Let me give him something.'

'No. Let him be. We'll never know unless he rides it out. Go back.'

Solomon retreated and the secret door closed softly.

After a few minutes, Hagan stopped rolling on the floor and was splayed out.

Sharp looked at the detective. The detective's breathing had stopped.

Bruce Hagan was dead.

Then he wasn't. Hagan stirred and got back up into his seat.

His hair was messed up and his face was lined with sweat. He looked at Sharp, but there was nothing behind his eyes, as if he'd died inside.

Sharp smiled at him. 'You're going to be okay, Bruce.'

'I believe you, doc,' Hagan said, softly.

Sharp nodded. 'I was talking about the parallax view. I said I'd tell you exactly what was wrong with you, and I meant it. I also said I didn't exist, and that's only partly true; I exist in your mind.'

'Of course you do, you're sitting there. I can see you.'

Sharp smiled at him. 'I want you to do something for me. I want you to go over to that door to my left and go through it. It's my bathroom.'

'Why?'

'Just humour me.'

Hagan looked at him and hesitated for a moment before standing. Thunder cracked again. He stretched his legs and walked over to the door.

'Don't close the door all the way just now,' Sharp said.

Hagan opened it and saw a small bathroom inside, just big enough to freshen up in. 'Now what?' he said, turning to look at Sharp who had swung round in his chair to watch him.

'Go inside.'

Hagan walked in.

'Can you hear my voice, Bruce?'

'Yes, I can hear you.'

'Good. Now close the door all the way. Stand still for around thirty seconds or so, and when you come out, tell me what you heard.'

SUDDEN DEATH

Hagan pulled the door closed after hitting the light switch. A small window with frosted glass kept out the night. He couldn't hear any sound but the thunder off in the distance and the wind howling.

'Right, you can come out now,' Sharp said, after exactly thirty seconds.

Hagan opened the door and came back into the office after putting the light out. He sat back down in his chair.

'So tell me what you heard when the door wasn't closed all the way, Bruce.'

'Just your voice.'

'What about when you were in the bathroom and had the door closed? Could you hear me then?'

'Were you talking to me?'

'No.'

'Then obviously I didn't hear you.'

'That's because I didn't exist.'

'Oh really?' Hagan's eyes were hooded as if his temper was going to come exploding out.

'You had the door closed for thirty seconds and I didn't exist for that thirty seconds.'

'Yes you did. You were right here.'

'Did you see me, Bruce?'

'No.'

'That's because for that thirty seconds, your mind denied any knowledge of my existence. That's what I've been trying to tell you. You *knew* I was here, but it was possible for your mind to deny my existence because it can't see me.'

'I'm not sure I understand, doc. Or that I *want* to understand.'

'I told you, it's the parallax view. Seeing something from a different angle. That's what you're doing. You see, you're sitting talking to me, because your mind says that's okay, but as you just demonstrated, when you were in the bathroom, I didn't exist. For you. I can make you think a different way so your nightmares don't exist. So you're not constantly thinking about what happened that night. You will be able to deny its very existence.'

Hagan sat and looked at him for a few seconds before speaking. More thunder rumbled in the distance. 'So what you're saying is it's all been in my imagination?'

'Freud said *psychic determination was the assumption that mental processes do not occur by chance but that a cause can always be found for them.* I agree with him. All the mental processes you have are made by your mind so it sees what it wants to see, nothing more. You couldn't hear me when you were in the bathroom because your mind didn't want to hear me. In fact, for that thirty seconds, it didn't want to recognise me as existing. Therefore, I didn't exist. I only took on the form you see now because your mind saw I was here and deemed it safe for you to come and sit back down.'

'And that's what you call my parallax view?'

'Now you're getting there! The parallax is the change in the position of an object resulting from the change in position of the observer. Your parallax view is the change in what you see in everyday life to make you exist. Soon, you won't be focusing on what happened, because I'll have trained you to think differently.'

'Doc, I don't mind telling you, this is getting a bit above me.'

Sharp smiled, getting into his stride. 'Stay with me, Bruce, this is getting exciting.'

'I'm trying to stay with you, but all this mumbo-jumbo is flying right over my head.'

'Nonsense. It will all become clear. Let me give you some examples of what I'm talking about.'

'I'm listening.'

'Right. Have you ever put something down then gone back to

get it and it wasn't there? Your car keys for example. You put the keys down on a table, then you went through to the kitchen to make a cup of coffee perhaps, then when you go back, your keys aren't there anymore. Where did they go? They were right there a minute ago. Have you had anything like that happen to you, Bruce?'

'Yes I have. Like putting the TV remote down somewhere.'

'That's a blip on your mind's mental radar. Let's stick with the car keys example for now. So you thought you'd put the keys down on your desk, but you retrace your steps and go back into the kitchen. They're right there, lying on the kitchen countertop. How did they get there? You would swear on your mother's life you had left them on the table and this causes momentary confusion. Your mind recognised the fact you were looking for the car keys and gave them to you. Do you follow me?'

Hagan nodded his head. 'Yes. The TV remote was down the side of the couch. I hunted high and low for it, and I only found it when I dropped a pen down the side and found the remote there as well. I could have sworn I'd already checked there.'

'Your mind had a blip for a moment. You actually put your car keys on the countertop but your mind was so focused on something else, for that moment in time, you can't remember moving them to there, so you thought they were still on the table. Your mind had automatically thought of something else, and it will do again, when it realises you're going to start thinking about what happened. It will block it out and you won't remember starting to have the thoughts, just as you didn't remember moving your car keys.'

'You're saying I can control what I see, is that right?' Hagan was starting to sweat again.

'Exactly. You only see what your mind wants you to see. It's a defence mechanism. If some people see something distasteful, something nasty on TV for example, they can immediately switch the image in their mind with something else, say a puppy playing. You'll be able to do that without thinking about it. You will be able to mentally transport yourself to a better place so you won't have to look at the horrible stuff.'

'What about my dreams? When I dream of being in the coffin?'

'Let me ask you, have you ever had a dream where, say, you were in Edinburgh doing something, and you knew it was Edinburgh, but where you were in the dream it looked nothing like the Edinburgh you knew?'

Hagan's eyes were beginning to look tired. 'Yes. I've had dreams like that before.'

'So your mind was telling you in the dream you were in Edinburgh, but in an *alternate* Edinburgh. Just like when you see yourself in that coffin, your mind can take you to a different place instead. It doesn't always have to be in the coffin.'

'You really think I can do this?'

'Of course you can. You will train your brain to think in a different way. Like some people are scared of the dark, your mind will tell you there's nothing to fear.'

Hagan jumped up, pointing a finger at Sharp. 'This is bril—' Before he could finish his sentence, foam appeared between his lips and he fell to his knees. Then he fell over for the second time that night.

Solomon came out from the room, syringe already in his hand. 'It's just as well he didn't make it out to reception like that Hollingsworth woman,' he said, rolling up Hagan's sleeve and injecting the contents of the syringe into his arm.

'I hope to God this one works,' Sharp said. 'Is it the different one?'

'That's what you asked for. He and the old woman have Type A and Type B. We'll monitor them closely.'

'Good.'

Hagan was stirring on the floor.

'Go now.'

Solomon moved back into the secret room. There was a staircase that led downstairs where Solomon would be able to move about without being seen.

'Wh-what happened?' Hagan said, getting to his knees.

'You passed out for a moment, that's all. It's just stress.'

'I want to go to my room now. Tired.'

'Of course. I'll have somebody escort you upstairs.' He pressed a button on his desk and a security guard came in.

'See that Detective Hagan gets back up to his room.'

Sharp closed his eyes for a moment. Maybe it was a mistake accelerating the program, but time was running out for Mama.

He hoped it wasn't too late.

FORTY-NINE

'There you are, daughter of mine!' Lloyd Masters said. 'Your sister wanted to come up here and see what the place was like. Didn't you, my dear?'

'I did, Dad.' I couldn't believe my eyes. Suzy Campbell as well. I wanted to ask them what they were doing here at the castle, but I had a feeling I already knew.

Julie smiled and looked at me, and although she had never met either of them, she grasped the situation right away.

Suzy hugged her and whispered into her ear, 'Inspector Suzy Campbell. I'm your sister, Sonia Kendal.'

'And who's this fella?' Masters said, looking at me, like any father would appraise a man who'd just appeared with his daughter.

'Dad, this is Frank Miller. He's a policeman from Edinburgh.'

'Well, don't you be expecting to show my daughter your truncheon, young man,' he said, and laughed.

I could feel my face going red. 'We're just friends, sir.'

'Good. My name's Lloyd Kendal. This is my daughter, Suzy.

Let me finish checking-in and we can have a drink at the bar.' He turned to the male receptionist. 'Can we get something to eat at the bar, young man?'

'Of course, sir. Now, I'll need to ask you to hand over any phones or computers you have.'

'Really? Why?'

'It's policy. This is a place of tranquillity. The management want people to relax away from their phones.'

'It said so in the brochure, Dad,' Suzy said. 'It was one of the conditions of booking.'

'Okay, okay. I don't know how to work the damned thing anyway.' He handed over an old flip-phone, while Suzy handed over hers.

'We don't have any computers or tablets with us,' Suzy said. 'I just want a massage and a swim.' She smiled at the man behind the counter.

He handed them their keys, and Masters took his and gave Suzy hers. 'Let's get to the bar. I need a couple of beers. What say you... er, what's your name again?'

'Frank,' I said.

'Frank! Come on then, it's your round.' He laughed again.

I ordered a couple of beers and a couple of soft drinks for the women and we sat at a table by the window.

There were other people around but not close.

'As much as I'm pleased to see you, Lloyd, I must say I'm surprised you're here.'

Masters clinked his bottle against mine as an older couple walked past. 'Purcell wanted Suzy to travel up here on her own tomorrow, but then he thought she should be travelling with somebody. He needed somebody who Hagan wouldn't recognise, so I volunteered my services when he called me asking for help.'

'So you came up early?' I said to Suzy.

'Lloyd was sending a group up for marksmen training to the training grounds in Perthshire, so we decided to leave with them this afternoon.'

'Why did they send you up?' Julie said.

'There's been a development. We found some stuff out about Hagan.'

I felt like I'd been punched in the guts. 'What about him?' I looked up as the concierge brought my car keys in and I thanked him.

Masters carried on. 'It seems he forged the report for him to return to work.'

'What? That can't be right. Jill White signed him off for his return.'

'No, she didn't. Kim spoke to her personally, and she most certainly did not. And this doesn't go any further than this table, but she doesn't think he will ever be fit to return.'

'Jesus Christ.' I was stunned.

'How has he been since he's been here?'

'Up and down. He had a setback and had to be taken to the infirmary. He was fine and he's going to be in a group therapy session tonight, but he's been all over the place.'

'That would explain it. He should never have been allowed to come back.'

'That was all my fault. I had a beer with him in Edinburgh and he seemed fine, then when he turned up with the report, I was on board with him coming up here. I should have known better.'

'You can't blame yourself, Frank. He's been very cunning about it.' Masters took a sip of his beer. 'Did you know he got married to another woman?'

'What do you mean, *another woman*?'

'He left Hazel. He's been living above Tanners bar with the barmaid from the pub. And they got married three weeks ago.'

'What? Bruce did?' I couldn't believe what I was hearing.

'Yes, he did. He and Hazel are well and truly finished.'

I was shocked. 'He didn't say a word to me.'

'We need to discuss what's been going on and what you found out,' he said.

I leaned in a bit closer. Told him about the fight with the man with the shotgun and the woman we'd seen in the basement. And Steffi's role in it.

'Where is she?' he asked.

'I assume she went up to her room,' I said.

'I think we should get up there.' He didn't touch his bottle again. We all stood and the women walked out ahead of us and I put a hand on Masters' arm.

'Why did Percy really send you up with Suzy?'

'He thinks you're in danger and although he thinks the women will have your back, there's safety in numbers.'

'Did Jeni Bridge sanction this?'

He smiled. 'Of course she did. She seemed relieved I was coming. If you see that arsehole with the shotgun again, I'll break it over his fucking head, trust me.'

'Well, if he says anything out of turn to you, you'll get the chance sooner than you think. He's standing at reception. Minus his shotgun.'

Masters laughed and clapped me on the shoulder as if I had just told him a joke, then turned round. We walked out of the bar and across reception. The man had his back to us. Masters walked close to the guy in camouflage and bumped into him.

The soldier turned round sharply.

'Sorry about that, son,' Masters said.

'Watch where you're going in future,' the man snarled at him.

'Easy there, fella,' Masters said, his smile still in place.

'Are you taking the piss?' soldier said.

Masters took a step towards him, his smile gone now. 'Twenty-two, sonny. It's your choice.'

The man looked like he was about to say something, but turned round and stormed out.

The women were waiting at the lift.

'Twenty-two?' I said to Masters as we caught up.

'Twenty-two, between the Paras and me leaving to join the Met. I served with them for three years.'

I hadn't known Masters had been in the SAS, but it seemed soldier boy knew the reference; 22 Special Air Service.

'Remind me not to piss you off anytime soon,' I said to him as the lift doors opened.

'You'll soon know if you have, my boy. You'll wake up in a body cast.'

The doors closed and we rode the lift up to their rooms, which were along the corridor from Steffi and Julie's rooms. Nobody spoke in the lift, in case it was bugged.

In the corridor, we walked along to Masters' room. He let us in and switched on a light.

'I'll go and get Steffi,' Julie said.

'I'm in the room next door,' Suzy said.

'Good,' Masters said. He opened his bag and took out a few mobile phones. 'Can't have a phone my arse,' he said, handing me one. 'Go and call Kim, she's worried sick about you.'

'You're a life-saver.'

'I just gave that tosser in reception some old piece of shite that was lying about in my office at the firing range. Can't have a phone. That laddie must be daft.'

'We laughed at *Can't bring a computer in.*' Suzy brought out an iPad from her bag. 'This one works like a mobile phone so we won't have to rely on their Wi-Fi. Your friend, Ian Powers, installed some software that will counteract anything they have that tries to capture the signal. They won't even know we have it here. Same with the phones.'

'Good job.'

I walked into the bathroom and called Kim.

'Oh, Frank, thank God you're okay. I've been so worried.'

'I'm fine.' I didn't tell her about the fight I'd just had, but explained about Masters bringing up the phones. 'How are you and Emma?'

'We're okay. Did Lloyd tell you about Hagan being married?'

'He did.'

'What a bastard. He's going to put your whole operation in jeopardy. Norma is having a fit. Hagan lying like that means he shouldn't be there and any evidence he gathers will be null and void.'

'We'll have to deal with him when we get back.'

'Where is he now?'

'He's had a setback, according to the doctor. He's not in the best shape, Kim.'

'I think it's about time you were thinking of wrapping it up, Frank.'

'I can't. There's something going on, just like we thought, and I want to see it through.'

'Okay. Just be careful.'

'Talk to you soon.'

I had just got out of the room when the bedroom door opened. 'There's no answer from Steffi's room. I think she's went exploring on her own,' she said.

'That's not what I wanted her to do. I told her it's too dangerous.'

'I'm sure she'll be careful. She'll be fine.'

I'm not sure any of us believed those words.

Suzy was on her phone talking to Ian Powers. After we'd told them what we had seen lurking in the basement, she wanted help getting the schematics for the place, including the mansion house.

'Let me go and talk to Hagan, see if he knows anything. Personally, I think he's gone over the edge.'

'Don't alert him to anything, Frank, for fuck's sake. He might blab.'

'I won't. As much as I like Bruce, I don't trust him anymore.' I left the hotel room and walked down to Hagan's room. I listened at the door. There was noise coming from the TV.

I knocked. He answered it a minute later.

'Can I help you?'

The man I knew as Bruce Hagan was standing in front of me, but the one I had known for years was long gone. This Bruce was dead behind the eyes.

I looked at his glazed eyes. You poor bastard, I thought, and then the guilt washed over me again.

There was an old Dracula movie playing on TV.

'Bruce, it's me, Frank.'

'Oh, sorry, I'm just tired. I had my session with that doctor, and to be honest, I'm fucked. I need to go to bed.'

'Will you be alright?'

'I'll be fine. I just need some rest. It's mentally exhausting.'

'Okay, I'll see you in the morning.'

He stepped back into the room and gently closed the door. I went back to Masters' room. They looked at me.

'What's wrong, son?' Masters said.

'Christ knows what's happened to Bruce, but he looks like shite. It's my fault. I should never have brought him here.' I looked at the women. 'First of all, we need to find Steffi, and secondly, we need to get Bruce home.'

'He's that bad?' Julie said.

'He is. He's washed out. He just went to his bed.'

'Jesus.' She looked at Suzy. 'We need to get him home, like Frank says.'

'I'll get onto it.'

'Don't go asking for help from Sergeant McTavish down on Main Street. Beardy bastard is a disgrace to Police Scotland.'

'Is he now? Maybe he'll be better off as a security guard on a building site, which is where he'll end up if he gets in my way.'

'Well, there's not much else we can do tonight. They'll be looking for two housebreakers on the prowl so we'd be better off keeping a low profile until tomorrow.'

'Agreed,' said Masters. 'We'll regroup in the morning. Check on Hagan before breakfast, then we can start wandering about this place.'

FIFTY

'Welcome to paradise,' Mabel Hollingsworth muttered to herself as she looked up at the old, red brick building in the distance. The bus ride had been its usual carriage ride in Central Park. She was sure one of those dirty freak shows was playing with himself, one hand holding up a newspaper, while the other one was under his long coat, giving himself a personal massage.

Dirty bastard.

It made her head absolutely boil. Well, what do you expect? That rag he was reading could hardly be called a newspaper. Tits and cartoons. What did any man expect anyway? That was why she, Mabel Hollingsworth, had never bothered to find herself one of those reprobates who only wanted to take her to dinner then rip off her underclothes.

She had gone out with one of those two-legged monsters once. *And what did I tell you?* she had said to her own reflection in the mirror afterwards. *What did I fucking say? That the daft old twat would only be after one thing! Didn't I just fucking tell you this? Yes you did,* she had said, answering herself.

Well, he very nearly had his way with you, didn't he?
No, no, he didn't.
Ha ha! Yes he did! And he would have bent you over the bed if he'd had his way with you!

Mabel had cried that night, the night she had gone out with Stanley. If that was even the fucking deviant's name. *Call me Stan,* he had said. *My friends call me Stan the Man.*

Even after all those years, she could still smell his aftershave. He'd dabbed it behind his ears like a woman, and he'd even put it in his underpants.

The dirty mutant had made her sniff his Y-fronts after what he'd done.

Just the thought of that now nearly made her boak. The smell of cheap aftershave and pish.

Mabel had to stop for a moment. Grab hold of the railings outside the primary school.

'You alright, darlin'?' the lollipop man said, walking across with his school crossing patrol sign.

'I'm fine,' she said, hoping she didn't look like a jakie.

Then she straightened up and hurried towards the nursing home, thoughts of *Stan the Man* still in her mind. The man's face just made her want to cry. Then she reached into the mental toolbox Doctor Sharp had given her.

Stanley had seemed a nice man as they got talking at the checkout in Asda. Then he asked her if she wanted to get a cup of tea. She did. They went to a little café she knew just along from the supermarket. And they'd chatted. *Stan the Man* was a widower. He'd been on his own for a few years, and he missed the company of a woman. Missed the nights out going to the bingo, missed sitting watching *Coronation Street* with someone. Missed having walks in the park with a woman.

Christ, she'd never met a man like this. So she jumped at the chance to go to dinner. *Going Dutch* she'd said to him. *I can pay my own way!* He'd agreed, and they'd gone to a little Italian place just off the high street in Glasgow's West End. He'd offered to pick her up, and although he seemed nice, the thought of being in the car alone with him right off the bat made her wary. So she'd got the bus.

He was wearing a blazer and a shirt and tie. On a Tuesday night! He looked shiny, as if he'd just stepped out of the shower, not like the smelly old bastards who lived in the home.

He'd opened the door for her, helped her with her chair, and again offered to pay the bill. She'd declined but she did accept a lift home.

She'd felt it only polite to offer him a coffee, not knowing that was the international signal for *Come upstairs and shag me.*

She could see there was a spring in *Stan the Man's* step, not knowing the old fucker thought he was getting his hole.

Up two flights of stairs to her flat.

This is a nice place you have here, he said, not meaning it.

Thank you. It's my mother's place.

His face fell for a moment – the second alarm bell should have been going off right then – and he looked awkwardly about the living room.

How old did he think my fucking mother would have been? Mabel had said to Sharp. *I'm fifty-nine and this happened a few years ago.*

Anyway, she'd assured him her mother had long since passed away. She couldn't use the word *died.* Some of those tarts in the home callously used terms like *popped his clogs,* and *kicked the bucket* when they were discussing patients who had passed on. One male nurse had even used the term, *got fitted for a wooden overcoat!* For fuck's sake, what way was that to talk about elderly people?

So Mabel always said her mother *was in a better place* if they ever asked, which they never did nowadays.

So telling *Stan the Man* about her mother had made her feel melancholy, and maybe she did need to sit down and just have him hold her for a little while. Just like her father used to do. Make her feel loved and wanted, but never in *that* way. In a *daddy comforting his little girl* way. And God help anybody who said anything bad about her dad, who had long ago moved on *to a better place*.

She had come through from the kitchen with a teapot on a tray, with two cups and a little fancy milk jug and sugar bowl, the one mother would bring out when her snooty friends came round. And by snooty, she meant the ones who didn't use the f-word. Mabel herself seemed to be using it more and more. She never used to swear, but after telling a motorist to *go fuck yourself you cocksucking prick*, she had felt strangely elated.

I hope you don't mind tea, but coffee at night makes me – piss like a horse – have nightmares, she started to say, but Stan wasn't in the living room. Maybe he'd gone to the toilet. She set the tray down and waited for him to come back. And waited.

Then she heard him calling her.

She went looking, hoping to Christ she hadn't used up the last of the toilet roll and forgotten to put a new one out, when she heard her name being called from the bedroom.

Oh sweet Christ, no, she thought, and she tried to swallow, but her mouth was going dry.

She opened the bedroom door. *Stan the fucking Man* was standing naked by the side of her bed, his manhood drooping. His clothes strewn about on the floor.

I'm sorry, love, but I was just wanting to get started so I'd be ready for you. And I got too excited. He had pointed to her clean sheets, at the wet patch there.

Her clean fucking sheets!

What are you doing, you dirty bastard?! she had screamed at him.

I told you, I was just getting ready!

By coming in here and doing this?

He grinned at her pun.

Get out! Get your clothes on and get the fuck out!

Don't worry, I'll be ready in a wee while.

Like fuck you will! Get out you dirty bastard!

His smile dropped and he picked up his underwear and had pushed them into her face. *See what you're missing?*

She had screamed and run through to the toilet where she threw up. By the time she came out, *Stan the Pervert* was gone.

And she'd never looked at another man again.

The chance to go and see Doctor Sharp was one she jumped at. She wanted to go and see him, get him to sort out the things in her head. And it worked.

Now she was walking through the front door of the nursing home. Her first day back since she had learned her new skills.

She felt like a new woman.

'You look happy,' the staff nurse said. 'Your break must have worked like a charm.'

'It was very enjoyable, thank you.' She smiled when she said it, even though this boot was an irritating cow at times. Thought she owned the fucking home. 'I'll get up and get started.'

'Actually, you'll be working in the west wing, level three,' the staff nurse said.

'Really? How did that happen? I've always been east wing, level two.'

'Well, we decided to shuffle things about when you were away on your wee holiday.'

'People have holidays, and when they come back, things aren't *shuffled.* What's-her-name went on holiday a few weeks ago and she's still in the north wing. How come she wasn't *shuffled?*'

'We know you've been at odds with some of the men up on three, so we decided to move you.'

'*At odds?* My God, one of them put his hand up my uniform!'

'That might be so, but the other women seem to handle it alright.'

That's because they'd drop their drawers for any man, so they get a thrill out of that! she wanted to scream at the staff nurse, but she knew it would be no good.

She went upstairs to her level, and took her coat off in the staff changing room. Then Sharp's words rang in her head; *They don't exist. You can't let them get to you. Not if you don't want them to. Up until now, you've let them in your head. Now you have to change your way of thinking.*

See? The money was well spent going to see him. He had shown her the way. Now they couldn't annoy her or do anything to her she didn't want them to. She walked along the corridor, skirting a maintenance man who was up a ladder fiddling with a light fixture.

In the ward where she now worked, some of the old men were sitting in the day room, watching TV or, if they were some of the more compos mentis ones, playing cards or dominoes.

Then she saw him sitting across from the TV. *Stan the Man.* And by God, strike her down if she was wrong, but he had his *thing* in his hand. Smiling at her and playing with it.

She shrieked and ran out of the room. What was she going to do now? Pretend she didn't see it. After all, *Stan the Man* didn't exist. He was only in her mind.

She went into a room. A man was lying in bed, asleep. She checked the chart to see when he was due his meds.

'Why, honey, you're back!' *Stan* said from the doorway. 'Did you miss me?' He was standing holding his joey. Doing things with it. Pointing it in *her* fucking direction!

'Put it away!' she screamed.

She tried squeezing past him in the doorway and he turned towards her, moving it faster and making a lewd face, sticking his tongue out.

'Look, even *he's* hot for you!' *Stan* said, pointing to the man in the bed. She couldn't help it, couldn't *not* turn her head. The man in the bed was sitting up, and one of his hands was under the sheet, pumping up and down as if he were trying to inflate a bicycle tyre.

'No! Stop!'

'Come on,' *Stan* said, 'you know you want it!' He was holding his underpants in his other hand and he shoved them towards her face, just like the last time.

She got past them before the cloth touched her face.

The maintenance man had a tool bag at the foot of his ladder. He was focused on the light, and didn't see her take the hammer from his tool bag.

Mabel walked back to the room where the two old men were hammering away at themselves as if it was a competition. Well, she'd show them a fucking good hammering.

'Stan,' she said, 'I think I do want it now.'

'See, didn't I say she did?' he said to the man in the bed.

Mabel stepped forward as *Stan* turned round. She swung the hammer with every fibre of her being. The round, steel head sank into *Stan's* skull, spraying blood over the cheap print in the frame on the wall at his side.

It came out with a sucking noise and she brought it down again on top of his head. It was enough to drop him. She turned her attention to the man in the bed. He wasn't moving now. *Had* he been playing with himself? Then he suddenly grinned at her. *Oh fuck, he was going to get out of bed and touch her! Christ, he was actually going to touch her!*

She stepped forward and hit him on the side of the face with the hammer. Swung it right round in a wide arc, putting everything behind it and the steel shattered his jaw on contact, throwing him sideways. He didn't fall out of the bed but made a screaming noise just before she brought the hammer down again and again on his head. Blood flew everywhere and bits of brain started to come out.

Fuck me, Mabel, that's some fucking turn on! Stan said from the end of the bed. Blood poured down his face but his teeth – obviously fucking false, if they were *that* white! – were grinning at her. His eyes were wide and he put his tongue out, licking his own blood.

Mabel screamed as hard as she could and charged back to the end of the bed, lashing out with the hammer again. This time, *Stan* fell down and stayed still.

Mabel was out of breath but she felt *good!* Hadn't Doctor Sharp said she would feel good when she reached into the mental toolbox and used some of the tools to keep her steady? Not only had she used her *mental* toolbox, but a real one.

She could tell his words would need tweaking. Maybe her own mind had given her a test by letting *Stan* come here.

She left the room and walked past the maintenance man who was down his ladder now. He looked at her funny. She still had the hammer in her hand and she wouldn't think twice about giving him a bloody good skelp with it, but then she mentally told herself he wasn't going to touch her, and just like that, she was past him.

Look at all the blood on your uniform! she said, but then when she told herself it wasn't really there, she looked again and it was gone.

She needed a hot bath. It was what *Charlotte* would do. Dear, sweet *Charlotte*. Mabel wanted to be with her now, so she could take her to speak to Grandmother in the library. Sip a cup of tea and sit by the fire that was always burning. Oh God, she couldn't wait to watch the episodes she'd recorded when she'd been away in caber-tossing land.

She'd have a hot bath first though. Make herself clean and presentable. Then she'd go home and be with *Charlotte*, the rightful heiress to the fortune.

The bathroom was empty. Mabel ran the hot water. Only the hot water. She didn't want to ruin the effect.

She locked the door. She didn't want any more *Stans* coming in and seeing her without her clothes on.

Steam billowed around the room. Water splashed into the cold tub, warming it up for her. When it was near the top, she climbed in.

The water was so hot, it started peeling her skin almost right away.

Mabel smiled as she sank deeper under the water, her face sliding below the surface.

Come on, Mabel! Charlotte shouted to her. I'm coming! She felt warm inside, as if her whole life had been leading to this point.

Under the water, Mabel didn't hear the screams as nurses, aides, and staff ran about, calling for help. Two men had been murdered in a room. The maintenance man had seen who had done it. The staff nurse was in shock.

By the time they found Mabel in the bathroom, her face now back up from under the surface, she had seventy-five per cent burns on her body, and she would succumb to her injury two hours later, before she could even be put on life support.

Both men in the room – neither of them called *Stan* – died instantly.

When one young detective constable saw what had happened, it reminded him of a case in Edinburgh recently. *Two* cases.

When he got back to the station, he would make a call through to their MIT office.

FIFTY-ONE

Julie Stott finished blowing her hair dry and made herself a coffee with the small kettle that sat on the dresser. Steffi had got in late last night. She had heard her moving about the room before she had fallen back into a fitful sleep.

She had told herself it was this case they were working on. They'd come up here to see if something happened to Steven Hubbard and Mel Carpenter while they were here, and so far, they had found out nothing.

Is that all, Julie? The case getting to you?

She stood and looked out the window at the Dornoch Firth. Let her eyes look skywards, imagining firing an arrow high up into the sky. Where would it land? Glasgow. She imagined a note tied to it, telling him she still loved him. That it needn't be like this. That they could spend the rest of their lives together.

It wouldn't change anything. He would still be married to that nurse, he'd still be the same arrogant lawyer he ever was.

He couldn't change the fact he had hit her.

The kettle clicked off and she poured herself a coffee, adding a little creamer to it. She knew she was just fooling herself, hanging onto the good memories, trying to erase the bad ones. The arguments that had turned into almost physical fights, until the day it did turn into a physical fight.

The old excuse had been trooped out: *I'm going to get a divorce, it just isn't that easy. You know, with the kids and everything.*

She'd waited for him for two years, waited for him to get his act together, but he never did. Always one excuse after another, always ending up in bed after the fight. The sex was good, but how good would it have been when she had been wife number two? There had to be a reason he was looking for sex with her; because sex with wife number one had gone out the window.

She had shouted at him one night after he'd had his way with her. She laughed at this expression, one her mother would have used. *Had his way with her.* After he'd *fucked* her. Definitely an expression her mother *wouldn't* have used.

He'd had a drink, but wasn't swaying about. He'd been fun when he came round, then they'd gone to bed, and he'd been fast and clumsy. Then he blurted out he wasn't going to leave his wife.

She'd been angry, accusing him of using her, and telling him he was an amateur in bed. He'd lashed out at her, back-handing her mouth. She had been shocked that he would hit her. Some women might have been scared, or run away to lock themselves in the bathroom, and she couldn't blame them. A lot of women were abused by bullies who were basically cowards.

However, Julie had been in fights before, and it was only because it was her boyfriend who had lashed out at her that she had been unprepared. After the initial shock, seeing him standing there with a grimace on his face as if it was meant to scare her, she took a quick step forward and shot her fist out from her hip, not giving him time to block it. Then she followed through with all her weight.

His nose broke.

He squealed and fell over, blood getting on her carpet. He held his face and cursed her out.

Then she felt sorry for what she had done, and knelt down to say how sorry she was, that she didn't mean it, that they could work things out, when he took his hands away from his face and looked at her with venom in his eyes.

'You didn't think I was really going to leave my wife for you, did you?' He got to his feet on unsteady legs. 'You were just good for shagging. Now even that's shite.'

'What did you say?'

'You heard. I've moved on to some other bint. But don't worry, I'll see you get arrested for this.'

'You assaulted me first.'

'You can't prove that. I can prove you hit me though.' He held out a hand dripping with blood.

'I have hidden security cameras, you prick. I'll have the recording on my phone by the time you get in your car. And it gets uploaded to the Cloud as well. So go ahead, call the police.' She held out the house phone to him.

'Oh, fuck off, Julie.'

And that was the last she'd heard from him. No phone calls, no coming round to see her to tell her how much he loved her. She'd nearly bumped into him in John Lewis in Buchanan Galleries one Saturday, but she'd managed to avoid him.

She drank her coffee and thought about the good times they'd had. The laughs, the drinks, the eating out. And all that time she'd thought he was going to leave his wife for her.

But they never do.

She shook him out of her mind. She'd moved on and was sure

the move to Edinburgh had been for the best. She hadn't been with him for over a year and wished she had made the move long before she had.

Yet sometimes, she couldn't shake off the melancholy she felt.

Putting her jacket on, she switched the TV off and knocked on Steffi's door. 'You up, Steffi?'

No answer. She knocked again, a little louder. No answer.

She turned the lock and opened the door into Steffi's room. 'Come on, lazy cow, time you were up and at it.'

The room was empty. The bed hadn't been slept in, and her clothes were gone.

Oh Christ, she thought, fighting back the rising panic.

She ran along to Suzy's door and hammered on it.

'What's wrong?' Suzy asked.

'Steffi's gone. Her room's empty and all her clothes are gone.'

'Come on, let's get Lloyd.'

Next door, Masters was finishing a coffee. He let the two women in.

'Ready for breakfast? I'm just waiting for Frank. He's away checking on Hagan.' Then he saw the look on the women's faces. 'What's wrong?'

'Steffi's not in her room. Her stuff's gone. Have you seen her?'

'No, I haven't.' He grabbed a jacket. 'Let's go and find Frank.'

FIFTY-TWO

'Are you sure Suzy's going to be alright up there in the middle of nowhere?' Lou Purcell asked his son.

'Relax. She'll be fine. She's an experienced officer.'

'Chivalry isn't dead, then.'

'She's a police officer. She's working undercover. Besides, Frank's up there and so is Lloyd Masters.'

'Masters? Never heard of him. You want to watch him. He might have a roving eye.'

'For God's sake, they're away to a wellness centre, not Butlins.'

'I'm just saying.'

'Well I'm not interested in what you've got to say.'

'Bloody charming that is.'

They were in the kitchen. Bear was eating his food in the corner, Percy was eating toast at the small kitchen table, and Lou was opening cupboard doors trying to find cereal.

'Bottom cupboard, far right,' Percy said.

Lou opened it and saw the bag of dog food. 'Oh, you're so

bloody funny. Maybe I'll rearrange everything in the cupboards when you're out at work.'

'Just try it, old man. I'd get a lot of money for you on the black market.'

'Here, enough of that talk.'

'I'm kidding. Besides, they'd probably pay me more to keep you.'

'Just tell me where the bloody cereal is.'

'Top left. If you're lucky, we might have something with a free toy in it.'

'Oh, don't worry, I won't take your wee toy. Big bairn.' He found the cornflakes. Poured himself a bowl.

'So when do you meet old fanny Annie?'

'You can't help yourself, can you?' Lou said between mouthfuls of cereal.

'I'm just interested in your love life.'

'You just said you weren't interested in what I had to say.'

'This is different. I want to watch when Elizabeth finds out you've been giving one to this new Judy and she kicks you right in the chuckies.'

'Jesus. Where did I go wrong?'

'A parent is a child's first teacher, so there's your answer right there. You failed me, old man.'

'Don't talk pish. Besides, we're just friends on Facebook, that's all. We're catching up with old times.'

'I thought it was Twitter.'

'Facebook's better. I can write more to her on the message page.'

'Well don't go taking photos of your ding-dong and putting it up on Instagram.'

'Is that how you met your first wife?'

'They didn't have Instagram back then, smartarse.'

JOHN CARSON

'So Margery and I have arranged to meet in the High Street. In Starbucks. Near the station, so I can pop in and say hello to all your workmates.'

'I don't think so. Don't drag me into this. And don't be bringing her back here

'I have no intention of bringing her back here. We're just having coffee.'

'Where did you work with her?'

'In the bank, in George Street, before they sold it and turned it into a den of iniquity.'

'A bar you mean.'

'Same diff. All banks will be bars one day, the rate they're closing them.'

'It's called progress, Dad.'

'Maybe it's a good thing, right enough. When you do your banking online, you don't get mugged. Which reminds me, I'll get some money for my keep. I can't have you buying me all my food.'

'You can share Bear's.'

'You'd like that, eh? Watch me kneeling down on the kitchen floor getting wired into a bowl of dog food. A right bloody laugh that would be.'

'I'm kidding. No need to be so sensitive. And I don't want any money. Besides, you'll be back on the bus tonight going back to Aberdeen.'

'Ha. You surely jest. I'll be here for a week. Think your heart can take the strain of having your old man around again?'

'No.'

'I'll be sure to have the paramedics on speed dial then.'

'Don't be sitting in that bloody lavvy reading your newspaper.'

'I like to do the crossword.'

'There's no crossword on page three.'

'You know I'm only staying here 'cause the Balmoral is full, don't you?'

'You wish.'

'Seriously, son, I don't want it spread around that I'm seeing Margery. Elizabeth might get the wrong idea.'

'I wonder why? Here you are, come all the way down from Aberdeen to meet a woman you used to work with, and you haven't told her. Because it's all innocent. Although she wouldn't believe that and might get the wrong idea.'

'Exactly!'

'That's called *having your cake and eating it.*'

'Sure, make it sound sordid.'

'Does Margery's husband know you're going to pump her?'

'Jesus. Your mind is a cesspit.' He finished his cereal. 'Besides, she's a widow.'

'Ah. The tale of true love.'

Lou looked at his son. 'No, that was with your mother. God rest her soul. This thing with Margery is just catching up with old times.' He got up and made to leave the kitchen.

'Dad, I'm sorry. I was just kidding.'

Lou stopped but didn't turn round.

'I feel bad now,' Percy said.

'Good. You can drop me off at the station. I'm meeting her in a wee while. After I've read my newspaper.' He turned and grinned at his son. 'In the lavvy.'

'You know I'm going to sign the paper for *Do Not Resuscitate*, don't you?' Percy shook his head and was finishing reading his copy of the Edinburgh morning paper, *The Caledonian*, when his mobile phone rang.

'Hello?'

'God, am I glad to hear your voice,' Suzy said.

'I like it when you think I'm a god.'

'This is serious, Percy; we can't find Steffi.'

'What do you mean, can't find her?'

'Frank and Julie went looking for something last night, and Steffi set off an alarm by opening a fire exit door as a distraction for them, and now there's no sign of her.'

'Wasn't she in her room?' Percy's heart started beating faster.

'No. Julie said she heard movement in the night in Steffi's room, which is right next to hers with a connecting door. This morning, her bed looked like it hadn't been slept in, and her stuff is gone.'

'What? Where the hell is she?'

'That's what I'm trying to say, Percy, we don't know. We're going to go down to reception to see if we can find out what's going on.'

'They took her, didn't they?'

Silence before she answered. 'I think so. There's definitely something going on here. Julie and Frank saw somebody who looked deformed in the basement of the mansion house in the grounds here. And Hagan, well, he's off the charts. We need to get him out of here.'

'I'm going to get Jeni to pull this operation, Suzy. I'm going to have reinforcements sent in from Inverness and Aberdeen. Hell, I can have people from here sent up.'

'Give us time. If they think we're suspicious, they might harm her, if they haven't already. And Frank doesn't trust the sergeant in Golspie.'

'The only time you'll have is until reinforcements get there. We'll get warrants drawn up so we can have the whole place locked down. I'll have every man and his fucking dog rip that place apart.'

'We'll have to try to find her. I just want to see what they have to say about her. They won't risk us calling in the police, so they'll have something up their sleeve. Little do they know we *are* the fucking police.'

'I won't be long getting this done. Hang in there. And for God's sake, be careful.'

'I will. I love you, Percy.'

'I love you too.'

'Don't worry if I don't hear my phone. They took our phones from us, but we gave them the fake ones. I can't have it ringing though. They mustn't know we have them.'

'Jesus. It's like a prison.' Then he had a thought. 'If Steffi had one, couldn't you track it?'

'I'm going to try. Although if they've taken her, I'm sure they would have searched her.'

'Fair point. Anyway, I'm going to get up to the station and get the ball rolling. You'll have company in a wee while. I'll have so many uniforms there they'll think it's a new training college.'

FIFTY-THREE

'Bruce, you in there?' I said, knocking on Hagan's door. No answer. It wasn't really surprising, since he had looked so washed out last night. I knocked again, calling out his name.

Nothing. I went back to my own room door round the corner and opened it. I went through the connecting door, knocking again.

'Bruce, it's Frank. You in there, mate?' I walked into the darkened bedroom and saw the bed was empty. The bathroom door was open and Hagan wasn't in there, but I switched the light on and looked in, just in case he was passed out in the tub. Empty.

Where the hell was he? I felt his bed sheet. It was cold.

I went back through my own room and up to Masters' room just as he was coming out with Suzy and Julie.

'Where's Steffi?' I asked.

'That's what we'd like to know,' Masters said.

'What do you mean?'

'She's gone,' Julie said. 'Her bed has been made and her clothes are gone. She's not here. I don't know where the hell she is.'

'Fuck. Hagan's gone too, although *his* room looks like it exploded. And it smells bad.'

'Suzy called Purcell,' Masters said. 'He's going to get Jeni Bridge to pull the operation and send reinforcements in here, but that's going to take time. I don't want to sit around and wait though. Let's see what these bastards have to say for themselves.' He was striding over to the lift.

I put a hand on his arm. 'Lloyd, let Julie and I go down to reception. Julie and Steffi are here under assumed names and they know me as a copper, so it would make sense for Julie – or Felicity as they know her – to come to me and ask if I'd seen her.'

'Right, good point. You go down with Julie first, then Suzy and I will come down to look for a bite to eat and we'll come across to you and ask if you've found your friend. Okay, Frank? Make it look like you're just a friend they made while they were here, and then you can casually ask where Hagan is.'

'Right. Julie, let's go.'

We took the lift down. At reception, the man who had checked in Masters and Suzy was still there.

'Can I help you?' he asked.

'I'd like to know what happened to my friend, Penny Blair,' Julie said. 'She's not in her room.'

'One moment.' His fingers skipped across the keyboard and then he looked at us. 'She checked out, ma'am.'

'Checked out? She didn't tell me. Did she pay for her room?'

'It says so right here. Under the explanations, it says she got a phone call saying she had to go back home.' He tapped the keyboard. 'And no, she didn't pay for her room. It says you'll pay for it. She did leave a message. *Felicity, I had to go home. My mum took ill. I'll pay you for the room when you get home. Penny.*'

'When did she go?' I asked.

'Last night.'

'How did she leave?'

'I believe one of the castle cars ran her up to the station.'

'Thank you for putting our minds at ease,' Julie said. 'I was worried when I saw her room was empty.'

'No problem, ma'am.'

Masters came out of the lift with Suzy and looked at me. 'Will you be joining us for breakfast?'

'Thank you. I'll be right through.' Masters smiled, but I could see the fire behind his eyes.

'I wanted to ask if you've seen my colleague, Bruce Hagan.' *Please don't tell me he left with Steffi or you and I are going to have a problem.*

'He was down earlier, sir, but he went away with Doctor Sharp.'

'I want to speak to Sharp.'

'I'll call and ask *Doctor* Sharp if he can see you.' He lowered his head as he spoke into the phone then hung up. 'He'll be able to see you in a little while, sir. Would you care for breakfast while you're waiting?'

'I'll be through in the dining room with my friends. Please direct him there if he comes through soon.'

'I will indeed, sir.'

I went through and was seated beside the other three.

'I ordered coffee for us. What did twinkle toes say about Hagan?'

'He saw him earlier, but Hagan is away with Sharp. I have a bad feeling about this, Lloyd.'

'Me too.' He looked around to make sure nobody was listening. 'We're going to have to do something today. We need to find Steffi, and I don't want to hang around.'

'Agreed. I'm going to have some cereal before we go.'

'I'm not hungry,' Julie said.

'Eat something,' I said. 'You don't want to feel sick later.'

'I feel sick now,' she said, but joined me at the self-serve table where little boxes of cereal were stacked. 'I feel responsible. I let her do this on her own.'

'Don't blame yourself for this. Neither of us knew what would happen. The idea was for *four* of us to be working as a team, and if Hagan had been honest, he wouldn't have been here.'

'You don't think she actually left, do you?'

'No, I don't. If you want my opinion, I think Steffi went exploring on her own and they caught her. Now we have to get a plan together and go look for her.'

We went back to the table. Masters and Suzy were eating toast and four cups of coffee had been brought.

'I'm going to get onto Ian Powers. He should have the schematics of this place by now,' Julie said.

'Where's your iPad?' I asked her.

She patted the outside of her bag that was lying at her feet.

Just then, Charles Sharp walked in, looking as if he didn't have a care in the world.

'Inspector Miller!' He walked over to our table and smiled. 'May I have a word with you in private?'

'Of course.' I stood up. 'If you'll excuse me,' I said to the others.

Sharp took me along to his office. 'Please, sit down.'

I sat opposite him. 'What's happened to my colleague?' I asked him.

Sharp sat with steepled fingers. 'I'm afraid he's had a little setback. As I said before, sometimes it's like trying to stem the dam with your finger. Once you pull your finger out, then there's the danger of the whole dam bursting. Bruce is at the stage where the dam has many cracks in it. He's about to burst. He's in the infirmary again.'

'I want to see him.'

'I can't let you do that, I'm afraid.'

I smiled what I hoped was my best *don't fuck with me* smile. 'I insist, doctor,' I said, leaning forward.

'You can insist all you like, Inspector. Bruce signed an agreement when you booked his trip here that should he need any medical attention, he gave permission for us to administer any attention he needed. That's what I'm doing. I have a medical doctor on staff, as well as nurses. He's being well looked after.'

I stood up. 'I want to see him.'

'Listen, you're an intelligent man. Your colleague is in a very fragile state of mind. Seeing you could drive him over the edge. Do you want to be responsible for that?' He smiled that sickening smile of his. 'When he's able to be transported, I will release him and you can take him back to Edinburgh.'

'I don't think I'll be leaving a very good review on Yelp, doctor.'

'As you wish.'

I left his office and went back upstairs. Julie was waiting near the lift.

'We're in Suzy's room,' she said, leading me in.

'What the hell was that all about? Steffi leaving of her own accord?' Suzy said, pacing the room. 'Her mother isn't ill, she died years ago. They didn't know that because the legend we had made for her gave her non-existent mother as next-of-kin.'

'Lloyd, we've got a big problem,' I said.

'Tell me about it, son. If they've fucking harmed her, I'll rip that doctor's nuts off.'

'Bruce is back in their infirmary again.'

'So what do you propose we do, sir?' Julie said to me.

'It's Frank while we're here, Julie, remember that. And I say, we go and find her. Suzy? Did Powers manage to get hold of the schematics?'

'He did. Believe it or not, this castle is hundreds of years old, but it was used during World War Two. There are old tunnels running underneath. Sometime during the war, they connected some of them, to make moving from the castle to some of the outbuildings a lot safer.'

'We were in the maintenance tunnels,' I said to Julie. 'That's where we'd been when you came in last night. Some of them are sewers.'

'I can see there are tunnels connecting the mansion house with the castle. There's also another officers' mess – a house in the woods – that connects to the castle.'

'What about this extension where we are right now? The rooms and the infirmary. Are they connected?'

She looked and moved her finger over the screen. 'Yes, they are. There's an old officers' quarters down at the bottom that is now connected to the base of this extension. A tunnel runs right underneath it and connects to the old house.'

'Was it built after Sharp bought the place, or was it already here?'

'Already here. The former castle owner had turned it into a hotel, and from what I can see that house attached to the base of this place was staff headquarters. However, when Sharp bought the place, he applied for planning permission to divide rooms in a couple of houses farther up the property. That wasn't that long ago. He's only been the owner for eighteen months.'

'How could he afford a place like this?' Julie asked. 'Where does he get his money?'

'I looked at his bio earlier, and it said his father was a Texan oil billionaire.'

'We need to get a plan together, people,' Masters said. 'Now, if this was one of my old army missions we'd go in under the cover of darkness. We could have a scout about first, get the lay of the land and take some photos with the phones, then compare them with the schematics. However, we don't have time for that. Percy might be sending the troops in, but we can't wait. We need to find out where they're keeping Steffi.'

'My guess would be in one of those houses. Far enough away to keep her out of sight, but close enough to keep an eye on her. I don't think he would be stupid enough to keep her in the mansion house.'

'Frank, what I want to know is, why did they take her in the first place?'

'I tracked Steffi's phone,' Suzy said. 'It just says it's in the castle.'

'We'll have to be careful today. They might still have extra security on, thinking they chased housebreakers last night,' I said.

'Okay, let's start moving,' Masters said. 'Suzy, you go with Frank. I'll go with Julie. We can take the south side while you two start at the north. We can meet up here in...' he looked at his watch, 'an hour's time.'

'Okay, everybody be careful. Make sure we have each other's phone numbers. We can send a text if we have to,' I said.

Masters nodded. 'Let's move out.'

FIFTY-FOUR

Chip Haines liked to jog. The older he got, the more important he thought it was to keep fit. He didn't know when his life was going to depend on it.

So every morning, he parked his car at the entrance to Cronomer Hill Park and jogged up the track, through the woods until he reached the fire tower at the top. It was a green, metal structure. Three short flights of stairs led to the first viewing platform, then another two to the top one. He ran up the five sets of stairs before starting his push-ups.

He was on his fourth set of ten when he heard the unmistakable sound of a diesel engine coming up the track.

A lot of people drove up here to go up the tower. It was a terrific spot for photographers, with views right over to the Stewart Air National Guard base and the Newburgh-Beacon Bridge. Bannerman Island lay dormant in the Hudson. The view was spectacular and Chip felt at peace up here. He had brought Ryan up here when he was a boy.

The thought filled him with sadness. Then anger at the thought of somebody touching his boy.

He jogged down the stairs. He'd run back down to Route 32 and then back up again. The noisy pickup truck sat idling.

The dirt road ran round the tower before connecting with the main track again. Chip ran round the bottom half of the circle. He couldn't see who was in the truck for the blacked-out windows. It wasn't moving at first, then it started to roll slowly.

Then suddenly it was going full speed.

The sudden movement took him by surprise, because it was coming right over the grass towards him. He tried dodging it, but it hit his leg before he had a chance to draw his gun. He was thrown through the air, landing on his back. He could feel his leg was broken, just by the angle it was at.

He screamed but there was nobody around to hear him.

The grey truck sat idling and then he heard the driver's door open. It was out of view, so he didn't see who got out.

He rolled onto his front, trying not to scream in pain. He tried to crawl away from the vehicle, not knowing what he was going to do when he reached the tree line.

He heard the boots on the grass behind him. He stopped crawling. His attacker was saying nothing. He struggled round to look. All he could focus on was the revolver. Black. Mean. Deadly.

Now he knew who had killed his son.

'Why?' he said.

The shot from the revolver was loud, the sound ringing out. So were the next five.

Four in the head, two in the heart.

Just to be sure.

Wendy Haines put her phone away. 'I can't get hold of Chip.' She sat back down on the bed. 'I don't want to buy Ryan clothes just so Chip can tell me our son wouldn't have liked them.'

The funeral director was waiting for Wendy to take some clothes along so her son could be dressed for the open casket viewing at his wake, but all the clothes had perished in the house fire.

'I can help you,' Samantha said. 'I mean, you did Ryan's laundry, so you know what he liked. But do you think he would want casual or a suit?'

'I think casual. Nice pants and a nice shirt, as if he was going to a family do but not too formal.' She couldn't believe this was happening. This sort of thing happened to other people not to people like her. Now she was talking about buying clothes for her dead son.

'Let's get some breakfast, then we'll go to Kohl's.'

'I'm not hungry. I feel sick.' Wendy took in a deep breath and let it out slowly. 'I wish to God Chip would answer his phone. I don't want to hear about it if I buy stuff and he doesn't approve. Cop or no cop, I swear I'll—'

'I'm sure he'll be fine, Wendy,' Jack said. 'I think he'll have more on his mind that day.'

They left the hotel and walked over to Jack's rental car. He looked around but there was no sign of the DEA guys.

They drove down 17K and along to Kohl's store next to PetSmart. The store sold clothes, bedding, and houseware. Jack dropped the two sisters off.

'I'll go up to where Chip's staying and see if I can talk to him,' he said. 'Or at least find out where he is if he's not home. I can call you and let you know what he says.'

'Okay, but be careful,' Samantha said. She leaned over the centre console and kissed him. 'I love you, Jack Miller.'

'I love you too.'

'Get a room,' Wendy said from the back, smiling. It was the first time she'd felt like smiling for the longest time.

The two women got out and went into the department store. Jack drove off, cutting back onto Route 300 and headed north. He wanted to know why Chip had called him earlier, wanting to talk to him. Wendy's husband had apologised for his behaviour and wanted to talk.

Fifteen minutes later, he was pulling up outside the house where Chip was now living. With his girlfriend. He shook his head. Some men didn't know how lucky they had it, and then they threw it all away.

He walked up to the front door and rang the bell. The girlfriend answered. She was dressed in a tracksuit and her hair was still wet as if she'd just stepped out of the shower.

'Hi, my name is—'

'I know who you are, Jack. Come in.'

He stepped in and Lois closed the door behind him. 'I was looking for Chip.'

'He goes jogging every morning. Some park. Would you like a coffee?'

'That would be great, thank you.'

They went into the kitchen and Lois turned the coffee pot on. 'So why don't you ask me, Jack?'

'Ask you what?'

'What everybody else asks. Why did I take Chip away from his wife?'

'I'm not here to ask you anything like that. I just wanted to let Chip know Wendy was trying to get hold of him. She wants to know what she should buy for her son to be dressed in for his funeral.'

Lois shook her head. 'I'm sorry the way things worked out, but the truth is, Chip and Wendy were already finished. Chip came to me, not the other way around. We work together and he started to confide in me, and then one thing led to another. By his accounts, his marriage had already failed.'

'You don't have to explain to me what's going on. I'm only here to support Samantha.'

'Okay.' She poured two cups of coffee and added milk. 'I have to go finish drying my hair. I won't be long.'

'Can I use your bathroom?'

'Sure. Down the hall on the left.' She walked away and went into her bedroom. Jack turned right and went down the hall. Opened the door on the left. Into the garage. Had she meant he should have turned left out of the kitchen? It would seem so.

The garage was a double affair, and in darkness, but some of the light from the open doorway shone onto the side of a vehicle next to Lois' Honda CR-V.

Jack reached in and hit the light switch. There were two steps that led down into the garage. He stepped down and looked at the big, grey pickup truck. A Dodge. With damage on the side.

He heard the hammer of the revolver being pulled back before he heard Lois approach.

'Find what you were looking for, Jack?'

FIFTY-FIVE

Purcell had only just ended the call with Suzy when his phone rang.

'DI Lester from Glasgow, looking for Superintendent Purcell.'

'Speaking.'

'Sir, I've been to a crime scene here in the West End. A woman who works in a nursing home killed two of her patients before getting into a boiling bath. She died an hour ago.'

'Okay.'

'You see, I thought it was similar to a couple of cases you recently had in Edinburgh; the guy who killed his boss and jumped off the roof. And the woman who set fire to the hotel.'

'It does sound similar, right enough.' Purcell sat up straighter. 'What do you know about this woman?'

'Well, she's fifty-nine, lives alone. A spinster. The thing is, although she could be a battle axe at times with other members of staff, she pretty much kept to herself.'

'Did she have problems with any of the patients?'

'No, but she did have a problem with a man who wanted to

give her... *attention*, a while back, according to the staff nurse who runs the wards.'

'Maybe she was depressed?'

'By all accounts, she seemed chipper enough this morning, apart from finding out she had been moved onto another level in the home. But she was just back from a wellness centre up north and she seemed okay.'

'Wait. What did you say?'

'She was at a wellness centre.'

'Do you know the name of this place?'

'Hold on.' Purcell heard the other detective flipping through a notebook. '*Paradise Shores.*'

'Christ. Do you know when she was there?'

'She was there for a week. Came back yesterday.'

'Thanks, Inspector.' He hung up and dialled Suzy's number, but there was no answer.

He got up and left his office. He had to make sure Jeni Bridge knew Suzy and the others were in danger.

Jeni was doing paperwork when Purcell knocked and entered.

'Come in, Percy. You look like you just found out the Nigerian King really doesn't have any money.'

'This is serious, ma'am.'

'Sit down. Tell me what's going on.'

'The operation has gone pear-shaped.'

'Okay, explain.'

'Steffi's gone missing from the castle. Hagan too. We need to pull this operation now and get people in there.'

'Okay, agreed. You did have a contingency plan in place, I assume?'

'I did. I'm going to enact it now. We have uniforms in reserve. The first lot are in Inverness. Actually, the first few were in Golspie itself, but that sergeant is worse than useless. I already made the call for the men to move from Inverness. Aberdeen too.'

'Good. I'll get onto the chief constable, keep him informed. I'll take any flack for this. He won't give me a hard time.'

'I wouldn't be too sure, ma'am.'

'Oh, I'm confident of it, Percy. He's not only my ex-boss, he's my ex-husband.' She smiled at him. 'Trust me, he won't give me the run-around. If he knows what's good for him.'

FIFTY-SIX

'No, actually, I didn't. I *was* looking for the toilet,' Jack said.

'Don't be a wiseass.'

'Seriously, I was. I just came in the wrong door. I didn't know this was the garage.'

Lois laughed. 'And to think you're going to die because you went the wrong way in my house.'

Jack kept his hands in view, not wanting to make her skittish. Her being a cop, he had no doubt she had fast reflexes.

'I didn't for one second suspect you had killed Ryan.'

'It was a pity. He was such a good boy. But he had to butt his nose in where it wasn't wanted.'

'What did he do that was so awful?'

Lois smiled but there was no humour there. 'I tried to befriend him. He knew me from way back. He'd met me several times in the past, just another colleague of his dad's. So it wasn't like I was a stranger. Then he started getting all annoyed because his dad left his mum for me. Jesus, it wasn't like he was a little boy. He was twenty-one, or something.'

'He was his mum's boy, Lois. She lost her little boy.'

'I could have lived with that, I really could have, but he had to go and take it one step further.'

'What do you mean?' He made to step up to her level, but she waved the revolver at him.

'Don't. I'm a cop. I'll shoot you dead long before you make it up here.'

'I'm not going to move. Besides, you have the advantage. I'm two steps down in the garage and you're standing over me in the hall. How can I fight that?'

'That's right. I could shoot you dead before you even got close to me.'

'You don't want to do that.'

'Why don't I?'

'Right now, you could say you accidentally hit our car with your truck. You got scared and ran. What will happen to you? A slap on the wrist? If you shoot me that's murder.'

'You don't get it, do you? I've already committed two murders.'

'What?'

'I killed Ryan. The little spoiled bastard took something that belonged to me and he wouldn't give it back. Then I told him I'd kill his mother and make him watch. So he told me it was hidden in the garage where they all hung out. I drove him over there, but the others were there. I drove him back home. I went into their garage when nobody was there, and I couldn't find what he had taken from me. I went back to his house, pretending to like him, then I overpowered him and injected him with Fentanyl-laced heroin. Fatal overdose. He'd been drinking so he was easy to overpower. Little bastard. But before he died, he told me he was lying, that he'd hidden my stuff in his house.'

'Let me guess, he was lying again so after you destroyed the inside of his car, you torched the house.'

'You guess correctly. I found the stuff up in their attic, but I wanted to cover my tracks.'

'What are we talking about here? Drugs? Money?'

'Both. I've been dealing to a list of users for a long time now. Not around here, but over in Duchess County. Where nobody knows I'm a cop.'

'So you and Chip are drug dealers.'

'No, Chip knew nothing about it. That's why Ryan took my stuff. He said he would give it back to me if I broke up with his father. Chip would have been so pissed at me for doing the drugs, but I was putting the money away for us so we could retire in a few years. Go to Florida and start a new life.'

'I don't believe Chip didn't know.'

'I don't care what you believe. It's no skin off my nose. However, he was going to talk to the chief after his morning jog this morning. Tell the chief he suspected his son was murdered. Christ, he would have had that asshole Chris Nolan snooping about here. Nolan's a good detective. He would have sniffed out something. I think he suspects Ryan was murdered, but the autopsy report says otherwise. For now. So I had to take care of Chip.'

'What do you mean?'

'I shot him up on Cronomer Hill, near the fire tower. I couldn't risk him going to the chief. Believe me, it was a hard decision, but I had to do it. I shot him with this very gun. The one I'm going to kill you with. Then I'm going to take you in that pickup and drive you far away and bury you. Then I'll bring the truck back and burn it somewhere.'

Jack laughed. 'You've got it all figured out, haven't you?'

'I'm glad you find it all so amusing.' She smiled back at him, as if the two of them were old friends talking about meeting up for coffee. 'I have to say, I think you're very brave. I know the police in

Scotland don't carry guns, so you didn't face them on a daily basis.'

'I'm Scottish. We're tougher than we look.'

'Well, tough guy, it's time for you to say goodbye.'

The doorbell rang.

'Move and you're dead.'

There was enough distance between them for her to turn her head quickly towards the front door, along the hallway. She turned back to face Jack. 'I guess they got bored—'

The door breacher was an expert. The hinges of the front door were blown to pieces just as the teargas canisters were thrown in. Next to the garage door was a bedroom. The window exploded inwards and more teargas came in.

It was when the front door was being blown in that Jack moved, knowing he had mere seconds to act. He threw himself over the bonnet of the small Honda, landing between the car and the pickup.

Lois was a police officer, and she knew the team leader of the department's SWAT team, but she had never trained to be one.

As the entrance was breached, her mind registered Jack moving, but then she didn't recognise him as a threat. No, *that* was coming from the front door. As she swung the revolver back, the teargas canisters exploding in the bedroom was just enough of a distraction.

It took her by surprise for a second, all the time the front SWAT officer needed. They were shouting warnings, but Lois knew her time was up. Prison? For a cop? Not for her. The gun wasn't pointed at the men in the dark blue tactical gear, but she started to swing it towards them, knowing they wouldn't have a choice.

Her finger was squeezing the trigger just in case they were in any doubt whether she would use it or not, but none of the rounds went even close to the first policemen.

The leader was shouting an order for her to drop it, his finger caressing the trigger of the M16. He saw the woman turn, saw the gun, issued the warning, but having been a Marine in Iraq, his reflexes were beyond sharp. His mind was perfectly focused on the woman and saw she wasn't going down without a fight.

He fired three rapid shots into her chest, throwing her backwards.

The next man was carrying the heavy tactical shield and ran forward, his sidearm out, ready to put her down if she moved.

Lois was dead.

'Police!' he shouted. 'Come out with your hands where I can see them!'

Jack's hands were the first thing above the Honda as he slowly stood up.

Chris Nolan came in behind them. 'Stand down, guys! I know him.' He looked at Jack. 'Anybody else in the garage?'

'Not that I know of.'

'Right, get in and sweep it.'

The three SWAT members searched the garage while the rest of the house was being searched. Jack heard them shouting *Clear!* as each room was confirmed empty.

'Put your hands behind your back.'

'No problem, but take my phone out of my jacket pocket. She told me everything. She even told me she killed Chip Haines. Up—'

'We know,' Nolan said, cuffing him. 'Somebody found him and called it in. He'd already spoken to the chief early this morning, and told us his thoughts about Lois. He was suspicious of her.' He led Jack outside and took his phone out of his pocket. The recording was still running. He stopped it and played it.

They went outside, through the dissipating teargas. The white, ex-military armoured vehicle sat growling at the kerb, surrounded by police cruisers and unmarked cars.

One of the assistant DAs came up. Nolan introduced Jack without taking his cuffs off.

'What brings you here, Mr Miller?'

'Chip not only called the chief this morning, he called me. He wanted me to come over and have a chat. Lois was going to be out. She obviously had other ideas. I just happened to go looking for the bathroom and went into the garage by mistake. She found me and thought I was snooping.'

The DA nodded.

'I know Mr Miller, sir. He's related to Chip's wife.'

'Okay, take his cuffs off. We'll need a statement from you. Detective Nolan, I'd like you to inform Mrs Haines of her husband's passing, and make sure she knows she will get all the help she needs.'

'Will do.' He took Jack's cuffs off.

'And you, Mr Miller, nearly blew this operation out of the water. If we hadn't been sitting here, waiting to go in, God knows what would have happened to you.'

'Believe me, it took me by surprise when Lois answered the door, and I don't get surprised easily.'

The DA walked away to go and talk to the lieutenant who was standing talking with some uniforms.

'She was ruthless. I suspect those DEA guys had an idea about her,' Nolan said.

'If they did, you'll probably never know.'

'We'll get you along to the station now.' Nolan looked at him. 'My grandfather was Scottish. He wasn't right in the head either.'

FIFTY-SEVEN

Steffi Walker lay in the room on the hard bed, the bright lights seemingly blinding her. She had woken up earlier but couldn't even think straight. Now she was wide awake but her head felt as if she'd been out drinking all night.

She tried to focus her thoughts. Where was she? In a room of some sort. A windowless room. The bed was the only form of furniture in here.

She looked at her wrist, but her watch was gone. There were no clocks in here either, so she didn't know if it was day or night. Then she saw the camera watching her from its position in the corner, high up and out of reach.

A few minutes later, the door opened.

'Ah, sleeping beauty awakes,' the man said as he came in.

'Where the fuck am I?'

'Oh, did you get out of bed on the wrong side?'

Steffi stood up and immediately regretted it. Her head spun, and she felt her legs give out. Two more men came into the room and caught her by the arms.

'Don't worry, the effect will wear off,' Doctor Solomon said. 'It was nothing that will have any lasting effects. Just something that made you sleep.'

The men held on until the room stopped spinning. 'I'm fine,' she said, shrugging them off.

'Let's go and get you some coffee, Miss Blair. Or should I call you Miss Walker?'

'You know who I am?' she said, as she followed him out into a short corridor.

'Of course we do. But before we go any further, please realise there is no point in you fighting us; this place is locked down tighter than a maximum security prison.'

They went through a set of doors into a canteen. Several other people were sitting at tables, eating breakfast. The food smelled good.

'Who...?'

'Are these people? They work here. Doctor Sharp was heir to his father's fortune. He pays these people a lot of money to work here. And I mean *a lot*. So, no, they're not being held here, and no, they won't help you escape.'

They walked up to the line and waited behind some other people, who were all wearing lab coats, and waited their turn to be served. The security men were still behind her.

'You guys can go. I don't think Miss Walker is going anywhere.' He smiled at her. 'I should say, *Officer* Walker though, shouldn't I?'

'If you know who I am, why didn't you just kill me?'

Solomon made a face. 'Because we're not animals, Steffi. You don't mind if I call you Steffi, do you?'

'Do what you like.' She was starting to feel really hungry now. She ordered a fried breakfast, and took orange juice and a coffee.

'You see, after we found you down here, we took your prints

from your room and got somebody to run them. And guess what? You're in the Police Scotland database. Not as a crook though. We have specialists who can access any system.'

Solomon took a cup of coffee. No money changed hands. They sat at a table away from the other workers.

'What is this place?' Steffi asked.

'This is where we work. Private work for Doctor Sharp and his wife.'

'What sort of work?'

Solomon drank some of his coffee and smiled. 'You know, I've been told to look after you, and make sure no harm comes to you. After this, you'll be transported back to Edinburgh by some members of our team, and you'll be put into your own home. I promise you no harm will come to you.'

'So you know I'm a police officer and you've abducted me. That's jail time.'

'Let me tell you something, you'll be given something that will erase all memory of this. You might dream it one day, but that's all it will appear as, a dream. I'll tell you anything you like, because I know you'll have no memory of it afterwards. And again, I promise you, there will be no after-effects, even though the stuff we make here is similar to Rohypnol.'

She was about to say something when he held up a hand. 'Two women from the lab will be travelling with your security detail. Just to put your mind at ease. They will be the ones who put you to bed at home, not the men. As I said, we're not animals.'

So, what sort of work do you do here?' she asked again as she drank some of the orange juice.

'Research work. Of a kind.'

'Come on. Research work in the bowels of a Scottish castle? Is this some kind of horror movie?'

Solomon kept on smiling. 'As you can tell, my accent is

English. I used to work at Porton Down. For the British Government. And if you think this place is secret, well, let me just say this, if you were caught in there, you wouldn't be having breakfast afterwards.'

Steffi felt the room spin for a moment and her eyes went slightly out of focus. She gripped the table and everybody around her carried on as if nothing happened. Nobody looked in her direction.

'Jesus, you spiked the orange juice.'

Solomon laughed. Took hold of her glass and drank some of the orange. 'No.'

'Then why am I feeling this way?' Then it passed as quickly as it had started.

'The stuff we gave you last night will remain in your system for twenty-four hours. We'll give you an additive in a little while, which will work in conjunction with what we already gave you, and you'll go to sleep. When you're home, we'll give you a counter measure, then you'll wake up normally a couple of hours later.'

'Just like you gave the additive to Steven Hubbard and Mel Carpenter? That worked out well for them.'

'They were given a trial dose of a new drug we were working on for Huntington's disease. That was a very different scenario.'

'How do I know you're not just saying this and you're not really going to give me the same as them?'

'You won't remember either way, but I can assure you we have other subjects who are on different trial drugs. You're not one of them. We know what we're doing here, Steffi. We don't want to harm you, but it's very important our work is kept secret.'

'You work for the government.' She lifted her coffee cup, but before she drank some, she lifted her eyebrows in question. Solomon shook his head. Apparently the coffee wasn't poisoned either. She decided to risk it as her mouth was dry.

'No, Doctor Sharp finances this place all on his own.'

'Why? So he can produce some chemical agent to sell to the government to be used on a foreign country?'

'Dear, oh dear, you are very sceptical, aren't you? No, Steffi, this is something far less complicated. Charles and Melissa Sharp have a daughter, who is twenty-nine years old. She's had Huntington's disease for ten years now. Doctor Sharp has been trying to find a solution that might slow down the progression. Hell, maybe we'll even find a cure.'

'So all these people here are scientists working on drugs?'

'In a nutshell.'

She laid her fork down. 'Apart from being illegal, it's highly unethical.'

'Doctor Sharp and his wife are extremely worried about losing their daughter.'

'I'm sure all of the parents of Huntington's patients are.'

'Are you a mother?'

'No.'

'Then you wouldn't understand.' He drank more coffee. 'Don't you see, Steffi? If we make a breakthrough here, then it can be used worldwide. Other sufferers can benefit from it. There are medications to try to alleviate chorea – that's the involuntary jerking and writhing movements patients suffer from – and there are antidepressants, anti-psychotic drugs, mood stabilising drugs, but those only alleviate the symptoms. We're trying for a cure.'

'Are you close to finding a cure?'

'We thought we were. But there was something not quite right with the dosage. It affected their daughter and made her look like an old woman. Her skin started to peel, amongst other things. We think we're on the verge of a massive breakthrough though.'

'So you're experimenting on your guests here without them knowing?'

'It's the quickest way to get results.'

'But these people don't have Huntington's I assume.'

'The drugs we test are trying to alter a gene that's already defective. To counteract depression. That's one of the symptoms of the disease. Almost ten per cent of sufferers kill themselves because the disease causes their mood to go downhill. We're trying to alter that. To give them a longer life.'

'Yet, a couple of the people you gave it to killed other people before killing themselves.'

Solomon nodded. 'We're rushing things, and sometimes when you do that, there are unforeseen complications.'

Steffi drank more coffee. 'If Sharp gets caught, he'll go to prison.'

'He won't get caught.'

'Money talks, right?'

'It does indeed. As Sergeant McTavish would testify to.'

'What about Bruce?'

'Ah, Mr Hagan. Madder than a March hare. It's sad really, but Doctor Sharp wants him out of here as soon as. There's nothing we can do for him here. He needs to be admitted into a specialist care centre.'

'A psychiatric hospital.'

'Indeed. There's no returning to duty for him for the foreseeable future. I'm not a psychologist like Doctor Sharp, but even I can see how troubled Bruce is. It's a wonder he can even function in day-to-day life. However, he's very good at concealing his illness.'

She continued her breakfast while Solomon watched in silence.

FIFTY-EIGHT

Charles Sharp walked along the road to his house, under the canopy of trees. His heart was heavy. Mama was getting worse every day, and nothing they had tried so far was alleviating the pain. God knows, they had done everything money could buy.

Their housekeeper was standing at the front door waiting for him. 'Mrs Sharp is waiting for you in the room, doctor,' she said. She always called Melissa *Mrs* even though his wife was a doctor too.

'Thank you.'

The house was warm, kept at a steady seventy degrees. He walked towards the grand staircase, then past it, stopping at the door under it. He opened it and walked down the stairs, making sure the door was closed behind him. And locked. It went down to the next level, where he turned right and headed towards the back of the house. Towards the maintenance entrance.

Then he turned left and walked along to the end of the corridor, where he unlocked another door. On the other side, was a large room.

Melissa Sharp was sitting in a chair next to another woman in a wheelchair.

Mama.

Their daughter.

She was called April, but the only word she had ever spoken for years was *Mama*, and that was her nickname. Well, *April* couldn't speak. The other one could, the thing living inside her. He couldn't remember the last time he'd called her by her real name.

'Hello, darling,' he said, coming into the room. Mama looked at him.

'How is Solomon coming along with the last batch?'

'He thinks this one will be better. His tech said they had altered it and it should be less potent.'

Charles could see a sudden switch in his wife's demeanour as she stood up. 'Really? Well, I beg to differ. Have you seen the news this morning?'

'No, I haven't had the chance—'

'The woman, Mabel?'

'What about her?'

'Your other guinea pig? She just killed two of her patients before killing herself. She lowered herself into a boiling bath.'

Charles hung his head. This couldn't be happening. This was supposed to be less potent than the last lot.

Melissa grabbed him by the lapels. 'You promised me! You told me my baby would be alright!'

'I thought she would be.'

'Look at her! She's like a ninety-year-old woman!'

'It just dried her skin that's all. And her hair just needs to be cut again. It's her mind we have the real problems with.'

'She got out, remember? Miller saw her. And he's a fucking

cop! You didn't lock the door again, and she got into the sewer. Luckily we got to Miller in time.'

'He's none the wiser. He thinks he tripped and fell down the stairs. He'll have dreamt he saw Mama.'

Melissa let him go.

'It's getting out of hand! We need to stop this nonsense and just go back to the States.'

'We've invested too much here.'

'It's bricks and mortar. You can afford to take a hit on it.'

'I don't mean this!' He swept his arm around. 'I mean invested in our daughter! I was lucky to find Solomon. We're knocking on the door. We've already slowed down the process. I won't stop until we can be sure it can be reversed.'

'It might never happen. You might be able to throw money at the best people, but nothing is guaranteed.'

'I won't stop! I refuse. I love her with every fibre of my being! And her condition is my speciality!'

Mama stood up from the wheelchair. 'Well, well, Doctor fucking Sharp,' she said, her teeth gritted.

Charles looked at his wife. 'Didn't you give her the meds this morning?'

'Shit. No, I forgot. It was seeing the story about that woman on the news—'

'Don't make excuses! She should have had her meds!'

Melissa turned to look at her daughter. 'Mama, sit down. Everything is going to be alright.'

'My name's April, you dumb fuck. Or can't you remember that?'

'Go and get my medical kit,' Sharp said to his wife in a low voice.

'April, honey, just let Daddy get you back into your chair.'

'*April, honey,*' she repeated in a mocking voice. Her face sneered, but it was her eyes that caught Sharp's attention. They were so focused, like laser beams, and he felt an excitement buzz through him. This was it! This was what they had been fighting for all this time! His team were on the verge of a breakthrough, just as Solomon had said. Now they just needed to tweak it, to add a suppressant to deal with the rage. Hell, the FDA wouldn't approve it just now, but with proper trials—

'Here!' his wife screamed, just as April launched herself at Sharp.

His reflexes were good, his wife's not so much. April grabbed her mother's hair and smashed her head against the wall. Again and again. Sharp grabbed hold of her.

She fought him off, pushing him against his wife and they both fell down.

Then she ran. She knew the way. After all, she'd been out and about often enough. She opened the door leading down to the tunnel, the one her parents thought was locked. She could run fast down here. The people who were wearing the black masks the other night had climbed up through the sewer maintenance pipe. She had watched them do it. If they'd only carried on round when they were down there, they would have come in here.

Now she raced down the stairs, into the tunnel, and ran as fast as she could.

Where she knew she would be safe.

FIFTY-NINE

We went downstairs. There were a lot of people milling about. I saw men in dark suits with walkie-talkies trying to corral them along to the lounge while others were trying to get them into the restaurant.

'What's going on?' I said to one of the apes.

'Just get along to the lounge, sir,' he said.

'He asked you what was going on,' Masters said.

'Listen, grandpa, shut your fucking mouth and get along to the lounge like a good boy.'

'They're closing the front door, Lloyd.' I turned to the two women. 'Go now.'

I briefly saw them turn and go into the hallway that led to the maintenance door. Whatever was happening, it was good cover. The fire alarm hadn't gone off and if it had, they would be getting people out, not ushering them farther into the building.

Masters gave the suit a look before we both fought our way through the crowd to the front door. There stood a couple more suits with the concierge.

'We need to get out,' I said to the first one.

'We're on lockdown. Nobody in or out.'

'Move your arse, sunshine,' Masters said.

'Going to make me?'

Just then I saw the blue flashing lights through the glass in the front door. I could see them through the trees, but the patrol car wasn't coming this way.

I nudged Masters and he looked. Then he decided no more words were going to be spoken to the suits. He moved forward, stepping slightly sideways, and hit the first suit with the heel of his hand, right in the guts.

The suit doubled over as air exploded out of his mouth and he fell to his knees. I didn't use as much finesse as Masters on the second suit. I hit him on the chin with the palm of my right hand and stuck my leg out, making him fall away from the door.

'Get that fucking door open,' Masters said to the concierge, bringing out his warrant card.

'Going to arrest me?' he said with a sneer.

Masters grabbed him by the hair, a lesson he'd learned in the SAS; *control their hair, control them*. He grabbed, twisted and pulled all in one fluid movement. The concierge tried grabbing Masters' hand to no avail, and the next thing he knew, he was on his knees, squealing.

'Keys,' was all Masters said.

The concierge's free hand gave him the keys, which Masters then handed to me and I unlocked the front door, putting the keys in my pocket.

Masters let his hair go after I opened the door.

We ran out into the cold morning and I saw the blue flashers drive past the far end of the car park. It was heading for the mansion house.

We ran over the gravel, our boots crunching the small stones.

At the other end, we continued along the track towards Sharp's house. The patrol car stopped in front of the mansion house and Sergeant McTavish and another uniform stepped out.

They rushed into the house, let in by the housekeeper.

I ran up just as she was about to close the front door. I brought my warrant card out. 'Police. What's going on here?'

Masters was right behind me.

'It's awful. Miss April has got out. You need to find her!' She didn't know we weren't with McTavish.

Masters and I brushed past her and I caught a glimpse of the uniform disappearing through the doorway under the stairs. We ran down and as we entered the basement, McTavish turned to look at me.

'You again!' he said, his face turning almost as red as his beard. 'Get out of here! This is none of your business.'

'Shut the fuck up,' Masters said.

'What did you say to me?' McTavish stepped forward.

'Superintendent Lloyd Masters,' he said, showing his warrant card. 'Stand down, sergeant. Tell me what's going on here.'

'Don't say a word, sergeant,' Sharp said.

'Charles!' his wife screamed. 'Don't be doing this right now! Help them find April!'

'Who's April?' I asked, but I had a feeling I already knew; the female whose face I'd seen in the basement window.

'It's our daughter. She's off her meds. She needs help!' Melissa Sharp said, as her husband stood dumbstruck.

'Where did she go?' I asked her. 'Down the sewers again?'

'Yes. Where you saw her the other night. I'm sorry for what we did to you, Frank, but we were only trying to protect her.'

I took a step closer to Sharp. 'It's over now, doctor. We want to know what you've done with our officer, Steffi Walker.'

Sharp looked at his wife.

'Tell them!' she said. 'I told you it was wrong taking a goddamn police officer, for Christ's sake.'

'I didn't know she was a police officer until it was too late!' He shouted back at her.

'Just tell them. You're the one who knows.'

Sharp's shoulders slumped. 'This house is connected to a staff house down the hill, by a tunnel. That tunnel also goes under the castle—'

'Which is connected to the house at the other end of the castle,' I said, finishing his sentence.

'What's along there?' Masters said.

'I thought it was the cure for my daughter,' Sharp said.

'Is that where Steffi is?' Masters asked.

'Yes.'

'If she's harmed in any way...'

'She's fine. We just gave her something to make her sleep. She's having breakfast right now. We were going to take her to Edinburgh and put her back in her apartment. No harm done.'

'What about Bruce?' I asked.

'He was in the infirmary, as I said, but we didn't want him scaring the other patients, if we had to bring any in. So he's down beside Miss Walker. He really is gone in the head. He needs to be in an asylum.'

'McTavish, take the doctor and his wife upstairs and call for backup,' Masters said.

Grudgingly, the bearded sergeant took the two Americans upstairs, with help from the uniform. We went looking for Steffi.

SIXTY

The nurse looked through the viewing port into the room before having her young assistant unlock the door. She saw the man Hagan lying on the bed, his eyes closed and his mouth open. He was very pale looking, and at first she thought he might be dead, but then she watched his chest and saw it rise and fall.

Just sleeping.

She was on the team that was overseen by Doctor Solomon. One of his trusted staff members.

Pushing the door open, she walked in. She was particularly happy this morning; this was her last day before going on holiday for a week. Her husband didn't get off very often, and now their son was away at university in England, they wanted to enjoy their time together.

A week in Tenerife would be just the ticket. Away from the cold, miserable Scottish weather. And now she worked here full time, paying for everything was a breeze.

'Well, well, we are Mr Sleepyhead this morning,' she said.

'Looks like I won't have to have an orderly come in and hold you down while I inject you with this medicine.'

She put the tray on the small side table and picked up the syringe, holding it up to the light and depressing the plunger a little until a squirt of the liquid popped out.

'Now, this isn't going to hurt you one little bit,' she said in a low voice.

'No, but it's going to fucking hurt you!' Bruce Hagan said. He sat up, fully awake, and grabbed the syringe out of the nurse's hand, gripping her wrist with his other hand.

She screamed but was powerless to do anything about the attack. Hagan pulled her down onto the bed, rammed the needle through her left eye, and depressed the plunger, pushing down harder onto the syringe until her eye popped.

Her body went into its death throes as Hagan threw her down onto the floor. The assistant was screaming and was so shocked she was rooted to the spot. There was nobody to help them. This part of the lab was soundproofed, to keep the screams from disturbing the lab staff.

As she saw Hagan get up out of the bed, she found she could move, and then she was running towards the door.

Then she heard the running footsteps from behind her. Hagan was fast and on her before she could even get the door open. He pulled her hair back, grabbed her by the chin, and twisted her head fast. The sound of her neck snapping would be unmistakable to anybody who heard it.

Hagan calmly opened the door.

When he opened the door, a young female assistant was walking by, but Hagan simply strode past her. When she looked in and saw her dead colleague, she ran screaming in the opposite direction and hit one of the alarms that were on the wall.

'Enjoy?' Solomon asked, smiling.

'As a hostage breakfast goes, it was pretty good, thanks.'

'You're a guest here, Miss Walker.'

'So I can leave here any time I want to.'

'Of course you can. Under escort.'

She wiped her mouth with a napkin, threw it down on the plate, and finished her coffee. 'So what is that other kitchen, through in the house where I came in? If everybody eats here?'

'That's if they're working late and feel like putting a pot of coffee on.'

'What about the other house on the other side of the castle? Below the mansion?'

'That's sleeping accommodation. They're brought back and forth in one of our Land Rovers, like a shuttle.'

Steffi sat and looked at the man, imagining he was across from her in an interview room. Which he would be, one day. If she had her way. She couldn't believe she wasn't going to remember any of this. If he had *his* way.

Solomon looked at his watch. 'Almost time to go.'

'What if I don't want to go?'

'Look, Steffi, you don't want to make this hard on yourself. If you say no, then some men will come here like they did last night, and hold you down again. I don't want you to get hurt.'

She could see he genuinely meant it, but it was hard to just let somebody inject you with something.

'I'm scared, Doctor Solomon.' Let him think she *was* scared.

'You don't have to be. We know what we're doing.'

And in that second, Steffi saw for herself they clearly *didn't* know what they were doing.

The alarm went off.

Solomon jumped to his feet. She expected him to shout *fire!* but he didn't. Instead, he shouted 'Fuck me, he's got out!'

Which didn't exude confidence.

Others started to get to their feet quickly.

She jumped up too, her head spinning for a second, but it passed and she followed Solomon to the cafeteria entrance and looked out. Then she saw a man running up the corridor towards them, and one of the lab workers stood in his path.

Bruce Hagan punched the man in the face, shattering his jaw, and carried on as if he hadn't even been in his way. Solomon tried to grab him, but Hagan shoved him, and Solomon went flying onto his back.

'Bruce!' Steffi shouted.

Hagan looked at her for a second, without stopping, but there was no recognition. He carried on running. She took off after him.

He got through a set of doors at the end of the corridor. Turned back to look at her. Then he hit the big, red emergency button that a staff member could hit to stop any patient from escaping.

Steffi reached the doors and grabbed the handles, but the doors wouldn't budge.

Hagan looked through the glass at her. Then, just for a split-second, his eyebrows knitted, as if he were thinking, *Where are we?* then he turned and ran.

Solomon was running behind her. 'They won't open without a staff member overriding the locking mechanism,' he said to her. 'Security's on it now.'

He seemed to have forgotten all about why she was here.

The doors clicked as they were remotely unlocked. Steffi stepped into the corridor leading down to where she had come in the night before.

Hagan was gone. Solomon went after him. Steffi saw her chance, and ran.

SIXTY-ONE

Mama was free! Free to run! Although she hated that name. *My name's April!* she had wanted to scream at them all those times.

Now she was out on her own again, running free along the tunnels. She wanted to run around the castle. It wasn't fair that other people got to play there and not her. Today, she was going to play whether they wanted her to or not.

She didn't have a light, but her eyes could make out the shapes in the tunnels, and she knew them like the back of her hand. Her feet slapped the cold, hard stone, but it felt good underfoot.

Round she went until she came to the area they used for storage. All the little rooms, and nooks and crannies. And the windows. Dirty, but they let the light through. She came here often, just to look out. Below here were the old pipes, but she didn't like it down there. The walls had no windows in them.

She walked along to the very end, past the old door that wouldn't open. She knew the other people were through there. She had put her ear to the door one day and heard them. Never mind, she knew another way into the castle.

She'd been there one time, and it had been fun. And scary. But she wanted to go there again. She felt an energy driving her she had never felt before. And her movements weren't erratic as they sometimes were. And the fog that was in her brain wasn't there anymore.

At the end, there was a door that opened up into the sky. There was nothing there but open air. She didn't like that. But there was a big door in the ceiling. A steel beam was on the ceiling and it stopped just before the door.

She jumped up and grabbed onto it, pulling herself up. There was a hatch in the door. She pushed on it and it swung upwards. It led into a small, dark room. It had been a large room at one time, but they had put up a wall and a door. It was through this door that she went into the castle itself.

She opened the door carefully. She couldn't hear any voices. Maybe her dad had asked everybody to leave so she could come and play.

This place was a kitchen like they had at the house, but much bigger. Look at all the shiny stuff! she thought, gliding a hand across a stainless steel work surface. *And look at the pots and pans.* She had seen people in kitchens like this, but they always wore white. Not like she was dressed, in an old black dress.

She knew how all of this worked. Especially the cooker. She played with the knobs, turning them one way, then the other way. Pushing another button, one of the rings burst into life. She clapped her hands and watched the orange flame turn blue. She loved to watch the flames dance. She made it dance with the knob. Then it went out. She turned them but couldn't get the blue one to come back.

April walked away in frustration. Leaving the kitchen, she walked through to the lounge. It was empty. It was so quiet! She loved the peace and quiet. Then she came to the bar. Walking behind it, she ran her hand along the smooth wood. Her other hand was running along the back counter and caught a bottle of spirits, knocking it to the floor, causing it to smash.

She yelped and jumped, careful where she stood. She didn't want her shoes getting wet. Looking under the counter, she saw them, matches. Her eyes went wide. She loved the little sticks that exploded at the end before settling down to a little ball of orange. She took some of the books of matches and scattered them on the bar top. Then she opened one and took out one of the little paper sticks and struck it. She laughed as the flame appeared. She held it to the others. They all exploded at once! This was so much fun. Then the flames burnt her fingers and she threw it down.

It landed near the spilt alcohol and before she knew it, more flames were appearing, getting bigger and bigger.

This was so much fun! She wanted to see more. The bottles made fire! She started throwing them all over, watching them smash into a million pieces. She struck more matches and threw them down, making more flames.

She ran from behind the bar as the flames started licking at the wood. Then bottles started exploding! She couldn't remember when she had been so happy. Then the curtains at the windows began to burn. More orange flames. This was spectacular.

But the smoke was getting thicker. She didn't like the smoke. She took a bottle from the end of the bar that wasn't on fire yet and opened it, leaving a trail. More matches then *Whoosh!* More flames! Leading out into reception now.

She ran up the grand staircase. This was so exciting. Just wait until her dad saw this! He would want to play too.

SIXTY-TWO

'Christ, do they actually know what they're doing?' Julie said to Suzy.

'They're a bunch of clowns. First they don't want us to leave, then they tell us they do.' They heard the sound of sirens in the distance.

'Everybody move to the side of the car park, please!' a security guard shouted. 'We have the fire brigade coming and they need room to get in.'

'Why is that police car over there, then?' a woman in the crowd asked.

'That's here on a different call, madam. Now move please!'

'I'm going over to the house, Julie. You stay here and keep an eye on things.' Suzy sprinted across the car park and up to the front door of the house. It was open so she went inside, looking for the officers who would have been in the car.

Charles Sharp was sitting in a chair with a glass of whisky in his hand. 'Who are you?' McTavish said.

'Inspector Suzy Campbell, Edinburgh Division. Where's Frank Miller.'

'Him and that other clown went chasing after *his* daughter.' He pointed to Sharp. 'God knows where they are, but they went after her in those fucking tunnels that run beneath this place.'

'I read that your daughter had Huntington's disease. Advanced stage. How can she be running?'

'It's a long story,' Melissa said, coming into the room. 'Sometimes she gets a burst of energy.'

'Do you know where Steffi is? Our other police officer?'

He looked at her. 'The one who was calling herself *Penny Blair*? I told Miller she's safe. We were just going to take her home and give her a little something so she wouldn't remember being here.'

'You were going to drug her after kidnapping her?'

'We do very sensitive work here behind the scenes. We just can't have everybody knowing about it.'

'It's still illegal, what you did.'

'I'm a billionaire. Nothing you can throw at me will stick. I have the best lawyers money can buy.'

Outside, the retained firefighters from the Golspie station arrived in their fire engine. The sub-officer jumped out of the passenger side.

'It's a false alarm,' Vincent Woo said. 'I'm head of security here. There's nothing to worry about.'

The windows in the bar exploded in a fireball as the flames licked out.

'You want to say that again, pal? I think you've got a real problem here. And I'm going to get reinforcements.'

But Vincent Woo wasn't listening; he was too mesmerised by the flames. How the hell was the place on fire? He'd been told to keep them all inside, then to clear the building. He hadn't asked why, he just did as he was told. But nobody had said anything about a fire.

SIXTY-THREE

My light bounced around one of the tunnels. And the one next to it. And the one next to that.

'Where the fuck did she go?' Masters asked me.

'She knows this place a lot better than us. I heard her coming up this way but I don't know what branch she took. I think we should split up.'

'Right, we can go down one each, but that still leaves one unchecked.'

'The schematics we looked at didn't show three, I'm sure.'

'Maybe some lazy sod didn't draw them properly. Either way, we might get lucky or we might be checking the two tunnels she *didn't* go down.'

'I'll go left. You can go right.'

'Fair enough.'

I ran into the left tunnel, my flashlight beam bouncing around the stone walls as I jogged along. The tunnel sloped down and seemed to go on forever. Then it flattened out. I thought I could see daylight farther along and ran faster. I heard a noise behind me in the dark and stopped. I whipped round, expecting to see somebody standing there, but it was nothing.

I carried on and then suddenly the daylight got brighter. There was a wooden door and two windows, with bars on them. This area was wider, and I could see the lawn-cutting equipment in here.

At the other end of this large room was another tunnel at right angles to where I was standing. Did April come down here? Maybe she did, knowing what was in here.

I heard it again. Footsteps. In the distance, like somebody was running. I walked quietly over to the other tunnel entrance with my light off. Then looked round.

The door to the tunnels in the old kitchen was wide open. There were people running about, but none had come here yet. They were looking for Hagan in the labs. But Steffi had seen him go this way. This was the chance for both of them to escape.

The shouts and the screaming became muffled as she entered the darkness. They had left her her keys and warrant card, but had taken her phone away. One thing she kept on her keychain was a little LED flashlight. You had to keep your finger on it for it to work, but her father had told her to keep it on her keychain, because you never knew when you were going to need a flashlight.

Like now.

The light from it was small, but gave her enough illumination to see where she was going. She ran as fast as she felt comfortable. There was no light ahead. Did Bruce have a light with him, or was he just running about in the dark? How could he see in here if he did? Maybe he didn't even come in here. Then why was the door open?

All these thoughts and questions went through her mind as she ran, not even sure if this was the way she had come into the house. It had to be though.

Then she heard the shout behind her.

'Miss Walker! If you're in here, I urge you to come back! It's not safe!'

It was Solomon.

His voice spurred her on. Not safe? Like going back there and being pumped full of God-knows-what was safer? No chance.

As each minute passed, Steffi felt stronger and clearer in the head. Obviously the stuff they'd given her last night was wearing off. She moved faster, having to keep moving the little light about to see where she was going, but she felt the adrenaline kick in.

She came to a point where the tunnels split. Had she come up the one on the left last night?

She turned a corner, her little, bright light aimed at the floor.

Bruce Hagan was standing waiting for her. It was the scraping of his shoe on the old, stone floor that alerted her.

Had he wanted to warn her? To make her look into his eyes before he challenged her? Or had he just been careless? No, this man wasn't careless. Everything was planned.

She lifted the light and shone it into his face, but the dazzling light had no effect on him.

His eyes were devoid of life.

'Bruce? We need to get out of here.'

'He isn't here.' The words were spoken in a flat monotone. The expression on his face made him seem like a grotesque figure from a bad movie.

'Where is he?' She didn't feel fear. She was past all of that. There was panic, the adrenaline fuelling her, making her burn inside.

'He's gone. Bruce isn't here anymore.'

Hagan was standing before her, but she knew the old Bruce Hagan was gone. She hadn't known him, hadn't worked with him, but Miller had told her all about him. It broke her heart to think of her colleague like this.

The light moved and caught the stainless steel of the large kitchen knife he was holding. The blade was eight inches long, going from a point to a maximum width of around two inches. So the wound would be deep and wide. Jesus Christ.

The sound of running feet behind her. She spun round, reflexes taking the light with her, but whoever was there was too far away for the light to find them.

She turned the light back, having only taken it away for a second, but it was enough for Hagan to have gone.

She saw a pinprick of light, moving away from her. He probably had a little flashlight with enough luminescence to show him the way without lighting up the whole tunnel.

Then he turned round a corner, and it was only darkness before her, her own little light not penetrating the blackness enough.

She turned the way the man had gone, but there were only more tunnels. No light. He could have ducked into any one of them and put his flashlight out, waiting to ambush her.

All her training was telling her not to follow, but her instinct told her to go forward.

Her indecision was answered by the sound of shoes catching up with her. She turned round, holding her light up, feeling just how vulnerable she was to attack from behind, but the figure approaching her had his own light, and he would surely see if the man with the knife was coming up behind her.

'Where did he go?' Doctor Solomon said. He looked exhausted, his eyes wild, sweat lining his face.

'In there. This whole place is a warren. There's no way we'll be able to find him, but he can't get out. Can he?' There was uncertainty in her voice.

'I can't even imagine where he would go when he gets up there. They'll be waiting for him.'

'We'd better go back the way we came.'

He nodded, and was about to turn when his eyes widened and he let out a gasp. He shoved her roughly to one side, and the steel blade that was meant for her sliced into his stomach, glancing off a rib. He'd saved her life, giving his own in the process.

She tried to scream, feeling doing so would bring her all the help she needed. All she had to do was crouch down, put her head in her hands, and close her eyes.

And wait.

But that wasn't her. She didn't back down. She'd learned to control the fear a long time ago, fighting a foreign war in a foreign land, but it was the fear that kept you sharp. She lashed out at the man in the dark, connecting with nothing. He no longer had his light on, and her own light was jittery.

As the knife was rammed in for a third time, her saviour managed to grab hold of his attacker and pull himself in close, leaving the way clear for her.

He made a garbled sound that may have been Run! but she couldn't be sure. But she ran. She was only a few seconds ahead. As she reached the room at the end, smoke seeped through the closed hatch in the ceiling.

There was nowhere else to go. Nothing she could use as a weapon, or hide behind.

There were no running feet behind her. Only the little LED light and the sound of his thick shoes on the stone floor, competing with the roar of the flames above. He knew she was trapped.

There were rails on the ceiling. The light picked out the rusted metal beams, and the equally rusted hooks. There were old pulleys and remnants of rope. They continued to old wooden doors built into the outside wall and carried on through.

She knew then this had been a place where deliveries were made by sea, probably two centuries ago. They'd bring the goods in and lift them through into what she guessed was the kitchen above.

Tendrils of smoke seeped through the cracks in the wood from above, and once more she could hear the roar of the flames. Going up through the hatch wasn't an option.

Then she heard the metallic scraping of the knife on stone. He was just outside. There was only one thing left to try.

She ran over to the old doors, which were held closed by an old, wooden bar. It wasn't as if it needed to be locked this high up.

The wind shot in like a hungry animal looking to feed, blowing her hair. The rusted rails stuck out into the night air. She stepped out onto a ledge where the goods used to be hoisted up from the boats below.

She could see breakers slamming the rocks, churning and splashing. How far was it to the water? A thousand feet for all she knew. No! Think. This was the lowest level. They wouldn't be hauling goods up a thousand feet.

Then, as her eyes adjusted to the darkness, she saw she had completely misjudged this. The sea wasn't directly below. The castle sat on an outcrop of rock, which sloped down, fanning out at the bottom. The goods were brought by boat, hauled a short distance across what was now the gardens, and then brought up.

She looked back into the room and saw the little light before she saw him. He was banging the steel blade against the stone, beating a tattoo, trying to scare her. She put her flashlight in her pocket and jumped up, grabbing hold of one the rails, and inched her way out farther, just as the flash of steel sliced towards her.

She was only hanging there for a few seconds before she knew she couldn't hold on. There was nowhere to go. Except down.

Looking past her feet, Steffi wondered if she would die quickly. Then she looked back at the man standing smiling at her. Holding his knife. Waiting for her.

Not this time, she thought, letting go.

Not ever.

SIXTY-FOUR

I ran up the tunnel, turned right, and almost tripped over the body. I kept my back to the wall, constantly moving the light around in case somebody was going to try to put me in the same position as this man.

It was the doctor who worked for Sharp. Solomon. His guts had been ripped open and it was obvious he was dead. His eyes were open, staring up to the ceiling, blood running out of his mouth.

I heard the roar of the fire getting louder the closer I got to it, and all my human instincts told me to run in the opposite direction. God knows how firemen did this on a daily basis, run into a burning building while everybody else was running out.

Smoke was filling the corridor I was running along, but there was a strong wind coming from an opening ahead, blowing it in my direction.

There was no sign of April Sharp.

But I saw Bruce Hagan.

'Bruce!' I called out. 'What are you doing here?'

I stepped closer. He had been standing looking at something, obviously an opening the way his hair was being blown about.

Windows let in a weak light. I could see old furniture stacked up. Could April have been hiding here? I didn't think so.

Hagan was standing watching me. Now I could see the knife and it sent a chill up me. If they had taken Hagan and Steffi, had he killed Steffi? Or just Solomon? He'd clearly killed somebody with it.

'Bruce. Drop the knife and come with me.'

He said nothing. The smoke was getting thicker. I was starting to choke on it. I walked forward, my only weapon my flashlight, compared to the knife he was holding.

He took a few steps towards me, then hesitated.

He'd seen the man coming up behind me before I heard him.

I turned and saw Masters coming towards me.

'Hagan's up there! With a great big bloody knife.'

'Where?'

I turned and shone my flashlight ahead, but Hagan was gone. 'Christ, he's away.' I started running with Masters behind me, but I didn't run blindly through the door opening. I wasn't stupid enough to run into a knife.

Carefully, I looked round, just in time to see Hagan's feet disappearing through the hatch in the ceiling.

Flames were licking around it, and smoke swirled around, making him look like a magician doing a disappearing act. I was about to follow when Masters caught my arm.

'We don't know what's up there!'

'I can't just let him go. He's killed Solomon.'

The door on our left was wide open, wind howling through it, feeding the fire above.

'We need to get out, Frank. Now!'

No sooner had the words left his mouth than there was a massive explosion above us.

Other fire engines started arriving to back up the part-time firefighters.

'Get those people right out of the car park,' the sub-officer said to the security guards as more patrol cars arrived from Golspie. The guests didn't need much telling as the flames were licking through the bar windows, and smoke was starting to creep out of other open windows.

One of the leading firemen ran over to the sub from the fire engine. 'Sir, we already have units from Bonar Bridge and Lairg arriving.' They turned as the aerial platform truck came barrelling down the main road towards the castle.

'Good. Did you get control to alert the others?'

'Yes, sir. Dornoch, Tain, and Helmsdale have already been alerted. There's a specialist crew coming up from Inverness.'

'Right.' The sub watched as the firefighter ran back to join his colleagues, and the police uniforms were shepherding the guests out of the way so the fire truck could get close. When he had told control to give him everything they had, they had sprung into action. They'd planned for this event for a long time. Years before, the castle had had its own fire service based in the castle itself, but that had been a very long time ago.

The sub had been at countless training exercises where men and women from all emergency services had got together and run through scenarios, such as *What if the castle went up and it was full to capacity? What if a small plane hit it? What if a truck carrying gasoline went out of control and ran into the front?* Some of the situations would probably never happen, but he had never wanted to be in the position of dealing with a situation where he thought, *Oh shit, we didn't think of that one!*

Now he had fire engines coming from towns close by as well as the specialist unit. Yet, despite all the training, he couldn't believe the castle was actually on fire. It broke his heart to see such a fine building go up like—

Oh fuck! He saw the woman's face in the clock tower, looking out from one of the windows. He ran to the platform truck, shouting and pointing to the officer who was in the passenger side.

'Up there! In the clock tower. She's—'

His thoughts were interrupted by the explosion. Windows blew out, throwing shards of glass like knives. The front door of the castle flew off in what seemed like a million pieces as orange flames and black smoke billowed out into the air. Masonry from the window frames was hurled with force, hitting the guests. Flames erupted from the windows where the woman was standing, tossing her outside where she landed with a thud on top of a car.

The sub shouted and ran as a piece of masonry smashed the windscreen on the fire engine. He was shouting orders as the first ambulance arrived, and he went into autopilot. Years of training kicked in and he didn't even have to think about what he was doing.

Everybody got out of the car park alive.

Except the woman who'd been standing in the clock tower. The sub ran over to her, along with other uniforms and the ambulance crew, but half her face was missing, and she was badly burnt.

Mama was gone.

SIXTY-FIVE

'Christ, I think you just saved my life,' I said to Masters as we lay on the cold, stone floor. The fireball had gone out of the open door.

He jumped to his feet and hauled me up. 'You can buy me a pint in Edinburgh, but right now, we still need to find Steffi. If April went up there, there's no way we can go after her. Let's get out of here, Frank.'

We ran back the way we came, the smoke thicker now. We heard more explosions from the oxygen cylinders in the small infirmary, but we were already at the end of the corridor and turning right. I had my flashlight out. We couldn't take Solomon's corpse with us, someone would have to get it later.

We ran down in the darkness, and I hoped we were going the right way, back the way we'd come.

When I saw the tunnel get lighter, I knew we had. Then we were back where all the grass cutting machinery was stored.

'Let's get that fucking door down,' Masters said to me. He jumped onto a ride-on lawnmower and started it up. He looked comical as he drove it towards the door, but it did the trick. The lock smashed easily and the door smacked back against the outside wall, and suddenly we were back out into the cool, refreshing air.

Then I heard the scream for help.

I thought it was coming from up in the castle and looked at the devastation up there. The back windows on the lower level were filled with fierce, orange flames, and smoke and fire was gripping the upper levels.

The scream came again.

There were thick bushes and trees at the base of the castle. I ran over to where the scream had come from.

I didn't know who it was, and thinking maybe it was April, I shouted out her name. 'April! Tell us where you are! We can help you!'

'Frank! It's me, Steffi! I'm in the bushes!'

Christ. Steffi! 'We're coming!' We ran over to the bushes and fought our way through them. I saw her lying tangled up. She hadn't hit the ground, which had saved her life.

'Christ, Frank, am I glad to see you. You too, sir,' she added when she saw Masters right behind me.

The two of us manoeuvred her out and onto the grass.

'I think my ankle's broken,' she said as we carried her well away from the debris that had been blown out from the castle.

I touched her ankle and she screamed. 'Yep, I think it's broken,' I said.

She slapped my arm. 'I just told you it was. I was an army medic, remember.'

'That's you put in your place, Miller,' Masters said.

'I don't know what this force is coming to. Hitting a senior officer. That's cause for concern. What do you think, Lloyd?'

'I'd say your goose is pretty much cooked, Miss Walker.'

'Will you pair of comedians bloody well get me to some help?'

I smiled, relieved to see her again. With help from Masters, we got her onto her one good foot and I gave her a piggy-back.

'See? I knew you were a gentleman,' she said.

'Don't go spreading rumours like that, Officer Walker.'

'I'm going to tell them you're both a couple of big teddy bears.'

'Don't you dare,' Masters said. 'We have our hard man images to keep intact. Isn't that right, Frank?'

'Correct,' I said.

'Handbags at dawn, gentlemen?'

'If you weren't on my back, I'd skelp your arse.'

'Big man.' Then she made a moaning noise and squeezed me hard. 'Christ, I need some morphine right now. I hope the ambulance crew have plenty.'

I didn't know if ambulance crews carried morphine, but they would give her something.

'Tell me how you happened to be hiding in the bushes,' I said, as we reached the track and it went uphill. I was already knackered but I had to dig deep.

'Frank, get her on my back,' Masters said.

'I'm fine, Lloyd.'

'That's not a request, son. I work out five times a week. Give her to me.'

'Well, fighting over a woman, eh? How your wives are going to hear about this,' Steffi said through gritted teeth. She got down onto her good leg, held onto me, then Masters had her on his back, making it look easier than I had done.

'You could do with losing a few, Officer Walker,' Masters said. Then he got a smack like I had.

'You never say that to a woman! Are you not married?'

'I am, and I would never dare say that to the wife.'

'Cheeky sod.' Then she let out a yell and squeezed him hard. 'I think I'm going to pass out, Lloyd.'

'Hold on, we won't be long.' He hunkered down and marched faster. Even in his early fifties, he was fitter than I could ever hope to be.

'So, you were telling me how you got there,' I said to her, marching at their side.

'Bruce tried to kill me. Although it was somebody else in Bruce's body. I know he didn't know me when we turned up at the castle because he's never worked with me, but he should have recognised me from when we had dinner. But he didn't. He was looking right at me, but all he saw was somebody else to kill.'

She started crying then. 'He killed the doctor. Solomon saved my life, but Bruce stabbed him to death. Then he chased me along to the end of the corridor. The only way I could escape him was to jump.'

'Christ, that's some jump.'

'I would rather jump than have him stab me to death. It wasn't as high as I thought.' She looked at me. Then she told us about the labs and the work they were doing here. 'Where's Bruce now?'

'He went up through a doorway in the ceiling. Then the place exploded. He's dead, Steffi.'

Just saying the words made me feel cold inside.

Then she fainted. I caught her and then she was in my arms. We made it to the car park and I fought my way through to one of the ambulances sitting on the edge of the car park. The place looked like the set of an action movie. Fire was raging out of the castle windows. People were covered in blood. Uniforms running about.

'I wonder where Suzy and Julie are?' I said, handing Steffi to a paramedic. They put her into an ambulance.

'There they are.' Masters pointed.

I turned and watched them march Charles Sharp and his wife into a police car. McTavish was also in handcuffs, having been placed under arrest by a uniformed inspector. They came over to us.

'April Sharp died. She was blown out of the clock tower when the building exploded,' Suzy said.

'What the hell were they doing in there?' Julie said.

'They were trying to get a cure for their daughter. To save her life. But in their quest, they ended other people's lives. And hers.'

I watched the castle burn. Watched as one man's dreams turned to ash. I hoped that Charles Sharp would spend the rest of his life in prison, but then I remembered he was a billionaire.

Men like him never get what's coming to them.

SIXTY-SIX

Five days later.

We were in the conference room along from the investigation suite. Jeni Bridge was at the head of the table like a matriarch. I sat opposite Percy Purcell, with Lloyd Masters on my right. Julie was there. Steffi was in the Royal Infirmary, having been transferred from Rigmore Hospital in Inverness. They'd operated successfully on her ankle but she was recuperating.

We'd written reports, had been interviewed by Professional Standards, and by Jeni herself. Everything had been gone over with a fine-tooth comb.

'I know you were planning to see Hazel this morning. How did it go?' Jeni asked me.

It had been a few days since I had told her Bruce had died in the castle fire. The place was a wreck. They were still finding pockets of fire and sifting through the rubble.

'She's beside herself. He was married to another woman, but

he was still the father of her children. She's going to need help attending his funeral.'

'We'll be there for her,' Purcell said.

'Good,' Jeni said, holding up pieces of paper. 'I wanted you all in here this morning for an update. Charles Sharp and his wife have posted bail. They're out and about right now.'

'What?' said Masters. 'They know he's a billionaire, right?'

'Of course they do. Why do you think he got bail? His lawyer said he's not a flight risk as he needs to organise his daughter's funeral.'

'He'll have her on a private jet and be away before we know it,' I said.

'That might be the case, Frank, but it's out of our hands now.' She looked at another sheet of paper. 'They haven't found Hagan yet. There is a ton of rubble to dig through. It will be another few days before it's safe enough. The fire chief thinks he was at the seat of the explosion when they worked out where you last saw him. So there's the possibility he won't be coming home in one piece.'

I shuddered at the thought.

'How did his new wife take the news?'

'She was upset. He was her husband after all.'

'What about McTavish, the sergeant from Golspie?' Masters asked.

'He's being charged. He's already been fired, but it would seem he was in Sharp's pocket. If he saw anything suspicious at the castle, he turned a blind eye. We have forensic accountants going through his personal bank accounts, but it seems he had a couple of hundred thousand in an account.'

Just then there was a knock on the door, and Paddy Gibb came in. 'Sorry to disturb you, ma'am, but I thought you would want to see this right away.'

'That's okay, Paddy, come away in.'

Gibb was holding a piece of paper, which he gave to Jeni before retreating.

'Christ almighty.' She read it and looked at us. 'One of the castle cars was stolen from the castle car park. A Land Rover. They were doing an inventory and found it was missing.'

'Have they any idea who it was?'

'They don't know.'

'There were quite a few staff who worked there,' I said. 'And staff we don't know about. The ones who worked in the labs.'

'So any one of them could have taken it. However, it was found parked on the hard shoulder on the city bypass just a little while ago by a patrol car.'

'Whereabouts on the city bypass?' I said, the hairs standing up on the back of my neck.

'By the Baberton exit.'

I was getting a bad feeling about this when she spoke again.

'That's not all; they recovered Doctor Solomon's body. And rammed into his head was a large, bloody kitchen knife.' She looked at me. 'You saw him, didn't you?'

'Yes, I did. And there was no knife sticking out of his head. Does it say what it looked like?'

She looked at the paper. 'Yes. A large kitchen knife. Wide at one end, running to a sharp point.'

'That's the kind of knife I saw Hagan holding. And I can assure you, Solomon did not have a knife sticking out of his head when I last saw him. But Bruce Hagan was holding one as he climbed through the hatch in the ceiling.'

'Jesus, you don't think...?' Purcell said.

I covered my eyes with my hand for a moment. Trying to envision the layout of the castle. Then I looked at Jeni. 'If he climbed up there and ran along the corridor outside the kitchen he could have found the doorway that led down to the basement on the opposite end to us. If he came down, he could have left the knife in Solomon's head, even though the doctor was dead.'

'He might have survived the explosion.'

Gibb was standing at the door again. This time he hadn't knocked. 'Not might have,' he said to Jeni. '*Did*. He attacked Hazel's babysitter and took the kids in the woman's car. She was at Hazel's house while Hazel was out. Now he's driven it onto the pavement on the Forth Road Bridge. And he has the kids with him.'

SIXTY-SEVEN

Police outriders did their best to make a corridor for us, and it was the first time I'd been in a car doing seventy miles an hour along Queensferry Road approaching Barnton.

Then we were doing more than a ton heading for the bridge, the pursuit driver moving the car like the expert he was.

Purcell was sitting next to me while Julie and Masters were in the car behind.

More of my team were behind them.

We made good time and I was hoping Bruce hadn't hurt the kids, but we were in constant contact with the patrols at the bridge. Traffic was being held back on the south side, and one lane was being kept clear for us northbound.

The car we were in cut right across to the other side and drove up and round his car to where Bruce was standing with the kids.

We pulled up short, not wanting to spook him. I got out and started walking slowly towards him. The wind wasn't blowing a gale, but it was cold. Baby Daniel was crying.

'Hey, Bruce, fancy seeing you here?' I said.

He looked at me but there was no recognition there.

'Why don't you come in the car and we can talk?'

'We're going swimming! The children love the water!'

I was maybe fifteen feet away from him then, too far away to rush him. I held out my hands for him to see them. The baby was cold and crying, and little Jane looked at me with tears in her eyes.

'Why don't you let them come with me, Bruce?' I edged a little closer.

'What? Who the fuck are you anyway?'

'I'm your friend.' Ten feet. That was all, ten lousy feet, but he had the baby up on the railings now. He was talking to him and pointing. He had let go of Jane's hand. I waved at her while Hagan was looking out over the Forth.

The little girl was scared. She shook her head. She couldn't move. I smiled at her and waved my fingers. Then it was like electricity shot through her.

She ran.

She came at me and I kept my eyes on Hagan. 'Run!' I said to her and she ran to whoever was behind me.

Hagan was holding the baby out above the water now. 'Monster!' he screamed at the boy.

I ran at Hagan and he saw me at the last minute. I threw myself at him, leaping up at the railings just as he let the baby go. I reached out blindly, yelling at the top of my voice, and I still don't know what it was I yelled, but I reached out, my hand and fingers stretching as my body was on the railings now, and I could feel myself going to my tipping point, but I reached and reached and I grabbed the baby, still holding onto the top of the railings.

Hagan punched me in the face, which by a stroke of luck, brought me back onto the pavement. I fell back, still holding the baby. I landed heavily on my back, thinking Hagan was going to kill me.

He was on top of me, and for a brief second, his eyes were clear. 'I'm scared, Frank. Help me. I'm trapped!'

Then his eyes clouded over again, and I knew the friend I'd had was gone forever.

Then a flurry of bodies were on top of him, black uniforms pinning him to the ground. He thrashed and kicked and screamed and cursed, but no matter how strong he was, he was outnumbered. The baby was okay. Hands took him away from me and I couldn't speak because all of the air had been knocked out of me.

'Jesus, Frank,' Masters said, coming over to me. 'As long as I live, I don't think I'll ever witness something like that again.'

'Come on, pal, let's get you sorted,' Purcell said, and the two men helped me to my feet.

'Is Jane okay?' I asked when I got my breath back.

'They're both fine. Thanks to you.'

I walked away with the two men and looked back once more at Bruce Hagan.

He was on his feet, still struggling, being handcuffed.

Then we locked eyes as he was being marched forward. Then he stopped struggling. And he looked directly at me.

'Whoever you are, we'll meet again one day. You can count on that.'

SIXTY-EIGHT

We were sitting round the table in Percy Purcell's kitchen. It had been a week since the bridge incident.

Lou Purcell was getting ready to go out.

'That must have been scary, son, watching Hagan on the bridge with the bairns.'

'It was, Lou. I have to say, it's sad that we lost a colleague we saw as a friend.'

'All because of that rich sod. I hope they lock him up for life.'

'He won't even see jail,' Percy said, sitting down at the table. 'But enough of that talk. We're here to celebrate. And to thank my friend here for bringing my fiancée back home safe.'

'Don't wait up,' Lou said, leaving us.

We all clinked our glasses and tucked into the food. Kim smiled at me and I wanted to focus on the here and now, and not tipping forward over the Forth Road Bridge.

'Lou's staying with us until his house is sold. His girlfriend found about his new female friend down here and dumped him.'

'I liked Elizabeth,' Suzy said.

'He was playing with fire,' Purcell said. 'So he's putting his house on the market and buying a flat here.'

'You won't have to worry about him up there on his own,' I said.

'That's one way of looking at it.'

'How's Jack getting on?' Suzy asked.

'Samantha's nephew was murdered by his father's girlfriend, as you know. So they've been wrapping things up. They had his funeral. And Chip's too. He told me he's moving in with Samantha when they get back. So we'll have a spare room.'

'There you go!' Percy said to me. 'You were just saying how much you enjoyed Lou's company! And now you'll have a spare room.'

'And ruin the chance for you and your father to catch up? I couldn't do that to you, Percy.'

'Oh well, I can only try.'

Kim squeezed my hand. 'As much as we'd love to have your father, we're going to need our other spare room after Jack moves out.'

'Are we getting another cat?' I asked.

'No, we're getting another child. I'm pregnant, Frank.'

AUTHOR'S NOTE

Thank you for reading the latest instalment of the DI Frank Miller series. It was fun to write and I hope you enjoyed it as much as I enjoyed writing it.

I would like to thank the real Julie Stott, Wendy Haines and Jeni Bridge. I hope you like the way I used your names! Thanks for all your enthusiasm. It makes this author feel very humble. Thanks also to Fiona Jackson and Evelyn Bell.

Back in 2016, I attended the Citizen's Police Academy at the Town of Newburgh Police Department, in New York State, where I live. We were given lectures and demonstrations by a number of police officers and civilian staff, and I decided to use some of that knowledge in this book. Each of them was a consummate professional in every way. The officer in this book does not reflect any Town of Newburgh police officer, past or present, in any way whatsoever. This is a work of fiction, and the storyline in here is not based on any real-life case. If there are any similarities, they are purely coincidental. I extend my thanks to Officer Henderson who took me on a ride-along in his patrol car, Police Chief Bruce

AUTHOR'S NOTE

Campbell, K9 Officer Lawson and his beautiful dog, Raven (RIP sweet girl). I salute you all for the hard work that you do every day. Stay safe my friends.

Thank you to Gregor Duncan of the Scottish Fire and Rescue Service, for his insight into what happens at a major fire in a large establishment.

All the people who helped me in my research know their job inside out, so if there are any mistakes at all, they are mine alone and not theirs. I also used what we writers call *literary license,* which means we take reality and bend it out of shape sometimes, just so it will fit into our story.

Thank you to my wife Debbie, who entertains our dogs while I write. Love you. And to my daughters Stephanie and Samantha. I bend their ears talking about plots and writing and I go on incessantly about Miller. Thanks for listening girls!

And a very big thank you to you, the reader, for coming on this journey with me. You all make it worthwhile.

And lastly, if I could please ask you to leave a review of this book on Amazon. Each review helps an Indie author like me, and each one, good or bad, is accepted with gratitude.

All the best my friends.

John Carson
New York
February 2017

Printed in Great Britain
by Amazon